'JESUS GOD, STEVE. HE'S DEAD. THEY'VE GONE AND KILLED HIM.'

Steve got to his feet, head spinning, and lurched across to Sunny. The mess that had been the back of his head, and his unfocused stare, showed it was true. He felt for a heartbeat and there was none. He thought of heart massage and mouth to mouth, but no first aid he had ever heard of could have put Sunny back together again. Finding his legs beginning to shake uncontrollably, he sat down on the pavement and took Sunny's hand in his own.

'I've got to get the camera,' said Pat. Shocked and hurt, his automatic response was to get the pictures, just like Oggy Lomas in the hill above Beirut, filming soundman Don Nesbit, unconscious on the ground after a mine destroyed their car. Then he looked around him.

'Where is it?' he said.

JAMES LONG

HARD NEWS

SIGNET

To Annie
and to all TV news camera crews

SIGNET

Published by the Penguin Group
Penguin Books Ltd, 27 Wrights Lane, London W8 5TZ, England
Penguin Books USA Inc., 375 Hudson Street, New York, New York 10014, USA
Penguin Books Australia Ltd, Ringwood, Victoria, Australia
Penguin Books Canada Ltd, 10 Alcorn Avenue, Toronto, Ontario, Canada M4V 3B2
Penguin Books (NZ) Ltd, 182–190 Wairau Road, Auckland 10, New Zealand

Penguin Books Ltd, Registered Offices: Harmondsworth, Middlesex, England

First published by Viking 1992
Published in Signet 1993
10 9 8 7 6 5 4 3 2 1

Chapter One

The Crown and Sceptre on Great Titchfield Street is an old-fashioned, serious drinkers' pub, and for many years it had been well placed to catch the serious drinkers' trade. Two hundred yards to the west, the BBC's Broadcasting House still provided the central London base of BBC Radio, though out in White City, next to Television Centre, the finishing touches were being put to the modern building which would, if budgets allowed, one day replace it. Just round the corner was ITN's headquarters in Wells Street, though that too was in the middle of packing its bags, moving towards the City in the search for more space. Three hundred yards east, Channel 4 was considering completing the hat trick by heading towards the river, to the consternation of all the small TV production and facilities houses which had clustered round the Charlotte Street area to be near the work.

On this evening in May, most of that was still to come. The Crown and Sceptre was filling up with its usual crowd. By the bar, three radio news reporters stood listening to a producer from the *PM* programme attacking the choice of the lead story on the *Six O'Clock News*. The producer was a pink-cheeked girl who had slipped from Oxford University into the BBC graduate training scheme without really noticing the difference. One year into her first proper job, she'd already learned there was more cocktail party mileage in saying she worked in BBC current affairs – hoping, by missing out the word 'radio', people would assume she moved in the headier reaches of *Panorama* or *Newsnight*.

'Now come on,' she was saying, with the bright confidence of Cheltenham Ladies' College, 'I just don't think it's very intelligent to treat unemployment statistics like that. It needed much more analysis. I mean, it's as if the BBC didn't even know there was a rational counter-view.'

There was a subtle unity of atmosphere about the three men surrounding her. They were all in their thirties, but this wasn't only a matter of physical similarity. They wore hard-wearing grey suits, shiny at the seat from a thousand rushed car journeys. Their pockets were baggy with overuse as storage for spare tapes, batteries, microphones. But it was their faces which linked them. With a bit less humour, you might have taken them for detectives. Their eyes watched and weighed up without giving too much away. They'd stood on a thousand doorsteps, asked ten thousand questions and turned it all into sixty-second chunks of spoken prose. Millions heard their voices. No one saw their faces. They looked cynical, serviceable, uncommitted and slightly unkempt. They were staring at the girl without really listening. Two were wondering if she'd go to bed with them. One was wishing she hadn't and looking for an excuse to leave.

'Anyway,' she said, 'I see Telly didn't make the same mistake.'

'Another one all round?' said the shortest of the trio, hoping to change the subject.

'Yes please,' she said. 'Oh, maybe I'll switch to Campari this time. No, they ran it after the halfway heads, right down the bulletin.'

'What did they lead on?' he asked, turning to wave at the girl behind the bar.

'It was another angle on this defence contracts fraud stuff they broke yesterday,' she said. 'They've got some follow-

2

up saying the Minister's going to announce a special investigation on it tomorrow. I suppose they've got it right, but I must say we've been chasing it all day and everyone we've tried to talk to says they just don't know anything at all.'

'What sort of people have you tried?'

'Oh, you know, all the defence correspondents from the national papers and ...'

He cut in. 'Bloody current affairs. You lot never change. You always rush off to interview some other hack first. What about the companies and the M.o.D. Did you go to them?'

She bristled. 'Of course we did. They just wouldn't say a thing. I must say I think Telly may have screwed up. Apparently it's all down to that reporter Steve Ross. Perhaps he made it all up.' Suddenly she had the full, and hostile, attention of all three of them. The tallest, a gaunt, fair-haired man with a scarred face, just beat the others to it.

'There's nothing wrong with Ross,' he said, and his tone said she was an outsider. 'He's a bloody good reporter. If he says it's true, then it's true and that's all there is to it. Steve Ross is not only one of the nicest guys in the business, he's also one of the best, though he's not the sort of person who'd tell you that himself. It's about time you and all the other current affairs wallies in this sodding organization learnt to trust your own reporters first and Fleet Street second.' He looked at her and snorted. 'Now I'm sorry to break up the party, but I've got to go and do some work.'

They watched in silence as he put down his beer and strode out. She wanted to run after him and apologize, because he was the only reason she'd come to the pub, but the presence of the others stopped her. She'd been hoping for a repeat of last time and had no idea that his indignation had been fanned with exactly this escape in mind. The other two watched curiously.

'What did I say?' she asked, with a failing attempt at jauntiness.

'Ross is a friend of his,' said the dark-haired one, who'd kept his silence so far, calculating that the odds had just improved sharply in his favour. 'Well, I suppose you might say he's a friend of all of us. He worked here for long enough before he went over to Telly. He helped pull Bob out of the shit once. Everyone liked him.'

'I didn't know he was ever in radio,' she said.

'Course he was. Before your time, but then so were most things,' said the short one.

She sniffed. 'So, he made it and you're still here. That's no reason to work it off on me.'

'Made it? What do you mean, made it? This is the thinking man's medium. That's just showbiz. He's a bit prettier than we are, that's all. When you've been around a bit longer, you'll see through all that TV crap,' said the short one, with more vehemence than he'd intended. The dark-haired one chortled to himself.

'Two down, just me to go,' he thought, and took her by the arm. 'Come and have a bite and I'll tell you the whole sad story of how Steve Ross made his name and lost his family.'

'Careful, he's an expert on losing families himself,' said the short one, but by that time he was already talking to their retreating backs.

Sitting at a corner table near the door, Eric Blackler watched them leave. He'd been looking at the blonde girl through his thick pebble glasses for a few minutes while he waited for his appointment. He was nervous. He never liked calls from Redman. It was usually about the money he owed, and, when it wasn't, it would be some grubby job for the porn trade. Most times Redman was offhand, but this time he'd been downright bloody rude. Meet the man, he'd said. Be polite. Don't give him any lip and tell him what he wants to know. If he's not happy, you're out of business, and there's a load of bent Sony gear in your stockroom that the Bill would just love to hear about.

'Who is he, anyway?'

'He's important, he'll know what you look like and he's not from round here, and that's all you fucking need to know, Blackler. Got that?'

'I just ...'

'I said have you fucking got that?'

'Yeah. OK.' He'd put the phone down in an impotent fury. Redman had financed his first purchase when he started up on his own. He could remember every detail of it. Four Ampex edit machines and a couple of cameras out of a Heathrow warehouse, hot enough to burn your fingers and they took an age to shift. Since then he'd got much smarter. These days the shop was eighty per cent legit, doing a lot of business with all the here today, gone tomorrow hopefuls of the professional video world, but Redman had found it suited him to keep putting up the money, and Blackler hadn't got the sort of books he could have taken to a more normal lender. Right now he owed Redman eighty grand on the video business and, when the man held up the hoop, he just had to jump.

He was thinking about it when a foreign voice said 'Mr Blackler?' and he looked up as a middle-aged man in an expensive suit sat down at the table.

'I'm Peter Müller,' he said, and Eric thought, 'Oh no, you're not.'

In place of small talk, the man who called himself Müller gave him an intense stare which lasted a good three seconds, then got straight into it. 'A friend of mine needs a portable television camera,' he said. 'He needs it for some specialized scientific work and therefore the exact type is very important. He has asked me to seek some professional advice on what model he should buy. The advice will be rewarded with a proper consultancy fee.'

Eric looked at the clothes, the Rolex on the wrist and the deeply ingrained tan, and thought 'banker' to himself. The man was in the wrong world, but the consultancy fee hit all the right buttons, so he leaned forward. 'No problem,' he said, thinking to himself that there was sod all difference between most of the ones on the market, but he put on a thoughtful look and went on. 'They're getting smaller and better all the time, and of course it's the subtle differences between them that matter. If you tell me what your friend needs it to do, I'm sure I can help you.'

The other man held up his hand. 'Ah,' he said, 'you see it may not be a current model that he needs. It could be that something older would be more suitable.'

Eric gazed at him wonderingly. 'Come on,' he said, 'every Japanese electronics genius has been burning the midnight oil for years to improve the damned things, and you think you want an old one? What on earth for?'

The man's mouth smiled, but his eyes frowned. 'That does not concern me, and I do not think it needs to concern you either. What matters is the specification of the camera. It might be best if you could start by outlining for me the main technical improvements in the past few years.'

'We are talking about ENG cameras aren't we?'

Müller looked blank. 'What is ENG please? I do not know the term.'

Eric looked at him in wonder. The distortion at the edges of his thick glasses and the tunnel vision they induced always gave him a sense of detachment from his surroundings, particularly in darkly lit interiors. Now, looking at Müller's privileged, insulated face against a swirling background of beer glasses and barmaids, he had a strong sense of two irreconcilable worlds. Why had this man flown, from who knows where, to ask him of all people these basic questions?

'Well now,' said Eric slowly, 'it sounds to me like you and your friend don't know quite as much about this business as you should. I'd better give you the quick, fools' guide.'

'That is why we are offering to pay you, Mr Blackler, but keep it concise please.'

'ENG means Electronic News Gathering. That means a camera you can hold on your shoulder and run around with. They record on tape, right? Now when they first came out, they had tubes inside to produce the colour picture, and the camera was a bloody great boxy thing. To start with, they were U-Matic format, that means they used cassettes containing three-quarter-inch tape, but the whole thing was very cumbersome. You had to be tough to have those on your shoulder all day. Then they came up with the Beta format. That meant smaller tapes, let's say paperback size instead of hardback, and a smaller camera and ...'

'Yes, yes, I know all about that. They put the recorder on the back of the camera, yes?'

Eric took a sip of beer. 'Well, yeah, on some of them. Made it bloody heavy again, though. Anyway, the point you need to get over to your friend is that the newer they are, the better they are, right? They gave up on tubes when they invented the CCD. Never mind the details but it's a more advanced way of scanning the picture – solid state electronics and all that. With modern Beta SP cameras the pictures are so sharp you could cut yourself, AND they'll more or less shoot pictures in the dark AND it all comes in a package that's half the weight and half the size of the old three-quarter-inch gear. I've got a couple of Betas lying around, not quite the latest, but bloody good for all that.

Nifty little cameras. I could knock those out to you pretty cheap.'

The man shook his head. 'There is a specific requirement here, Mr Blackler. I can only say it is for ...' He paused a moment and leant further over the table. '... aerospace applications. From what you say it is clear that a tube camera would be necessary, and U-Matic format could be a positive advantage.'

Eric looked at him in growing exasperation, not unconnected with the fact that he didn't have access to any tube cameras and he could see a valuable bit of extra business going out of the window. 'That doesn't make much sense, if you don't mind me saying so, and anyway they're getting like hens' teeth these days.'

'Hens' teeth?'

'Rare. Hard to find, you know?'

'That is why we need you.'

'Well, I suppose we've got to go out looking for an old Ikegami. That was pretty much standard issue for the BBC up to the mid-Eighties. There's the French Thomson and there's hordes of old Yank stuff, but God knows where you'd find one of those.'

'I am glad you confirm our views. That is exactly the conclusion my friend came to.'

Eric looked sharply at the man opposite, realizing he'd just gone through some sort of test.

Müller went on. 'He tried advertising and various other avenues and had no success. So the question now is, where should he go to buy an Ikegami?'

Eric could smell money a mile off, and he smelt it now. 'Hard to say really. There's very few around. The BBC still use them a bit for training. I might just be able to lay my hands on one, but it's not going to be easy.'

'My friend needs it within two weeks. Money is less import-

8

ant than time. He thought twenty thousand pounds ought to be enough.'

Indeed it ought, Eric thought, in fact about four times too much. 'If you're lucky,' he said.

Müller reached into his pocket and gave him an envelope. 'This contains ten thousand pounds as an advance, and my telephone number. Two weeks, Mr Blackler.'

In his office off Wardour Street, the following day, Eric hit the phone. He turned up two Ikegamis quite soon, but that was that. One of them was being used to shoot a Navy training film and, though it was definitely for sale, it wasn't due back on dry land for another three weeks. The other sounded like the business, but the owner was a total prat who wanted twelve grand for it. Eric had done the sums. He reckoned he needed fifteen grand clear on the deal to keep Redman off his back, and he wasn't about to throw away his profit margin. In fact, it occurred to him, maybe he didn't need to throw away much of the money at all.

He sat thinking for a while, then made a few discreet enquiries. When he got the information he needed, he reached for a street map, then picked up the phone to a hard man who owed him one.

Chapter Two

At 7.30 on a Saturday morning, four days later, the phone rang in an Earls Court bedsit. The traffic down the Redcliffe Gardens one-way system was already shaking the loose-fitting sash window. The room had impermanence stamped on every corner of it, from the stained orange wallpaper to the institutional bed and the coin meter for the electricity. It wasn't a grown man's room, but it was undoubtedly a grown man who reached out from under the blankets.

He sat half up in the bed. He looked sleepy but weary, as though he had slept without much refreshment from it. He was on the gaunt side of handsome, somewhere in his thirties, with piercing, pale blue eyes, blazing through the half-closed sleepy puffiness of their lids. He groped around on the wrong side for a while, then, sitting completely up, suddenly remembered where he was and just how bad things were. Then he picked up the receiver and they started to get a whole lot worse.

'Morning, is that Steve Ross?'

'Yes it is,' he said, trying to keep the sleep out of his voice, though he didn't really need to ask 'Who's that?'

'It's Doug Muir, Steve. I'm standing in as News Organizer today. I wasn't sure because I haven't been on the desk for a while, and the number in the file isn't the one I had in my book. Have you moved or something?'

'Or something, yes,' said Steve. 'What's going on?'

'We need you in, I'm afraid. Richard's had to go up to

Stafford because of the bomb, Martin's called in sick and Kate's on a plane to Cyprus. I know you're off, but it's all hands on deck and Mike Page said to call you.'

'What's the story?'

'It's the health cuts demo. If you can get going towards the East End as quick as you can, I'll fill you in when you're in the car.'

'What? It's only a demo, what's the panic?'

'Believe me, there's more. Just get going.'

'All right,' said Steve, because you had to be bulletproof to say no and he was still a few years short of being a household name. He put the phone down and lay for a while, staring in dejection at the ceiling. A stranger would have said he had a lot going for him. He had what most people would consider a good job. Though he would never have thought it, he was good-looking in a sharply drawn way which was somehow magnified even more by the camera, so that people who knew him from the screen were just very slightly disappointed to meet him in real life. That morning, though, he was in a mood to count what he'd lost, not what he'd got.

He cursed his reputation for always saying yes. There were some reporters they simply wouldn't have dared call up at short notice on a weekend. That word 'weekend' triggered an uneasy feeling about what he'd just agreed to do, but it was only when he got out of the narrow bed, searching for his clothes in the open suitcases strewn across the floor, that he saw the brightly wrapped parcel on the table and felt his stomach tighten with anxiety. 'Oh shit,' he said, then picked up the phone and dialled the Intake Desk number.

'Doug? It's Steve again. Listen, I completely forgot. It's my son's birthday. I'm meant to be taking him out this afternoon. I can't do it.'

'You'd better talk to Mike Page. Hang on a minute, I'll transfer you.'

The Birmingham accent of Steve's line boss, the head of BBC TV News Intake, came on the line. Page ran the UK-based team of reporters, as well as the Planning Desk and the Intake Desk itself, the nerve centre of the TV newsroom, which controlled the activities of all the crews out on the road.

'Morning Steve, how's life in Kangaroo Alley?'

'It'll do for now. Listen, Mike. Today's a problem. It's my kid's birthday. I promised I'd take him out this afternoon. I can't jack out now, Maureen would kill me.'

'Jesus, Steve, don't do a bleeding heart on me today for Christ's sake. I shouldn't be here myself, but I've got no one to whinge to when it's not convenient. Tell the kid you'll take him out tomorrow. He won't know the difference. Anyway, what are you worrying about your old lady for? I thought you and her were past history.'

The words made Steve shiver. 'I don't know. Maybe we are, but this is a bloody good way of making sure of it. Surely you can find somebody else?'

'There isn't anybody else. That's all I can tell you. It's a three-line whip, Steve. The word's out that the people who caused all the bother at the Poll Tax demos are out looking for more blood. If you've got problems, we can talk about them over a beer on Monday, but right now I need you to stop talking and shift your ass. Right?'

There was a silence, then Steve found himself saying 'Right', because apart from saying 'I quit' there didn't seem anything else to say. He put the phone down, then picked it up again and dialled what had, until a month before, been his home number. Maureen answered on the third ring, and from the tone of her voice he knew it was a bad moment.

'It's Steve.'

'Yes?' she said, and there was ice clinging to the monosyllable.

'Look, I'm sorry but the bloody office has just called and I've got to go in.' He waited for her to say something, but she didn't so, knowing he was heading deeper into dangerous waters, he plunged on. 'It means I can't take Tom out this afternoon. I'll have to do it tomorrow instead.'

'Have to? What the hell do you mean, have to? He's your son, Steve, for God's sake.'

'You know I didn't mean it like that. Look, I've tried to get out of it and I can't. Mike Page won't listen.'

'I don't feel like listening either. They've always come first. You'd better tell Tom yourself. I'll get him.'

There was a short wait, and then he heard his five-year-old son.

'Daddy? When are you coming? It's my birthday today.'

'Happy birthday, Tom. Listen, sweetheart, I can't come this afternoon, but I'll come tomorrow and we'll go out and have a lovely time. I promise.'

'Ohhh. Why can't you come today, Daddy?'

'Because they're making me go to work. I'm very sorry.'

'Ring them up and say you can't come.'

'I tried that, Tom, but they said I had to. Never mind, we'll have a great time tomorrow. Where would you like to go?' But by that time Tom had started to cry, and suddenly it was Maureen on the end of the line instead.

'Go on, just piss off to your precious work and leave us alone. I should have known you wouldn't turn up today. It's always been the bloody same.'

Steve took a deep breath. 'I'm sorry. It's out of my hands. I just can't do anything about it.'

'You should take a long look at yourself. Of course you can do something about it. You're just so tied up in being "this is Steve bloody Ross for the Nine O'Clock sodding

News", you do whatever they want you to. I think it's pathetic.'

'I'll call you this evening about tomorrow.'

'You've run out of tomorrows.'

In the BBC issue Rover 216, heading east through the thin traffic, Steve felt no clear emotion except depression and sadness. His anger was undermined by the feeling that Maureen was largely right. Their first years together had been fine when he was a radio news sub-editor, working shifts on the desk, rewriting stories from news agency copy. The pressure had started to crank up when he was made a reporter and she gave up her job in an architect's office to have Tom. Then the midnight calls and the long trips began, but it was when he made the leap across the gulf to television that the monster began to take over his life, and the first cracks appeared soon after Tom was born. An impartial outsider would have said it wasn't all his fault, that she had begrudged his sudden success as well as his time away from home, but he wasn't an impartial outsider and it was in his nature to give more weight to her side of the problem even if he couldn't do much to change it.

He cut down a side-street to avoid a traffic jam where a truck was picking up a skip. Time was tight. Time was always tight in television, where the logistics of getting the pictures shot, rushing them back to base and editing them into a story burnt up five times as much time and adrenalin as the simple world of radio. In radio, if it happened and you weren't there, you could still talk about it. In TV, if you didn't get the pictures, you were dead in the water. As he got back on to the main road, pushing his way into the traffic, the harsh electronic bleat of the car phone went off. He pressed the button, answering it hands-off, the mike on the screen pillar picking up his voice, leaving him free to drive.

'Steve, it's Doug. I've been calling you on the Storno. Couldn't you hear me?'

He glanced down at the Storno two-way radio – one of his lifelines in this world where fast communication was everything – and saw with a guilty start that he'd forgotten to switch it on. He put that right, then for belt and braces checked his bleeper too.

'Sorry, Doug. Bad morning. It's on now.'

'OK. I'll give you a call with some details and the rendezvous in five minutes. In the meantime, Mike wanted a quiet word on the phone.'

Mike Page came on again. 'Steve, just a little word of caution. I know it's been quieter this year, but this one sounds like the bad old days again. You know what it got like on these demos when the boys in blue started screwing around. Just be a bit careful, that's all.'

'Thanks, Mike, got any other eggs you want sucking?'

'No need to get sharp with me.'

For all the sarcasm of his reply, the warning was serious. In the past two or three years, the police had got more and more hawkish about seizing camera crews' videotapes after violent demonstrations, to help them identify those involved. News editors wouldn't hand the tapes over freely because it put their crews into new and direct danger, but the authorities had begun using the courts to get the tapes. As expected, the backlash from the demonstrators had turned the crews into targets. Soundman Robin Green had been seriously injured by a shotgun blast, and the number of violent incidents had risen steadily. The authorities seemed totally unconcerned by the effect of their actions, and the crews now had to assume they were right in the firing-line.

The radio net was alive with distorted conversations

between camera crews, the lighting men, who travelled in separate cars as they weren't needed for every job, and the Intake Desk back in Television Centre, where all this activity was coordinated.

'Ariel Three Eight, do you read? Over.'

He picked up the mike and thumbed the button. 'Three Eight here, Doug. Go ahead.'

'Steve, the march starts at ten o'clock. There's about a zillion police along the route and they're expecting lots of bother. It's forming up on Whitechapel Road and heading for Hyde Park. You go with it all the way, and Diana Pugh's got the other crew around Westminster to cover anything there.'

'OK,' he said. 'How are we getting the stuff back?'

'You'll have a dispatch-rider with you for anything early, but if it starts to shape up big we'll send down links or the OB.'

Links vehicles were Land Rovers with microwave dishes on the roof. They could bounce a TV signal off various strategically located reflectors on high buildings, straight into the Spur, a wing of BBC TV Centre in White City where, on the sixth floor, the TV Newsroom was situated. For the big stories, needing more resources and using live injects into the news straight from the scene, the OB van was brought into play – an outside broadcast truck with its own generator, cameras and mini 'gallery' or control room. If there wasn't such a hurry, a dispatch-rider would pick up the tape from the crew and take it back to the Spur by motor bike.

'Who's the crew?' Steve asked.

'Sunny Jordan and Pat White. The RV's in Fieldgate Street.'

Steve pressed the disconnect button, pleased to get one of his favourite crews. News attracted the best, but even then, among twenty-odd teams consisting of cameraman and sound recordist, there were one or two who insisted on seeing the bad side of everything. Crew chemistry was all-important. If they didn't get on, you didn't get the best pictures, and that went for the reporter too. Steve had spotted early on that the prima donnas among his colleagues were shooting themselves in the foot. If the crew didn't like your attitude or didn't think you were professional enough, their patience would soon wear thin and, at that crucial second when a bit of extra speed, courage or endurance were needed, that might make all the difference between just another report and something truly memorable.

The crews liked Steve, regarding him as a good old-fashioned hard news man, good to be with out on the road, and fun during long stake-outs on cold doorsteps. If they noticed the way the faintly public-school accent of his on-camera performances shaded to something more streetwise in their presence, they never mentioned it. Indeed they would probably have mistaken the former for the affectation, not the latter.

Half an hour later, he was parking the car down a side-street opposite Sunny's Ford Granada. Sunny was standing by the open boot, a big, white-haired man, near retirement and tending to fat, but with the near-permanent smile on his face which had given him his nickname. Sunny strode across to Steve as he got out of the car, and clasped his arm.

'How's my favourite reporter? I haven't seen you for weeks,' he said, and then with a more serious look, 'I hear you're living out of a suitcase. How are you making out?'

Steve shrugged it off. 'It's not the best. I should have seen it coming.'

'But you're such a reasonable bloke.'

'That's not the way Maureen sees it, Sunny. She thinks I've put the job before the family.'

17

Sunny looked at him with sympathy showing on his broad, generous face. 'You don't get much choice, and she should see some of the others.' He shook his head. 'I've been so lucky. My wife's always kept her sense of humour. Let's you and I sit down for a beer when we've got this lot out of the way. I'd like to hear more about it.'

'Yes, I'd like that.' Steve glanced towards the end of the road. 'Is there much going on yet?'

Sunny shrugged. 'Not a lot, but the hordes are starting to gather. I've done you a few shots of police buses unloading, and people with pink hair sticking banners together, but that's about it. There's a crew from news training down here with a few of their youngsters, too. Anyway, we only did about ten minutes, then we had a camera fault.'

'Serious?'

'Serious enough,' said a soft Devonian voice, and Sunny's soundman, Pat White, unwound all six and a half feet of himself from where he'd been bending over the camera in the open boot. Upright, he towered over Steve by some five inches, and he was known in the business as the 'unfair advantage' from the time he'd hoisted Sunny onto his shoulders for the crucial shot everyone else missed, over the back wall, during the dramatic ending of the Iranian embassy siege.

'Every bloody light came on at once,' he said, 'head clog, humidity warning, battery. It looked like Christmas. I think it's got AIDS.'

'We've been on the blower, but they've asked us to see if we can do anything at this end, then they'll send another one down in a car if we can't,' said Sunny.

'Nice to know they've still got our interests at heart,' said Steve sarcastically. 'I'm surprised you didn't get some teenager with a First in Media Studies asking why you couldn't manage without one.'

18

It was a running sore among the crews and reporters out at the sharp end. Changes at the top of the BBC had filtered down through the News Division, stressing a new, intellectual approach to news, which to most of the experienced hands was pure anathema. Every day, it seemed, there were more people calling the shots who believed you could get the right perspective on a story by sitting in White City reading old newspaper cuttings rather than going out to see for yourself what was happening on the ground. An anonymously written subversive poem had gone the rounds. It detailed the story of a reporter, ringing in urgently from a call-box, who couldn't get his message through the plethora of desk people, all anxious to give instructions instead of listening. The last verse ran:

> Mike Page says you're going to lose your crew this
>   afternoon,
> We need them for some shots of a rabbit farm in Troon.
> They're needed for the backdrop of a graphic we've got
>   planned
> For a piece on rabbit farming up in North Northumberland.
> We've only got a cameraman called Jordan free just
>   now,
> But Fiona could direct him, tell him what to shoot and
>   how.
> The hapless correspondent, though, can't take it any
>   more –
> He has no more 10p pieces and his ear is getting sore:
> *Can you listen just a minute? Well, if you can or not, I'm
>   going to get this message through: The sodding Queen's
>   been shot.*

Sunny grinned at him. 'Well, you know what they say about

our dear bosses, don't you. If you haven't got any big ideas ...'

'... buy a bigger pair of glasses,' they all chorused together, and laughed with only a touch of bitterness.

'OK,' said Pat, 'I've done everything I can. Let's go and give it a try.'

They locked the cars and walked down to the main road, which was packed with demonstrators and policemen. An ITN crew and a small gaggle of the news trainees with their crew were already there. Sunny hefted the camera on to his shoulder, switched on and started shooting. Within seconds he stopped, switched off and put it down. He looked at Pat, who shook his head.

'It's had it, hasn't it?'

'Yup. What do we do now?'

Sunny pulled a mobile phone out of the equipment bag and punched the short code for the desk. He had a rapid, monosyllabic conversation, then rang off, looking unhappy. 'Would you credit it? They haven't got a spare camera that's serviceable?'

Steve looked at him in disbelief. 'So what do we do?'

'Believe it or not, they want us to go and take the one the news training crew are using.'

Steve glanced across the road. 'But that's an old Icky.'

'Yup, back to the steam age for us. Never mind, just as long as it works.'

It took a few minutes to persuade the trainees that they were serious, but then their cameraman handed over the gear and took the dead Sony in its place. Sunny busied himself checking the camera over, and Pat repacked his shoulder-bag with the bits and pieces for the different rig. Steve was watching the demonstrators. None of them noticed the three men in the Vauxhall Cavalier studying them from an unobtrusive parking place down a side-street, and, if they had noticed it, they would have had no reason to think anything of it.

Sunny had switched the camera on to warm up the tubes, plugged in the umbilical to the heavy recorder which Pat had slung over his shoulder, and was playing with the controls. He caught Steve looking at him, and smiled.

'Funny, isn't it. I remember when these seemed like Star Trek after all those years on film. It doesn't half seem old hat now.'

He hefted it on to his right shoulder, fitted his hand through the steady strap on the lens assembly, and fingered the rocker switch to zoom the lens backwards and forwards. Then he put it down carefully on the pavement and inspected the filter settings. 'Mustn't forget my trade mark,' he said, and from his pocket he took out a little metallic rising sun motif. For years, wherever Sunny had been, he had marked his equipment with his own personal emblem, to the despair of the facilities unit which serviced the cameras and was forever having to peel them off again. Once or twice they'd tried to get someone to stop him, but Sunny was a veteran of twenty-five years' service, with as many war zones to his credit, and the scars still on his leg from some Beirut shrapnel. He was allowed a lot of licence. He peeled the backing paper off the adhesive sticker and put it carefully on the side plate of the camera next to the logo which identified it as an Ikegami 79D.

'There. Looks as if it was made for it, doesn't it?' he said, and, in truth, the metallic gold of the little badge made it look just like part of the logo. 'OK,' he said, shouldering the camera, 'let's go and earn a crust.'

The next two hours were a hard slog. Steve and the crew, working closely together, were everywhere – covering all the angles on the developing demo, running to get ahead of it, looking for the vantage points and the shots to make sure the pictures told the tale. By the time it moved off, it was already massive, and more people joined it every step of the way. Most of the marchers were there to make a peaceful political point and the ranks included many nurses and doctors, but there also were plenty of hard cases, cheated of street aggro by the diluting of Thatcherism into Majorism and the shading of Poll Tax to Council Tax.

When the vanguard – the first thousand out of a total crowd maybe fifty times that – reached the section of the Embankment just before Waterloo Bridge, the trouble began. The police, still smarting from the sacking of the West End during the Poll Tax riot, had decided the march should turn south over the bridge – and keep south of the river for a while before heading towards its eventual destination in Hyde Park. The march leaders wanted to go through Parliament Square, and weren't having any of that. A bit of designer malice from them, a bit of clumsy police work, plus the effects of an isolated hot day, and the whole thing boiled over into mayhem in the space of two or three minutes. Sunny was right in there, in his element, charging around, taking Pat with him on the end of the umbilical in that complex two-step at which crews become masters. Steve too had to move smartly around them, staying close to Sunny's ear to guard him from jostling, and acting as an extra pair of eyes for the next shot when fresh incidents flared outside Sunny's viewfinder-blinkered line of sight.

The march split, with the violent element racing north towards the Strand, round the side of the police cordon, while the vast bulk, away from the trouble at the front, seemed happy to stay where they were and take a breather for a while. The crew worked northward too, shooting scenes of increasing violence – smashed windows in Northumberland Avenue, a British Telecom van being tipped on its side, and then a police car, trying to reach it, being pelted with bricks from a building site. They paused for a minute in a narrow side-road to change tapes, and Steve saw an opportunity in the pitched battle now raging ten yards away, across the end of the street they were in.

'Hey, Sunny, what say you we knock off a quick piece to camera with that lot going on behind?'

Sunny squinted at the sun and nodded. 'Perfect. Says it all, and the light's good on your face. Think up some words a bit sharpish, though, or they might all go away.'

They'd left the tripod back in the car. It was far too bulky to carry through a demo, but Sunny made do by bracing his shoulder firmly against a wall to hold the camera steady on the head and shoulders shot of Steve with the riot going on behind him. Steve quickly pulled out a comb and – checking his reflection in Sunny's lens – straightened out his hair and his tie. As he did so, he noticed three figures turn into the narrow road from the other end, behind Sunny, and start walking towards them.

He thought quickly, looking for worthwhile words to say to fill fifteen seconds in the middle of a story whose structure and script wouldn't be decided for a few hours yet.

'OK,' he said, 'ready when you are.'

'Give me a quick white-balance, would you?' asked Sunny. Steve held a white sheet of paper from his notepad up in front of his face, the sun bright on the paper and in his eyes. Sunny zoomed in on it, pressing the button so that the camera took that as a datum level for its three colour-tubes.

'Right you are,' he said, 'Go whenever you're ready.'

Steve stared into the camera lens, went blank for a second, then got the words back and began to declaim.

'The violence started right here, just north of the river, at about 11 a.m. The police couldn't stop a ...' He paused, annoyed. The three men were right up to them now, black outlines against the bright sunlight, and, instead of giving them a wide berth, were clearly intent on messing around. It was an occupational hazard of shooting pieces to camera in the street. Then, just as he was preparing to be angry, he saw with incomprehension and sudden fear that all three had donned full-face balaclavas, bank-raider style, with nothing but small holes for their eyes.

Sunny thought that Steve had simply forgotten his lines, and kept the camera pointing at him.

'Go again, whenever you like,' he said, but by then Steve was shouting and trying on what seemed leaden feet to spring forward. A descending cosh had appeared in the hand of the nearest man. Sunny muttered and had just started to turn when the cosh hit him with a muffled, splintering sound. As his knees buckled, his attacker grabbed the camera from him, letting him slide to the pavement. Pat was on his knees with the recorder and the mike, and he only began to react when he heard Steve's yell through his headphones. Before he could do anything, he too was down. By that time Steve was on the one who'd hit Sunny, who didn't try to fend him off but concentrated on keeping secure hold of the camera. Steve landed two hard punches to the side of his head and the man grunted in pain, but then his own head exploded from behind in obliterating blackness, and he pitched head first to the pavement.

A hard pain in his cheek was the first thing he became aware of as he came round. He opened his right eye, the other being gummed shut, and lifted his head with a huge effort. The pain in his cheek came from the sharp, unsquashed corner of a flattened cigarette packet between his face and the pavement. Pat was on his hands and knees, swaying and shaking his head slowly as he called to Sunny, who was lying flat on his back. Pat crawled over to Sunny, looked closely, and felt his head. He straightened to his knees, stared for two or three seconds more, then turned slowly to face Steve, his eyes wide in a white face.

'Jesus God Steve. He's dead. They've gone and killed him.' Steve got to his feet, head spinning, and lurched across to Sunny. The mess that had been the back of his head, and his unfocused stare, showed it was true. He felt for a heart-beat and there was none. He thought of heart massage and mouth to mouth, but no first aid he had ever heard of could have put Sunny back together again. Finding his legs beginning to shake uncontrollably, he sat down on the pavement and took Sunny's hand in his own.

'I've got to get the camera,' said Pat. Shocked and hurt, his automatic response was to get the pictures, just like Oggy Lomas in the hill above Beirut, filming soundman Don Nesbit, unconscious on the ground after a mine destroyed their car. Then he looked around him. 'Where is it?' he said.

Chapter Three

A month earlier, the autobahn from Chur to Zürich had been full of opportunist skiers scurrying home to Zürich after grabbing the last – melting – snow of the season. In the narrow tunnel, the traffic was slow moving, and the big overhead fans were turning, blowing out the carbon monoxide. As the tunnel ended, brightening to fading evening light, the road curved left into the open, straight into the setting sun. Ahead, directly in her line of sight, a man stood on the hard shoulder, dark and distorted against the bright backlight of the sky.

Before she could identify it as mere coincidence and block it out, the perfect match of sun, man and road brought vicious memories crashing in on her. She saw again the windscreen craze and mushroom in, saw her hand on the steering-wheel, thrown back towards her face, numbed and spraying blood as it came. She remembered the hot, invading stings in her shoulder and her hip. Then, as the car slewed sideways, she had turned in slow motion to see Pedro, her husband of just three hours, flopping towards her with one eye gone and his forehead smashed to pulp where the heavy machine-gun bullets had found their intended target.

She was brought back to the present by indignant Swiss horns, to find herself slowing down as she stared across the empty passenger seat of the Hertz Mercedes, sorrow sharp in her throat and behind her eyes. A parking place came up on the right and she threw the Mercedes into it, holding tight on to the wheel long after she had stopped, and beginning to burn with the anger which had long ago become her anti-dote to sorrow.

'Four years,' she said out loud, 'four bloody years.' She looked around her at the foreign landscape and fought to repair the little patch of vulnerability. That's half a world away, she said to herself, silently this time. Just stick to the job in hand. Just think about the money, nothing but the money. Her native tongues were Spanish and English, but the English prevailed in her when her emotions were raised.

She got out of the car, looked with distaste at the neat picnic tables, and glanced briefly, and with little interest, across the rippling, picture-postcard width of the Walensee to the Churfirsten mountains beyond, where the high snow-fields were burning with orange and pink in the setting sun. Her mind was still thousands of miles away when some symmetry in the landscape caught her professional attention and brought her back to the present. To any casual passer-by it would not have merited a second look – a chance conjunction of clearings through the trees on the hillside, leading to two anonymous barns. To her, though, ballistics, overlapping fields of fire, enfilades, ambushes and sudden death had been the stuff of life for four years now. From Beirut to the Bekáa and even to Belfast, and wherever else man's inhumanity to man takes explosive form, her genius for bloody innovation had gone before her. Her first act of revenge in her Colombian home town had brought her the nickname that stuck to her, and the warped legend of the Bang Lady was born.

She was a stranger to Switzerland and the all-pervading militariness of its neutrality, but the careful camouflage of the gun emplacement controlling the tunnel entrance in front of her was an open book to her specialist eye. She spotted a missing element. Surely there would also need to be a mortar somewhere straight ahead, for backup? She looked harder. Yes, there, in a small clearing on the steepest part of the slope, was a lone tree stump. Glass fibre for sure, she thought, and hiding a nasty surprise for any hostile power which chanced its arm in this section of the Alps.

She reflected on the day. The overnight flight across the Atlantic into Zürich's Kloten airport. The familiar and unnecessary moment of tension as her passport was checked with what seemed more than usual care, but then she'd been warned that the reaction of Swiss immigration to anyone with skin darker than their own tended to be hostile. Then the two-hour drive east in the hire car. Knowing nothing before leaving home except the name of her Zürich hotel and her first rendezvous in Liechtenstein, she had taken care to check that out. Vaduz, the capital of the toytown principality, was just what she'd been given to expect. Its winding main street was dotted with restaurants, tourist shops and the discreet banks which were the power-house of the tiny place. Behind those dull walls, under the shadow of the Disneyesque castle of the Crown Prince up on the hill, was one of the most receptive homes in Europe for hot money – where the laundryman bankers could wash any stain clean as long as there were enough noughts on the bills.

Even though it was Sunday afternoon, the bank's side-door opened at once to her buzz. A polite middle-aged man, dressed so painfully well that it was hard to believe his clothes had ever been worn before, showed her to a room furnished with antiques of a self-conscious fragility.

'You are Miss ...?' he enquired in English.

'I am your four o'clock appointment,' she had answered, curtly.

'Yes,' he said, accepting the rebuke. 'I wonder if you would mind ... the glove,' he added, gesturing towards her hand with embarrassment. She left it on, holding her hand out so he could inspect its incomplete shape through the black leather. He looked quickly at it, then away.

'I'm sorry,' he said. 'You will understand, I hope. I was given precise instructions about identification.'

She waved the mutilated, gloved shape in front of his face, controlling her own feelings by deliberately, childishly, adding to his discomfiture. 'Don't worry,' she said, 'three fingers are enough for most things,' and he looked as if he wanted the ground to swallow him up. With sudden briskness he turned to the attaché case on the side-table and brought out the package.

'I am instructed to give this to you, to be opened only when you are back in your hotel room. You must follow the instructions on it. I do not, of course, know what is contained in it. Here also is fifty thousand dollars in cash. I am further instructed to show you this deposit statement to the sum of one hundred thousand dollars. This is to be held in an escrow account until the other signatory is satisfied that you have completed your contractual obligations.'

She looked briefly at the paperwork, aware of his eyes studying her. She knew he was wondering what degree of sexual service she could possibly provide to be worth so much money. Her beauty was a great disguise, she mused, not for the first time. Looking like she did, dressing like she did, tended to stop people asking serious questions about her travels and the source of her wealth. It was so much easier to leap to the conclusion that she was just a *poule de luxe* with a small added attraction for deformity freaks. Then she met his eyes and realized with slightly alarmed amusement that his speculations had obviously stirred the man somewhere inside the suit and he was starting to contemplate some clumsy form of advance.

'Please don't get too excited,' she said. 'You couldn't

possibly afford me, and anyway I'm sure your wife would like you back home in one piece.'

He looked horrified. 'Madame,' he began, 'I hope you don't think ...' but she cut him off. 'Just show me the way out, please. I need to be on my way.' Anyway, she thought, as he led her to the door in a strained silence, you're far too nasty, and so has everyone else been for such a long time now.

She felt calmer now, and took one last brooding glance across the evening landscape before getting back in the car for the final leg into Zürich. She wondered briefly who her employer might be, but soon gave up that pointless pursuit. It had been her own decision to take the anonymous offer, breaking her own safety rules. She didn't need a lot more money to reach her goal, and this one paid as much as four jobs in South America.

Once, she reflected, the black and white of good guys and bad guys had been so much simpler. She had been an explosives specialist in DAS, the Colombian internal security police. Pedro had been her commander, then her lover, then finally, and so briefly, her husband. Since his death, all that had mattered to her was the money building up, job by job, and the revenge it would one day help to buy her against those who had killed him.

The sun set while she was still driving, and though she restlessly checked her mirror and the cars she passed for any sign of threat, the effortless ride had lulled her halfway to most people's normal level of alertness. So it was that the sudden blinding glare from the road's edge, which filled the windscreen, caught her off guard for the second time that day – shock pumping her instantly full of adrenalin. Pulse racing, she floored the accelerator and took the slip-road at 140 k.p.h. and rising, tyres swaying on the limit of adhesion.

She searched the road in front and behind for any further sign of trouble – gradually letting herself conclude with relief that, whatever it might have been, she was past it and unscathed.

Back down the road, rocking in her wake at the wheel of his old Renault, Gerd Winistoerfer, chocolate salesman, shook his head in disbelief. Only an out-of-towner would have fallen foul of that obvious speed trap. The big steel box containing the radar and the flash camera stood out like a sore thumb, but usually people hit the brakes after the flash. He'd never seen anyone react to it like that before. Still, he'd noticed the exotic profile reflected by the instrument lights as the car had wafted past him, and the hire-car number-plates provided a completely satisfactory Swiss explanation for the strangest behaviour. 'Bloody foreigner,' he said to himself.

In her room at the Nova Park Hotel, she calmed down and decided to dismiss the incident for want of any reasonable explanation, though she stayed on a high level of watchfulness and prowled the room more than usual. Over a glass of wine, she opened the package. It contained a VHS videotape, carrying no outward identification except for a printed label saying 'Erase after viewing'. A machine had been provided in the room, so she slipped it in and settled back to watch.

An hour later she had seen it through twice, and she had a block of paper covered in neat notes in front of her. The tape described a type of target without precisely identifying the person. It described a venue and an event in detail, and listed all the formidable security precautions in force there. It listed problems and more problems, and it demanded a foolproof solution. The voice on the tape was a man's voice, and he didn't sound like a nice man, but in the light of the subject matter it would have been odd if he had been.

She put the tape in the machine, to erase it by recording over it. She flicked casually across the cable channels and found CNN just starting a news bulletin from Atlanta. As she settled back to watch, the phone rang and that now familiar, not-nice voice said, with no preamble, 'You've watched it by now, I hope.'

'Of course,' she said, but her attention was distracted by what she was seeing on the screen.

'You see the special nature of the problem then. I hope you're up to finding a solution.'

'Oh yes,' she said, staring in fascination at the magical answer which had just appeared before her eyes. She reached for a pad of paper with her free hand, already thinking dimensions, considering materials. 'Yes, I am sure that will be possible.'

Chapter Four

There was no one else in the side-street, just the two of them and Sunny's body. All the equipment had gone. Steve's first impulse was to run back down the street to the turning from which the men had come. He had no idea how much time had passed since the attack, but his legs would barely work and, after two or three stumbling steps, dizziness forced him to slow to a painful walk. There was no one there. He went back the other way. Pat was sitting on the pavement, staring at Sunny.

Steve had a strong sense of the time-driven machine for which they worked, its wheels whirling around in White City, not knowing that one of its vital cogs lay in pieces on the ground. He wanted to tell them. He wanted help. Like a child turning to an adult to mop up the spilt milk, he wanted someone in comforting authority.

He walked out on Northumberland Avenue and realized several minutes at least had passed. There was a lot of noise coming from the right, up towards Trafalgar Square. In the road immediately around him there was nothing but a trail of destruction – broken glass, half-bricks and other missiles. An acrid smell came to him, and a hundred yards to his left he saw a group of firemen hosing down a burning work-man's hut. He headed for the uniforms.

He had only gone a few steps when a white Transit approached at high speed with its siren going. He waved, but his reactions were slow and it went by, policemen in riot helmets turning to look at him through the back windows. A second Transit followed it, and this time Steve stepped out into the road, arms waving, to force it to stop. His rubbery legs took him off balance, a step or two further than he intended. The van swerved violently round him, then braked sharply to a halt. As the side-door opened, a sudden wetness on his neck brought it home to Steve that there was blood all down the side of his face.

A man in a helmet, its visor pushed up, wearing dark blue overalls, ran up to him.

'What the bloody hell do you want? We nearly ran you over, pratting around in the middle of the road like that.'

'We've been attacked,' said Steve. His voice sounded thick and strange. He tried to go on. 'My cameraman's dead,' but only the last word came out clearly.

The policeman looked him up and down. 'You're not dead,' he said. 'Drunk maybe. If you don't want to get hurt, don't come out on days like this. Now, we've got better things to do.' He was turning back to the van when Steve got his tongue to work.

'My friend's been killed,' he said. The policeman stopped in his tracks. 'Down there,' he went on, and pointed.

Everything happened in a rush then. More policemen jumped out of the van. Two of them held him and sat him down inside it. Others ran off. In a minute, two of them were back with Pat between them.

'Mind this one, he was there too,' said one. 'There's a dead one down there all right.'

'HN Unit 14,' said the driver into a microphone. 'Northumberland Street, corner of Northumberland Avenue. Assistance needed. Ambulance and CID. We have a body here. Over.'

'Why did they do it?' Pat started to ask Steve, but the Sergeant next to him interrupted.

'Don't talk to each other, you two. You can talk to me

instead. I've got lots of things I want to know from you.'

So much for comforting authority. It suddenly came home to Steve that being found with a corpse in the middle of a riot was not going to lead automatically to hot sweet tea and sympathy. He tried again.

'We're a camera crew from BBC TV News. I'm the reporter. This is the soundman. The ...' He couldn't bring himself to say the words. 'The other one is the cameraman.'

The Sergeant looked at him hard. 'Let's see some ID then.' Steve reached inside his jacket for his wallet, with his press card and his BBC identity card. There was no wallet. 'They've taken it,' he said. 'Show them yours, Pat.'

But Pat was already trying his own pockets and shaking his head.

'If you're a camera crew, where's the camera?' the Sergeant said, as if talking to a child. He had a wide, round face with small eyes, and was sweating hard.

'They took it, and all the rest of the gear,' said Steve, and his words swam thinly in the silent atmosphere of disbelief. 'Look,' he said, 'ring the TV newsroom. I'll give you the direct line number. They'll tell you.'

The Sergeant shook his head. 'All in good time. They can do that at the station when we get you back there. In the meantime, you give me your names and addresses for a start.'

Pat lurched to his feet, banging his head on the roof of the Transit with a dull boom. 'I'm going to be sick,' he said indistinctly, 'Let me out.'

'Cuffs on him,' bawled the Sergeant, and a young police-man jumped to obey. 'Out of the van, quick, and watch yourself.' Metal handcuffs were snapped on Pat's wrist and he was pulled, stumbling, down from the back of the van so fast that he tripped and fell awkwardly to the ground.

Steve tried to get out to help. 'Watch out. He's been hit on the head, for Christ's sake.'

The Sergeant caught his arm and forced him back in the seat. 'You keep quiet. You are a suspect. Got that? A suspect. You just do what you're told, and we'll sort you out later. We've got a body down there and two men with no means of identification found in its close proximity. That means you sit still and shut up, right?'

'But I came to find you.'

'You were wandering about in the road, that's all I know.'

Steve watched Pat on his knees, retching in the gutter. The young policeman, forced to stand close by him because of the handcuffs, was trying to keep his trousers out of the line of fire, turning his head away with distaste.

Help came from a wholly unexpected source, with a loud American voice from round the side of the van. 'Steve, Steve Ross. What the hell are you doing in there?'

Steve turned in surprise and found himself looking through the side-window into a face he hadn't seen in a year or more. A mane of curly brown hair sprouted from under a battered baseball cap with a lager advert on the front. Pale blue eyes and a well-chewed walrus moustache topped a surprisingly naked chin. Relief flooded through him. 'Nick Nielsen,' he said, 'the Seventh Cavalry.'

Nielsen's face disappeared, and a moment later reappeared at the back door. The Sergeant moved to block him off. 'You can't come in here.'

Nielsen looked at him and smiled a slow smile. 'Why not?' he asked politely.

'Because we have two suspects in here and you'll be hampering our enquiries.'

Nielsen turned and whistled. In another second, the snout of a TV camera was peering over his shoulder and a gun-mike was being thrust in the Sergeant's face. 'Now, Chief,' he said, 'would you care to tell CBS News just why you're holding this man in the back of your truck here?'

The Sergeant gaped, then put his hand over the end of the camera lens and tried to push it away. Nielsen used the moment to climb into the back of the van. The other policemen were standing round, unsure what to do, and the Sergeant gave up on the camera and grabbed him instead. 'Out, you, now, or you're in a lot of bother.'

'And you're on camera, Chief, in the middle of a diplomatic incident involving the manhandling of a prominent American citizen. Now why don't you just tell me why exactly you're holding one of the British Broadcasting Corporation's top reporters in the back of your crummy little paddy wagon, and how come he seems to be leaking a little blood?'

He cut an unlikely figure now he was in full view. A dirty T-shirt invited the world to stay at the beautiful Summerland Hotel, Beirut. A patched pair of jeans, and running shoes which were down at heel from the weight of his beer gut, rather than from any strenuous exercise, completed the ensemble.

Steve intervened. 'Nick. He won't believe who I am. Someone attacked us. They've killed Sunny Jordan.'

From then on, under the relentless eye of the American's camera, all the things happened which should normally have happened straight away. The Sergeant put a call through to Television Centre and confirmed Steve's identity. He became ingratiating instead of aggressive; it was no great improvement. Pat had recovered a little, and his handcuffs were quickly removed. Nick, conscious of the state of shock that both Pat and Steve were still in, sat in the van talking quietly to them while his crew got some more shots of the scene.

It was a surprise to see him in London, and Steve said so. 'Yeah, well, I moved over last month from Rome. There wasn't much freelance there, so I decided to try my luck over here. I tried to phone you but Maureen said you'd

37

moved out and she hung up on me when I asked for your number. I was going to try you at the Beeb.'

'So how come you're working for CBS?'

Nick looked round, but the policemen were all outside the van now. The Sergeant and a couple of the others had stayed to wait for the CID men, and the rest had gone on up to the riot in Trafalgar Square. 'I'm not. I'm doing a cheap documentary for some Canadian outfit, called *The Thatcher Legacy*. I just didn't think that would cut much ice with the rozzers.' He looked towards Trafalgar Square. 'If you guys are up to it, I'm going to have to hit the road. We need some riot piccies.'

Steve smiled. 'Of course. And thanks, Nick,' thinking that's the second time you've pulled me out of the shit.

They exchanged addresses. Nick's was a smart one in W8, but he waved it away. 'I just borrowed it for a while. She's gone shopping for a month or two.' Then he was gone.

The first concrete effect of the Sergeant's phone call was the breathless arrival on the scene, four or five minutes later, of Diana Pugh and the other BBC News crew. The crew were old friends of Sunny and Pat and were clearly very shocked by the events. Diana was one of the last people Steve wanted to see, a brassy lady, trying hard to be the next Kate Adie but lacking the natural talent to balance the assertiveness. She confined herself to an unanswerable, 'Are you all right, Steve?' before trying to rush him into an interview.

'Come on, Larry,' she said to the cameraman, 'let's put Steve against the police van.'

Larry Moss, the cameraman, grimaced apologetically at Steve and hoisted the camera on to his shoulder.

Steve found himself shaking his head. 'Diana, I don't think I want to do this now,' he started, but she interrupted.

'Oh come on, Steve. Just a couple of quick questions. We

may not get the chance later.' Then she broke off, looking past him. 'Hold on. Look, they're going to take the body into the ambulance. Get that first, Larry.'

Without enthusiasm, Larry turned and shot the picture of the ambulancemen carrying a stretcher into the alleyway.

'Come on,' she said, 'we'd better go and get the close-ups as they put him in. We'll do the interview after.'

Larry put the camera down on the ground and turned to her.

'No, Diana. I'll do you a long shot from back here, and I don't mind shooting the ambulance, but that's all.'

Her voice went up half an octave. 'Get on with it. We're missing the shot. We can argue about it later.'

He picked up the camera and offered it to her. 'Here you are. If you know how this works, which I doubt, you go and do it.' Larry was a calm man, but there was an edge creeping into his voice. 'If you think I'm going to go down there and take close-ups of someone I had a beer and a laugh with yesterday, you can forget it. You know damn well they'll never use them on the news anyway.'

Diana didn't know when to stop. 'That's not very professional. You were at Zeebrugge. You've been in Beirut. So what makes this so different?'

'Friendship,' said Larry simply, and turned away. Diana gave an exaggerated shrug and turned to Steve as if seeking support, but Steve found he couldn't meet her eye.

'Let's do the interview, then,' she said, but at that moment the Sergeant, who'd been on the radio, came up.

'Sorry to interrupt,' he said, 'but they want these two gentlemen down at Vine Street straight away,' and Steve felt huge relief.

At Vine Street, they were inspected by a young doctor. He put a dressing on Steve's head wound, but something he saw when he peered into Pat's eyes made him uneasy and he sent him straight off to hospital for a fuller check-up. Steve gave a statement to another Sergeant, aware that it was painfully thin on detail. The outline and movement of the man who'd hit Sunny was etched in his memory, but he had trouble even estimating the heights of the other two.

'Did they say anything?' prompted the Sergeant.

'No, nothing.'

'Do you have any idea why they might have done it?'

The door opened during the question. 'Not really,' said Steve and looked round. Mike Page came into the room with a PC who spoke to the Sergeant.

'This is Mr Page from the BBC, Sarge. He's Mr Ross's boss. He asked if he could come straight in.'

Page put his hand on Steve's shoulder and gave it a squeeze.

'I thought I'd just sit in, then we can talk later.'

The Sergeant picked up his pen again. 'So you don't have any idea of why the attack happened?'

'It's obvious, isn't it?' said Mike Page, and the Sergeant looked at him with slight irritation.

'Why do you say that, sir?'

Unabashed, Page went on. 'Well, it's not the first time someone's tried to get rid of the evidence. We were talking to the Assistant Commissioner only last week about this sort of thing.'

But Steve was seeing the scene again in his mind.

'I'm not sure it was that,' he said. 'They didn't just take the camera. They took all the kit, even the bag with the spare batteries in.'

'They probably thought that was the only way they could be sure to get all the tapes,' Page objected.

The Sergeant cleared his throat. 'Sir, we are trying to get Mr Ross's statement down. Now it may well be that you should make a separate statement as to what you have just said, but we can leave the CID to decide if that is necessary, if you don't mind.'

The rest of it took another half-hour, and then they were told they could go. Page's car was in the yard and, as they drove out, Steve spotted a crowd of reporters, photographers and camera crews waiting at the street entrance. It was only when the lights came on and the flashes started that he realized he was their target. He turned and looked back as they drove slowly through, spotting Diana Pugh and Larry among their number.

They headed past Marble Arch, then Paddington and up on to the elevated section of the Westway, Steve telling the story again in detail for Page's benefit.

'Jock's gone to see Sunny's Missus up in St Albans,' said Page. 'We've sent a car to get Pat's sister up to the hospital. I didn't know if you'd want me to ring Maureen under the circumstances, so I thought I'd better wait and talk to you first.'

Steve stared out of the window at the shabby North Kensington roofs passing below. A momentary and tempting vision of reconciliation, with him cast as the wounded hero, came into his mind. He knew it was immature and he pushed it away.

'No,' he said, 'let her hear it on the news,' and as he saw Page's eyebrows lift slightly, he knew he'd succumbed to the even worse temptation of the macho opposite extreme. He also knew, from Page's thoughtful silence, that the remark would be around the building in no time – part of the legend of the day's events – and he wished he hadn't made it.

They swooped down the White City exit and left into Wood Lane. There was another small knot of photographers waiting at the gates, but the security man had been forewarned and raised the barrier for them almost before they had stopped. They pulled up the circular drive to one of the spaces reserved for news camera cars, next to where the Director-General's Jaguar was parked. Bypassing the newsroom, they went straight to the Editor's office, where Terry Conway, as well as his deputy and the head of administration, were all waiting, their casual dress showing the traces of their abandoned weekends.

Conway was young for the job, almost a contemporary of Steve's, and, though bright, tended to retreat into mild pomposity to cover up the missing years. 'Bad business,' he said, walking over to Steve. He seemed unsure whether to shake his hand, put an arm round his shoulder or hug him. He got around the problem by pushing his glasses higher up his nose with a finger, repeating himself, 'Bad business,' and retreating to his desk.

More practically, Mary Pickersgill, the head of administration, poured Steve a glass of corporation whisky from Conway's drinks cupboard. Their discomfiture started to give the day a surreal flavour. Steve found himself wanting to laugh, but a sudden image of Sunny killed that before it started.

He had just finished telling the story again, to a reverent hush, when the door burst open. A large man with a shaggy beard and horn-rimmed glasses strode through and glared around him. Dennis Daley, the editor of the weekend news bulletin, was a ferocious man in late middle age, not noted for his subtlety. He nodded at Steve. 'Sorry to hear about it,' he said, ''fraid that makes you the story tonight. Hope you're feeling up to it.'

'That depends what you mean.'

Daley handed round sheets of paper. 'That's the running order at the moment.'

Steve looked at it. RIOTDEATH was the first entry, at

number 6, with gaps above it in case any hotter story came in. He looked around, saw all the others studying the paper with deep concentration, and felt a sudden sense of revulsion at their readiness to turn his tragedy into the arm's-length stuff of their everyday business. Then Mike Page looked up, caught his eye, gave him an exaggerated shrug of exasperation and a big wink, and he felt a little better.

Daley glanced around, just missing the exchange of looks, and continued. 'Sylvia's the newsreader tonight. We'll do the headlines, then go to a wide shot in the studio showing Steve next to her to trail the interview.'

'What interview?' Steve asked, and the others glanced up at him.

Daley looked at him in surprise. 'The interview with you, of course. There'll have to be a bit about our man on the spot. We'll do Diana's report at the top. She'll do a minute and a half just on the killing. Then we'll do a graphic sequence showing how the attack happened. I've got Ed working on that, Steve, and he'll need a bit of help from you to get it right. Then we'll do an obit of Sunny Jordan. That's being cut now – and we'll want a word from you, Terry, as well. Then it's the interview with Steve, followed by the rest of the riot coverage.'

There was a silence filled with sage nods. Steve wanted to object, but found he was now feeling extremely tired in the aftermath of shock and couldn't cudgel his brain into working out the basis of his objection. Terry Conway spoke first.

'Where are the pictures for Diana's piece going to come from, if all the tapes were taken with the camera?'

'We've talked to ITN,' said Daley. 'Under the circumstances, they're giving us a dub of their coverage. In fact, they offered it straight away when they heard. I said I was sure Steve would do a turn for them in return.'

Mary Pickersgill was a relative outsider in this group. Middle-aged, and looking fresh from the pages of a 1950s women's magazine, she had recently joined TV News from the more cloistered atmosphere of BBC World Service. 'Perhaps we should ask if that's OK with Steve?' she suggested mildly.

Daley looked at her uncomprehendingly. 'Of course it's OK with Steve, isn't it Steve?' he said.

Steve shook his head. The movement hurt it. 'I don't feel too great,' he said.

Terry Conway looked at Mike Page in concern. 'I thought he'd seen a doctor?'

'Yes, he has. But he's been knocked unconscious, AND he's been on the wrong end of a murder,' Page replied, with a touch of sarcasm in his voice. 'I'll take him down to my office for a bit.'

The two of them went slowly round to the newsroom. Every head turned when they walked in the door, and one or two people started towards them, but Page, unseen by Steve, shook his head at them, and they returned to their desks.

Steve sat in a soft chair in the corner of Page's little office, sipping coffee to wash down two aspirin. Page put his feet on the desk.

'Are you going to be all right?' he said.

'I expect so,' said Steve listlessly. 'I suppose I can't disappoint Daley.'

'I'm sorry about all that,' Page said, 'they do all care about it really. It's just that they didn't know Sunny like we did. If you think about it, none of them have been out on the road in living memory, and they don't have much to do with the camera crews.' He scratched his head. 'It's like this lot in here. Some of the producers only believed it when they

44

read the story off the wires, just like it was happening to somebody else.'

'It's running on the wires?'

'Of course it is. I'm afraid it's going to be everyone's lead story. PA have been running yards of it. They got your age wrong to start with, but the rest of it is pretty accurate.' He turned his computer screen round and called up the Press Association news wire. 'Here, read it for yourself.'

The phone rang. Page spoke for a second, then looked at Steve. 'They want you down in graphics, as soon as possible. OK?'

The graphics department on the floor below was a dark gallery full of Quantel Paintboxes, expensive electronic graphics machines, lined up in a long row with their operators seated in front of them. Usually Steve quite enjoyed spending time in there. Despite the fact that he regarded graphics as a very inferior alternative to moving pictures, it was absorbing to watch the graphics artists picking up colours from an electronic palette, mixing them with a light pen and conjuring their images from nowhere. He saw the producer standing over one of the graphics staff, staring at a TV monitor. He walked quietly up behind them, looked at the screen, then looked again in disbelief. A series of cartoon-like images showed a map of Northumberland Avenue and the surrounding area. At the press of a button that changed to the outline of a man with a camera, then to the silhouettes of three figures, and then finally to another, very fanciful, silhouette picture of the attack – a comic-book attempt at an arm finishing an arcing blow, and a starburst impact point on the cameraman's head.

'You can't do that,' he said, 'that's terrible. It's just …' Words left him for a moment. 'It's just trivial. For God's sake let's have a bit of dignity in this.'

They both turned round in surprise at the bitterness in his voice.

'It's Dennis Daley's idea,' said the producer, deciding after one quick look at Steve's face that he was glad he had someone else to blame. 'Which bit don't you like?'

But Steve was out of the room and heading upstairs to Daley's desk before he'd finished the sentence. Daley was checking through stories on his computer screen and was taken aback by the ferocity of Steve's attack.

'Dennis, if you put that heap of crap on the air, I'm not going on your show. Sunny's dead, right? The way you want to cover it isn't news, it's the fucking Beano.' He suddenly became aware that the entire newsroom had gone quiet and every head was turned towards him.

Daley looked at him. 'All right, all right,' he said, 'I'll have a look at it. Just calm down, this isn't like you at all.'

The rest of the afternoon went by in a haze. Fifteen minutes before news time, Steve was asked to go into the studio for make-up and for the studio director to set the camera shots properly. On a normal day it would have been an unusual experience for him. Reporters don't get much time in the studio; that's for the newsreaders and the specialist correspondents who get called in to give expert opinions. He sat down and the make-up girl came and looked at him.

'You HAVE been in the wars,' she said.

He looked at her. 'I suppose the dressing might come off my head now.'

The floor manager, standing off to one side, cocked his head as a message from the gallery came through on his earpiece. He pressed his talkback button and said, 'OK, I'll tell them.' He walked over to them. 'They're saying leave the dressing on.' He took the make-up girl by the arm and led her away, whispering to her. Steve was expecting heavy pancake make-up to cover the damage of the day, but when she came back she simply put a little pale powder on his already pale face. He realized he was meant to look the part.

Sylvia Carroll, the newsreader, came in from doing her own make-up, moving slowly and stiffly as if to avoid disturbing the intricate architecture of her hairstyle, and sat down in the middle chair, next to him. She had her moulded earpiece already in place, and pushed its jack plug into the socket just under the desk before turning to Steve and giving him a thin smile. She was a brittle brunette, fresh out of regional TV and trying to make her mark. Steve felt even sleepier under the hot lights, and let it all wash over him. People were rushing in and out with fresh scripts. Sylvia was having frequent, one-sided chats with the gallery through the open mikes. The Floor Manager was conducting urgent, low conversations with her and the director. Steve, cut off from the chaos in the gallery by the lack of an earpiece, felt himself in the calm eye at the centre of a storm, the only quiet spot in the maelstrom of the approaching bulletin.

They rehearsed the headlines quickly, then there was a sharp. 'One minute to air' from the floor manager, and it all went quiet. There was another warning at thirty seconds, and a curse as the floor manager tripped over a cable, then he counted down aloud for seven of the final ten seconds, ticked off the last three on his fingers and the title music started.

Steve watched the monitor in front of him in a torpor which was broken abruptly as Sylvia Carroll began to read the introduction to Diana Pugh's report. He looked closely to see what changes Daley had made to the repulsive graphics of the attack, and stiffened in appalled indignation when he saw precisely the same sequence of cartoon images being spread across the screen, exactly as he'd seen them earlier. He waited for the introduction to end and the recorded soundtrack of the report to begin, then addressed himself to the gallery through the microphone in front of him.

'You shit, Dennis,' he said. 'You said you wouldn't do that, you stupid bastard. That was bloody unforgivable.' He could see by the expression on Sylvia Carroll's face that someone was talking urgently into her ear. She looked hesitant, turned to glance at Steve, and said, 'Yes, yes. I think so.' Then she spoke to him directly. 'Dennis Daley said he'll talk to you about that later. Just concentrate on the interview.' The floor manager brought him a glass of water as though that was some kind of solution.

He watched the monitor glumly as it went through a short obituary of Sunny. First some famous film footage he'd shot in Vietnam, then Beirut and finally the Iranian Embassy siege. Terry Conway's face appeared, its mouth opening and closing silently, and then Sylvia Carroll's voice, from next to him, in a new, synthetic tone of concern. 'And in the studio we have our reporter Steve Ross, who, as you've heard, was injured in the same attack. Steve, we're very glad you are well enough to be here. When did you first realize what was happening?'

He heard his voice replying, and found in the cathedral-like stillness of the studio that he could listen as though it came from a separate person. Out of the corner of his eye, he could see his own image on the monitor. She asked him a series of dry, factual, what, when, where and how questions, then, with a wide-eyed look, slipped in a final question: 'How did you feel when you saw he was dead?'

Steve looked at her aghast. His mind churned to find an answer. The main thought in his head was that this was a ridiculous and insensitive question, but it wasn't until he saw the newsreader flush and turn back to the camera to start the next story that he realized he had said it out loud.

Chapter Five

Professionalism kept him in his seat, still and silent, until the newsreader got through the introduction to the next report, stumbling twice over her words, and the tape began to roll. Professionalism ensured he carefully removed the mike which was clipped to his tie instead of wrenching it off. Professionalism made him pick his way slowly round the cameras and over the cables to the studio exit, following the safe path to stay out of shot if the director in the gallery should suddenly need to cut back to the newsreader before the tape ended. He didn't hear the sudden hubbub in the studio as Sylvia Carroll frothed into lightweight indignation and the floor manager moved in to calm her down.

Once beyond the heavy, soundproof door, however, blind anger took over and professionalism went out of the window. As Steve headed down the narrow passageway outside, the gallery door flew open and Dennis Daley, scripts in hand, erupted from it to block his way. 'You bloody little ...' he began, but that was as far as he got. Without any conscious decision on his part, Steve found his hands reaching out, seizing Daley by the front of his sweater and hurling him out of the way against the wall.

Through the next set of doors and into the newsroom, where he walked into a frozen tableau. Three or four people were still working hard, finishing or changing breaking stories. The rest would normally have been slouched in chairs, watching the news going out on the nearest monitor. Instead they were on their feet in small groups, chattering.

As the doors creaked closed behind him, they all swung round. There was a moment of silence; then, from the foreign news area off to one side, a loud Australian voice said, 'Bloody good, Steve. That bitch needed telling.'

Thirty pairs of eyes swivelled towards the Foreign Duty Editor, a grizzled Queenslander who'd been everywhere, done everything and always spoke his mind. No one else felt so brave. As Steve walked through their midst, Mike Page appeared through the doors at the far corner of the room and beckoned him through.

'Post mortem,' he said, 'Conway's office. He wants you right away.'

Steve stopped just inside the newsroom, aware that every word they said was being committed to memory by every ear in range. His first surge of fury was past, but a colder anger mixed with exhaustion was now in its place.

'Where the hell do you think I'm going?' he said. 'I've got a bloody sight more to say than he has.'

It was perhaps forty yards down the corridor and round the corner to the Editor's office, forty yards in which some remaining natural reticence and respect for authority on Steve's part tried to reassert itself and failed. He went through the secretary's ante-room at speed and opened the door. Terry Conway, insulated from the rest of the room by his huge desk, was in the middle of an expansive gesture towards his deputy, an older man, who was slouched in one of the rows of couches lining the walls. The words '... just downright embarrassing' trailed off as he registered Steve's presence and frowned.

'Ah, Steve,' he said, 'I think we need to talk about your, er, rather unfortunate phraseology to Sylvia.' He paused for a second, waving towards a chair, but Steve gave him no chance to continue.

'I think we need to talk about the obscene pile of crap

Dennis Daley put on the air tonight.' He stood in front of the desk, leaning over with his hands on its edge, getting his face as near Conway's as he could. 'I think we need to talk about that bloody graphic which turned Sunny's death into something out of a Batman comic. Daley told me he'd do something about it. He didn't. Then simpering Sylvia comes along with her stupid question and I thought it was time we stopped the circus act, so don't start telling me what *I've* done wrong.'

Conway moved back in his chair as far as he could and tried to avoid looking at Steve. 'Fine, fine,' he said quickly, 'let's watch the rest of the show and talk about it when Dennis gets here. Get yourself a drink.'

He turned to the screen again, where a dismembered coach lay spread across a Midlands motorway, and launched into a discussion of camera angles with unconvincing enthusiasm. Mike Page came in and sat down quietly. Steve sat, crouched sideways on the couch, staring down out of the window at the forecourt of Television Centre, the wasteland of Wood Lane beyond and the roofs of North Kensington and Notting Hill. He wondered how many of those roofs covered people now discussing his outburst. A steady stream of cars drove past on Wood Lane. At least they hadn't been watching, he thought, then realized he didn't really give a toss.

He was aware just how tired he was, and how little the rest of the day now held for him. No one to go back to. No one to listen sympathetically. No one to take his side over a day in which he, the victim, seemed to have inexplicably become the villain. The news ended. It seemed that barely a minute passed before Dennis Daley burst into the room, chin thrust out, beard bristling, full of affronted dignity. He ignored the others and swung round to face Steve.

'I'm not used to being manhandled by some little prat

who's just screwed up my show. I want an apology from you first, then we'll start talking about what you said on the air.'

Steve found himself staring up into Daley's face. He noticed that the hairs of his shaggy moustache were curling into his mouth and there was a patch of congealing food in his beard. He rose slowly to his feet and Daley stepped back a pace. 'Dennis,' he said, 'I'm sorry I pushed you out of my way. I really am ... I wish I'd hit you.'

Daley blinked, and everyone else started talking at once. Conway raised his voice over the rest, his usually concealed Welsh accent coming out as ever in times of stress. They fell silent and looked at him.

'I'm sure you don't mean that, Steve, so let's all simmer down, boys.' They waited for something more, but nothing came. Conway seemed at a loss. Mike Page, always practical, stepped into the breach.

'The point is, Steve stepped over the line with Sylvia. He's had a rough day to say the least, so let's not go overboard about it.'

'That may be the point to you,' broke in Daley. 'The point to me is that he manhandled me after behaving in the studio like a cabinet minister in a huff.'

It seemed to Steve in that moment of utter weariness that Page was the only one of them worth a damn, so he spoke directly to him. 'Mike, just a couple of points. First, I wasn't really in there like a normal reporter, was I? I was there like some kind of circus exhibit and, if Sylvia asks me that kind of insensitive personal question, I think I'm fully justified in giving her an insensitive personal answer. Second, I told Dennis that if he didn't change that foul bloody graphic then I wouldn't go on. He said he'd look at it, and then he did nothing about it.'

Daley jumped in. 'That's for me to decide, not you. I'm

the editor of the day and I'm not used to having some reporter telling me what I should put in my show.' He nodded emphatically as if in endorsement of himself and looked at Conway for support.

Conway rocked back in his chair, looked at the ceiling for a while, and cleared his throat. 'Well, of course Dennis has the final say, and we certainly won't run the interview again on the late bulletin. Maybe the graphic needs another ...'

At that moment the phone on his desk rang, and he seized it with obvious gratitude. As he listened, he leant forward sharply, looking from Steve to Dennis Daley and back. He went on listening for a couple of minutes, then said thank-you and hung up.

'That was the ...' He stopped and looked again at Steve. 'I'm sorry, Steve, would you mind waiting in the outer office for a minute, something's come up.'

Reluctantly, Steve went outside and sat down, wondering what it meant. He could just hear the voices within, but couldn't make out what they were saying. He looked idly at the secretary's in-tray, thinking that on any other day he might have been tempted to rifle it for interesting titbits. Then, suddenly, the voices within were raised, angry voices. The inner door flew open and Daley burst out, sniffed at Steve in passing and vanished down the corridor, leaving an almost tangible cloud of disgust in his wake.

The door closed, and stayed closed for another two minutes, then Mike Page came out, jerked his head for Steve to follow, and went out into the corridor. Steve followed him to an empty editing suite, and Page perched on the table. He was grinning.

'Come on, Mike, what's happened?'

'That was the duty officer on the phone. It seems that as soon as you did your little number on Sylvia, the switch-board lit up. The calls are still coming through. Two-thirds of them say it was the best thing they'd ever heard. It seems Sylvia isn't exactly the audience's favourite.'

'Hang about, does that mean the other third were on her side?'

Page grinned even wider. 'No, it does not. The other third were complaining about the nasty graphic in the intro.'

Steve felt a sudden bubble of savage exultancy. 'I bet Dennis didn't like that. No wonder he went storming out of there.'

'You haven't heard the best bit. He stormed out when Terry told him the only change he wants made for the last bulletin is that graphic. Everything else stays. They're going to replay the whole of your interview.'

Steve was startled. 'That's a bit over the top. I mean, doing it live is one thing, but that sounds more like showbiz.'

Page made a face. 'Whoever told you TV news isn't showbiz?'

Left alone, sitting in the edit suite, Steve stared at the phone for a long time, then picked it up slowly and dialled his old home number. Maureen answered immediately, then sounded disappointed when she recognized his voice.

'What do you want?'

'I just wondered if you watched the news.'

'Of course I didn't.'

It would have been easy if she had. She would surely have put recent rifts aside, he thought. 'It's just that we had a bad time,' he began, then stopped. His voice rang hollow in his ears, the voice of someone not just seeking sympathy, but demanding it.

Into the silence, her angry scorn poured over him. 'So did Tom,' she said. 'Why should I care?' And for once, he hung up on her.

He took the lift down to the ground floor and threaded his way through the corridors, where trolleys of lights and scenery stood ready for the next studio turn-round. He was in the section of the car park reserved for the news cars before he remembered that his car was still parked in the East End, where he'd left it that morning. He stood still, utterly dejected, and heard footsteps behind him. It was Diana Pugh.

'What's the matter?' she asked. In the sodium light she looked eerie, her make-up too dark, her face like hard plastic.

'I left my car there this morning. I forgot.'

'Come on,' she said, 'I'll drop you off. Where do you live? Fulham?'

'Used to,' said Steve, 'it's Earls Court now.'

'Sorry,' she said, 'I forgot.' But it didn't sound as though she had.

She said nothing more until they were alongside Shepherd's Bush tube station, heading for the roundabout. Then she looked at him sideways and said, 'Is there anyone else there? At your flat, I mean?'

'It hardly counts as a flat,' he said. 'No, there's only me.'

She looked at him again. 'Not a very good evening to be on your own.'

Steve felt himself a passenger in every sense of the word. Sitting there, barely in touch with the swaying of the car around the corners, his responses were lagging behind, but the ambiguity of this remark got through to him nonetheless, and it surprised him. He had never had much to do with Diana, but no one would describe her as the caring kind. The simpler variation on that – that he had been at the centre of the main event of the day and she wanted to be there too – didn't even occur to him.

'Let's stop off,' she said. 'I think the best thing for you is a strong drink.'

He let himself be led to a noisy pub just off Holland Road. He reasserted himself enough to get the drinks and, standing at the bar, he looked across at her. She was sitting at a table, sideways on, looking a little bit away from him. All he could really see through the crowd was her hair, thick, but bobbed at shoulder level. It was slightly curling, blonde, and darker in streaks. Carefully calculated to appeal, he thought. But then that impression was broken as, still looking away, she tilted her head and ran one hand up through her hair, lifting it up and back to reveal the long, pale curve of her arched neck and a delicate ear. For the first time he felt a stir of interest at the unconscious gesture and stared for a second or two before the barman came to get his order. Turning away, he didn't notice her eyes had been on him all the time in the big wall mirror.

They were both drinking whisky and his sense of unreality became stronger with each sip. Diana was quiet, solicitous, hanging on his every word. Her eyes, unnaturally wide, never left his. The pub lighting was soft on the sharp profiles of her face, and her voice was low, with a note he had never heard in the acid-sharp newsroom exchanges when she used her words as carefully weighed weapons to get her way. He told her the whole story all over again. At the end, she reached across and squeezed his hand on the table, letting her own hand stay resting lightly on his. He looked down at it lying there, thin pale fingers ending in darkly painted nails, so unlike Maureen's. The thought provoked a pang of guilt which he pushed away. Why the hell should he feel guilty?

'By the way,' she said, 'what happened in Conway's office? First you're on the carpet, the next thing you seem to be public hero number one and Daley's stalking around with a face like thunder.'

He would probably have answered, but, before he could, a shadow fell across the table and an unsteady hand came down on his shoulder. He looked up, but the intruder's gaze was focused on Diana. He was a middle-aged, round man with little in the way of a neck. His head seemed to be surrounded by his shoulders like a face painted on an egg. Everything on that face was moving, eyes blinking, nose sniffing, lips twitching wetly, all framed by the rolls of inert flesh surrounding them. He swayed on a slow ocean swell of alcohol.

'You're on the telly, aren't yer?' he said.

Diana put on an exaggerated and sarcastic smile. 'No, I'm in a pub, talking to a friend in private.'

He was too far gone to take any notice. 'Course you are, you're that Diana something, aren't yer? I always watch when you come on.'

Diana raised an eyebrow. 'How clever of you to know,' she said.

Steve shrank in his chair, nine-tenths glad it was Diana and not him who had been recognized, one-tenth peeved by the same fact.

The man sat down next to Diana. 'Here,' he said loudly to the bar in general, 'it's that bird off the BBC.'

Diana got to her feet. 'We were just going actually. I wish I could say it was nice to have met you, Mr ... ?'

'Er, Candless, but ...'

'As I was saying, Mr Gormless, have a perfectly horrid evening.'

'No, I said ...' But by that time they were on their way to the door.

On the pavement outside, Diana stopped. 'Have you got anything to drink at your place?'

'There might be a bottle of wine.'

'That'll do. Let's go and drink it in peace.'

She hung back a bit as the door opened on the bleak communal hallway of the house in Harcourt Terrace. The stairs had a violent red carpet with yellow sunbursts, or perhaps they were flowers. You could only see them clearly on the vertical sections. The treads had been worn down to the underlying structure of coarse matting.

Steve remembered as he opened the door into the room that he hadn't cleared up when he left so quickly that morning. He flipped the lids of suitcases closed and took stock. There was only the G-plan chair and the single bed to sit on. He waved at the armchair and went to the little sink in the corner where there was an uncorked bottle of Lambrusco left by a visiting friend. He poured it into two plastic beakers which were all he had. It was flat and had the pinkish-purple colour of Ribena.

He gave one with apologies to Diana, and sat on the bed. His head began to ache ferociously and he rubbed the back of his neck gently. Diana came over to him and put an arm round his shoulders. 'Hurting?' she asked. He nodded. 'Lie down, I'll give you a back massage. I'm good at it.'

It was easiest to do just as she said. He rolled over and stretched out and felt her fingers kneading the muscles of his shoulders and his neck with something approaching but not quite reaching pain. He felt himself relaxing as her fingers pulled his shirt free of his trousers and slid underneath them to dig into his skin.

'Steve?' she said. 'You were going to tell me what happened in Conway's office.'

It suddenly became very clear to him that the story wouldn't be safe with her and that, when it began to spread, he would be seen as the obvious source.

'Oh, not much,' he said. 'I just said I wasn't happy about the intro to the story and I didn't like the question, and I suppose he finally took my point.'

There was a doubtful silence, then some movement behind him. She went back to rubbing his back.

'Do you like this?' she said.

'Mmm, yes.'

'I've got a nicer way,' she said with a voice that sounded like a purr. He tried to look round, but she said, 'No, just lie still.'

Until then she had been sitting on the bed. Now he felt her swing up on to it, kneeling over him with her knees straddling his thighs. She pushed his shirt up to his shoulders and her weight came down on to his back, skin on skin, bare breasts warm below his shoulder blades as she began to nuzzle the back of his neck with her lips.

Then the phone rang and they both froze. He slowly reached one hand out to the floor and picked up the receiver.

'Hello, Steve?' said an uncertain and anxious voice. Maureen's voice. 'I just saw the late news.'

'Oh, right,' he said.

There was a short silence. 'I didn't know what you meant when you rang me before. I'm sorry.' She sounded restrained and formal.

'You didn't know,' he said.

'If you want, I can come over and see you. Are you hurt?'

He became aware that Diana, who had been still, listening, was now gently moving against his back and her hands were moving slowly around his hips.

'No, I'm just sore,' he said, 'don't worry. I'm planning to go to bed soon and sleep it off.'

Diana giggled and Steve felt a flash of irritation. He waved his other hand behind him in caution. She stiffened and kept silent.

'Is there somebody else there?' asked Maureen sharply.

'Someone from work just gave me a lift back,' he said.

'Who is it?'

'Oh, no one you know,' said Steve.

There was another silence, then she said, 'Tom's coming down the stairs. He keeps waking up. He wants to talk to you about tomorrow.' She turned away from the phone and he heard some mumbles, then Tom's voice.

'What are we going to do tomorrow, Daddy?' He sounded sleepy and muddled.

'Something nice. I'll think of something.'

Diana's hands started moving again and Tom said, 'Will you come in time for breakfast?'

Steve found he couldn't cope with two such complete contradictions. He rolled out from under Diana and hunched over on the edge of the bed. As he tried to concentrate on planning the day with Tom, he could hear Diana moving around, putting on her clothes. He looked behind him to see her pulling a jacket over her blouse and realized with a feeling of only mild disappointment that the moment of intimacy was past and his total experience of Diana Pugh's breasts looked likely to remain the feeling of them against his back.

She blew him a derisive kiss and walked out, closing the door sharply behind her.

Chapter Six

It's easy to spot the estranged fathers in the Science Museum. They're the ones talking to their children. Complete families are mostly content to wander round, sometimes together, sometimes separately, knowing that an infinity of breakfasts, lunches and bedtimes stretches before them for sharing, arguing about or simply forgetting what they've seen. For the others, though – and Steve was a learner in this – it was a precious island in a bleak sea.

He talked to Tom endlessly of trams, aeroplanes, veteran cars and steam engines until Tom became so disconcerted by the unrelenting attention that he started hanging back, then wanted to go. They walked up to the park and watched serious adults sail model boats on the Round Pond.

'Uncle Lawrence says you can get aeroplanes like that,' said Tom.

'Aeroplanes like what?' asked Steve, who had been momentarily locked back into thoughts of riots and death.

'Aeroplanes that you can steer like that with a box.'

'Yes, that's right,' said Steve. 'They're called radio controlled aeroplanes because ...' He broke off, struck by a thought. 'Who did you say said that?'

Tom looked hard at him. 'Uncle Lawrence. He's a friend of Mummy's.'

'Oh, yes, of course.'

Tom went on studying him. 'You don't know him, do you, Daddy?'

'Oh, I'm not sure, Tom. I probably do.'

'What colour is his hair then?' Tom challenged.

Steve knew he was caught up in some roundabout test of Uncle Lawrence's legitimacy. 'I can't remember, Tom. Why?'

Tom was silent for a while, looking at the pond, then said, 'I don't like him', and began to cry.

Steve hugged him, but he wouldn't stop for a long time. There wasn't anything to say that would help.

'I want to go home now,' Tom said when he finally sobbed himself to a standstill.

In the car, which Steve had retrieved from the East End that morning, on the way back to Fulham, through the Sunday streets, Tom withdrew into himself, sitting in the back, looking at the books Steve had bought him. Steve thought about Maureen. She had been hard to read when he'd arrived that morning, shocked at his appearance, tender when she asked about Sunny, but impatient and distant when he tried to build on that. She opened the door to them.

'You're home early,' she said to Tom.

'I want to have tea with both of you,' he said. 'Together.'

They each tried hard to make it work, seeking safe ground. They talked to Tom and only occasionally to each other. They played games, made up jokes and avoided eye contact, then at Tom's request they all watched a video, with the boy sitting between them. By further request Steve gave him his bath, read him a story, then sat with him as he went to sleep, before going downstairs to face an inevitable encounter alone with Maureen.

'I made you a cup of coffee,' she said.

'Thanks.'

'Have you seen Sunny's wife?'

'No, not yet. I'll go and see her in a day or two.'

'I thought you were right to say what you did to that newsreader.'

'Well, I didn't really mean to. It sort of slipped out.'

She looked at him in exasperation. 'That's a pity. I thought all that business might have made you start to see the error of your ways.'

'What do you mean?'

'Don't you understand really, Steve? There you were again, going out to play cowboys and indians. Getting your kicks standing next to your silly riot pretending to be Mister Hero reporter, and all it achieves is there's a widow where there used to be a nice couple. Then when your real feelings show just for a moment, when you tell that damned newsreader your private feelings are none of her business, you say that was just a mistake.' She paused, flushed and breathing heavily. 'I'm very sorry for what happened. I'm very sorry for Mrs Sunny, but don't you see if you would only lead a normal life, you wouldn't have even been there. You would have been with us, here where you should be on your son's birthday, and it would never have bloody well happened.'

Steve recognized the element of distorted truth, which made it sting all the more.

'It's not cowboys and indians,' he said, and even to himself the tone of forced reason in his voice sounded nothing but annoying. 'There is a point.' But then he thought, here we go again. He took a deep breath. 'Look, let's not start all that.' He thought about Tom's face at bedtime. 'Listen, Mo,' he said, 'do you think we could get a babysitter? I'd like to go out and have dinner. Why don't we?'

She looked at him coldly and defensively. 'I've got a babysitter,' she said. 'I am going out to dinner, but I'm afraid you're not invited.'

Steve nodded. 'Ah, this is Lawrence, I suppose,' and he saw her surprise.

'Did Tom mention him? What did he say?'

'Only that he didn't like him,' said Steve, heading for the door.

He drove aggressively and much too fast back to Earls Court. He parked a hundred yards away from the door and noticed that there was a wino slouched on his doorstep, drinking. Then he got nearer and recognized the baseball cap covering Nick Nielsen's woolly hair. Nick waved to him as he walked up. He was holding a pint tankard of beer, clearly liberated from the pub across the square. Nick patted the step next to him. 'Take a seat, my friend. I watched your little party turn last night so I thought I'd come and deliver my congratulations to you in person. Terrific.'

'That's not what they thought in Wood Lane.'

'Well, the hell with Aunty. I was watching it at ITN and they all stood up and cheered.'

'What were you doing at ITN?'

Nick looked slightly, but not very, embarrassed. 'Well, I hope you don't mind, but I sold them a bit of the stuff we shot when we found you with the police. All very tasteful, I assure you, and strictly in the interests of keeping the Nielsen body and soul together.'

'I believe you. Is it still women, wine and steak, or has the order changed with the advancing years?'

'No, I guess that's still about right.'

Nick Nielsen had a reputation, created in his wanderings around the world and amounting to almost mythical proportions, for lowlife tastes and legendary generosity. His propensity to borrow was only exceeded by his tendency to spend the money on making sure other people had an equally good time.

Steve smiled. 'Nick, believe me. You're the only good thing that happened yesterday. That makes two I owe you.'

Nick laughed, 'Yeah, the first time was funnier though, wasn't it?'

It had been two years before. The occasion was the second North–South summit between the leaders of the rich and poor nations, at Cancún on Mexico's Yucatan peninsula. It was one of those offbeat jobs that no one really wants despite the exotic location, because it's not clear there'll be any real story, and, when that happens on an expensive jaunt, it's the one doing the jaunting who tends to carry the can.

Steve's name had come out of the hat, and he'd spent three frustrating days there in stifling heat, trying to bend the rules of the press pool to get a few shots no one else had and trying to get the briefers to tell him something no one else knew. The trouble is, there wasn't really anything to tell because nothing of any great importance was happening. So the story started near the top of the bulletin for the glitzy arrivals at the airport and the pompous declarations of intent, and gradually slipped further and further down successive running orders as it turned out to be even duller than it looked. By the time of the final communiqué it barely rated a mention, and certainly didn't rate the cost of a satellite link to get the pictures back.

It was about then that the regular phone conversations with the foreign desk began to turn to how soon he could get back, rather than what was happening in Cancún, and the travel news wasn't too good either. There was a severe shortage of seats with everyone trying to leave at once. Steve found himself with an enforced thirty-six hours of idleness, as the detritus of a major news jamboree – the temporary briefing rooms, the satellite ground stations and the extra phone exchanges – disappeared around him like snow in spring.

The first morning on the beach was fine, an unexpected bonus after a lot of largely pointless activity. By lunchtime

Steve was bored with it. He met Nick at the bar, equally bored and too drunk to use the old Jeep he had hired. On impulse, and with Steve driving, they headed south down the coast towards some Mayan remains, down mile after mile of dead straight road, with mangrove swamps on either side, Steve's slight reserve melting under Nick's hell-raising approach to everything around him.

It was on the way back, after a day of yarning, sightseeing and more drinking, that they nearly came unstuck. They had left it until after dark – a bad mistake because the Jeep's lights were feeble and the road was filling up with strange nocturnal wildlife. They had been tearing along at an unwise speed, singing loudly, when Steve, who was still driving, saw something in the road ahead. He started to slow down, then realized with horror that the road was completely blocked by some kind of army checkpoint. There were soldiers behind an improvised barrier of oil drums, lit by a lantern whose battery had dwindled to the level of a glow-worm. Without realizing it they were back to the junction of the approach road to Cancún airport, and this was the security detail closing the road for some late departing head of government.

Steve had hit the brakes hard, only to find those on the left worked a lot better than those on the right. The Jeep slid sideways into the oil drums, scattering them and lurching to a halt in the middle of the remains of the barricade. There was a dead silence in which they heard the sudden clicking of rifle bolts. Aware that they'd just given a pretty fair impression of a terrorist attack, Steve had raised his hands slowly, staring at the frightened soldiers and their levelled weapons. Nick, however, stood calmly up in his seat, bowed and produced a coin out of his ear. As the soldiers stared, he put on an impromptu conjuring show which soon had them lowering their guns, clapping and laughing.

It was much later in the evening, in the pub, by the time they stopped swapping old war stories and turned introspective. Nick came back to the table with two more pints after a long and increasingly friendly discussion with the barmaid. He placed them on the table, sat down and waved a finger in Steve's face. 'It's time you broke out of all that news crap, Steve. You write too well to get stuck with ninety second wonders. Go and do some proper TV.'

'Easier said than done.'

'That's what losers say when they don't want to try. Anyway, now you've discovered the special catch-22 of TV news, haven't you?'

'Have I?'

'Sure you have. You can't keep the family happy with the job, and you can't stay happy in the job when you don't have a family any more. In the first case you come home beat when you come home at all, and that's no fun for them. In the second case, you come home beat and there's no one there to give a shit, and that certainly isn't any fun for you. Some people marry the job, and that's the fast track to sad old age.'

Steve shrugged. 'Some people marry other people with the same job. How does that rate as a solution?'

'OK if you can stand the competition. Got anyone in mind?'

Steve remembered Diana's fingernails and shuddered slightly. 'No.'

Nick waggled his finger again. 'You should have said no more often.'

'Easier said ...' but Steve trailed off, remembering what Nick had said last time.

'Crap. You always underrated yourself. I bet every time you go on air you worry about screwing up. I'll bet deep down you're scared that some day someone will point their finger at you and say, Steve Ross, we've found you out. You're just an imposter pretending to be a TV reporter. You don't really know what you're doing at all.'

'Of course I am. So is everybody.'

'Only if they're dumb. It's something you have to get past, otherwise life ain't worth living. One day you have to look at yourself and say, hell I really CAN do it, and if I can't, I can sure as hell fool most everyone into thinking I can. Then you get to start calling the shots and that's when they stop treating you like the doorstop.'

At the end of this speech Nick turned and blew a kiss to the barmaid, who blew one back to whistles from the others at the bar.

'Fine words, Nick,' said Steve, 'but I'm not in a very strong position right now with just about everything I earn going to Maureen. That sounds to me like it's time to toe the line.'

'When you finally see the error of your ways, give me a call. We could make some docos together.'

'I've never done a documentary.'

Nick reached across with both hands and tweaked his cheeks. 'You don't listen too good, do you? I told you, you're a natural. You write to pictures like an angel. Other people who've been in the business far longer sweat over it. You could do it standing on your head.'

'Maybe one day. What sort of stuff are you planning to do?'

'The sort of thing you'd enjoy. A bit of muckraking, a bit of investigation. The first one's kind of a portrait of a top cop. There's this guy who's about to retire from running the Serious Crimes Squad, or something like that. Got a million inside stories.'

'How did you meet him?'

'I didn't. I met his daughter.'

Chapter Seven

The phone bell broke her concentration for a second and the parallel rule skipped just a fraction on the big draughtsman's board. She suppressed an exclamation of disgust and picked it up.

His voice said, 'We've got it. It came this morning.'

No 'Good morning', she thought. None of the niceties of life with Cheeseman. Just the barest essentials.

'Good,' she said. 'I need to see it.'

'You'll have to come over. It's best that it should stay here. Less chance of an accident that way. Come after two,' and the phone clicked into a dialling tone.

She put the phone down and stared out of the window of the rented apartment. A tram rattled down Sihlstrasse below her. It's just like a big blue battleship, she thought. It's Zürich all over, impregnably solid, unknowably serious, old-fashioned, powerful, clean and secret. She pushed the swinging table away from her and stretched. When she thought of cities it was usually through the caricature of their transport systems. The past four years had been a riot of impressions, of fast, furtive journeys, of jobs done well and quickly. In that time she had added thin layers of selective and curious sophistication to the quickness which had always been there.

No one's life story seems strange to themselves, but hers was truly quite a tale. The town of Cali produces Colombia's most beautiful women, and she was the illegitimate product of a short and steamy affair between an aircraft mechanic from San Diego and the local woman who came to keep house for him while he was on a foreign assignment there. Complications killed her mother in the maternity ward and some deep-rooted seed of her father's Quaker parentage made him assume complete responsibility for her, although it would have been easy not to. He took her back to California, where, looked after by a series of his girlfriends, she remained until she was fourteen.

Once a year he would take her on a pilgrimage of guilt back to see her aunts, uncles and cousins. In between, she spent her leisure time surrounded by bits of machinery, regarding an aircraft hangar as the ideal playground and developing a keen sense of basic, practical engineering.

The day he died was one she would never forget, but tried never to remember. Standing with the latest girlfriend, a plump divorcee, in the crowd at the airfield, she watched him take off in the back seat of the old Grumman warplane he had just rebuilt for its car-dealer owner. She watched the car dealer's test flight with pleasure, then felt a tightening sense of anxiety as he went into an aerobatic routine.

'Don't worry, Elena honey,' said the kindly divorcee, 'they know what they're doing.'

But they didn't. The steep dive was followed by a late pull-out, but she could see it was too late. The plane, flattening out at tremendous speed, was still sinking, mushing down towards the ground, which suddenly met it in a bang, a blinding flash, with small flaming pieces of metal pouring forwards out of the tumbling ball of smoke.

The girlfriend was good to her for a while, but another man came along and that was when the tempers started, the fits that seized her when the stress proved too much. Then she would clench her fists while the little white storm invaded her mind, and she would let rip in insensate fury at whoever provoked her. Afterwards, calmer and trembling, she would not like to admit that she had no memory of what had happened or what she had said, so she was never given the medical attention which could have helped her.

In six months the girlfriend washed her hands of her and sent her back, with a small part of her father's savings, to the uncles and aunts in Cali.

By this time her beauty was starting to show and the cousins took to her, despite the frequent tempers which she gradually and painfully learned to control. They taught her how to live on the streets, because none of them had money in Cali. But she had the advantage of her American upbringing and education, and she did so well in school that a friendly teacher with good connections got her into a civil service training course. The recruiter for the DAS internal security service found her working as a government interpreter. It was probably her looks that first attracted him, but her aptitude carried her beyond the grosser aspects of his patronage.

The mechanics of weaponry and explosives came naturally to her. Bomb disposal was an unusual specialization for a woman, but it didn't occupy her for long because Pedro Aragones saw her and recruited her to his specialist anti-terrorist unit. The unit became both the scourge and the target of the Medellín drug barons, seeking to anticipate and prevent their attempts to destabilize the government, and fighting off many attacks on its own personnel. Two years to the day after she joined, she married Pedro Aragones. Three hours after that, she was a widow.

At two o'clock, on the dot she presented herself at the gates of the house. She was inspected and allowed to enter. It was the smooth sidekick, Heller, who took her to the workshop, where the camera she had long imagined but never seen sat on the bench with all its equipment. She looked it over, took the side panel off and checked inside, noting with relief that the layout was just as she had assumed from bad diagrams in the technical manuals.

The door opened behind her and Cheeseman's voice said, 'Just what you ordered, eh?'

'It's the right one, yes.'

He looked at her with that now familiar mixture of sexual interest and racial disdain which cut her to the soul. In that, he was no different from the other older men she passed on the streets of Zürich. No one could call him attractive, she thought, that thick neck, the bristly hair and the harsh guttural tones behind the voice.

'Time for you to start earning your money then. The man will be here in two days. His name is Pfister.'

'He will need training, or does he have the skills?'

'Skills? He is a machinist and a fitter, that is all. He is also a thug, but I doubt you would regard that as a skill.'

'He will need training.'

He stopped looking at the camera and half turned to her with a raised eyebrow. 'That's your job.'

She shook her head slightly. 'It seems my job is getting bigger all the time.'

He looked at her, weighing her up. 'Come and see me when you've finished here. I'll be in my study. We had better talk.'

He left. The sidekick in his banker's suit stayed, watching her silently. She checked measurements, inspected the recorder and delved into the equipment bag. In a side pouch, under the spare battery, was something which brought a frown to her face. It was a leather-covered address book. She pulled it out and opened the first page. Written in block letters it said, 'Property of Sunny Jordan. If found please return to BBC TV News, Television Centre, Wood Lane, London W12 0TT.'

She turned to Heller. 'Where did this camera come from?'

He looked back calmly. 'Does it matter?'

She waved the address book at him. 'Shall we say it sounds a little bit hot?'

He crossed the room, took the book from her and looked at it. He wasn't fast enough to cover up his surprise, then he put the book carefully in his briefcase and shrugged. 'Don't give it any thought. It is here now and that is what matters. One camera, after all, looks just like another.'

When she had finished he took her to the study, through the stale rooms stuffed with the evidence of unwise wealth, ill-chosen, ill-matching pictures, antique furniture whose only common thread was its price. It was so far removed from the world of back rooms and hidden-away huts to which most of her jobs had taken her since she started on her dangerous quest for revenge, but it struck her that her employer was not so different. Beneath the expensive suit he had something of the same smell, the lack of humour and, judging by the wariness of those who worked for him, the potential for explosive anger. She wished she had asked more questions beforehand, but there hadn't been the opportunity. It had always been on her own terms before, a brief visit from an expensive expert whose time was money, and, if her employer stepped out of line, she was gone leaving the job undone. Well, she thought, I can do that again any time I want to.

In the study's anteroom the secretary forestalled them, a sharp-nosed, metallic woman of forty suffering from the best attentions of the couturiers of Zürich.

'Wait,' she said, with absolutely no attempt at courtesy. 'He is occupied on a call,' and she let her gaze linger for a contemptuous second before looking down at her desk again and fiddling with a recalcitrant typewriter. Heller left her sitting there, and several minutes went by before a buzzer sounded. The secretary nodded at her and she went in.

The study, like the rest of the house, was over-furnished. Cheeseman stood up for her and waved her to an ornate Louis XV couch, sitting down in a chair opposite her.

'I think it is time to get some things straight,' she said. 'You are not my usual type of client and I don't have as much information as I would like. I need to know your timetable and how long you expect me to stay. I told you from the start, I am a planner. I organize things on paper. Others carry them out. Now you want me to do the training too. That was not our agreement.'

He looked at her impassively, and she went on. 'Above all, I need to know the identity of the target. That is most important.'

'Forgive me,' he said, 'but we seem to be getting off on the wrong foot here. I have paid you a very large sum of money. For that I expect a lot of work and not too many questions. If you will excuse the analogy, I have hired you as a worker on the shop floor, not as managing director.'

'Then you have been badly informed,' she shot back. 'I would say I work as a management consultant, and that is the only way I work.'

He was silent for a while, considering. She let the silence lengthen. Then he seemed to make up his mind.

'All right,' he said. 'On the question of the timetable, I will need you here for a while yet. That is clear. You will have to oversee this man Pfister, but I assume if I pay you pro rata that should be acceptable.' It was an assumption, not a question. Before she could agree, he went on. 'On the question of the target, I am not sure why you need to know. You have enough information on the security involved already.'

'This may surprise you,' she said, aware that using sarcasm on him was like a fly-swatter against an elephant, 'but there are some principles involved and I always …'

She was right. His temper could be quickly triggered. He rose to his feet. 'And you suggest I have no principles? Is that it? Is that what you mean?' Ill at ease, she watched him as he crossed to his desk and stood leaning over it with both hands. 'I have principles. Do you think I would be held in high regard in this country of all places if I did not have principles? My wife comes from one of the best Swiss families. I am invited to the best houses in the Canton. What I do is done for the love of my country, nothing less. Do not ask me about principles.'

He reached into a drawer of the desk and produced a wad of banknotes, then walked over and dropped it in her lap. 'I will tell you what you think you need to know at the time of my choice, not yours. Is this enough principles to keep you quiet until then?'

She looked down. There must have been fifty notes in the wad. They were one thousand Swiss francs each. What was that? Four hundred dollars apiece? She turned them over. On the back was a gigantic picture of an ant. She laughed, and he just looked at her in incomprehension.

Chapter Eight

For the first time ever, Steve went to work on Sunday morning even though he wasn't on the rota. He knew there would be plenty of loose ends to tie up, and the bedsit held little enough attraction for him. Driving into the car park and knowing he was free to drive out again any time he wanted was an oddly luxurious feeling.

He arrived in the newsroom just as the morning meeting began. The shift was gathered round one of the big tables, mostly standing. He joined in quietly at the back. A ripple spread through the room when he was noticed, and this time there were smiles, winks and thumbs up. Terry Conway walked into the room and an expectant hush fell.

Conway glanced around and pushed his glasses higher on his nose with a stiff forefinger. 'You will all have heard of the sad events of Saturday,' he said. 'It goes without saying that we are all greatly saddened by the death of Sunny Jordan, and we intend to give the police all the assistance we can in the search for his murderer. At the same time we will make the point to them yet again that this kind of violence is a direct consequence of their policy of insisting on access to our untransmitted video material.'

Steve shook his head quietly to himself. Conway continued. 'Pat White is still in hospital, though I am pleased to say he should be released later today. Steve Ross is taking it easy at home with his family.'

'Jesus!' thought Steve. 'No, he's not,' someone said, 'he's standing over there,' and Conway looked up in surprise.

'Oh, hello Steve. Great to see you. We weren't expecting to see you today.'

He paused and seemed to rethink his words. 'You will probably all have seen or at least heard about the bulletins on Saturday night which I'm told are already passing into legend.' A little expectant stir ran around the room. Conway smiled a mirthless smile intended to show he was one of the chaps. 'They were unusual to say the least but, under the special circumstances, Steve's very human response seems to me to have been entirely understandable.'

Yes, but is that what you were planning to say before you found out I was here? thought Steve.

'Terry, is it true that Sylvia has resigned?' asked the Australian who'd backed Steve on Saturday.

Conway looked irritated. 'Oh really,' he said, 'I do wish ...' But what he wished was destined never to be heard because at that moment the newsroom loudspeaker came alive with a buzz and, with a deeply ingrained response, he and everyone else turned to listen. The General News Service, based in the main BBC Radio newsroom, was the quick tip-off service for the whole of BBC News. It kept a close eye on the wire services from the Press Association, Reuters and the other news agencies for breaking stories and, when they rated it, passed them on round the chain of newsrooms and current affairs offices.

The speakers clicked and the woman on the other end of the mike cleared her throat. 'GNS here.' Papers rustled. 'A PA snap says the Metropolitan Police are holding a man in connection with the death on Saturday of BBC cameraman, Arnold Jordan.' The rest of it was lost in a spontaneous cheer right round the newsroom, and every face swung towards Steve. He felt only surprise, and an odd sense of distance at hearing Sunny given the name with which he'd been christened.

The meeting got back to its set pattern. The home news organizer ran through the diary, explained what they were expecting, how they planned to cover it and what facilities were in place, complaining in the same breath that he had no spare crews and only one reporter left at base to cover anything unexpected. The foreign duty editor did the same for his list, and Steve felt a sense of relief when he heard Diana Pugh had been sent on a short-notice trip to Holland to cover an extradition hearing. An argument developed with the lunchtime news editor questioning the timing of one of the satellite bookings, which he felt short-changed his programme in favour of the *Six O'Clock News*. Then it broke up and the *Nine O'Clock* and *Six O'Clock* teams went away into separate huddles.

While all this was going on, a girl strolled over from the Intake Desk and tapped Steve on the shoulder. 'The Foo wants you,' she said.

The man still known in these days of video as the Film Operations Organizer had a phone in his hand with the mouthpiece buried in his shoulder. 'Steve,' he said, 'it's the police down at Vine Street. They're saying can you go over there?'

'It's Brian Kitto here, Mr Ross,' said a voice which sounded unused to having to explain itself. 'I'm the DCI in charge of the Jordan murder investigation. We're holding someone, and I'd be grateful if you could get straight down here, OK?'

Detective Chief Inspector Brian Kitto held sway at one end of an open plan office. He was a burly man with a flushed complexion which made him look a bad risk for life insurance. Sitting down, he looked like the Rugby-playing army sergeant he once was. It was only when he stood up that the years of Rotary lunches and Masonic dinners could be seen to have taken their toll. He exhibited his personal style of authority by being pointlessly rude to one of his team within seconds of Steve being shown in. He showed a perfunctory courtesy which said clearly that Steve was a means to an end, and the end was to get his suspect put away.

'Mitchell Gardiner,' he said, 'is our man. It's fairly open and shut, but I can't show you his mug shot because you're going to have to pick him out of a line-up, and it's not allowed.'

'I'm afraid that's not very likely. The men were wearing Balaclavas. I said so in my statement.'

Kitto looked across the desk at Steve and gave a half smile. 'I've read your statement. Let's say it's not completely clear from it that you couldn't have seen bits of their faces at some point in the ruckus.'

'Well, I didn't I'm afraid.'

Kitto leaned back in his chair, looked up at the ceiling and steepled his fingers with a sigh. 'Look, Mr Ross. There's not a lot of doubt about this one. This man Gardiner was telling his mates in the pub last night that he was there when your friend got it. Went into it in great detail, he did. Even described how he coshed him. What he didn't know was that a sharp-eared young PC from Tottenham nick was right behind him in plain clothes. Soon as he could, he whistled up some support and there was an almighty ruck pulling Gardiner out of the pub with all his mates joining in.' He stopped and tossed a sheet of typed paper over to Steve.

'When we finally got our hands on him down here, the computer came up with the interesting fact that he was one of the other suspects when PC Keith Blakelock was murdered in the Broadwater Farm riot. Not only that but we found him on our own video of Saturday's merry events not two hundred yards from where your mate copped it.' He paused again and looked hard at Steve. 'All I want is what you want,' he said, 'I want someone to go down for killing your friend, and Gardiner's already said it was him. Come and have a look, and you never know, something might click.'

Steve followed Kitto down through the building towards the large room where the identity parade had been set up. Just before they got there, Kitto stopped and had a loud conversation with the Sergeant in front of the door.

'All ready for us?'

'Yessir.'

'Any problems over the height?'

'Couldn't find any as big as 'im sir. We came as close as we could.'

So that's how it's done, thought Steve. A bit of heavy-handed prompting for the doubtful witness who wants to help, and bingo, an instant guilty verdict for some poor sod who was just talking big at the wrong time. It all became even clearer when he looked at the men on parade, Mitchell Gardiner's name and the reference to Broadwater Farm should have given the game away. They were all black. There was no doubt which one was Gardiner. He stood a clear two inches above all the rest and was the only one looking frightened.

Steve went back and faced Kitto. 'I can't help you,' he said 'and anyway, there's another thing I realize now. The man who killed Sunny Jordan was white, not black.'

Kitto rounded on him with contempt in his voice. 'Well, look here now, what have we here. One minute it's I'm sorry, I couldn't see their faces, they all had Balaclavas on. The next it's, Oh I'm sure it's not this one because I can tell you what his fucking skin colour was. Anything else you'd like to tell us now, Mr Ross?'

Steve held on to his temper and answered in a level voice. 'I hit the man. I tried to hold on to him. I was pulling his

Balaclava around. I could see the skin around his eyes through the slits. I know he was white.'

Kitto nodded slowly. 'But you don't know the other two were, right?'

'I think they were. Anyway, you said Gardiner described how he was the one who coshed Sunny.'

'Too right I did. All the way, just like you said it happened in your statement. You tell me how else he could have known that.'

'By watching the early evening news last night for a start. We described it all in detail. There was even a sequence done with computer graphics showing it.'

Kitto shifted his ground. 'How come you left all this important information about skin colour out of your statement?'

'Because I made that statement just after I'd been hit on the head, and it never occurred to me you'd start off by assuming it was black guys.'

Kitto leaned towards him. 'I'm not assuming anything, Mr Ross. There's no prejudice here, I can assure you, but I must say I am a bit surprised. I would have thought you'd want someone to go down for this one, but you're not being exactly what I'd call helpful.'

'Look, I do want someone to go down for it. I want that very badly, but I want it to be the right person. I don't think the people who did it were just rioters trying to hide the evidence.'

Kitto rocked back. 'Well, well. I don't remember reading this in your statement either.'

'I did try to say it but people kept interrupting. I think they wanted the camera for some other reason. They were very careful to grab it and stop it falling when they hit Sunny, and they took every bit of our gear with them too.'

Kitto glanced at the Sergeant and shook his head. He was

clearly barely even listening. 'It'll be at the bottom of the Thames by now,' he said, 'or if not they'll be trying to get a few quid for it from someone in the skin-flicks game. There's no point in dreaming up fancy ideas about it. If you want to nick a camera you do a break-in, not a bloody murder, don't you?'

'I wouldn't know,' said Steve wearily.

'No, you wouldn't. Anyway I expect I'll get a confession out of Gardiner, but I'll tell you straight it would make things a whole lot simpler if you were on our side.' He considered Steve for a minute with his eyes screwed up. 'You'd better come back up to my office,' he said, 'there's something else I want to show you.'

Steve was glad to leave the subterranean vault with its grey pipework like the inside of a ship. Back at Kitto's desk, he was handed a folder. He opened it and wished he hadn't. The first thing in it was a glossy blown-up photo of the wound to the back of Sunny's head.

'He had a thin skull, did you know?' said Kitto in a conversational tone. 'Otherwise he might have got away with it.'

'Look, do you need me any more?' said Steve angrily. 'I need to get back.'

'Need you? It looks as if I'd better not need you at all for all the help you're likely to be,' said Kitto with heavy-handed sarcasm. 'You just run along then, but if you suddenly get a bit clearer as to which side you're on, do call me, won't you?'

When he got back to his car, there was a ticket on it.

It was lunchtime before he walked into Television Centre, and all the people with whom he might have gone for a drink or a bite had already headed off. He joined the queue at the snack bar for a sandwich and a mug of soup, opening the post from his pigeon-hole as he did. There was a series of friendly notes, from people he barely knew, about Saturday, as well as a circular on the effects of tax changes which barred the private use of mobile phones in their cars. Leaving the best until last, he opened a very official letter in a white BBC envelope marked PRIVATE.

'It's herogram time,' said a girl's voice with a Scots accent just behind him, and he turned to see Terry Conway's secretary next to him in the queue.

'You know about this, do you Sarah?'

'Go on, just read it,' she said smiling. 'It's very flowery.'

It was. Conway had gone over the top, expressing deep condolences for Steve's sad and painful experience, and admiration at the professionalism with which he'd met his broadcasting commitments and retained his personal integrity on the air.

'Is that Conway-speak for slagged off Sylvia?' he asked.

Sarah looked over his shoulder at it. 'Yes, I think it's a line he stole from one of the letters that came rolling in.'

'There were letters?'

She laughed. 'Only two hundred and forty so far. That's on top of the phone calls. You seem to have touched a nerve. It appears the whole nation's been dying to tell Sylvia to get stuffed for ages.'

'Hence the herogram?'

She smiled again. 'Loyalty prevents me from saying anything unsupportive of my beloved boss, Steve, but he's a great one for checking which way the wind's blowing before he bolts the stable door.'

He looked at the letter again, then crumpled it into a ball and chucked it into the nearest bin. Sarah shrugged.

The following day Steve was given the all-clear to go back to work by the BBC doctor. He went to see Mike Page.

'Mike, I want to get back into the swing as soon as I can. I hate sitting around here with nothing to do. What's coming up?'

Page looked through the diary and shook his head. 'Not a helluva lot, truth to tell.' He held it out to Steve, who glanced through it.

'What do you mean? There's lots going on. What about the Loach, Baines fraud case at the Bailey?'

'Come on, Steve, you know that's a specialist job. That's for the Business Unit.'

'Well, OK, but how about the Concorde story?'

'That's the Business Unit too. The Transport Correspondent's name is already down for it.'

'All right, here's one. The Mitterrand visit.'

'Diplomatic Unit.'

Steve scanned further down the list. 'OK, safety in soccer grounds. The Commission's press conference. Sounds dull as hell, but it's better than nothing.'

Page looked unhappy. 'Well, I'm afraid the Sports Unit is down for that one.'

Steve looked at the last item on the list. 'Customs figures on drug seizures. Don't tell me we've started up a narcotics unit now?'

Page looked even shiftier. 'Nooo, but Terry's decided that should be done by the Home Affairs Unit.'

'For God's sake, Mike. You and I both know half the people in the units don't know how to put a story together to save their lives. It's not so long ago that they didn't even exist. What the hell are us old-fashioned types meant to do, sit here on our butts waiting for planes to crash? Next thing you'll be telling me there's going to be a specialist unit for unexpected events, and we'll all be out of a job.'

'Don't go over the top, Steve. You know I have to support my lord and master's plans to put some intellectual gloss on the murky world of news. I'll find you something to do, I promise.'

By Wednesday evening, however, Steve was going stir crazy, sitting at the reporters' desk in the newsroom, praying for something to happen. Mike Page watched him unobtrusively, reassigned one of the home affairs specialists to a no-hoper of a story in deepest Kent and pencilled Steve's name in to cover a joint press conference by the Foreign Office and the Home Office on diplomatic protection and new police measures to safeguard foreign embassies. It wasn't much but it was a lot better than moping around and, on a quiet day, it looked like being one of the few contenders for the lunchtime news's lead story.

It was just after 10 a.m. on Thursday when Steve parked his car in King Charles Street and, even before he could get the door open, he was set upon by the over-eager young producer sent down by the lunchtime bulletin to get him out of their hair.

'Great. Glad you're here, Steve. The crew's inside setting up. The presser starts in half an hour.'

'Yes, I know – Richard?'

The producer looked crestfallen. 'David,' he said reproachfully.

'Sorry, I meant David. Have you talked to them about when we're doing the interview yet?'

'Er, no, I didn't know there was one, but I would like to go over the graphics with you when you've got a moment. There's some useful figures in the press release.'

'Look, David,' said Steve gently, 'forget the graphics for a second. Graphics are just acres of electronic nonsense set up by people who never stir out of the building, to give them the illusion of control over a story happening somewhere else. This is real life, right?' He looked around. 'Well, that's a slight exaggeration seeing this is a Government department, but still there will be real people here, saying real things, and our first job is to make sure we report what they say, and then think about the graphics when we've got that sorted out.'

'But I've been working on this since Tuesday with Peter Taylor, when he was down to do it, and we thought ...'

Steve was already striding towards the Foreign Office and David had to run to catch up. 'I'm not Peter Taylor and we'll do it my way. I'll be pleased to look at your graphics, but it would be a very good idea if we made sure first of all that the Minister knows he's going to talk to us, OK?'

Two press officers, one from each of the departments, were acting as minders in the reception area. 'Hello, I'm Steve Ross from BBC TV. I think we've got an interview with the minister set up for straight after the presser?'

The Home Office man consulted a list. 'Yes, we've got you down third after ITN and Channel 4.'

'Oh, hang on,' said Steve. 'I don't mind following ITN. They're on before us, but I'm not going to hang around for Channel 4. They're not even on the air until seven.'

'I believe they wanted to use ITN's lights.'

'Never mind that. They can use ours if they have to. Or we can all use ITN's. That's quickest, but if we don't go second, it won't make it on in time for the lunchtime news.'

That settled, Steve went through to the conference room and walked over to the camera crew, Ken Minchin and Peter Maddox, who had the tripod set up between the other two crews in the middle gangway for the head-on shot of the ministers at the table. He had a quick chat with them, but there wasn't much room for creativity.

'So it's the ministers walking in, then close-up for the first part of the spiel, then you'll give us the nod on the questions and answers?' said Ken.

'Yup. I'll sit next to you so I can cue you when I want

you to roll. Then you can grab the wide shots and the cut-aways of the audience when we've finished with the interesting stuff. It's going to be a bit tight on time, so we don't want to shoot more than we can help.'

Ken nodded. The physical editing time spent spooling through lots of tape looking for the right shots was something to avoid when up against a tight deadline. Steve sat down to read the press release, but Dave appeared, as puppy-like as ever, and thrust a mobile phone at him. 'The desk wants you.'

It was the lunchtime news editor. 'Hello Steve, I'm scratching around for a lead,' she said. 'The Mallory verdict isn't going to happen in time, and everything else seems to be dropping like flies. Any chance of this one?'

'Not really, Jenny,' he said, 'it's only a few small tweaks. Pretty much business as usual. I can't see much of a headline in it, but I'll get back to you if anything comes up.'

Some editors would have pressed the point, giving a covert nod to hype up the story for all it was worth to dig their bulletin out of a hole, and some reporters would have done it, but Jenny wasn't one of those and nor was Steve. 'OK,' she said, 'put David back on, will you, I don't much like his graphics.'

The story ran its predictable course. One of the Home Office junior ministers, Timothy Hitchcock, tipped as an up-and-comer, arrived, was filmed walking to the table with his Foreign Office counterpart and sitting down, flanked by his advisers and acolytes. He exhibited all the signs of someone newly groomed in the art of dealing with the press on a higher plane than that needed in his previous incarnation as a mere Member of Parliament. They shot four minutes of an interminable opening statement on the aims of the changes before Steve muttered 'cut' a bit too loudly, earning a sharp glare from the nearest of Hitchcock's press officers.

During the questions and answers which followed, Steve listened carefully to each of the questions, getting Ken to switch on for anything which looked likely to produce a usable answer. It was dangerous, an easy way to miss the odd unexpected quotable quote, but the only way to deal with a tight schedule. He asked one question for safety, just in case anything went wrong with the interview, then kept his powder dry.

Sitting waiting for ITN to finish their session with Hitchcock, he wondered how on earth to inject some life into it. The trouble was that embassy safety hadn't been a hot issue for ages. When his turn came, Hitchcock showed he had read his briefing notes. He came over with a big smile and shook Steve's hand warmly. 'How's the head, Steve? I'm glad you're on your feet, and I'm very sorry about Mr Jordan.'

It was a disarming performance and, despite a cynical voice within him, Steve felt touched and slightly hampered by it. Then, halfway through the interview, Hitchcock overplayed his hand. 'You of all people, Mr Ross,' he said, 'after your own recent experience, should be convinced of the need for a strong police force, able to deal with violence in a satisfactory manner.'

Steve stopped him. 'I think we'd better retake that one. Any convictions I have one way or the other don't matter. I'm just the reporter. Let's keep it to what you think if you don't mind.' At the end he thanked him, but some of the warmth had gone out of the minister's demeanour.

As soon as they were out of the room, David reappeared with several sheets of paper. 'Steve,' he said, 'I've reworked these graphics and I think they're OK now. If you start your script with the statistics on the rise in ...'

'Later. We've still got work to do.'

'Piece to camera?' asked Ken, grinning.

'Yes. Outside across the street I think. Then we'd better start editing a bit sharpish.'

With more time to spare, the 'rushes' or raw video material would have been taken back to Wood Lane and the editing done there. But it was now 12.05, with just fifty-five minutes to the start of the lunchtime news, and, because of the tight deadline and the lack of other competing stories, one of the mobile editing vehicles had been assigned to the story so that all the work could be done quickly, on the spot. It was parked down a side-street, a Renault Espace with the back seats taken out and an equipment rack installed in their place to carry the edit machines and monitor.

They crossed Whitehall quickly, zigzagging between the traffic. David was half walking, half running beside Steve.

'I really should read you this bit,' he said. 'You'll have to write the script in a minute.'

'If you must.'

David began. 'The worldwide rise in the incidence of violence against diplomatic staff in the course of their official duties has itself been on a steepening trend, with the year-on-year rise showing a compound increase over five years averaging 8.7 per cent ...'

A motor cycle courier swerved round them, and then they were separated by a bus. When they reached the pavement and David caught up, Steve looked at him. 'The start doesn't make too much sense,' he said.

'That's because you weren't concentrating,' yelped David.

'No, of course I wasn't and nor are most of the other people who are watching TV, especially lunchtime TV. If you want people to concentrate, go and write for a news-paper where they can read it five times if they have to. Just make it simpler.'

Ken set up the tripod on the pavement, squinting at the built-in bubble to get it level, then clipped the camera on to the top plate. 'Hey Steve,' he said, 'there's one of the Jags waiting at the front over there. If you're quick, we might get someone going off.'

They were in luck. Just as Steve started his fifteen second spiel, Hitchcock himself came out of the building, clearly visible over Steve's shoulder, got in the car and was driven off. Ken, watching it all through the viewfinder, was just congratulating himself on one of those little touches which add an indefinable something to a story when a speeding van, going far too fast, squealed its tyres over Steve's final words and ruined the take.

They did it again, cursing, but halfway through a distant noise intruded, so it needed a third take which wasn't so good without the departure shot of the minister. It was 12.10 and it was just then, as they prepared to cross the road again, that Steve looked up towards Trafalgar Square. He saw people running towards two cars entangled in the middle of the road some two hundred yards away, and saw that one of them was the ministerial Jaguar.

'Come on,' he yelled to Ken and Peter, and grabbed the tripod.

They ran up the road, with David, who had been far slower on the uptake, bellowing, 'What are you doing? You haven't got time.'

They made it to the cars before the police did, camera up on Ken's shoulder and already running. It was a mess. A blue pick-up truck lay buried in the back offside door of the Jaguar, T-boned across its bows. The driver of the van sagged over its wheel with his head half through the windscreen. The Jaguar's driver was being helped out of the passenger door. Steve looked in to the back of the Jaguar. Hitchcock lay across the back seat, white-faced and unconscious, one arm bent awkwardly under him and blood oozing steadily from a rent across his sleeve.

Steve straightened and took the portable phone from David, who'd just caught up. He was torn between dialling 999 and calling the newsroom, but an approaching two-tone siren showed someone was already on the ball, and he saw the minister's detective lying on the ground next to the car, talking painfully into a two-way radio as someone supported his shoulders.

He called the desk. 'It's Steve. Get Jenny for me, as fast as you can. The story's changed.'

'Hang on, she's busy,' said an unfamiliar voice.

The adrenalin was getting to Steve now. He was conscious of every second passing and of just how much could be achieved in each one. 'Make her unbusy then. She needs to hear this NOW, and pass the word we've got a big story.' While he waited he turned to David. 'Get back to the Espace. Tell them to get ready. I'll be there in five minutes.'

Jenny came to the phone. 'What's happened, Steve?'

'Hitchcock's been badly injured. Rammed by a car on the way out of the Home Office. We're right there.'

She was excited and alert immediately. 'IRA?'

'I doubt it. Hold on.'

He took three paces across to the pick-up truck and looked in the back. There was a box of floor tiles and a power saw. In the front, the driver was slowly picking himself out of the windscreen, groaning and opening his eyes. He was an old man and he stank of whisky.

'It looks like a traffic accident to me,' he told Jenny. 'The car was turning right and an old drunk in a van tried to overtake it.' Then he looked again at the van and a thought struck him. 'Jenny, ask the desk to get us some cover down here, will you? I'd better get back to the Espace and start putting it together.'

She passed him on to the news organizer. 'OK Steve, there's a DR and the links vehicle on its way to you. They weren't far away. I've pulled Lesley off a story and she'll be with you in three minutes.'

An ambulance arrived and they shot the unconscious minister being carefully loaded into it, then Steve took the tapes, left Ken filming, and started running back down the road towards King Charles Street. It was 12.21, and he was badly out of breath when he arrived at the edit vehicle. David was pacing up and down outside it looking at his watch. Martin, the picture editor, was ready at his seat inside. Steve climbed in and gave him the tapes. 'Spin it back to the first piece to camera, will you? I want to have a look at it,' he said.

David stuck his head in through the open door. 'You mean the third, don't you? The first one was spoiled by the noise.'

'Shut UP David,' said Steve, 'keep quiet and watch. I meant the first.'

Then he concentrated hard on the pictures of what had been happening behind him while he'd been saying his piece. They saw the minister's car leave, then the speeding van whose squealing tyres had spoilt the take. It was the blue pick-up truck.

'Bloody hell, we've got it.' Then another thought struck him. 'I think we may even have got the sound of the crash. Play the second take.' And there it was, the loud thud which had made them start a third time.

Steve scribbled a rough script while Martin quickly copied off a few shots of the wrecked cars for the headlines, then they started, working intently as a team. Martin laid the shots one by one, giving Steve the exact length of each one, and Steve wrote the sentences to fit, trimming words one at a time. It began with the minister at the press conference, but the angle was different now. The original story would be just a couple of lines on the end, delivered by the newsreader.

Now the press conference was only important in the way it set the scene for what followed. Next, over a shot of the outside of the building, Steve's script explained that they had accidentally shot pictures of the truck and caught the sound of the crash, and they ran the first two pieces to camera, back to back.

Martin shook his head doubtfully. 'It really needs a freeze frame to give you a chance to see the truck. It's all a bit subliminal.'

'Save that for the *Six O'Clock*,' said Steve. 'We can add the bells and whistles then. It's 12.40, let's just get it done, even if it is a bit rough-and-ready.'

They laid down the last shot and put on the final line of Steve's voice track at 12.47. The DR was waiting at the door with the motor bike to take the tape, and they chased after him in the Espace round to Horse Guards Parade. There the Land Rover was waiting, its mast extended to beam the pictures back. The engineer was already playing the tape over by the time they arrived, talking to the Spur VT area while he was doing it. 'Hello VT3, are those levels OK? ... Right, I'm spinning back to the start again, are you rolling? ... Coming in five seconds from now.'

It was 12.56 by the time they were satisfied that they had a good recording at the other end, and Steve could picture the rush in the dark glass boxes of the VT area to get the tape cued up and ready in time. They switched on the TV in the back of the Land Rover and watched anxiously as the *One O'Clock News* titles rolled. The newsreader went straight into it as the first headline. 'A Government Minister has been seriously injured in a car crash in Whitehall.' The newsreader glanced down at his own monitor and paused for a moment to see if the headline picture would roll. The screen went to black for a tiny fraction of a second, then came up on their shots of the wrecked car and the minister being removed.

Out of vision, the newsreader went on. 'Home Office Minister Timothy Hitchcock was rushed to hospital with a broken arm and leg and suspected internal injuries. He is now undergoing surgery. This eyewitness account from our reporter Steve Ross.'

The tape ran perfectly and they all breathed a sigh of relief, then it cut back to the newsreader, who handed over live to the familiar and knowledgeable figure of the BBC's political editor, who spoke of Hitchcock's rising stature in the party and the political impact of the accident. While that was going on, Steve rang the direct line to the studio gallery and spoke to the bulletin editor again.

'Jenny, I'm just going back down there to see if there's anything else.'

'Good. We'll take you on the phone for an update into the end of the programme, unless you can get hooked up in time for live pictures. I don't have to tell you everyone wants to know if it really was just an accident.'

'I'll be right back to you.'

'Oh, and Steve, very well done. When I told you I needed a lead story, I didn't expect you to go that far.'

Steve looked around. The police had now sealed the street off and the crash was a five-minute walk away. He looked at the DR standing there. 'Tony, lend us your bike, will you, just for a minute.'

The DR looked shocked. 'I'm not allowed to. Anyway, have you got a licence?'

'Of course I have. I was brought up on these. Just look the other way for a minute.'

Ignoring the mild protests that followed, he jammed on the DR's helmet, thumbed the BMW's starter, and kicked it into gear.

Back on Whitehall, he swung round the roadblock, gesticulating urgently at the policeman manning it, who looked at the BBC crests on its panniers and left it at that. Lesley Downing, the reporter sent to cover for him, was standing by the cars, and she did a double take when he took the helmet off.

He walked up to her. 'Lesley, any word on who the truck driver was or how it happened?'

'Nothing suspicious, Steve, or that's what they think. Hitchcock's been taken off to Guy's and they've had people crawling all over the truck.'

'Who?'

'Bomb squad, anti-terrorist branch, you know.'

'Is anyone talking?'

'Not much. The most useful guy is the head of the Serious Crimes Squad, who just happened along. He's over there.'

Steve looked and saw a trim figure in his late fifties or early sixties who was just walking around the back of the wrecked van. He went over to intercept him.

'Excuse me, have you got a second? My name's Steve Ross from BBC TV News and I've got to be on the air in a minute or two. Can you help me?'

The man looked him up and down and stuck out a hand. 'I know who you are. I'm Keith Brice. How can I help?'

'I just need to hear someone say this was a pure accident and not anything to do with terrorism.'

'Well, don't quote me, but it wasn't PIRA.'

Steve noted the army acronym for the Provisional IRA. 'You're sure?'

Brice pulled a face. 'That driver's only acquaintance with Ireland was the pint of Old Bushmills whiskey he drank for his breakfast. The anti-terrorist branch are happy. In fact they're about to pack up and go home.'

'Thanks. I won't say who I got it from.'

Steve was putting the helmet back on when Brice called after him. 'Where are you heading for?'

He turned in surprise. 'Our links vehicle, down in Horse Guards.'

'I'll follow you down.'

He had no time to wonder. It was 1.12 and there wasn't a second to lose. It was just after 1.14 by the time he got the bike back on its stand next to the Land Rover and, frustratingly, it took three attempts to get through to the gallery. At 1.18 he was talking to Jenny and at 1.21, at the end of the next tape, he was on the air being interviewed down the phone by the newsreader, with the definitive, if unsourced, news that the crash had no sinister, terrorist overtones. The news ended with another phone two-way, this time from Guy's Hospital, to report that Hitchcock was still in the operating theatre, where they were trying to stem internal bleeding.

Steve was sitting back enjoying the relief that follows a rushed job well done, and yawning as the adrenalin drained out into weariness, when a voice said, 'Mr Ross?'

He turned to see Chief Superintendent Keith Brice, whom he had completely forgotten, standing at his elbow.

'Oh hello,' he said, 'what can I do for you?'

'I think it's rather the other way round,' the policeman answered. 'If you've finished, I thought you might like a quick drink.'

Chapter Nine

In a crowded pub across Whitehall, they fought themselves into a corner. Brice bought the drinks. 'Cheers,' he said, and raised his glass. Steve tipped his glass to him in silence, wondering what it was all about.

'I know your friend, Mr Nielsen,' said Brice. 'He's been seeing a bit of my daughter.' He looked gloomily at his beer, and Steve finally made the connection.

'Oh, right,' he said, 'Nick mentioned it vaguely.'

'Unusual fellow,' said Brice, 'not the steadiest of types I imagine?'

He was clearly hoping for a form of reassurance which Steve didn't feel in all honesty he could give. He searched for words. 'Heart of gold, Nick,' he said, 'a bit unlikely on the surface, but a thoroughly good guy.'

Brice looked at him with a jaundiced eye and nodded, thinking about it. 'Well that's as may be,' he said, 'but that's not really why I wanted to talk to you.' He seemed to cheer up then. 'I'm a bit of a fan of the BBC,' he said. 'Come to that, I'm a bit of a fan of yours. I liked that stuff you did on the insurance fiddles. Much better than ITN.' Steve looked at him in some surprise. He looked around him, and dropped his voice level. 'I just heard that Brian Kitto is running the investigation into your cameraman's murder. Has he seen you yet?'

'Yes, on Monday,' Steve said. 'He's a bit forceful, isn't he?'

Brice fidgeted with his glass. 'Look, I shouldn't say this, but I'm leaving the force and I've seen too many people like him over the years. They're all being found out now. He's a bit bloody dangerous if you ask me. I thought I'd just mark your card for you.' He looked all round him again. 'Kitto fits people up. Time was, there were a lot more like him and it isn't always just the blacks and the Irish they go for. If Kitto decides someone's a wrong 'un, he thinks the end justifies the means, and, if he can hang someone else's rap on them, he will. You being the chief witness, that might well put you in a hot spot.'

'Yes, it already has. I'm afraid I was a bit of a disappointment to Mr Kitto. I just couldn't help him at all over the man he's pulled in.'

Brice looked hard at him. 'Well, don't expect him to give up trying, that's all. He's a man who always thinks if you're not for him, you're against him. We're getting rid of people like that slowly, but no one's ever had anything but suspicion to hang on him so far.'

'I appreciate the warning. I just wish he was a bit less convinced about Mitchell Gardiner.' Steve paused, then spoke with sudden feeling. 'He's looking the wrong way, and I want the man who really did it arrested more than anything else I can think of.'

Brice looked at him with sympathy. 'I lost a man once myself, killed on a job I was running, and the man that did it got off scot-free.'

'How come?'

'Nobbled a jury at the Bailey. They make it all too bloody easy there by handing out the jury's names and addresses. I always thought I'd get him one day, but it's too late now. Anyway, for what it's worth, I know how you feel. If there's any way I can help on the quiet, give me a call. Here's my number.'

'There is one thing,' said Steve, a little hesitantly. 'I'm sure they were after the camera – not to destroy it but because they wanted it for something. Kitto won't even give that idea the time of day. If you happen to know of anyone who deals in that sort of stolen gear, I'd very much like to hear about it.'

'If I do, and I'm not promising, you'll have to promise not to do anything stupid. The law usually bites you when you take it into your own hands, you know.'

'Understood.'

The afternoon and evening were a whirl of activity. Steve went down to the hospital, then back to the Spur to put together the *Six O'Clock* version of the story. There was an unpleasant five minutes with the *Nine O'Clock News* when he discovered one of the specialist Parliamentary Unit trying to take over the whole story. That was only resolved when Mike Page stepped in to point out the absurdity of running an eyewitness story without the eyewitness. It left a nasty after-taste of ill-feeling with Steve as he sat at the reporters' desk watching the news finish.

He didn't hold out much hope that Brice would be able to help him, so it was a complete and gratifying surprise when the phone on his desk rang.

'It's Keith Brice, Steve. I thought I'd wait until the news was out of the way before I called.'

Steve took his feet off the desk and reached hopefully for a notepad. 'That was thoughtful.'

'No names, no pack-drill, right?'

'Right.'

'You didn't hear this from me, you didn't talk to me and we've never even met, right?'

Steve's pulse speeded up. Whatever it was, it was worth something. 'Agreed,' he said.

'Right. Get this down. There are hundreds of villains who are known to deal in bent video gear, but that's all your home movie stuff. Easily shifted. We've only ever had a sniff at four who do the professional stuff. One of those is doing a five-stretch and won't be out for another year. The second went to Canada when it got a bit warm for him here, and that leaves two. They're called Stuart Seymour and Eric Blackler. Neither has ever been convicted, but they've both been fingered by informants several times.'

'OK, I've got that,' said Steve, taking notes.

'There is, however, one more thing, and if this gets back to Kitto I'll have your balls. Some time in the last month there was a request made through the Foreign Office for surveillance of someone who came over from Switzerland on a one-day trip. The funny thing is, apart from shopping and eating lunch, the bloke only did one thing all day.'

'What was it?'

'He met Eric Blackler in a pub and talked to him for just over half an hour.'

'What did they talk about?'

Brice chuckled. 'This isn't James Bond stuff. Seems our watcher couldn't get close enough.'

'Who was the other man?'

'Don't know. That's locked away in some Foreign Office file.'

Steve thought fast. 'Who made the request, the Swiss?'

Brice's sudden pause told him he'd hit the target. 'No, the Americans.'

'Why on earth ...?'

'Look, I have no idea, and I can't ask without ringing a lot of bells in places that might have their fingers on my pension, so don't push it. The only reason I know all this is that there's a coded cross-reference in Blackler's files, and I once had a job where I had to know what the codes mean. Most people don't.'

'I see. When you say the Americans, which Americans do you mean?'

'I don't even know that. Could be the FBI, could be anybody.' He was sounding a bit twitchy, and Steve knew from long experience of coaxing out information that one more question might well push him too far, but then he went on of his own accord. 'There's a contact name for the Yanks. Hang on a second. I'll look at my notes.' There was a scuffling noise, then he was back on. 'The name is M. Rhinehart, but be bloody careful about quoting that around.'

'I appreciate that.'

'That's OK …' He hesitated again. 'I think I've stuck my neck out a bit too far. Don't embarrass me, will you?'

Steve put the phone down and went to the BBC club bar, where there was a buzz of congratulation all round on the Hitchcock story. It seemed unimportant against what he'd just heard. He'd always followed hunches and now all his senses were screaming at him that there was a definite connection here. That sense of excitement lasted him through a quiet weekend and only ended when Brian Kitto rang him at seven-thirty on Monday morning to see, as he put it, if he felt like being a bit more helpful by getting his memory back.

He called again on Tuesday. Steve presumed he must be having problems holding Gardiner. On Wednesday the pace hotted up with three calls, getting more hostile each time as Kitto tried every tactic under the sun. The final one was at 6.30 p.m.

'Mr Ross?'

'Yes, Mr Kitto, what can I do for you now?'

'You know very well what you can do for me, and not just for me but for Mr Jordan's wife and everyone else who cared about him.'

'I'm sorry. There's no point in going over it all again. I'm not going to say I saw something I didn't see, and that's the end of it.'

'Look, I've got someone who saw a man answering Gardiner's description putting a camera into the boot of a car half an hour after Jordan's murder.'

'Well, you don't need me then.'

'Maybe I don't. I don't need you saying you can ID him, but what I do need is for you to go quiet on the rest of it.'

'I don't follow.'

'Maybe you've had a hard day. I mean I don't want to hear you telling anyone that you're sure it wasn't Gardiner, because in my book that puts you over the line, and once people go over the line with me they usually regret it. I think you're forgetting what really happened because your nice little socialist sympathies make you think anyone with black skin must have angels' wings.'

Steve had had enough. 'Mr Kitto,' he said, 'this phone has a recorder built into it and I am pressing the button right now. Do you want to say again what you just said?'

'I don't know what you're talking about, Mr Ross, and I do wish you wouldn't keep making these calls when you haven't anything helpful to say. Good night.'

Steve put the phone down, making a mental note that from now on he must only take Kitto's calls on the other phone, the one that really did have a recorder. He was frowning, going over the conversation again, when Mike Page's hand fell on his shoulder.

'I've been watching you from my office. Whatever that was all about it looks as though it needs a pint or two to wash the taste away.'

'It's just this bloody policeman. He thinks I should help him frame Mitchell Gardiner because he doesn't have any other way of doing him.'

'He can't force you.'

'He's having a bloody good try, Mike. I've just told him I'm going to record all his phone calls from now on.'

'Serious stuff. Be careful how you go about it. There's still a disturbing tendency to think our police are all marvellous, even when the bad ones keep being found out.'

'I know. Frankly, I'm up to here with the whole bloody thing.'

'I hate to say the obvious, but do you need a holiday?'

Steve shook his head. 'On my tod? No, thanks all the same. I'd rather be kept busy, preferably as far away from Brian Kitto as possible.'

Page thought about it. 'Anywhere special?'

'You mean I can choose?'

'I didn't say that, but you do seem to be flavour of the month in spite of telling the Editor's favourite newsreader to take a running jump.'

'Well, since you've asked, I don't suppose there's any chance of a trip to Washington?'

Page drew in his breath. 'You don't ask much, do you? I was thinking more of Cardiff, or maybe even Aberdeen if you got really lucky. We've got a perfectly good Washington correspondent in residence who isn't very likely to welcome you on to his patch with open arms.'

'No chance then?'

'I didn't say that either, did I?'

Steve woke on Friday morning to a blank day, a light rain falling and nothing in prospect apart from a trip to the launderette. He wasn't on the rota again until Sunday. He felt like he'd seen every film in town, and there wasn't a museum, art gallery or shop left in central London which held any surprises for him at all. There wasn't even a comfortable place to read library books in the bedsit. He tried to stay in bed dozing for as long as possible, but that's never satisfying when you're not defying some external pressure to get up. The morning post showed his bank account virtually empty even though it was another two weeks to pay-day. He'd just decided to catch up with his expenses when the phone rang.

'It's Father Christmas,' said Mike Page's voice.

'Let me guess, I'm going on a day-trip to Stockton-on-Tees.'

'You're an ungrateful bastard. I've been bending heaven and earth on your behalf, so get ready to feel grateful.'

'Stop fooling about, Mike, just tell me.'

'Washington DC. Leaving on British Airways this afternoon for two weeks. Get a move on.'

Steve's heart soared. 'Brilliant. How did you pull that?'

'By going on my knees to Foreign News and cheating a bit. Gareth's out of the Washington office for a week covering the East–West Summit and he had a leave request outstanding. Foreign were borrowing Paula to stand in for him, but I persuaded her she'd rather stay here.'

That didn't sound easy. Washington, even as temporary cover, was a post any reporter would kill for. 'How did you manage that?'

Page chuckled. 'Between you and me, I told her she'd made it to the short list for the Southern Africa job, and the appointments board is next week.'

'Was she really on the list?'

'She is now.'

After packing hastily, Steve drove out onto the A4, country-and-western music playing loudly on the car stereo, and left the car at the off-airport parking service where TV News kept an account. Even the boredom of the increased security at Terminal 4 couldn't take the edge off the day.

*

Elena put the phone down, pleased with the minor impersonation she had just successfully carried out with the accreditation bureau. She jotted the necessary details down on the pad and turned to the typewriter to start composing a suitable fax of confirmation. The front door to the apartment banged open and closed, and she groaned. She knew who it was. Only he behaved as if he owned everything about her. The others always rang the bell, even though she knew they all had keys.

She swivelled round in the chair as the door of her room opened, wishing she was wearing more than the T-shirt and shorts she'd put on that morning.

'It would be nice if you could remember to ring the bell,' she said.

He ignored her. 'How is the work going?'

'There's no problem. The working drawings are almost finished. The fabrication won't take too long now we have all the materials. Then it is just testing and preparation.'

She thought of asking about the target once more, but here, in the flat, away from the other people, she was nervous of arousing his anger again. Be businesslike, she thought to herself, keep him at a distance.

He walked over to the desk and looked at her drawings. 'Pfister will be here tomorrow,' he said. 'Concentrate on getting him into good shape.'

'My agreement with you was just for planning. Now it's training too. That will be finished in a few days.'

He took two steps nearer. She resisted the temptation to back away, feeling the implied weakness might be dangerous.

'I've changed my mind about that,' he said. 'I need you here for longer. I need you to ...' He made an exaggerated play of dreaming up an excuse. '... Let's say to supervise the operational side. You know I'll pay you well. You have no cause for complaint.'

'That is my decision, not yours. I have commitments. I need to be back home in two weeks.'

'Commitments?' he said sarcastically. 'Commitments in dago land? You should be pleased to stay here in nice, clean Switzerland. You should be grateful that we let you stay.'

Her voice rose. 'I must go. That's all there is to it.'

That was when he dropped all pretence of persuasion, and the colour rose in blotches on his harsh cheeks. 'Listen well, you are staying as long as I want you to and that's it. It is time you understood that you have no choice. I know enough about you to put you inside with one phone call to the Fremdenpolizei. You just remember that. If I say you stay, then you stay.'

'And what of you? Don't you think I know enough of you?'

He moved right up close, looking slightly up at her. 'You know nothing of me, bitch. I am a pillar of the community here. I keep my nose clean. I help the government of this country in ways you cannot begin to imagine. The police look after my interests and I look after theirs.' He reached forwards and pinched her right breast painfully through her T-shirt. 'You watch your step, bitch.'

'You watch yours too,' she thought as he walked to the door, but she did not say it. There was something in his cocky manner that made her think he had kept some low blow in reserve, something that made him feel master of the situation. She tried to think what it could be, but then he told her.

'By the way,' he said, turning at the door, 'I should have told you before. I've had to take your passport for, let's say, administrative purposes connected with Swiss immigration.

I do hope that is not inconvenient. After all, you weren't thinking of going anywhere, were you?'

When the door slammed behind him, she ran to her case. The passport had gone. When in hell did he do that? she said to herself, but she was half amused by the thought of how clever he believed he had been, and how wrong he would find he was.

She strode out of the apartment past the glittering shops of Bahnhofstrasse and into the twisting lanes of the old city around Augustinergasse and the St Peters Kirch. She headed for the river, seeking safety and solitude in the crowds, thinking how to play it. She was resolved not to stay. The easiest way was to go, and let him try to wreak any petty revenge he could. She had one or two cards up her sleeve. She had already reconnoitred some escape routes. She was inclined to believe that he really did have powerful links with the Swiss authorities, and it would be safer not to leave via the airport. The land crossings into Germany would be easiest, the maze of little lanes around the Rhine with half-attentive border guards who had no fancy computer systems to warn them.

If she wanted to take even less risk, there was the hydro-electric dam north of Glattfelden, where you could cycle across into Germany past nothing more impressive than a closed-up wooden hut. That would get her out of Switzerland, but it would be useless with no passport to take her further. She was too uncertain of what the computer systems of the European countries might have on her to go shopping for fake documents in a foreign land. But that wouldn't be necessary thanks to her trump card. The Colombian passport was expendable. In her shoulder bag, she carried the one that never left her presence, the passport of the US citizen.

I can go any time I want to, she thought. I'll go the very next time he steps out of line. He's not all-powerful. I can just go to the airport and get on the next flight to anywhere I like, and he won't even know until it's too late. She arrived at the Quaibrucke, the final bridge where the Limmat flows out of the great lake of Zürich, and looked down the long expanse of the Zürichsee, crowded with all kinds of boats, glinting in the sun. Just below the bridge there was a pontoon where there were motor boats for hire. She looked again at the lake and thought, why not. It would be nice to have some clean water between her and all this. If she really was going to walk out on the job, and all the signs pointed that way, then the lake would be a good place for calm consideration of the pros and cons.

At the counter she asked in faltering German if she could hire a boat. The woman looked at her and reached for a form.

'May I have your name and your hotel please?' she said in English. They filled in the form, then the woman made her read a list of regulations. Do not approach the shore closer than 100 metres except for the purpose of landing. Do not land anywhere except at a designated landing area or you will receive a ticket from the lake police, and so on. They finally came to an end and the woman said, 'Now I need only your passport.'

That was when she reached into her shoulder-bag for the American one and found that it too was gone.

Chapter Ten

Stretched out in the relative luxury of the 747's Club World Business Class, Steve was feeling relaxed in the pleasant limbo of not being expected to do anything. He always felt a little guilty about the expense of travel, imagining entire streets paying their licence fees so that he, Steve Ross, could be on this plane. Turning down the free champagne, because it made his eyes dry and his head ache in the cabin's dehydrated atmosphere, made him feel only slightly more virtuous. The only cloud on the horizon was his next-door neighbour.

Steve's preferred method on long flights was to acknowledge his neighbour as briefly as politeness allowed, then settle ostentatiously into a book to create the gulf which he could then choose to bridge later if that seemed desirable. No such approach stood a chance against Victor Bowler, sales director of a Midlands stainless steel fixings company, with two children, both at boarding-school, though one was rather asthmatic, who always went through Washington at this time of year on his way to some trade show. He told Steve all of this and plenty more within five minutes of settling his huge girth into the next seat and, most annoying of all, allowing his overstuffed briefcase to stray over into Steve's floor space.

The breathless flow of information allowed Steve to avoid even giving his name, and when Bowler asked the stewardess for a 'Cognac, and make sure it's Rémy – no, better make it two' before boarding had even finished, it began to look like a horrible flight. Steve was trying to get into Caris Davis's book *Stealth* when Bowler reached across with a fat hand and stabbed a finger at the picture on the cover.

'Stealth bomber, isn't it?' he said. 'You a plane spotter or what then?'

'No,' said Steve coldly, 'it's a novel. It just happens to have that picture on the cover. It's a pun on the title.'

Bowler wasn't happy to leave it there. He'd fronted up with his curriculum vitae and he wanted an equal trade from Steve in return.

'So what game are you in then?' he asked.

Steve sighed inwardly, knowing exactly the sort of conversation which would now follow. He thought of lying, but decided he probably couldn't sustain it all the way across the Atlantic.

'TV,' he said, as uninformatively as he could.

'What? You sell them do you?' persisted Bowler.

'No,' said Steve putting the book down, and this time the sigh was probably audible. 'I work for the BBC.'

'Oh yes? What as?' persisted Bowler, and Steve wished he knew how to be really rude without feeling guilty.

'I'm a reporter for TV News,' he said, and the cat leapt, miaowing furiously, out of the bag.

Bowler was hugely and loudly delighted. 'Let's have a look at you then,' he said, and Steve, who was familiar with this turn in the conversation, pretended not to understand.

With complete insensitivity Bowler plunged onwards. 'Go on,' he said, trying to lever himself forward in his seat and peering round at Steve. 'Turn round and look straight at me. See if I can recognize you like you are on the telly.'

Thank God for the relative anonymity of profiles in a full-face world, thought Steve. You're most at their mercy when you're sitting down. Standing up there's a good chance you'll be shorter, taller, fatter or thinner than they think and that will throw them off the scent.

'Yes. I've got you now,' Bowler said in a satisfied tone, and went on peering at him as though the normal rules of politeness were suspended and there was no person behind the features he was studying. 'Course I know your face, you're er …'

Steve opened his mouth to introduce himself, but Bowler stopped him. 'No, hang on a minute. Leave it to me. I want to get it right. You're Keith Graves, aren't you?'

'No, I'm …'

'Wait, he's got a beard, hasn't he? No, you're John thingy, John … Simpson.'

'No. Look, really, this is …'

A voice from behind his shoulder said, 'Can I get you a drink, Mr Ross?' and he looked up in grateful surprise to see a stewardess smiling at him.

'Oh, thank you, I'd love an orange juice,' he said, and she gave him a small, private wink as she turned.

'Of course,' said Bowler, 'I remember now, it's Nick isn't it? Nick Ross?'

'No, he does *Crimewatch*. I'm Steve Ross actually.'

Then he watched with even more excruciating alarm as the slow process of association with recent events made itself plain across Bowler's face. Whatever stainless steel fixings may be, he thought, they must walk off the shelves and sell themselves without any help from this man. Take-off interrupted the conversation, such as it was, and Steve was gratified to see Bowler's hands clenching and unclenching in sudden tension that explained the two brandies.

It's fake fame, isn't it? he thought to himself. People find nothing odd in chatting away about how well or poorly they remember your face, as if it had nothing to do with you at all. They pay to have you in the corner of their living-room. They feel they know you. They feel they own you. You're not really famous after all, you're just familiar – part of the B team.

A year before he'd been walking along a city street and seen one of those almost-familiar faces approaching, the sort that has you racking your brains for when, where and why you last met. At an approach speed of eight miles an hour, he had twenty seconds to come up with an answer, and he could see all the signs that the other, a man of about thirty-five, was going through the same sort of process. Steve's memory was no clearer when they reached each other, and he could only search for clues.

'Well, hello,' he said.

'Haven't seen you for a long time,' said the other.

'No,' replied Steve with what sounded inside his head like almost hysterical *bonhomie*. 'Where was it now?'

'Anyway, nice to see you looking so well,' said the other in equal panic, and they waved their goodbyes.

Steve had only gone ten yards when it came to him that the other man was in fact a supporting actor in a TV cops and robbers serial, and they'd never met before. Two faces from the B team, passing each other in the fog.

Bowler recovered his nerves as they rose through the cloud tops, and got back his memory at the same time. 'Steve Ross,' he said with a tone of delight. 'You were the one in that riot, weren't you? The one when the cameraman got the chop?'

It's now or never, thought Steve, or I'm going to have to move seats. 'The cameraman was a close friend of mine,' he said in a cold voice. 'Got the chop is not an expression I would care to use.'

The rest of the flight was spent in something satisfyingly approaching silence.

*

There was a long, slow queue at the Dulles airport immigration desks. It was a beautiful, sunny late-afternoon, and Steve found the experience of driving into Washington as vivid as the first time he'd done it as a junior radio news reporter years before. The hire-car waiting for him was a Pontiac, and he tuned the radio to DC101, the raucous, vulgar Washington rock station.

Flying into New York, San Francisco or Chicago puts you into at least the fringe of urban North America straight away. Washington's own scary, in-town National airport puts you cheek by jowl with the businessmen and politicians using the New York shuttles like a city bus service, but Dulles is different. It's quiet and expansive, easing you down into the heart of the soft, wooded Virginian countryside. The airport expressway isn't the most exciting of roads, but it makes up for it with a cyclorama of exit signs whose romance completely obscures the suburban American reality hidden by the trees: Wolf Trap, Cabin John, Spout Run, Leesburg Pike.

Used to being alone on foreign trips, Steve found he'd stopped feeling lonely, and only then realized how deep and familiar that feeling had become. He crossed Key Bridge into the bustle of the Georgetown end of M Street. He stayed on M all the way over the dividing gulf of Rock Creek into serious, important Washington and checked into the Omni by Dupont Circle. He had a shower, drank copious quantities of orange juice to get rid of the itchy aridity of the plane, then walked down 19th Street to the BBC's office, just a few blocks away.

It was a small, efficient, friendly operation, and he was pitched into it with barely time to draw breath. He had a day's overlap with the regular correspondent before he had to head off for the Summit. There was a flurry of diplomatic activity going on in the aftermath of the Gulf War, plus a rush of arms limitation initiatives ahead of the Summit and, as a sub-plot, an unexpected change of position from the Commerce Department on the long-drawn-out GATT trade row.

The time difference between the US and the UK is an awkward one for news. Steve was up early every morning, getting ready for the *Six O'Clock News*, which is 1 p.m. East Coast time and demands satellite feeds to get the pictures over to London at around 12.45 p.m. That in turn means editing has to start by midday at the very latest, so the story has to be shot early. After that they would usually get a take out salad or sandwich from one of the fast food palaces around the block if there was time, before going out to shoot more for the 3.45 p.m. feed to hit the 9 p.m. UK news. Once upon a time it used to ease up then, before some idiot decided that what Britain needed was breakfast TV. That means, just when it should go quiet in the evening, the process starts all over again, watching the US networks for anything promising to keep the morning bulletins, which have few other sources of breaking news overnight, full and happy.

In the middle of the week Steve was complaining mildly about the latest request from Breakfast to Angie, the fixer, producer, secretary and lynchpin of the office.

'Come on, knock off the complaining,' she said. 'You can't say we don't make it easy for you – NBC, CBS, CNN all spoonfed to you to record, chop up and turn round as you wish. Feeds coming in on video from the White House, the State Department and everywhere else that matters, just so you can sit here in comfort with a cold Budweiser in your hand and not even have to stir out of the office.'

'Ah, but that's just what I don't like,' he said. 'Unless it's a really big story, that's exactly what you wind up doing, rushing to turn round other people's material and just putting your own words on it.'

'You don't know when you're well off,' she said. 'You're just too darned conscientious, Steve.' She was probably right. The regular correspondent would have divided his time more judiciously and felt freer to turn down the more outrageous requests from the Breakfast team. For all that, Washington was a great place to work. The local camera crew were fast on their feet, enthusiastic and fun to work with. The editing, one floor away, was state-of-the-art – a big video facility built up by a former cameraman who'd cut his teeth with the BBC. His picture editors had a sure eye for what shots would cut together. Pushed, they could cut a one and a half minute story and put the voice track on inside twenty-five minutes, and have it on the machines in London, ready to run, just three minutes later.

In the odd quiet moments Steve started the search for M. Rhinehart. The obvious places all turned up blanks. The FBI admitted to several Rhineharts, but not one that fitted. Angie was curious, but took Steve's reticence on the subject as a warning not to ask for explanations, and she contented herself with finding him lists and directories of any official agency that might lead to the man. She knew all about Sunny's death and decided early on that Steve's quest stemmed from that.

After three or four days Steve felt he was at a dead end. One M. Rhinehart, listed as a congressional aide, had called him back on getting his message, but had sounded convincingly blank when he hedged round the subject. Apart from that, nothing. That was when Angie said, 'There's always the CIA?'

Steve laughed. 'Sure. They're really likely to help me out.'

'Stranger things have happened,' she said. 'After all, they're listed in the phone book.'

Feeling silly, he called the number at Langley, explained that he was trying to trace someone, and was put through to a woman with a voice that sounded like Donald Duck's.

'Yes?' she said.

Steve wished he'd thought out a clearer plan of attack. 'My name's Steven Ross,' he said, 'I'm with the British Broadcasting Corporation here in DC.'

'Would that be Steven with a v or a ph?' she said.

'Er, v.'

'Yes, Mr Ross. How can I help you?'

'It's a rather awkward personal matter. I'm trying to trace someone called Rhinehart. Initial M. I'm sure you don't usually discuss your employees with journalists, but it's a matter of considerable personal importance to me, and I was wondering if there might be any way you could help?'

'What would the M stand for, Mr Ross?'

'I don't know, I'm afraid.'

There was a pause. 'In that case, if you don't mind my saying so, it doesn't sound too personal.'

'Well, it is, but I can't really go into it.'

'Mr Ross, I doubt that I can help you, but perhaps you could start by giving me a few personal details of yourself.'

In the next five minutes Steve gave them everything except his inside leg measurement. They wanted to know his mother's maiden name and his parents' places and dates of birth. In the end he hung up, rightly certain that he would never hear from them again.

Angie looked at him sympathetically. 'No luck, eh?'

'Less than no luck,' he said. 'They've now got a great big file headed "Steve Ross (asks silly questions)" – and I've got zilch.'

'Come on,' she said, 'let's find a nice dark bar and go over it again.'

In a cosy, wood-panelled bar on 18th Street she said, 'Let's just check that we haven't missed anything. We've tried the

FBI, the CIA, the Justice Department, the State Department, the White House ... Where else?'

Steve ticked them off on his fingers. 'The IRS, the DEA, the Customs Service, Immigration, and every other likely Government department.'

'What about the SEC?' she said.

'SEC? The Stock Exchange Commission?'

'Nearly right. In fact it's the Securities and Exchange Commission. Cowboys in white hats and grey suits who specialize in scaring the shit out of corporate criminals. You know, Levine and Boesky and all that.'

'Wouldn't be them, surely?'

'I don't know, Steve. Your business is your business. I'm just looking for any stone you might have left unturned.'

He smiled at her then, aware of how much she was trying to help him, and thinking if she didn't have a boyfriend he would have asked her out.

It was too late to reach anyone that night, so, as soon as he could the following morning, he called the SEC's number. He took the full-frontal approach. 'Could I speak to Mr M. Rhinehart please?'

'I'm sorry, sir,' said a standard American telephone voice, 'we have no such person,' but then, as Steve was on the verge of apologizing and hanging up, she laughed and became human. 'That's a gender error, I believe, sir. We do have a *Miss* M. Rhinehart. Hold on and I'll put you through.'

The woman who came on the line had a deep, assured voice, and Steve knew he was holding one end of a single, slender lifeline which would be broken for ever if he played his cards wrong now.

'Miss Rhinehart, my name is Steve Ross. I'm sorry to ring you up out of the blue. I hope you're not too busy?'

'I'm always busy, Mr Ross. What can I do for you?'

'I'm with the British Broadcasting Corporation, and I'm

here in Washington for a short time and I'm trying to trace someone who may, by chance, have some information which could help me concerning the death of a friend of mine. The only lead I have is the name, M. Rhinehart.'

'That's a little startling, Mr Ross. I don't think it's me you want to see. Deaths don't usually come into my business.'

'No, but you wouldn't necessarily know about that aspect of it.' He paused, thinking. 'Look, it's hard to talk about this over the phone. Could I possibly see you for just five minutes. I promise to get out of your hair if it isn't you.'

'Well, you've come a long way, Mr Ross, but I'm very short on time. I'm going to Atlanta this evening for four days and I have meetings all afternoon.'

'Suppose I came down right now. I don't mind waiting,' he said, desperately hoping that there wouldn't be an urgent story to stop him.

She sighed. 'Well, all right. I can't promise anything, though.'

He told Angie he would be an hour and gave her the SEC's phone number. The office mobile phone had a flat battery because he'd forgotten to put it on charge, so he took a bleeper and hailed a cab. It was a long, slow journey east, past Union Station and down to the SEC's headquarters. He kept checking neurotically that the bleeper was working, imagining major stories breaking in his absence.

He remembered the tale of the newspaper columnist who'd covered a political rally in America, filed his story and gone to bed to get a good night's sleep, taking his phone off the hook. With earplugs in, he slept through the sound of someone knocking persistently on his door and woke refreshed to catch an early cab to the airport. It was only as the plane got airborne that he opened his paper and read that Bobby Kennedy had been killed the previous night in that very hotel.

He gave his name at the reception desk and stood looking at the old, ornate stock certificates which decorated the walls. Then a male voice said 'Mr Ross?' at his elbow. He turned to see a glossy young man in a Brooks Brothers suit.

'Yes?'

'I'm Randy McLernon from the press office. Mary Rhinehart asked me to meet you and sit in on your meeting.'

Oh shit, thought Steve. That blows that one. Why on earth did she have to bring in the bloody press office, she can hardly bend the rules in front of them. But he followed, resignedly, through a corridor to a door marked Office of International Legal Assistance.

Mary Rhinehart was a sturdy, tough-looking fifty-year-old with her hair back in a tight bun, and a tweedy look out of the run of the normal DC female business suit. She shook hands and waved them both to a chair.

'I asked Randy to step in, Mr Ross, because that is the rule we have here when we see a journalist. Now perhaps you could tell me a bit more?'

Steve didn't want to take the plunge, knowing the odds were loaded against him, deprived of the one-to-one chance to strike up a sympathetic relationship, but he had to say something.

'Miss Rhinehart, I haven't really come here as a journalist at all. Last month, a cameraman I was working with was killed during a riot in London. I've made some roundabout enquiries into his death, and there may be a link to a man called Eric Blackler.'

Her head lifted just a fraction, and he knew the name was familiar. He ploughed on. 'I wanted to talk to you completely off the record to see if you could tell me anything helpful about Blackler. I know you, or maybe someone with your

119

name, expressed an interest in him to the police in London, and it's the only clue I've got.'

It was Randy McLernon who jumped in. 'Mr Ross, I should tell you straight away the SEC has rules which prevent background briefing to journalists. If the Commission has anything to say, it says it on the record. If it doesn't, then it keeps quiet. We can discuss general policy if you like, but we can't go into individual cases.'

Mary Rhinehart, however, was sitting back considering her own thoughts and clearly not listening to this. She waited for McLernon to finish, then looked curiously at Steve. 'It sounds like the kind of question the police should be asking, not you, Mr Ross.'

'Yes, they should be, but they aren't. They've arrested a black guy who had nothing to do with it, and they don't seem too interested in taking it further.'

She raised her eyebrows and started to speak, but whatever she was about to say was cut off by the sudden startling sound of Steve's bleeper going off.

'I'm sorry,' he said, 'that's my office.'

She picked up the phone and passed it over. Angie answered at the second ring. 'Thank goodness, Steve. I paged you twice. Didn't you get it first time?'

He felt the nervous rush of adrenalin. 'No, that was the first time as far as I was concerned. What's going on?'

'You've got to make tracks fast. The State Department's making a statement on the Middle East. The crew's on its way. Can you meet them at Foggy Bottom? You've only got fifteen minutes.'

'I'll be there.'

He hung up and looked at Mary Rhinehart. 'I'm sorry, I've got to go. There's a story.'

'That's all right,' she said. 'I'm sorry I couldn't be of more help.'

Aware that he had no time left, he made a last attempt. 'The reason I came was that Sunny, the cameraman, was a good friend. It really matters to me that the man who killed him should stand trial.'

She smiled at him and, getting to her feet, reached out a hand. 'I do understand, Mr Ross, and I wish you the best of luck.'

In the taxi he cursed loudly. A London cab driver would have been astonished. In Washington it barely made the driver's eyebrows twitch.

He leapt out of the cab on 21st Street and ran round to the main entrance to the State Department. He saw the crew, Ricky and the Spanish girl Teresa, the far side of the barrier, waiting with their equipment alongside the other crews for the go-ahead to enter.

'Let me see your accreditation, please,' said the man at the desk. Steve produced his BBC card.

'No, I need your State Department accreditation,' said the man impatiently.

'I don't have it. I'm a temporary replacement for the regular man,' said Steve. 'Here's a letter from the BBC and my passport.'

The man looked at them and shook his head. 'I'll have to get someone down from Public Affairs,' he said, and picked up the phone.

Steve looked at the group on the other side of the barrier. They were picking up their gear and preparing to move off. 'There's no time for that,' he said. 'Look, it's about to start.'

'That's all I can do,' said the man, 'it's security. Someone will be down directly to see to you.'

Steve waved his hands and Ricky came over. 'Listen,' he said, 'I can't get in. I'll try and join you later. Just shoot everything you can.'

It took ten minutes before someone arrived to deal with

him, ten minutes which Steve spent pacing up and down, imagining the worst and swearing at himself for wasting his time at the SEC. It was a further fifteen minutes of check calls and filling in forms before Steve was inside the room where the Secretary of State was just taking the last of the questions. He took a copy of the hand-out giving the transcript of the statement. That was fine as far as it went, but it was the detail from the question and answer session that mattered, and he'd missed it. He went over to Ricky, who looked at him pityingly.

'Gave you a hard time, huh?'

'My own fault, I should have been here earlier, what did I miss?'

'Well, it's all on the tape. I just kept rolling. Some of the guys were getting pretty excited in the Q and A.'

'Any idea why?'

Ricky spread out his hands. 'Sorry, Steve. I guess you'll just have to look at it yourself. You know what it's like when you're trying to get the pictures straight, you don't have time to think of much else. Why don't you ask one of the guys?'

Steve looked around at the departing press corps. There were a few faces he recognized, but none that he knew well. It was hard to go up to another journalist and ask what the story was, but he tried it with a little balding man still sitting in the front row of seats, who was trying to get his pocket tape player to rewind.

'Excuse me,' Steve said diffidently, 'I missed the questions. You couldn't give me a quick run-down, could you?'

The man looked up, irritation showing clearly on his face. 'No, I goddam well couldn't,' he yapped and, gathering his sheaves of loose paper and his tape player to his chest with both arms, he ran out of the room, short legs pumping. Steve thought of trying elsewhere, but decided they would be better off heading back and viewing the tape.

The traffic was agonizingly slow. Time ticked by far too fast. It was 11.30 when they pulled up outside the building on M Street, and the picture editor was waiting in the edit suite.

'Lots of time,' she said.

'Not really,' said Steve, 'I wasn't there. We need to whizz through the Q and A session so I can hear what happened.'

'Oh,' she said, and put the tape in the machine.

The phone rang, and she picked it up then passed it straight to Steve. 'It's Foreign News.'

'Steve, it's Jacko. I'm Foreign Duty Editor today.' It was the Australian. 'The bulletin wants to know how strong the story is.'

Steve decided honesty was the best policy. 'Jacko, I'm not sure yet. We had a problem. They wouldn't let me in.'

'Oh, what? Why not?'

'No dog tag. By the time they checked me out, it was all over.'

'Shit. That's never been a problem before. You should have been there early enough.'

'Well ... I wasn't. Anyway, I'll get back to you as soon as I can.'

'Yeah, well, do that. Dennis Daley's doing the bulletin today because Eileen's sick. I wouldn't want to give him any sticks to beat your back with, mate.'

The first five minutes of tape was the statement, covering the version issued on the press release almost word for word. The next fifteen minutes were questions and answers, and it was clear straight away that the focus of the press corps' questions was fixed on one single aspect of the statement. The issue was whether the US administration was prepared to threaten Israel with serious cuts in economic support if Israel refused to play the part the US wanted in a Middle

East peace conference. Steve was making notes furiously, jotting down the time codes which appeared on the bottom of the screen so they could go straight to any section of the tape he wanted to use.

The question was asked five or six times in five or six different ways. The Secretary of State ducked and weaved in his impassive Texan style. That was a theoretical question, he said. It would be a matter of consideration at the right time, he said. It would not be appropriate to comment while negotiations were still in progress, he said. Then a very blunt question from ABC's White House correspondent seemed to get under his skin. 'All right,' he said, holding up both hands, 'I hear what you're saying. Let me be as plain as I can on this and then let's move on to something else. The first priority of this administration with regard to the Middle East is ...' and the tape ended.

Ricky, standing behind Steve's chair in the edit suite, groaned. 'Sheeit. I thought that might have been a bad moment. We had to change tapes.'

He'd done well. The tape change had only taken some twenty seconds, but the damage was done. The Secretary of State had said what he was going to say and they hadn't got it. 'I'm sorry, Steve,' said Ricky.

'It certainly isn't your fault,' said Steve, trying to think through the growing feeling of panic in his head. He looked at the picture editor. 'Janie, would you start putting together about twenty seconds of establishing shots. Let's say two outside shots and a couple of wides of the presser. I'm going to check what the agencies are saying.'

'OK Steve. I hate to hassle you, but it's twenty minutes to feed time.'

'I know.'

He took the lift one floor to the BBC office, unsure if the fire doors on the stairs could be opened from the other side.

Angie looked at him in concern when he burst in.

'Everything OK, Steve?'

'No, not at all. Hang on, I've just got to read the wires.'

It then became a question of who to believe. Reuters had just started running a strong story saying the Secretary of State had given a firm and unequivocal warning to Israel that peace in the Middle East was its first and overriding priority. Another agency had a very different interpretation. The Secretary, it said, had resisted pressure to name Israel as the foot-dragger, and restated existing US principles on Middle East peace. The panic reached Steve's stomach.

Then the door of one of the smaller offices opened, and the unkempt figure of Duncan Frayling, BBC Radio's Washington correspondent, shambled out, half-moon glasses low on his nose, clutching a script and heading for the small, sound-proofed studio from which he broadcast his dispatches. In the heat of the moment Steve had forgotten all about him, and relief washed over him.

'Duncan. Have you got a second? I'm deep in the shit.'

Frayling checked his stride and peered over his glasses. 'Dear boy, how uncomfortable.'

'Were you listening in on the State Department?'

'I was watching it on CNN.'

Steve explained his problem, and Duncan, with a certain air of lofty satisfaction at scoring over the other side, turned to the photocopier and made him a copy of his script. It took the same line as Reuters.

Angie had been listening to this. 'Hasn't Ricky got it on tape?' she asked. Steve explained about the tape change. 'Ah,' she said, 'lucky I was recording CNN then wasn't it,' then shrieked as Steve grabbed her and kissed her on the cheek.

'I'll bring it up,' she said, and he was already running through the door.

He'd never worked so fast before. With a second-rate picture editor he wouldn't have stood a chance, but Janie worked at the speed of light, getting each individual edit right first time. Normally, Steve would have been thinking up script lines on the way back to base. Now he had to go from cold, but suddenly the story had fallen into place, and he knew where to start and where to finish. Angie came in with the CNN tape and they edited in the vital answer. It had CNN LIVE emblazoned across it, but that seemed a small price to pay.

At 12.42, with the start of the satellite booking three minutes away, Janie said, 'It needs a stand-upper. I've got no more shots to cover your conclusion.'

Ricky was already on the move. 'We'll set up right outside the front door, Steve. Ready in two minutes.'

Steve looked at Angie. 'Ask them to extend the feed by five minutes.'

'Ouch,' she said. 'They won't like that.'

'Never mind the money, there's no choice.'

He went after Ricky, walking at a deliberate pace, knowing any time saved in running would be wasted getting his breath back before he could say his piece to camera. He concentrated on getting the words right. Outside, the camera was already on the tripod and Ricky was focusing on Teresa, standing in for Steve. He took her place, an anonymous Washington cityscape behind him, and a minute later, with no more need to conserve his breath, was tearing back in through the doors with the tape. Up at the edit room Janie snatched it from him and shoved it in the player.

'One take?' she asked, running back to the start.

'Yes,' he said, and they watched tensely as the machines copied it on to the end of his cut story. Then Janie rewound it, pressed the eject button, and they waited what seemed an agonizing age as the machine unlaced itself and lifted the tape, in slow motion, up and out of the slot.

Janie ran round the corner to the feed point where Angie was waiting, phone in hand, talking to London.

'Yes, it's here,' she said, 'going in the machine now. Are you getting our tone and colour bars?'

They switched over from the audio and video test signals to the tape, and played it twice, once with Steve's soundtrack and once with natural sound only so it could be used for headlines or anything else London needed. It was two minutes to news time when they finished.

'Jeez,' said Janie, 'I can do without ones like that.'

The phone buzzed. 'Steve, it's Jacko. Glad you made it. The story looked good in the end. I don't need to tell you Daley was on the rampage. He's not your closest friend, is he?'

'No. Look, Jacko, it took me a bit too long to get there, that's all. Angie had to bleep me twice because it didn't work first time.'

'Well, there's bound to be a bit of an inquest. You know what things are like at the moment with the overspending on the Gulf. I've got to have a good story to explain any satellite extensions, because that's real money. Where were you when Angie was trying to get you?'

'I was over the other side of town, at the Securities and Exchange Commission.'

'Oh good, I thought you were about to say you'd gone shopping or something like that. What was the story?'

'Well, there isn't one, Jacko. I was just following up something somebody told me. It might come to something or it might not.'

'Christ, Steve. I can't turn round to Daley and say you were off chasing hunches. He's gunning for you. He'd love to prove that we should never have sent you in the first place.'

'Oh. I didn't realize.'

'I'll cover for you. I'll tell him you were doing some research for a story next week.'

'It's a bit heavy, isn't it? I mean, we made the bulletin and it would have been bloody tight anyway.'

'Yes, but he's going round saying you didn't have a headline for him until you'd read it on Reuters.'

Steve hung up feeling depressed, but there was no time to linger on it. The *Nine O'Clock News* was already on to them, keen to set up interviews with Washington Middle East watchers and Congressmen on the significance of the State Department's stance. They spent lunchtime and the early afternoon rushing from place to place, getting what they needed, and put together a comprehensive two-minute piece for the lead. It was finished on time and, apart from a technical problem which held up the satellite feed for an agonizing five minutes, all went smoothly.

It didn't, however, take away the bitter taste of the earlier problems, and Steve was now acutely aware that Daley, still smarting from his defeat on the night of the riot, was actively trying to rubbish him behind his back. At 4.05, with the lead story safely on the air in London, Angie looked at him with a twinkle in her eyes.

'I've been holding out on you,' she said. 'I didn't want to distract you while you were working. There's a message for you to ring Mary Rhinehart.'

Chapter Eleven

Steve found a phone in a quiet side-office and called Mary Rhinehart's number.

'Mr Ross,' she said, 'after our conversation I took the liberty of checking the press cuttings, and I now know what happened to you and your friend Mr Jordan. I'd like to help you, but there is a very strict limit on what I can say, as I am sure you will appreciate.'

Steve breathed in, aware he was treading on very thin ice. 'Miss Rhinehart, I quite understand. I promise you I'll be very discreet about anything you tell me.'

Unexpectedly, she chuckled. 'I'm sure you said that to whoever gave you my name too. You may not think what I'm going to tell you is very useful, but please listen for all that. Your man Blackler is a mystery to us. We don't know why our man went to see him, and he wasn't at all what we expected.'

'Who is your man?'

There was a short silence, then she said, 'I'm sorry, I don't think I can tell you that.' There was another pause, and he waited it out, knowing he had no more cards to play but that she seemed to want to give him something.

'I'm going to give you some advice,' she said. 'You haven't been in Washington long, I guess, so you probably don't know how the system works. Can we do it that way?'

Steve had no clear idea of what she was getting at, so he agreed.

'Regulators like us have to answer to the great democratic

dream,' she said. 'There has to be someone to watch over our shoulder, so on the Hill they have what are called Oversight Committees. Stop me if I'm telling you something you already know.'

'Not at all,' said Steve, 'Please go right ahead.'

'Well, we have a Senate Oversight Committee chasing our tail a lot of the time. There's a man called Dave Berkowitz there who has the right to call me up and ask me to provide all kinds of files and documents that I don't really care to give him, so that he can make sure I'm doing my job properly and not infringing the Constitution. There are all kinds of things which I'm not allowed to tell you, but which he can insist, or at least try to insist, on knowing. You would be very well advised to see him. I'll give you his number.'

Steve put the phone down, unsure whether he'd made any progress or not. The chance that Berkowitz would have asked for the right documents to help him seemed slim in the extreme. Nevertheless he called Berkowitz and made an appointment to visit the office. The earliest Berkowitz could manage was the following Monday, so, with the day's painful experience behind him, Steve made an appointment for 4.30 p.m. to be on the safe side. That turned out to be just as well because he was run off his feet during the intervening days by the developing Middle East story and then, on the Saturday evening as he was preparing to go to a movie, by a major plane crash on the West Coast.

On Monday, with the last of the day's business for London hopefully behind him, Steve got out of a cab on Independence Avenue, with the Capitol Building partly hidden by the trees behind him in the late-afternoon sun, and, with his portable phone in his hand, went into the Rayburn Office Building. It was a monolithic, old-fashioned rabbit warren of Senate and Congressional offices, with wide corridors thronged by earnest-looking aides all acting roles in their own private movie. He was shown to the third floor, through a double wooden door with frosted glass panels, and immediately it was as if the script had changed from *All the President's Men* to *Hill Street Blues*.

A large open-plan office with a small screened-off waiting area by the door was full of men and women barking down phones or sitting on the edges of desks, swinging one leg and talking to each other. They looked like screen cops. He was directed to a small, balding man with a broken nose and a shiny blue suit. White jogging shoes showed incongruously below it.

'Glad to see you, Steve. I'm Dave Berkowitz. How can I help you?'

'I'm not exactly sure. Mary Rhinehart at the SEC suggested I come and see you because you might have some information I need.'

'You may not be sure, Steve – I love your accent by the way – but I'm sure. She must like you.' Here he gave Steve a slap on the back, which involved reaching upwards, and a lewd wink. 'Though I heard tell that men weren't exactly her first choice.'

Steve gave him a 'we're all men together' grin, unsure how else to respond, and Berkowitz went on. 'I guess she told you how it works, Steve. We keep an eye on what they do over there, *pro bono publico* and all that. That means we get to see all kinds of things.'

'So you're the watchdog's watchdog?'

'Yeah. Hey, I like that. Watchdog's watchdog. That's good.'

'So how do I find what I need, considering I don't even know the name of the guy I'm looking for?'

'I guess that would normally be a pretty big problem, Steve. In the normal way of things that would be just about insurmountable, I guess. Luckily for you though, this ain't the normal way of things.'

Steve raised his eyebrows, and Berkowitz grinned at him. 'Watchdog's watchdog. Yeah, that's a good one. So anyway, I got this envelope sent over by Mary and with it was a note saying these were the documents I had insisted on seeing, which was a little surprising seeing I haven't been insisting on anything much for a week or two. Then she said, because it was a current investigation, she wanted me to think very carefully before I showed them to anyone else in the office. So I started thinking very carefully like she said, and I thought this wasn't completely unconnected with the other note she sent me in the same post, asking me to give you any help I possibly could when you called me.'

Steve looked at him in wonder. 'That's great, but it seems a hell of a strange way of going about things.'

Berkowitz laughed out loud. 'Not so strange when you think about it. It protects her back, and she can pin the blame on me if it leaks. It ain't going to leak is it Steve?'

'Not on to the airwaves, no, Dave.'

'Well, here it is. The ground rules are these. One, you sit here at the desk looking at them and you don't photocopy anything or take it away. Two, if you make notes, you don't put in the time, date and place you are making them.'

Steve looked at him questioningly. Berkowitz explained. 'Subpoenas. In case anyone forces you to hand over your notebook. Three, you give everything back to me before you leave the office. Four, if you turn anything up later, remember one good turn deserves another, so you call Mary. Five, you buy me a beer some time.'

Berkowitz got him an institutional coffee in a plastic cup, with one of those stirrers that looks likely to melt into the liquid as you use it, and left him to it. Steve opened the envelope with a keen sense of anticipation. It contained six photocopied sheets of paper. Some names had been whited out and some others highlighted with a marker pen.

The papers were a summary of an investigation into share dealings on Wall Street and elsewhere by a company known as Dandycap Holdings. Dandycap's address was on the island of Sark in the Channel Islands. There was a long list of dates, times and amounts of share trades, and the profit they had netted. It ran into millions of dollars. Attached was a note concerning a Swiss citizen believed to be connected to Dandycap. His names were variously given as Huber, Morgenstern, Müller and Heller. He was said to be associated with a private bank, and lived in Zürich with another address in Paris. Surveillance had been mounted on him in the course of two trips to New York. He had met shady US investment bankers, and further Dandycap share dealings had immediately followed. On the third and most recent occasion, he had gone to London where he had met a man, later identified as Eric Blackler, in a pub. There was no record of what was discussed. A further sheet of paper summarized all that was known about Blackler. Someone had drawn a series of large question marks in the margin next to it.

Steve was halfway through making notes on the main points when his phone went off. He thumbed the button. 'Yes, Steve here.'

Angie's voice said wearily, 'Sorry, Steve, but Breakfast is on the phone. They say can you get back here soonest. I asked them what for, but there's some self-important airhead there who doesn't want to talk to me.'

Steve sighed. 'Bloody wonderful. I need another half-hour here. I'll call them.'

He pushed the numbers and got through to one of the producers. 'There's nobody here at the moment, Steve, but there's a big note on the desk. I'll get it.' He came back. 'It just says, if Steve Ross calls, tell him I must speak to him urgently.'

'Who's it from?'

'It doesn't say.'

'Damn. OK, if whoever it is comes back, tell them I'm on my way back to the office.'

He raced through the rest of the notes and gave them back to Berkowitz with thanks, then went outside and spent fifteen minutes in the DC rush hour before he managed to find an empty cab. Back at M Street, the phone was ringing when he walked in to the office. Angie was nowhere in sight. He lifted it, but there was nothing except confused mumbling at the other end, then he heard a voice say, 'Can you hold on a minute?'

'What do you mean?' he said, annoyed. 'You're calling me.'

There was more mumbling, then he heard the voice at the other end say distinctly, '... and make sure you get peas with it. I can't stand baked beans. Hello?'

'It's Steve Ross.'

'Sorry to keep you. Something that couldn't wait. Look, we need a bit of fixing done.'

'What sort?'

'Well, we need someone to interview tomorrow about the Middle East talks, and we hoped you could fix us up with a senator or a congressman or someone.'

'Who are you?'

'Oh sorry, it's Tim Bradshaw.'

The name meant nothing to him. 'Yes, Tim, fine. What I mean is, what function are you performing?'

'Oh, I see. I'm standing in as breakfast news organizer while Katie's ill.'

'Well, I think that's a bit of a problem, because I've

already stood the crew down. They've got a very early start tomorrow on another story.'

'Oh, you wouldn't need a crew. We want someone to come in live.'

'Tim, have you been on the desk for long?'

There was a silence, then he said defensively, 'No, why?'

'What time would you want this person on live?'

'About 7.30 for a two-way.'

'7.30 a.m. That's London time. How's your arithmetic?'

'Fine, why?'

'Well, what time is that over here?'

'Er, about mid-day.'

'No, Tim. You don't ADD the five hours, you take it away. That makes it 2.30 a.m., and if you think I'm going to be able to persuade a senator to come in at 2.30 a.m. for a breakfast show he's never heard of, on a channel he's barely heard of, from a country he hardly ever bothers to think about, then you've got another think coming.'

'Well, there's no need to be like that.'

'Yes, there is. I was doing something important at the other end of town, and you've dragged me back for this.'

'Oh ... Well anyway, is there anyone else you could get in for us?'

'Like who?'

'Well, you know. How about an academic or a journalist or someone?'

'Whoever it is, it will still be 2.30 a.m. It really is a bit late to be trying to set that up. Everyone's leaving their offices and going home.'

'Well, you could at least try.'

Steve held on to his temper. 'OK, I'll try,' he said. 'Come to that, why don't you try too? You've probably got more home numbers than I have. I'm only standing in, you know.'

He tried fruitlessly for ten minutes, then Angie came back

135

in from the other floor and she made a few suggestions. No one who was contactable wanted to do it. They phoned London and left a message, then went round the corner for a drink.

'Steve,' said Angie in the bar, 'you've been riding yourself pretty hard. I was thinking. Next weekend is your last weekend. Why don't we go out into the mountains?'

He teased her. 'I thought you and Jim were about to get married? Wouldn't he mind?'

She made a face. 'Oh come on, I meant all together. I know Jim would like to come.'

'I'd hate to be a lemon.'

'Well, you wouldn't be. There's this girlfriend of mine who's just split up. She's called Gina …'

Steve put on a mock frown. 'Angie, are you matchmaking by any chance? If you are, you've left it a bit late.'

Angie put on an irresistible look of wide-eyed innocence. 'I just thought you'd enjoy it, that's all.'

'Well, it sounds great, but I'm still meant to be working. I can't really cover from somewhere up a mountain and Gareth's not back until Sunday night.'

'Wrong. He was just keeping quiet about it. He gets back on Thursday and he'll be home over the weekend. I can sweet-talk him into covering just in case.'

The remaining days went fast. The stories were unexciting, but they kept him busy. As Friday drew nearer, Steve began to wonder a little about the weekend. Despite the ill-timed evening with Diana Pugh, he'd lived the life of a monk since he and Maureen had split up, and indeed for quite a time before that. He imagined a weekend with a clone of Angie, all-American wholesome sexuality, an outdoor advertiser's blonde dream of a girl. Then he felt ashamed of himself and went to buy an absurdly expensive present for Tom.

On Friday evening, hunky Jim, Angie's husband-to-be, arrived at the office to collect them. He was a football-playing lawyer, and Steve found himself envying the spontaneity with which he and Angie laughed into each other's faces as they hugged. Jim drove them out onto Interstate 66 in his Plymouth station-wagon to a neat housing development in Falls Church, where he pulled up outside a small, white house and hooted.

The woman who came out was as neat as the house, dressed more for the city than the mountains, gilt clasps flashing on her jacket, her shoes and her shoulder-bag. She placed a Louis Vuitton case carefully in the back of the wagon and climbed in next to Steve. Angie leant over from the front to make the introductions. 'Steve, this is Gina. We were in school together.'

'Hi, Steve.'

She had a slightly nasal voice, and Steve looked at her as they made small talk. She was dark-haired and slim without being at all fragile. She looked made out of hard rubber. Her face was an attractive creation, the work of a practised artist starting from a fairly blank canvas. Steve tried to imagine her without cosmetic help, but his imagination kept air-brushing her head completely out of existence as it tried to work backwards from what he could see. There was nothing to go on.

'So what's the big secret, guys?' she said to Angie and Jim. 'Where are we heading?'

By this time they were on the outskirts of the western suburbs of Washington, going through a last hiccup of concrete cubes dispensing fried chicken, discount shoes, transmissions and pet cremation services. Angie sounded a little evasive. 'We thought Steve should see some real Virginia countryside before he goes back, so we're going up on the Blue Ridge.'

137

There was a querulous note in Gina's voice. 'Are we staying in the Shenandoah Valley somewhere?'

Angie looked at her doubtfully. 'No, we've booked a cabin up at Skyland.'

Gina let out a squeal, which Steve mistook for a moment of pleasure until she said, 'Oh Angie, how could you do that? That place is so ... so *rough*.' She turned to Steve. 'It's full of bugs and splinters.'

'Oh come on, Gina,' said Angie, 'you've never even stayed there. It's great. Give it a chance. You both look like you could use some mountain air. You wait for tomorrow. We'll climb Stony Man Mountain. It's so fine up there.'

They turned off 66 and went through Warrenton. The scenery was getting interesting, sweeping grassland, old wooden houses and horses behind immaculate, white post-and-rail fencing. The traffic contained a growing proportion of pick-up trucks, and they could see foothills ahead. Steve would have been quite content to sit quietly, drinking it all in, but Gina wanted to talk. She told him about her job in real estate, her boss who wanted to take her out, her husband who'd found out he was gay and moved to Venice Beach, and her analyst who said she shouldn't be so afraid to reveal her innermost feelings to others. Steve cursed her analyst privately, but wasn't called on to put in much more than the occasional yes and no, and tried to take in the passing scenery.

They began to climb increasingly steeply around Sperry-ville, past roadside stands selling cider, sorghum and honey. Jim pulled off on to the gravel by one of the stands. 'Anyone thirsty?' he asked. They got out and bought glasses of the fresh apple juice.

'Not for me,' said Gina when he passed her one. 'I don't think its hygienic. Do they have any Diet Coke?'

The last, climbing section of highway to Thornton Gap

took them up through forest to a saddle in the steep slopes of the Blue Ridge. They paid at the entrance gate to the National Park and twisted slowly south down the first part of the Skyline Drive, along the spine of the mountains. Steve was entranced by the plunging, thickly wooded slopes and the rocky crags. Gina, who had not yet asked one question of Steve about himself, mostly to his relief, was telling him about her allergies when they drove into the Skyland parking area. He liked it immediately. It was a collection of solidly built log cabins amid the trees, with winding paths connecting them to a central lodge.

Jim picked up a key and they drove round to a cabin poised on stilts on the edge of a wonderful, sheer view northward over the Shenandoah Valley, the dusk filling it with a pool of deepening shadow. It had a sitting-room and two bedrooms, each with a double bed. Steve looked quickly around, holding his bag in his hand. There seemed to be no other beds. Gina didn't help by going straight into one of the rooms and starting to lay out a long line of cosmetics on the shelf. Angie and Jim went into the other. No book of etiquette Steve had ever read covered this situation, so he sat on the couch in the sitting-room and put his bag down beside it.

Angie came out and looked at him thoughtfully. 'That must be the one that unfolds into a bed,' she said. 'I guess we can leave you two to sort that out.' He looked at her with eyebrows raised, and she gave an exaggerated shrug. They went down the path to the lodge and sat drinking strange cocktails from Mason jars. Gina was reading a fashion magazine and occasionally showing Angie pictures of clothes. Steve was sitting next to Jim, who with considerable sensitivity steered the conversation round to Sunny's death and all that had happened since. They talked about it for the best part of an hour. Jim was a good listener, and Steve found himself telling him more than he meant to, about the link to the SEC and what had followed from his visit to Mary Rhinehart.

At the end Jim looked at him. 'Don't let it go, Steve,' he said, 'I don't believe in coincidences of that kind. It takes a lot for the SEC to go to that kind of trouble in a foreign country. If they're on to something and your man is in it somewhere, it's got to be worth chasing.'

They ate a good meal, and then Jim and Angie stood up. 'We're just going for a little walk around before bed,' said Angie. 'See you for breakfast in the morning, people.'

Set up, thought Steve. Gina smiled at them. 'Sleep well,' she said. They had a final drink and walked out on to the wooden balcony overlooking the valley. 'You know, Steve, I was wondering,' said Gina, 'why did you and your wife split?'

The question took him by surprise; he'd been expecting another bout of obsessive introspection. 'Pressure of the job, mostly. She's seeing someone else now.'

'Was she seeing them before you split?'

Steve realized he didn't know, and said so.

'So it wasn't any kind of sex thing?'

'No.'

She nodded. 'Mine was,' she said. 'In the end, he always wanted to pretend I was a boy. He just didn't like straight screwing any more.'

'That can't have been too good,' said Steve, and thought, that's pretty inadequate but what the hell am I supposed to say.

'My analyst says I should talk about it more, so I get to recognize it was his problem, not mine.'

They walked back to the cabin. Jim and Angie's light was off. Gina walked into her room and stood there. Steve felt a sense of profound detachment and turned to pull out the mattress of the sofa bed. She watched him.

'Well, I suppose it's bedtime,' he said. She nodded and pushed her door shut. He didn't usually wear anything in bed, but for once he left on a T-shirt and pants. He had barely settled down when her door opened.

'Steve,' she said quietly.

'Yes?'

'I think there's some insect under my bed. Would you mind looking?'

He went in and looked. There was nothing. When he straightened up, she was standing there close to him. She wore a short, sheer nightie, frilled and very see-through. She looked like a mannequin in a lingerie shop, her breasts clearly visible through the nylon. 'I don't really want to sleep by myself,' she said, 'do you?'

Oh well, he thought, here goes, and put his arms round her. Her body felt alien. She smelt slightly sharp and her flesh was as firm and rubbery as it looked. She kissed him and then stopped, and he remembered he hadn't cleaned his teeth. They got into the bed and he still felt far away, as if this was all happening to someone else. She reached down and felt him. 'You're not too excited about this,' she said, and it was true. Then, as he lay there in the quietness, he heard Angie and Jim through the thin wall in the next bedroom, and Angie's mounting moans of pleasure. A sudden clear image of her came into his mind with a little pang of jealousy.

'Oh, that's better,' said Gina. 'That's much better.' She reached under the pillow and came out with a condom, and he simply lay back and let it all happen.

He woke around seven in the morning, after disturbing and complicated dreams of disaster, looking in surprise at Gina, asleep with her smeared make-up still on. He got

carefully out of bed, dressed and went outside. The air was
fresh and chill with the altitude. Small animals he'd never
seen before scuttled around the pathway, and he decided
they were probably chipmunks. He sat still on the porch for
a long time and there was a rustling as a deer walked
carefully out of the trees and browsed among the plants. He
watched the animals in a limbo, and took vague stock of
himself. He'd scratched the growing sexual itch of enforced
celibacy but swapped it for some kind of unspecified
emotional debt to Gina for the rest of the weekend. On
balance, he decided, he was glad he was flying back on
Monday.

He was even more glad of that later. Angie and Jim
appeared, asked him with studied detachment if he'd slept
well, and took him off for breakfast. Gina wafted in, made
up with more care than ever, at the same moment as the
Virginia ham and hot cakes, embarrassing the hell out of
him by kissing him on the cheek and putting an arm round
his shoulders as she sat down in the chair next to him.
Angie nearly succeeded in covering up her grin and Jim
talked on manfully about the history of the Allegheny mountains.

They discussed the day ahead. Jim, Angie and Steve
wanted to climb a mountain. Gina wanted to go down to
Luray in the valley and go shopping. It turned out that she
had no driver's licence and no intention of walking up
anything steep. With enormous forbearance, and to Steve's
great relief, Jim agreed to take her.

It was a crisp, clear morning with the westerly wind
bringing with it the smell of mile upon mile of pine forest.
Steve and Angie headed up the track, through the trees.
Steve looked at Angie as she climbed the rocks with athletic
ease and contrasted her with Gina, moving stiffly through
her chosen, artificial world. They came out on a flat slab of

rock overlooking the valley and stopped to get their breath.

'You've got me worried, Steve,' said Angie. 'I have this suspicion I might not have done you a big favour.'

'How do you mean?'

'It seems to me Gina isn't exactly your ideal woman.'

'Well, no. That's true, but that's not your fault.'

'It is, in a way. I didn't realize how weird she's got lately.' She looked at him and smiled. 'Anyway, if I read the signs right, that didn't stop you guys getting it together last night?'

Steve pulled a face. 'An Englishman has to behave like a gentleman when it's expected of him. That's drilled into us at school you know.'

'So what is your ideal woman?'

'That's not so hard. It's sitting pretty close to me right now.'

'Don't tease,' she said with a smile. But he wasn't and she knew he wasn't, and there was a slight sexual buzz that neither of them tried to build on or define for the rest of their walk.

They all met up again in the afternoon to find Jim had persuaded Gina to buy some walking shoes. They went down through the easy paths of the old hemlock forest, Gina clinging unnecessarily to Steve's arm. He played the dutiful game with her, and it didn't require much except to go on listening. Angie and Jim made sure it stayed a foursome, so all in all it wasn't too bad. When night came, Steve again did all that was required of him while Gina made love with an odd determination that convinced him she was merely following her analyst's orders.

On Sunday they loafed around, then left at lunchtime and visited the Manassas battlefield park on the way back to Washington, Steve discovering he knew more Civil War history than any of the three Americans. He made a hollow excuse about pressure of work to get out of Gina's invitation to stay at the house in Falls Church. Angie knew it was a fib, but backed him up. At the hotel, he said a fonder farewell to the two of them and sat in front of the TV watching mindless movies until it was time for his last night's sleep in Washington. The next day he packed up, had lunch with Angie and Gareth, the regular correspondent, and headed for the plane home. It was only when he was in the air that he began to feel a sudden pain of departure. The holiday, for all its problems, was over. The bedsit and emptiness beckoned. What a fool I am, he thought. Gina was a lot better than no one, but even as he said it to himself he wasn't sure it was true.

Chapter Twelve

At half past nine on Monday morning Elena was exercising to music, giving herself a workout to soothe her nerves after a bad night of worrying. The dilemma was simple. Should she run the risk of crossing the border with no passport and trying to get a replacement from an embassy in Germany? The Colombian route was ruled out, her Colombian passport being in someone else's name, but the American embassy would help if she reported that one missing. So long, that is, as her activities hadn't earned her a special mention in the computer and so long as Cheeseman didn't guess what she would do and start blowing whistles. Also there was the not inconsiderable matter of the escrow account in Liechtenstein. She had no illusions that Cheeseman would let her get her hands on that money if she went.

The rhythmic exercise pumped oxygen into her blood, bringing the animal quality back into her body and the sharpness to her mind. She'd tuned the radio through several rock stations, rejecting them in turn until she found a local station playing traditional Swiss music. The banal thumping rhythm was perfect for what she wanted. In mid-stretch, the Swiss band hit a sour note and she frowned at the radio. Ten seconds later there was another strange discord, and this time she turned the volume down and heard the doorbell ringing. She slung a short coat over her leotard and went to answer it, knowing that, if someone had bothered to ring, at least it wouldn't be him.

It wasn't, but it was the next worse thing. Heller, the sidekick with the Teflon style, stood there. She looked at him enquiringly.

'I would like to come in,' he said. 'I have something important to say to you.'

She made coffee to give herself time to set up her mental defences, but he hadn't come for battle.

'My employer,' he said, 'and yours of course, is aware that you do not see your contract with him in quite the same way that he does. He has asked me to come and, shall we say, pour oil on troubled waters.'

Oil, she thought, is something you are not short of, but she contented herself with raising an eyebrow, and he went on.

'He has asked me to tell you that he would like to maintain a proper professional footing. He wishes, as he has said, that you should take full responsibility for the technical programme, the training programme and the testing. When that phase is over, you will be free to go.'

'And what guarantees are there for me in this?' she said. 'Taking my passports wasn't the sort of behaviour that inspires much confidence so far.'

Heller gave a thin smile. 'He is used to getting his own way. He also knows that you must pay for what you get and that contracts should be honoured. As a proof of goodwill he has asked me to return your passport to you.'

He held out an envelope. She took it and opened it. Inside was the Colombian passport, and she looked at him quickly. He smiled again. 'He will keep your US passport as assurance of goodwill on your part until the contract is completed. In addition, he has increased the balance in the escrow account by a further fifty thousand dollars.' He handed over another envelope. 'This is your copy of his instructions that the bank will transfer that to the account of your choice on receipt of a photocopy of your passport, showing a Swiss exit stamp dated no earlier than one month from now.'

The music held no attraction for her after he left. She curled up in a chair and thought hard for a long time.

9.30 a.m. Zürich time was 8.30 a.m. in London and 3.30 a.m. in Washington. As Flight BA 228 touched down at Heathrow, Steve was trying to shake off the mental quagmire of an extremely broken night. He'd done all the right things, rejected all the offers of alcohol, picked only at the lightest parts of the meal, and ignored the movie, but his life in London was speeding towards him at six hundred miles an hour with all the attraction of a knee in the guts. Back on the rota, waiting days for a job worth doing, opening bills he knew he couldn't pay and going back to the bedsit to do just that, sit on the bed and stare at the wall. Gina and the Blue Ridge mountains seemed suddenly a romantic dream which he'd been foolish not to savour, though it was Angie's face that came into his mind when he thought about it.

Heathrow did nothing to make things better. His bag was nearly last off the carousel. The courtesy bus for the car parking service took an age to struggle through the traffic to pick him up, and the journey into London once he'd got his car back was very slow. Whenever the car stopped in the jam, he could feel his eyelids drooping shut with an extreme of jetlag which set the inside of his head fizzing with fatigue. He let himself in to the bedsit, put the pile of letters as far out of sight as possible, and fell deeply asleep.

The phone woke him, to complete disorientation and an immediate return to depression.

'Yeah, hello?' he said, with his tongue sticking to the roof of his mouth.

'Steve. It's Nick. Just thought I'd welcome you back. Hey, you weren't asleep were you?'

'Um, yes. What time is it?'

'Seven o'clock. Time you woke up anyway.'

Steve couldn't make sense of it, his brain was crawling along far behind the conversation. 'Seven in the morning or the evening?'

'In the evening. Hey, you are in serious need of a big drink. Get some clothes on. I'll pick you up in a half hour.'

The water in the dirty bathroom down the hall was not much more than warm, and someone had broken the lavatory seat while Steve was away so that the cracked plastic pinched agonizingly when he sat on it incautiously. He found a fairly clean pair of jeans and a sweatshirt and was looking out of the window when a shining new Audi drew up outside. That Nick should get out of it seemed merely unlikely in his fuddled state, but it undoubtedly was Nick under the baseball cap.

He went out. 'Nice car,' he said, 'where did you get it from?'

Nick wasn't saying. 'So how did it go, champ?'

Steve told him all about it, and the account took them right through the West End, into the City and out the other side to the East India Dock Road before he thought of asking where they were going. Nick, driving one-handed with careless abandon, reached into the top pocket of the rough reefer jacket he was wearing and pulled out a crumpled piece of paper.

'Newham,' he said, 'some pub near the old docks.'

'It's a hell of a long way for a drink. What's so special about it?'

Nick grinned at him. 'You just wait and see and if in doubt, play dumb.'

It was a grimy, desolate street with half the houses on one

side boarded up and a corrugated iron barricade hiding the wasteland of a forlorn development site on the other. The pub was on the corner, unremarkable in Victorian brick except for the line of flashy cars parked outside it. Further down the road they were all old Cortinas, Escorts with rusting wings and Morris Marinas occupying a temporary purgatory of semi-legality on their way to an inevitable appointment with the crusher. Here, though, there were new Jaguars, custom Mercedes, even an Aston-Martin Volante.

When they went into the bar, there was nothing to explain it, just ten or a dozen old regulars, slumped in their chairs over pints of beer, and a raucous old lady with a large mongrel on a lead, trying to get them all to watch while she fed it a pickled egg. They went to the bar and Nick bought a couple of pints from a thin, lined man with slicked-down hair and one eye that looked in the wrong direction.

'Where's the fun?' he said to the barman. 'I was told to say that Tozer sent me.'

The barman looked him doubtfully up and down, then shrugged. 'Through the door and up the stairs,' he said. 'It's in the club room.'

The door opened on to a scene of extreme concentration. There were forty or fifty people packed in to the long room. Most were men, tough-looking men in their thirties and forties, wearing expensive leather jackets. The women were East End glamour, the magnifying mirrors for their menfolk. In the middle was a table where two men sat facing each other, elbows on the table and hands locked together. They were younger, in their twenties. Their faces were red and wet. Their arm muscles bulged. Slowly, one arm was being forced down, until its owner seemed to give up and it banged hard on the table.

There was an exultant shout from one side of the table,

and a few expletives from the other. Then some of the watchers looked round and saw Nick and Steve at the door. A bearded man with a shaven head came over to them and held up his hand.

'No offence, lads,' he said, 'but this is a private function.'

'Tozer sent me,' Nick said, and his American accent seemed more pronounced than usual. 'He said it would be all right.'

The man looked him up and down. 'Did you wrestle Tozer?' he asked.

Nick laughed. 'Sure. I met him in a pub down in Putney last night. We had the best of three.'

'Who won?'

'I did, two—one. He said if I wanted to do some serious stuff, I should come down here.'

Everyone round the table was listening. Looks were exchanged. The bald man reached out his hands and felt Nick's biceps like a butcher inspecting a carcass. 'All right, then,' he said, 'come and try it.'

Space was made for them at the table. The bald man spread talcum powder on his hand and offered some to Nick. They took up the position and an older man at the head of the table said, 'Ready ... away.' Nothing seemed to happen for fifteen seconds, though Nick was making quiet grunting noises. Then he slowly began to force the bald man's hand down towards the table. It hovered above it for a few seconds while the bald man's face began to turn pink, then gave way.

'OK son,' said the man, 'you're worth the game. Now do you want to play for real?'

'What's it worth?'

'Fifty says Blue Boy can beat you.'

'Who's Blue Boy?'

He nodded towards the end of the room where a huge

man silently waved a finger in acknowledgement. Nick looked at him and reached in his pocket. 'Here it is then, let's see yours.'

The man took it and counted it. 'You're five short.'

Nick turned round. 'Lend me five will you Steve. That's all I've got.' It was half of what Steve had, but he handed it over.

Blue Boy put up his money and won the first after a long-drawn-out tussle in which each man came within an inch of victory several times. Nick won the second very quickly, seeming to put everything into an opening lunge which caught his opponent off balance. There was some side-betting going on amongst the audience by the time the final match began. Nick tried for the quick lunge again, but his tank-like opponent was ready for him. It see-sawed to and fro until Nick seemed on the edge of victory, then slowly his hand was forced, half inch by half inch back up, over the vertical and all the way down to the far side to the table.

The other man looked a little surprised to have won, but took the money and left the table. 'Tough luck, son,' said the bald man to Nick. 'That your lot then?'

Nick looked around, taking the measure of the room. 'I'm only just getting the hang of it,' he said. 'Anybody want a real go?'

'I hate to mention it, son, but you don't appear to have the readies,' said a man near him. 'No stake, no play is the rule here.'

'What about other things?'

'No cheques, no credit cards,' said the man, and there were laughs around him.

Nick smiled. 'I was told you wouldn't say no to some solid assets – like maybe a car?' and Steve groaned.

The room fell silent. 'Tozer told you that, did he?' said the bald man. 'Did he tell you the rest of the rules?'

'No.'

'You have to have clear title. Documents go to our Reginald over there for checking.' He waved towards a fat, pink man in the corner. 'He's our legal eagle. If it's someone we don't know, we want to see the stake first. Where's the car?'

'Outside,' said Nick. 'Want to check it?'

A small delegation was chosen to go with him and look over the car. They came back in two or three minutes. The bald man was one of them, and there was a buzz as he held up his hand. 'All right, then,' he said, 'what we've got here is an Audi 80. Nearly new, call it six months, and 4,000 on the clock. No problems and the Yank's got the ticket on him.' Nick waved a car logbook in the air and the man continued. 'Reg? What have we got in the pot? The car's got to be worth ten big ones min.'

Reg opened the file and there was a buzz of conversation. A man shouted out, 'I'll put up a Golf cabrio,' but his girlfriend shouted, 'You fucking won't. That's mine you pig.' Then a big man stood up. 'I put the XJS in. I'll go for it.'

Reg shook his head. 'Yeah, but the Yank has to put up another four grand to balance it.'

Nick looked at him doubtfully, but another voice broke in, 'What about me then?'

At the back of the room an unshaven man in shabby clothes lounged by himself against a wall. 'I've got a boat,' he said.

Reg pulled some bits of paper out of the file. 'Says here it's a launch-cum-house-boat, down in Sussex. Haven't had the valuation yet. You been promising that for two weeks.'

'Yeah. It got held up. It's worth all of ten grand though.'

'Says here you've got title on you. Let's see it.'

The man reached into his pocket and slapped papers down on the table. 'Deeds are here,' he said. 'I'm good for it.'

Nick looked doubtful. 'I don't know,' he said, 'could be a

pig in a poke.' There were a few supportive murmurs.

'OK then,' said the man, 'I'll put in two grand in cash as well.' He reached into his pocket and slung a roll of bills across the table to Reg, who counted it, nodded and tossed it back.

The man stood in an island by himself. Nick looked at him, then around at the crowd. 'Do they know you here?'

'You're Brian's mate, aren't you?' said the bald man.

'That's right. He'll stand for me when he gets back.'

The bald man turned to Nick. 'That's all right. By our way of doing things, Brian's responsible if anything don't come through.'

'Who's Brian?' said Nick, and the room exploded into shouts of laughter.

'Brian's the man round here. Don't worry about it. He likes fair play.'

Steve just wanted out, but Nick bent and began to write out a detailed agreement about the stake, dictated by Reg, who was watching intently. Reg looked at the car registration document, then turned to Nick. 'OK, just sign it there, Mr Brice,' he said, and Steve's stomach turned over.

The other man took off his coat and sat down at the table. He had massive arms, with tattoos all over them. Nick looked powerful, but definitely weaker in comparison. There was complete silence when the referee gave them the go. The atmosphere had changed to something feral. It took five minutes, and the advantage seemed to be moving in Nick's direction, when the other man turned his body hard to the right and bent his full weight on Nick's arm. Nick began to give way, but the referee got to his feet.

'Stop there,' he shouted, 'that's a foul.'

They unlinked hands and stared, panting and flushed. The referee pointed at the tattooed man. 'None of that here,' he said. 'Arm muscles only. No leaning. Got that?'

The man looked at him and nodded unhappily. They started again and it went the same course, with Nick slowly gaining the upper hand. This time, with a straight contest, the other could do nothing about it. Once beaten, he asked for a break. 'Got to take a leak,' he said.

'Go with him, Lenny,' said the bald man, and one of the two who'd been wrestling when they arrived nodded and followed him out, to the evident displeasure of the tattooed man. 'Might have done a runner,' said the bald man to the room.

'Best thing for him,' said the referee. 'He knows he's beat. It's only when they know they've had it that they pull stunts like that.'

He was right. Within two minutes of the restart it was all over, and Nick was collecting the cash and the papers for the boat. The crowd gave the tattooed man no chance to argue.

'Thanks all,' said Nick to the room. 'Gotta fly now. See you again.'

'What, no time for one more?'

'Sorry, writer's cramp. Some other time.'

Steve felt enormously relieved when they were back in the car heading out into the brightly lit main road. He turned accusingly to Nick. 'Brice,' he said, 'they said Brice. You're not telling me this is Keith Brice's car?'

Nick nodded. 'Well, yeah. I just needed some stake money. He's away this week. Sally let me borrow it.'

'You're completely off your trolley. You could have lost a brand new car belonging to the head of the Serious Crimes Squad in there. Then what would you have done?'

Nick laughed. 'Well, I figured I could report it stolen, and if anyone could get it back, he could. Anyway, I've never lost yet.'

'But you did lose. You lost the first game.'

Nick looked at him and winked. 'Oh, did I?' he said.

'Well, whatever you were playing at it cost me five quid.'

Nick reached in his pocket and drew out the thick bundle of bills. Steering with his knees, he pulled off ten twenty-pound notes. 'Here you are,' he said. 'With interest.'

'I'm surprised they let us walk out of there with all that cash,' said Steve.

'Whatever it is, back room crap games, bare knuckle boxing, cock fights, there's always a code of honour or they don't work. Anyway, I took him up because he was a loner. He didn't have mates there. When it came to it they were just as much on my side as his.'

They went for a meal in an Indian restaurant and looked at what Nick had won. There wasn't much to go on, just a bunch of papers, a key, and a letter signed by the tattooed man assigning the title to him. The boat seemed to have an address rather than a name: Number 42, The Houseboats, Shoreham Beach.

'I know that place,' said Steve. 'I went to school down there. It's a little muddy creek off the river. I used to wander along there sometimes and look at them. They used to be real old wrecks in my day.'

'Easy come, easy go,' said Nick. 'It was the cash I wanted anyway.'

They went back to talking about Washington again, and Steve gave Nick the rundown on his meeting at the SEC. 'So it all points to Sark and this guy from Switzerland,' he said. 'It's not much to go on, but it's a lot better than nothing.'

'I never heard of Sark. What's Sark?'

'It's just a tiny island off the coast of Guernsey.'

Nick looked equally blank, so Steve explained about Britain's Channel Islands, a short way off the French coast. 'I don't know much about Sark,' he said, 'except that it's very small and it's always been run by this feudal family set-up, which means no one's allowed cars there, just tractors and bicycles.'

'If you could get a bit more, there might be a doco in this,' said Nick. 'International insider dealing and funny little islands. It sounds perfect.'

Steve snorted. 'They'd never let me. News aren't going to lend me to some programme for long enough to put together a documentary. Anyway, the doco people think all we're good for is sixty seconds from some street corner in a dirty mac.'

'So why not ask News to let you go to this place Sark and take a look-see?'

'Some chance, unless I pay for it myself. They already think I'm chasing shadows. Anyway, if I mentioned the words "insider trading" they'd have it off me before I closed my mouth. They've got hordes of highly paid specialists sitting around in their Business Unit killing each other to get on screen once a month.'

'Well, find a reason to go to Switzerland then.'

'Oh sure. Anyway, all I've got is a name, or rather three names for one man, and an address.'

The food arrived and, by the end of it, his flight began to catch up with him all over again and Nick drove him home.

He woke the following day feeling a bit more human, and went out with the balance of Nick's two hundred pounds in his pocket, suddenly feeling rich. He spent the afternoon in the library, trying without much success to find out something useful about Sark, then went to give Tom his present in the early evening, to find him in the care of a babysitter.

The next day he went to work and was summoned almost immediately into Mike Page's office.

'Morning, Steve,' said Page. 'Take a pew.' He seemed to be searching for words. 'How was it?'

'It was a really good break, Mike. It did me a lot of good.'

'Well, I'm sorry to undo some of that, but there are a couple of things.'

Steve had been smelling trouble since he walked in. Page had the reluctant air of someone told to perform a distasteful deed. 'Dennis Daley's been making trouble behind your back.'

'Oh? How?'

'That State Department story. He's been saying you weren't in the office when you should have been.'

'Hey come on, now. The story made it. I know we had problems, but the main reason was I didn't have the right dog tag and you know that's always difficult with visiting reporters.'

'I know that, Foreign know that and you know it, but Daley thinks you humiliated him last time and he's out to cause trouble.' He stopped and looked at Steve. 'Anyway, the fact is you *were* out of the office, and when I asked Jacko where you were, he couldn't give me a very convincing answer.'

'Can I tell you, just between us?'

'Go on, try me.'

So Steve told the story of what happened at the SEC, and Page listened in silence.

'I thought it must be something like that,' he said in the end. 'You don't think you're getting a bit obsessive about it, do you?'

'I'm not making it up, Mike. There's some link there, and I'd love to find out what it is.'

'Well, I'm afraid there is one other thing. I've been told to give you this by Terry Conway.'

It was a letter. Page watched as Steve opened it. 'Dear

Steven,' it started, 'I have been instructed at a high level to talk to you concerning the aftermath of Sunny Jordan's death. It has been drawn to the BBC's attention that the police feel you are not being as cooperative as you might be in your dealings with them. I would ask that you give them as much help as possible and would remind you that this is a matter of great concern to the whole News Department as well as a personal matter of your own.'

'This is a joke,' said Steve. 'What bloody right has he got to write such crap ... instructed to talk to me, indeed. Is this what he calls talking, and who's instructing him?'

Page screwed up his face and wiped a hand across his forehead. 'Someone's pulling his strings from a great height. I don't know whether it's the DG or the Governors or who, but someone has been leaning on him and now he's leaning on you.'

Steve saw red. 'Well this is a sodding insult, Mike, and I'm going to go and tell him so right now.'

'Simmer down. You can't. He's gone off to Berlin for a conference. He won't be back until Saturday.'

'I'll see him then.'

'I don't know that you will. I think I'd like you out of the way by then, for both your sakes.'

'Where?'

Page pulled the computer screen round and brought up the planning diary on it. 'Well I had this, er, disagreement with Daley, you see. I was defending sending you to Washington, and he got on my wick, so I said I wouldn't hesitate to recommend you to Foreign for any story anywhere.' He looked at the screen for a while. 'There's an OPEC meeting in Geneva at the weekend,' he said. 'The Business Unit's down to cover it, but it means Iraq and Kuwait are sitting down at the same table again, so there's every reason to

158

send a good reporter instead. That seems to fit with what you want to do.'

'I seem to spend all my time these days saying thanks, Mike.'

'It starts Saturday and it's meant to end Monday night. I won't expect to see you back until Wednesday. After Monday your bills are down to you, but I'll cover a hire car for you. And Steve ...' He looked at him hard. 'My neck is out a very long way on this one. If you screw up, there's not much I can do to protect you, understood?'

Chapter Thirteen

In a corner of the lobby, the hotel's deputy manager was having a tantrum. Being a very expensive hotel it was a very discreet tantrum, and being Swiss it would wind up costing someone a lot of money. Around his feet lay the wreckage of what had been, until two minutes before, a very expensive light – the sort of mini-chandelier, dangling from a wall bracket, that it's hard to imagine anyone designing, making or selling, but which nevertheless looks perfectly natural in a row of ten spaced along the walls of an expensive hotel lobby. But now there were only nine.

The deputy manager was finding it very difficult to decide which of the many rules he had learnt in the service of the Intercontinental Hotels chain applied to this situation. He hated having the OPEC oil ministers disrupting the smooth-running machinery of his hotel by holding their meeting in it. On the other hand they paid a fortune for the privilege, and part of the hotel's special cachet came from the frequency with which it appeared on TV screens hosting important international events.

It was the means by which it got on the TV screens that really bugged him and was the reason he had to thrust his hands into his trouser pockets so that other guests wouldn't see his fists clenching and unclenching. The TV crews and journalists covering the meeting were making a pigsty of his hotel. They were slouched in his chairs, laughing raucously in his restaurants, and above all they were so *scruffy*. The worst of it was, he couldn't even throw them out. Not only did OPEC want them to be there, but most of them were staying in the hotel.

He resented the smile on the face of the Englishman before him. He resented the man's size and his lean good looks. He resented the fact that the man wouldn't take the blame. 'Look,' the man was saying, 'it was one of those things. If you force all the camera crews to stand behind barriers all day, you're bound to get this happening. Ali Khalifa came out wanting to say something, and the only way the crews could get it was to rush down here after him. I know it was a scrum, but that's tough.'

'But who is going to pay for the light?'

'Beats me. It wasn't my crew that broke it.'

Steve turned away from the irate little man, still trying unsuccessfully to hide a grin. It had been the only entertaining moment in a deadly dull morning. Fifty stills photographers and a score of camera crews from all over the world were jammed behind steel crowd-control barriers on a long, narrow platform against the wall. From there they could see and shoot the oil ministers as they came out of the lifts, along the corridor towards them and then turned a corner past them to disappear into the conference room.

By Monday, two days in, it was like watching paint dry. They wandered through in the morning, wandered back again at lunchtime, and repeated the whole dull process in the afternoon. The writing press from the papers and the specialist oil journals were gathering in secretive huddles talking to junior delegation members to get off-the-record hints as to what was happening behind the closed doors. The junior delegates didn't have a clue either, but liked to give some false substance to their speculation by pretending they did, so the stories doing the rounds were legion and, on the whole, totally misleading.

Into this tedious process, with barely a moving picture

worthy of the name, had stepped one of the better oil ministers, who had chosen to reveal the setting up of a special OPEC task force intended to ensure its members stuck to the production limits agreed. He had a sense of humour and a certain love of drama, and announced it on the hoof, tearing down the narrow side-aisle of the hotel lobby with a hundred journalists in hot pursuit. It was inevitable that one cameraman, trying desperately to force his way through the fast-moving crowd into shooting range, had taken out the wall light on the way. The crash could easily have been a bomb. The minister's security man certainly thought so and sent his master sprawling to one side. Steve's cameraman was Larry, who'd been with Diana Pugh at the London riot, and he was perfectly positioned to catch it all. That may have been why, when it was all over, it was Steve who found himself buttonholed by the irate deputy manager.

As he walked off, he saw Micky Freeborough, the picture editor, coming out of the lift and looking around. 'Over here, Micky,' he said, and waved.

'Message from the desk,' said Micky. 'The *Six* are sounding a bit hungry. They want two and a half minutes.'

'Oh Christ Almighty. It's worth about thirty seconds at the moment.'

'I told them that, but they keep saying there must be a big Iraqi angle.'

'If there is, they're keeping it to themselves,' said Steve. 'I reckon they're all sitting inside playing backgammon and laughing like drains at the rest of us.'

At the start he'd done a big set-up piece, but that was the easy bit. Lots of security, plus oil sheikhs arriving, flashy cars and the empty conference room waiting for the talking to start – all topped off by a short interview with an oil specialist speculating on the outcome, and a quick piece to camera from Steve bringing it back to prices at the petrol pump, to give some justification for inflicting it all on the viewer. The problems started when the meeting started. The pictures were all much the same, and no one was saying a thing.

'Sounds like there's not much going on in the world. We're the lead, so we'd better come up with something.'

It was 2.45, just after the second session started, when something seemed, for just a moment, to be coming up all by itself. Steve was standing in the crush behind the barriers, at the end nearest the closed outer doors of the conference room, when the doors opened and one of the Gulf oil ministers walked slowly out by himself. An American reporter called out to him, 'What's going on? Will you have an agreement here?'

The minister smiled vaguely, in nervous reaction to the challenge, and spoke quietly. Steve heard him say 'No comment', but the second word was spoken much more quietly as he drifted off towards the lifts on the other side of the barrier. A few people raced after him, but he wasn't a man renowned for the accuracy of his comments, nor the seriousness with which he took these meetings, so many of the old hands simply didn't bother. There was a small buzz of speculation. 'What did he say? Did he say no?'

The short fuse at all such news events is held by the news agencies. For Reuters, AP Dow Jones and the rest, being five seconds ahead of or behind the opposition in getting a breaking story out on the wires makes all the difference between glorious success and ignominious failure. That's magnified tenfold if the subject is in any way financial, because the jam on their bread and butter comes from the financial markets who buy their services, and the first news break on the OPEC meeting would have the potential to push the oil markets and the currency markets sharply one way or the other.

Steve's experience made him keep a close eye on the main correspondents for the wire services. He saw them cross-checking with each other as they sometimes did when something wasn't quite clear. One of them had been standing close enough to hear what the minister had actually said, and none of them seemed to be heading for the phones, so he relaxed.

Fifteen minutes later Micky Freeborough came down again. 'The *Six O'Clock* want you on the phone upstairs. They're going ape-shit.'

Steve left the crew and went upstairs with Micky. They had rooms side by side, on the fifth floor, but Micky's was now less a bedroom than an electronic jungle. Big aluminium carry cases were stacked on top of each other. On them sat the mobile edit machines, controllers and monitors, linked by a spaghetti of wiring. On the table was a microphone surrounded by plastic tape boxes, old scripts, half-eaten club sandwiches from room service and empty beer cans. Rearranged in detail only, it was an environment they'd each lived in on scores of occasions all over the world.

The editor of the *Six O'Clock News* was well known for his affected style – monogrammed, handmade shirts, all-weather sunglasses and Grecian 2000. His manner of speech was equally studied.

'Steve boy, you've got a hot one. Let's hear the low-down.'

'Sorry?' said Steve, startled.

'It's on the wires. Don't tell me you haven't heard?'

'Whoa there, Martin. Let's start again. What's on the wires exactly?'

'What do we pay you for, Steve? Have you been having a long lunch? Here it is ... Oil Minister quits meeting. Says no deal likely. Sounds pretty strong to me.'

'Just tell me which agency ran that, will you Martin?'

'Yeah, it's on F F E.'

Steve breathed a sigh of relief. Fast Facts Europe was a new agency trying to break into a tough market and not doing it very well. The financial group behind it had put the bulk of the money into the software. What was left over they spent on the staff. The reporters were young and inexperienced, and it was already becoming a byword for mistakes.

'It's just garbage, Martin, and I'll take a bet it's not on any of the other agencies. I tell you, they've got it wrong. I was there. The man said no comment. Nothing else. They misheard him. Forget it. There's still nothing happening.'

'Well, I hear what you say, Steve, but are you sure? I checked with the Business Unit and they say it's quite likely that the whole thing's going to screw up at any moment. Michelle's been going through the cuttings from News Information and she says they all agree. She's ordering the graphic for a bexpo on what failure would mean for world oil prices.'

Steve sighed. A bexpo, or brief exposition, was just what he hated most. All too often it meant an explanatory package put together as far away as possible from the story, based on flawed newspaper cuttings from the library rather than the expertise of the reporter on the spot. That style of journalism reached its fullest flowering on the evening that followed the I R A's attempt to kill Margaret Thatcher with the Brighton bombing. On the evening news that night, the reconstructions, computer graphics and the newsreader's own version of events ran for nearly ten minutes before they got to the real pictures and the reports from the team on the spot.

If ever there was a time to lay down the law, Steve decided, this was it. 'Martin,' he said, 'I am here, you are there. I don't know what's going on here and nor does anyone else except the bloody O P E C ministers themselves, but I *do* know that report is a load of old cock and so is your bexpo. Call me when you read it on Reuters. Until then I suggest you stick it.'

'There's no need to be offens ...' But by then the receiver was back in place.

Micky passed Steve a can of beer and smiled. 'Same old story, eh?'

When Steve went to go back downstairs, he found the lifts closed off by a small squad of Qatari security men. Their minister was on the move, and they didn't give a damn about inconvenience to other hotel guests while he was moving. Despite the fact that nothing had happened for hours, being away from the lobby gave Steve a feeling of nervous concern that he could be missing something, and he didn't want to wait. He saw the sign to the fire exit and went through the door. Concrete steps stretched downwards. He went down to the ground level and pushed the door. It was latched and there was no handle on the inside. An exit sign pointed further down. He sighed and went on down.

It came out in a far corner of the underground car park. A vulgar Lagonda with Arab plates stood half-covered by a dust sheet, with two Rolls Royces flanking it. Further up the ranks of expensive vehicles was a silver-grey Range Rover, so tall that its open tailgate nearly touched the pipe-work projecting down from the low ceiling. Two people were standing by the tailgate. One was a short, thickset man, with close-cropped hair, a moustache, and long stubble on his chin which was much greyer than his hair. The other was a youth in his early twenties in a tightly cut grey suit and a pock-marked face.

Steve walked towards them, knowing they were slightly

familiar and searching for the association. Then he got it. They'd been standing at the far end of the lobby during the morning, some way from him. They hadn't looked at all like a camera crew, but they had a camera with them and seemed to be staring at the rest of the press more than the OPEC delegations. He'd marked them off in his head as a security detail in clumsy cover. It was just as he drew almost abreast of them that he saw they were loading a camera into the boot. He glanced down out of professional curiosity and noticed with slight surprise that it was an old Ikegami. Then he saw the little red and gold rising sun badge on the side plate.

How he kept walking and how he kept silent in that astounding moment of recognition, he never knew. He continued on for perhaps ten paces, then slowed down, patting his pockets as if searching for something. He turned back to look again, and saw they were getting into the Range Rover. He turned again and walked towards the exit ramp, feeling the excitement of certainty about the past mixed with terrible indecision as to what he should do now, and no small measure of fear.

The ramp led up to the end of the hotel's forecourt. He heard the Range Rover's V8 engine come to life with a dull, uneven rumble amplified by the acoustics of the garage. It idled for a moment or two. Then he was round the corner, out of their sight and running, up the ramp, across the flower-beds and into the side-street where his hired Peugeot was parked. He scrabbled the keys into the lock, started the engine and pulled out just as he saw the Range Rover come out of the car park and take a left and right on to the main road towards the centre of Geneva. He realized he hadn't done the most basic thing of all. He hadn't taken note of its number.

Everything left his mind except the need to get close

enough to see its plates. A clear cold anger came over him. He cut ruthlessly in front of a Citroën coming down the side-road, and reached the junction on to the main road in time to see the Range Rover disappearing a hundred yards away. A huge truck with a column of cars behind it came down the hill from his left, and he had to wait for it, chafing at the bit. He pulled out after them with screaming tyres, taking three of the cars before the lights at the bottom of the hill. There was only one more car and the truck between him and the Range Rover, but the lights turned red.

The Range Rover was the last one through, swaying as it took the right turn at some speed. He saw CH plates on the back of it, but then it was too far round and he was too far back to make out more. If the split decision of one second can make your life diverge, then this was that second. Steve was still closing up on the nearly stationary cars ahead. He swerved to the left of the bollards, on to the wrong side of the road and, as the drivers on the other road let in their clutches to come across his bows, he accelerated hard round to the right after the Range Rover.

The two policemen who stepped into the road in front of him didn't think that was at all the right thing to do. They waved Steve over to the side of the road. He sat with the adrenalin draining out of him, in a cold sweat, thinking that of all the places he needed to be at that moment, this was not one.

One of the policemen started looking slowly around the outside of the car. The other took his time about coming to the window, and bent down with a very unfriendly look. '*Qu'est-ce que vous faites, Monsieur?*'

Steve took a quick decision to play the innocent foreigner. 'I'm very sorry, I don't speak much French,' he lied. 'The traffic sign confused me.'

The policeman answered in English. 'Then you must be

168

easily confused. Give me your papers please.'

Steve handed over his driving-licence and the hire documents. The policeman studied them impassively. Steve tried again. 'I'm very sorry. I'm not used to driving on this side of the road. I panicked. I am in a terrible hurry.'

The man slowly lowered the papers and looked at him with disconcerting blankness. 'That was clear enough. I would say your speed was 80 kilometres an hour at the least.'

'I am here for the OPEC meeting, I have to get back to it. I am a reporter.'

'Then I cannot think why you were trying to leave it so fast.'

The man finished looking at the papers and reached into a deep pocket, from which he brought a printed book of forms. He flicked the cover forward and began to write. 'You will pay a fine, Monsieur. A fine of four hundred Swiss francs. When do you leave Switzerland?'

'Tomorrow probably.'

'Then you must pay the fine immediately.'

Steve felt in his wallet. He had three hundred and twenty francs and some traveller's cheques. 'This is all I have.'

The man looked at him. 'Wait here,' he said. 'You will have to be taken to a bank.'

It took an age. A police car arrived and took him on a ten-minute drive to a bank which was shut. They found another one, and Steve had to queue. By the time he got back to his car, over an hour had passed since he had left the hotel, and it was getting near time to start cutting a story for the *Six O'Clock News* which he hadn't even started to think about.

He abandoned the car on the forecourt and rushed in through the doors to find his crew. Then he stopped as if he'd been sandbagged. In that second he knew he was in deep trouble. The scene had changed completely. There was almost no one in the lobby. Hotel staff were clearing away the crowd barriers. Where there had been a hundred journalists milling around, there was just a handful. The doors of the conference room stood open and there was no one inside.

'Where *have* you been?' said a voice, with a heavily resigned stress on the second word. Stan, the lighting man, got up from a seat and came towards him. 'I've been waiting 'ere for you. You'd better get upstairs double quick.'

Steve felt his mouth go dry. 'What happened, Stan?'

Stan looked at him with an expression of professional censoriousness which Steve had never seen before in anyone he respected. 'You disappeared. That's what happened. Then the Iraqis walked out, didn't they?'

'How long ago?'

'Must be an hour at least. Everyone's chased them off to the airport.'

Steve took the lift to the fifth floor, sweating out the thirty seconds it took to get there with a stop on the way, and rushed into the room. Micky Freeborough was on the phone. 'He's here now,' he said, looking round, and waved the phone at Steve. 'It's Mike Page,' and he pulled an unhappy face.

'Where the fuck have you BEEN?' said Page.

'No time for that now, Mike. I got stopped by the police.'

'*Stopped?* Where, in the hotel lobby? Everyone's going up the wall here. Have you got the story?'

'I will have. I'll talk to you later.'

He put the phone down. 'What have we got?' he said.

'Aside from a huge problem, not much,' said the picture editor. 'Larry did the best he could downstairs without you. Everyone was shouting their mouths off on the way out, but he didn't really know who mattered. He thinks he got the Iraqis saying something, but it's not much, and he just had to pick up what he could of other people's questions. I hate to ask the obvious, but where were you?'

'That can wait. I really was stopped by the police. Where's Larry now?'

'He chased off to the airport with the rest. I've got his tapes.'

They looked through the material. It told little bits of the story. It was just like Washington all over again but, this time, Steve knew it was far, far worse. He went back to the lobby looking for anyone he knew, and in his desperation found the OPEC correspondent of an oil traders' newsletter coming back in through the doors. She was a larger-than-life New Yorker with lipstick to match.

'Steve,' she cried, 'what a bun fight. Did you see it?'

'No,' he said quietly, 'I didn't, Shona, but if you've got five minutes to spare you might just save my bacon.'

She looked at him and saw the desperation in his eyes. 'OK,' she said, 'tell Auntie Shona your problems.'

Shona finished giving Steve her detailed and dramatic account of the walk-out just as Larry came back in from the airport with his camera in his hand and a big chip on his shoulder about Steve's absence. 'This is the biggest bloody foul-up I've ever been dropped in,' he said. 'What sort of reporter pisses off without a word just when the story's breaking?'

'Larry, I am really sorry. There was a very good reason and I couldn't do anything about it, but I'll tell you all about it when we've cut the story.'

It was a tense and unhappy team that put together what they could. Larry had done his best but, in some of the shots without guidance, he'd focused on the wrong man, and what they crucially lacked was their own questions to get the full-face attention of the ministers in the scrums that followed the walk-out. Steve had to spend far too much time fending off the angry bulletin editor on the other end of the phone, and the edit inched its way along, shot by shot and script line by script line as the clock ticked round. There was very little time to spare, as the finished tape had to go across town to SRG, the Swiss TV network, to be fed to London.

Micky was putting on the final shot as Steve put the phone down on a terse conversation with the desk giving them the details they needed, the in and out words of the piece and its length. The anger crackled at him over the phone. Micky pulled the tape out of the machine.

'We've got to get there,' he said, 'I've already checked. They can't get an extension on the bird. It's block booked right through.'

'I'll drive you,' said Steve. 'The car's right outside.'

Missing a bird – not getting to the feed point in time for the satellite booking – was the ultimate crime. The chances looked slim.

The car was accompanied by an angry hotel commissionaire. They ignored his protests, jumped in and tore off. It was the end of the Geneva rush hour, but the traffic was still bad, and Steve had to throw caution to the winds to get across town. He jumped lights, cut round queues of traffic and, at one blocked intersection, drove slowly down the pavement with his hand on the horn to get round the glaring commuters in their stationary cars.

They got to within a block of the SRG building, and Micky, who had been cowering in the other seat, groaned. 'That was wrong,' he said. 'You should have turned left and left again. It's one-way the wrong way.'

'Fuck that,' said Steve, and swung into the street anyway. It was narrow and clear, and he accelerated hard up it towards the junction at the other end. It was two minutes to feed time. Three-quarters of the way up, a Volkswagen turned in towards them, going the legal way, filling the road. Steve didn't slow. He started flashing the headlights and blowing the horn as they tore down the road towards it. The VW driver slowed, stopped, then, looking aghast at the Peugeot still racing towards him, slammed his car into reverse and got out of their way.

They ran in, straight past the security guards, waving the tape box at them. Steve shouted, 'BBC. Satellite. *Vite*,' and the guards goggled at them. They took the lift, then sprinted down long corridors, bursting into the sudden darkened placidity of the satellite control room, where two unfussed technicians, completely used to this kind of thing, took the tape from them and fed it to London.

They were back in the car before Micky said anything else. He was a small, impish man, who normally had an excellent, dry sense of humour. There wasn't much of that in evidence now. He turned and looked at Steve. 'There's going to be hell to pay for this. It wasn't very good was it?'

'No it wasn't, but it's all down to me. You don't have to worry.'

'Come off it, you know that's not what I mean. I've worked with you enough times to know you're bloody good and you don't do stupid things. When you get back the *Six O'Clock* are going to try and crucify you, particularly after your little spat with them earlier on, so you'd better start practising on me.'

Steve searched for a way into the story, and knew the impossibility of it all. 'OK,' he said, 'but you won't believe it. When I went downstairs again, I came out in the car park, and I saw two guys loading a camera into their car. It was Sunny's camera, the one that went missing in the riot. It had his little sticker on the side plate. I chased them, but the police stopped me.'

Micky looked at him in surprise, then chuckled. 'Oh shit,'

he said, 'couldn't you just pretend it was something simple, like Martians taking you prisoner?'

In the hotel room, he phoned the foreign desk, to get in first. As soon as they heard his voice, they switched him straight to Mike Page. Page's voice had a quality of cold fury in it which Steve had only heard directed at other people before now.

'ITN walked all over us, Steve. Do you want to hear what they had which we didn't have?'

'I can imagine.'

'Oh no you can't. They had the Iraqis at the airport saying they were glad they blew the Kuwaiti wells, and they'd like to do the same to the Saudis. They had the Kuwaitis saying Iraq must be thrown out of OPEC. They had a fight between two Kuwaiti security men and an Iraqi. They had the Saudi oil minister losing his cool and shouting. What did you have? You had nothing except what Larry shot when you were off on some bloody jaunt.'

'I know. Mike, I am truly sorry. I took a decision on the spur of the moment to chase a car. It would have only taken five minutes, but I got stopped by the police and they wouldn't let me go.'

'Why the hell were you chasing a car?'

For a second Steve thought of lying, but nothing convincing came to his mind, and it went against the grain. 'I saw two men get in it, carrying Sunny's camera.'

There was a long silence, then Page spoke again with a remote, cold voice. 'I can't help you any more, Steve. I think you need a different sort of help. I stood up for you and you've let me down. You be on the first flight back tomorrow, and you think very hard about what you're going to say to me then.'

Chapter Fourteen

The corridor between the newsroom and the Editor's office in the Spur is a good litmus test. It is a main route to many destinations, and walking down it you can always count on running into a cross-section of news people. Arriving back from a foreign trip, Steve could normally have expected several friendly greetings and a quick gossip or two between one end and the other. This time it was as if he carried plague. People passed him with quick nods, in a terrible rush to get to somewhere else.

He went into the ante-room of Conway's office. Sarah looked up from her desk, and when she recognized him the expression of someone in the presence of bereavement came over her face.

'They're waiting for you,' she said and, tapping on the door, went into the office. She came out again a second later, holding it open for him. Steve had been expecting no more than two or three people, but the room seemed so crowded he wondered for a moment if he'd walked in on some other meeting. He saw Conway, his deputy, the Foreign News Editor, Mike Page, the editor of the *Six O'Clock News*, and the head of personnel, and suddenly recognized it for the court martial it was.

Conway was ill at ease, and over-jocular, which clashed badly with the circumstances. 'Come in, Steve,' he said, 'have a seat. Did you have a good flight?'

'Yes, thanks,' said Steve and took a place on the opposite side of the room, as far away from the others as he could get.

Conway looked down at a piece of paper. 'We need to get to the bottom of yesterday's mess. Would you like to kick off by telling us just why you left the hotel when you did?'

'I didn't intend to leave it at all,' said Steve. 'I saw something I wanted to check out, and I went off in the car for what was meant to be no more than five minutes. Unfortunately, I fell foul of the Swiss police, and they held me until I paid a fine.'

Conway was looking at him, nodding, clearly unable to make much sense of it. Mike Page cleared his throat. 'Steve,' he said, 'I think it might save a lot of time if you told everyone what you told me over the phone.'

So he did and, as he did, keeping it short and simple, he could see it was going down like a lead balloon. The *Six O'Clock News* editor kept shaking his head in disbelief. Mike Page stared at the floor, Conway was fiddling with a piece of paper in front of him, and the personnel man was making rapid notes on a large pad.

Steve came to the end, and the *Six O'Clock News* editor jumped in. 'Steve, I have to say that in all my years I've never heard such a cock-and-bull story. You know very well that we were across the story of the walk-out before you were and . . .'

'Oh no you weren't,' said Steve. 'Come off it. You were reading a heap of old rubbish on a wire service which hadn't a clue what was going on. It wasn't true at the time, and it had nothing to do with what happened later.'

Conway stepped in. 'Let's leave that aside for the moment. Steve, you will admit that your story sounds very far-fetched. I know you've gone on about it to the police before now, but you are the only one who believes in some kind of wild conspiracy. I have to say I think it's clouding your judgement.' He looked down again at the paper in front of him. 'I'm afraid what we have to decide now, without any better explanation from you, is how we deal with this matter.'

Steve looked around at all the faces staring at him. Only Mike Page was looking away and, at that moment, the sudden certainty that he was right, conceived in the SEC office and born in that brief moment in the Geneva car park, came boiling to his rescue. These people weren't going to listen to him, and he wasn't going to give way. 'This looks a bit like a kangaroo court,' he said.

The personnel man spoke first as the other faces hardened. 'Come now. What makes you say that?'

Steve groped through his memory of procedures. 'Well, if this is a disciplinary matter, as you obviously think it is, then I believe I'm entitled to have someone from the NUJ here on my side. Isn't that right?'

The personnel man smiled a lofty smile. 'Well, you could say that technically I suppose, but we were hoping to solve this more informally.'

Steve looked round at all of them. 'You mean you were hoping I would lie down quietly and take my medicine?'

Conway held up both hands. 'Hold on. I think this is getting a little out of hand. Let's take it a bit at a time. Perhaps the rest of you wouldn't mind adjourning to the other office for a moment while I have a word with Steve by myself.'

When the door closed behind them, Steve found himself facing Conway across the entire length of the big office, but he wasn't going to budge and it was Conway who was forced to stand up and move to a nearer seat. He was clearly trying to choose his words carefully.

'Steve,' he said, 'I don't want you to take this wrong, but a number of us have felt that, since you were attacked, your behaviour has been not quite what we have grown to expect. I've been quite concerned about it.'

Steve broke in. 'There's nothing wrong with me apart from a wish to see a little justice done.'

'That's not the way we see it, or indeed the way the police seem to see it.'

I'm just one against them all, Steve thought. What can I hope to achieve? But he felt a new independence within him, a growing awareness that he'd been a victim for weeks and that it was time to take the upper hand.

Conway passed him a letter. 'This is what I've decided to do,' he said. 'I think it's in the interests of us all for a while, until it all settles down.'

Steve took the letter and read it. 'Dear Steven,' it said, 'I regret to inform you that following your absence at a crucial moment in a developing story in Geneva yesterday, I have decided to suspend you from the post of reporter for an initial period of three months. During that period you will work as a producer on the news desk. If at the end of that time I am completely satisfied that you deserve reinstatement, I will consider that possibility.' It was already signed.

Steve looked over at Conway. 'You wrote this and signed it before the meeting even started.'

Conway shifted on his seat. 'It was there in case,' he said. 'Of course your account could have made it unnecessary.'

'Crap,' said Steve. 'You had already made up your mind. Anyway, I don't accept it.'

'Well, I'm afraid you don't have that option.'

Then Steve laughed. 'Oh yes I do,' he said. 'I resign. Right here and now. Understood? I quit.'

He didn't wait for Conway's reaction, but rose to his feet, opened the door and went out to the ante-room where the others stood frozen, looking at him. He reached into his pocket for his car keys and handed them to the personnel man. 'I won't be needing these any more. Goodbye to the lot of you.'

Mike Page came after him as he went down the corridor, calling for him to stop, but he looked straight ahead of him and, with others in the corridor, Page gave up the pursuit. Every eye was on him as he walked through the newsroom, taking the contents of his pigeon-hole on the way. He packed his briefcase with a few personal things, then took the main lifts down. It felt odd walking out of the front gate which he was so used to driving through, and even odder to think that he wouldn't be coming back.

Undecided for a minute, he turned left and headed for the tube station, then a thought struck him and he stopped and checked in his briefcase. There, in an inside compartment, was the bunch of keys he needed. He caught the Central Line tube from White City to Oxford Circus, in a light-headed state of near joy. He could hear his voice saying 'Understood? I quit' over and over again. At Oxford Circus he switched to the Victoria Line and headed out north-east. An old lady sitting opposite him in the dark, swaying carriage leaned forward and rapped him imperiously on the knee. 'You're on the telly aren't you. I've seen you.'

'No,' he said, and smiled as he shook his head.

He got out at Tottenham Hale, and found his way down streets he hadn't trod for months, until he came to a long row of old concrete garages on the edge of a builders' yard. He counted down seven from the left-hand end, and then had to sort through his bunch of keys to find the right one. The garage door creaked up and over to reveal the back of an old, dark-green sports coupe. Letters on the back spelt Scimitar GTE. It was dusty, but there was still air in the tyres, and the driver's door-lock turned with a little persuasion. He settled into the cold leather of the driver's seat, instantly almost as familiar as it had been when he'd stored the car two years before. His hand fell automatically to the gear lever.

Smell is the most powerful sense when it comes to stimulating memory, and the mixture of glass fibre, old oil and neglected leather gave him, quite unexpectedly, a sudden keen sense of what had been happening to him. He remembered clearly the emotions with which he'd locked the old car away when it became so much easier to rely on the car provided by the BBC. He remembered how the slight sense of regret had been outweighed by the attractions of free transport, free insurance and free servicing. He reached out and stroked the top of the Scimitar's dash, and remembered a dozen involuntary stops by the roadside – the petrol fire under the bonnet in Knightsbridge, the time a front suspension mounting sheared on him on the Yorkshire moors.

It came to him then that he had just moved out from under a huge, sheltering umbrella – an umbrella which covered his daily needs as long as he reciprocated. He thought for a moment of a world which didn't include foreign trips, expenses and a monthly pay-cheque, and for a moment it daunted him. Then a new mood of resolution came and settled on him. No more playing by the organization's rules. It had been a freer spirit who parked this car here and locked it away. It was time to let that person back out into the open air again.

He put the key into the ignition, looking for an omen, and the big V6 engine churned for just a few heartbeats before it burst into ragged life.

It took him the rest of the afternoon and a horrifying amount of money to get the car insured, taxed, tested and more or less roadworthy, but he knew he needed mobility to keep the blues at bay, and he wrote the cheques regardless. He had only ten pounds left in cash, and he went to an automatic cash machine to get some more. Lately, he'd found himself increasingly nervous whenever he used one, certain that it would keep his card, perform the electronic equivalent of shouting for the police, and leave him to walk away empty-handed, facing the casual mockery of others in the queue behind, who would know exactly what that meant. This time, thinking of other, greater problems, it took him a moment to register that where it usually said 'Please take your card and wait for your cash', the screen was instead displaying 'No credit available. Please contact your branch. You may try again if you wish.' He was suddenly so unprepared for this reality that he actually did try a second time.

He sat in the car for a long time after that. Ten pounds and half a tank of very old petrol were all that stood between him and immediate crisis. He became very calm and thought of his responsibilities. Tom was what mattered, just Tom. Paying the mortgage to keep a roof over Tom's head, paying the Sainsbury's bills to keep Tom fed, that was where the shoe pinched first. He drove to Fulham.

Maureen opened the door to him in jeans and an old shirt of his own. She looked happy, but her expression changed sharply when she saw him. 'What do you think you're doing, just turning up? You agreed you would always phone first.'

'Yes, I know.' He almost apologized, but decided it was time to break the habit. 'I need to talk to you. Something serious has happened.'

'Not now. We'll have to meet tomorrow.'

'Now, Maureen, not tomorrow. I've just been fired. No job, no money, no mortgage payments, right?'

That stopped her. She looked at him, open-mouthed, then seemed to come to a conclusion. 'Just wait here for a minute. I'll be right back,' and started to close the door to leave him standing on the step, but he put his foot in the way.

She looked at him in surprise and went down the corridor. He waited in the hall and heard two adult voices from the kitchen, one of them male. When she came back, she wore a look of anxious determination. 'You can come in, but there's someone else here you'll have to meet.'

'Lawrence?' said Steve.

'Yes.'

'I'm not sure I want to discuss this in front of Lawrence.'

'Well, it sounds as though it's going to concern him too. But you'll have to promise to behave yourself.'

'What do you think I'm going to do, attack him?'

But that was what some unexpectedly territorial part of him wanted to do when he walked into the kitchen and there was Lawrence sitting at *his* table, drinking *his* coffee from *his* mugs. Lawrence, worst of all, discussing the finer points of an unfamiliar toy boat with *his* son and Tom looking up almost casually to say 'Hello, Daddy' before going back to the boat again. The worst of it was the sudden realization that he had a preconception of Lawrence – short, sallow, older, warped, appealing to some dark recess of Maureen's mind – but this tall, cheerful blond man didn't fit that picture at all.

Maureen stuffed Tom in front of a video in the next room, and Steve suppressed the impulse to suggest she give him a book instead. She came back in. Lawrence looked at Steve.

'I hear you've lost your job. I'm sorry.'

'Oh thanks, Lawrence,' said Steve with entirely false *bonhomie*. 'Hey, why don't you apply for it? That would be neat. Then you could just take over everything all in one go. In the meantime why don't you go and wait next door?'

Lawrence looked a little hurt and kept his silence. He and Maureen exchanged looks. Maureen said, 'No, Steve. Just say what you came to say.'

'I've said it. I got fired.'

There was a silence while the kitchen clock ticked oppress-
ively. Maureen fiddled with a can-opener. 'How does that
leave you for money and so on?' she said.

'You mean you, not me,' he said. 'It doesn't leave me any
different. I was broke before and I'm broke now. But it leaves
you with nothing, because there's nothing in the bank.'

'Will you get another job?'

'I haven't a clue.'

'So what are you proposing?'

'I'm not proposing anything at all, Maureen, I'm just here
to warn you that there's a problem, and I can't pay the bills
this month.'

Another look passed between Maureen and Lawrence,
and he stepped in a little hesitantly, speaking slowly and
watching Steve's face for a reaction. 'I don't want to butt
in, but I might be able to help there, Steve. It may be a bad
moment to bring this up, but I want Maureen and Tom to
come and live with me.'

Steve stared at him in silence, and he went on. 'I've been
asked to go and set up a new office in Dublin. There's a
house that goes with it. You could let this one to somebody.'

So that's how it works, thought Steve. In the end it's not
an emotional decision, it all comes down to interest rates
and cash flow. How strange. 'I want to go and talk to Tom
about it,' he said.

'Don't upset him about it all,' said Maureen with a sudden
edge in her voice. 'We want to make this very positive for
him.'

Positively leaving Daddy, thought Steve. It sounds like a
film title. He nodded and went into the other room. Tom
was playing with the boat, apparently ignoring the video.
Steve turned the sound down. 'Tom,' he said, 'do you like
Uncle Lawrence now?'

Tom looked at him and smiled. 'Uncle Lawrence gave me

this boat. Look, it's got ...' He searched for the word. ' ... porkholes.'

'Yes, but do you like him?'

Tom looked at him judicially. 'Mummy doesn't shout when he's here.'

'Yes, but ... Oh, never mind.' He tried another tack. 'Tom, would you like it if you and Mummy and Uncle Lawrence all went and lived in a new place?'

Tom looked at the boat. 'Would it have a pond?'

'It might have, I don't know.'

'Would you come and see me?'

'Well, sometimes.'

Tom began to cry, and Maureen rushed in with an exasperated look and picked him up. Steve went back to the kitchen, and Lawrence stood up from his chair. 'I'm very sorry it should work out like this,' he said, 'but at least you won't have to worry about the bills. If you want I'll handle letting the house.'

Steve took a last look at him and left the house thinking, how dare you? How dare you be so bloody reasonable and pleasant and difficult to dislike? Can't you see I need to hate you? Then he thought of Maureen and realized, apart from their common link to Tom, there was no emotion left, just yawning months of dull time wasted.

It was after seven o'clock when he pulled into Redcliffe Square, the exhaust bellowing through a growing split in the silencer, and he was pleased to see Nick Nielsen once again in place, sprawled on his step, surrounded this time by four pint mugs full of beer.

Nick watched him park and walk up the pavement. 'Hi. I got you a couple, too. Figured you could use them.'

'Have you heard?'

'Me and everyone else in the business. It's the only story in town.'

184

'Exactly what did you hear?'

'You got the chop. The Beeb version is you had it coming. You've been acting like a loon ever since you got the bang on the head. ITN are enjoying the story, but the jury's still out.'

'And what do you think, Nick?'

'Welcome to freedom, Stevie, you should have done it years ago.'

'Freedom's all very well, but you can't eat it. I've got to pay the rent here tomorrow.'

'Why bother? Chuck the place in. It stinks anyway.'

'It's better than sleeping in the park.'

'You don't have to. Remember the boat? Go and try it out, while I scratch around for something to keep the wolf from your door.'

'I can hear the wolf, and it's already doing the scratching. It's amazing how it costs so much money just to stand still. I've got this feeling everything I own is just waiting for the most inconvenient moment to fall to pieces, unless I pour money all over it.'

Nick laughed. 'What you need is a simpler life, free of the domestic burden. That's why the boat is so perfect for you.'

'You don't even know if it's really there.'

'Of course I do. It's on the phone. The phone rings, therefore it must exist. The deeds are real. Anyway, I rang the local council to check it out. Give yourself a seaside holiday.'

Steve looked up at the window of the bedsit and came to a conclusion.

'Can't be worse, can it?' he said.

Steve woke next morning with dim recollections of a night before which had included several pubs, a club with some extraordinarily large women in it, and a great deal of singing. He crawled out of bed and saw an envelope propped on the table. On the outside it said 'There's no turning back' in huge letters. Inside were the keys to the boat and a hundred pounds in ten-pound notes.

His suitcases were on the floor, their lumpy shapes showing they'd been not so much packed as force-fed with his possessions. He dressed, wrote a note to the landlady, and took the bags outside into the noisy warmth of a London summer Wednesday. Through a muzzy head, he looked the Scimitar over. At least, it's not rusty, he thought. That's one good thing about plastic cars.

He opened the rear hatch to put his bags inside, and there was a sudden ripping noise as its support strut tore out of the glass fibre. It took five or six attempts to start the car on the last of its battery power, and there was a new screech when he put his foot on the clutch pedal. Like a particle flung off by some giant urban centrifuge, he headed out of London to the south, driving slowly to save petrol.

Chapter Fifteen

At just after 8 a.m., the River Adur was still carrying the heat of a long June yesterday. Coming down from the gentle chalk swells of the Sussex downs, it ran under the colder sea air just north of Shoreham harbour and divided the old village of Shoreham on its east bank from the new estates on the west with a miasma of mist hovering over the water.

To the postman cycling over the bridge and looking down, the mist was an elixir of youth to the long line of houseboats lying end on to the bank of the creek just below him. It hid the mud on which they rested. It hid the ramshackle gangways which connected them to the concrete path along the bank. It hid the piles of old bicycles, spare timber, plastic cans and rotting dinghies which covered the bank around each gangplank. It gave them life again, and what a life it had been.

He'd been on this post round now for eighteen years, and he loved these boats, the greyhound lines of the war surplus torpedo-boats which made up fully half their number, their mahogany hulls staving off the slow decline of the years, just as they had once staved off the German E-boats out in the Channel. Here and there among them were different craft of the same vintage, motor gunboats and air-sea rescue launches designed by Vosper or Fairmile. Their hulls kept a purity of line which gave the lie to the square cabins added to their decks, the window-boxes of geraniums and the doors hacked into their sterns, liberties taken with sleeping wolves.

Here and there along the row were other boats, veterans of an earlier time, a wooden oyster smack, a two-masted barque still carrying its long bowsprit, and some modern interlopers, steel barges – even a catamaran ferry retired from the Isle of Wight run. He wheeled his bike along the path, noting the new 'For Sale' sign outside number 21, delivering a letter to Motor Gunboat 618, otherwise known as number 23, and so on, along the row, then went on his way.

Behind him, not much was stirring. Many of the boat folk were late risers. A cat was let out, a kettle on a gas ring started a tremulous whistle, a hatchway was slid open, but most of the noise came from the outside world. Cars and trucks rumbled across the Adur road bridge. Half a mile north, faster traffic droned over the high arching span of the A27 flyover. A bell clanged in the old public school up on the hill until it was drowned by the sound of a Cessna engine being run up in one of the hangars of the little airfield in between.

The sounds had that clarity of cool morning air in summer, a poignancy that rarely penetrates the rushed adult world but leaves indelible impressions in the memories of children waking in strange bedrooms. Then, in the foreground of all those noises, the old boats began to come to life, lifting, stretching and creaking as the rising tide inched their hulls yet again from the mud's suction and pulled frayed mooring ropes tighter.

Forty-one of them rose on the tide. The forty-second didn't. It sat on the very end of the line, nearest to an open sea which it hadn't seen for over thirty years. Its neighbour was a sleek, grey-hulled MTB more than sixty feet long. It was not much more than half that length – a stubby harbour launch with a boxy top built on. An old, red-painted kitchen door more or less fitted in the rear of it. Inside, the upper cabin was a half-painted mess, white emulsion covering some of the pink rose motif wallpaper, as if someone had lost heart and abandoned it for ever. A stairway, which was not much more than a ladder, led down into the lower part of the hull.

Phones don't ring under water. The tiny click of a solenoid dispersing its burst of electrical energy into the river was the only indication that Nick Nielsen, far away in London, was trying to reach Steve. It didn't wake him. What did wake him was the floating rush matting, rising gradually from the floor and brushing the fingers of his left hand where they trailed down from the side of the bunk. The hand was still greasy black, despite his best efforts, bearing the marks of the struggle to fix the brake cylinder failure which had stranded him beside the road at Bolney until well after dark the previous day.

He opened his eyes. Light was pouring down from the hatchway. He couldn't work out where he was, and then he began to put it together. Arriving late, after the breakdown, driving through the housing estate into the potholed car park, searching along the bank by torchlight for number 42, he'd let himself in, turning a light switch, knowing that nothing would happen, to smell the damp. Everything was cold and slippery to the touch. He had climbed down the ladder, stumbling at the bottom and coming up against the panelling with a sound of splintering wood. Then, depressed, hungry and tired, he had laid out a sleeping-bag and crawled in.

There it was again, something bumping against his fingers. He looked down and could make no sense of the moving matting. He pulled his legs up out of the sleeping bag, swung them over the side of the bunk straight into two feet of cold water, and, slipping on the oily scum which coated the floor, he sat down in it heavily.

He levered himself to his feet and looked around at a scene of ruin. The cabin was slowly filling with water. He scrambled up the ladder into the deck-house and wiped off as much of the viscous scum as his towel would take, leaving a streaky grey effect. He found a pair of swimming trunks in his case, put them on and went out on deck. The morning sun made him feel better for just a second, then he looked at the high tide mark on the bank next to him and it dawned on him that the boat was going to fill up completely in the next two or three hours if he didn't do something about it. He began to curse his lot with deep feeling.

'Now come on,' said a woman's voice, 'it's a bit early for that sort of thing.'

From the path along the bank, a woman was studying him.

'Sorry,' he said, 'I seem to have a bit of trouble.'

'I'd say you were sinking,' she said, and laughed. 'If that's any way to describe something that's already resting on the bottom. I expect you could use some help.'

She walked across the gangplank and looked at him. She was a neo-Rubens blonde, slightly too plump, slightly too everything. Still, thought Steve, she's not that long past her Best Before date.

'I'm Rosie,' she said, 'I live a few boats down. You're not Ted, so why are you slumming it in his wreck?'

'Ah well, I only met Ted once. I didn't even know that was his name. A friend of mine called Nick won it from him and he lent it to me.'

'I should get yourself some new friends. Still, I bet I know what's wrong. There's a soft spot halfway down your port side. That twerp Ted was always shoving in Polyfilla and painting over it. He didn't have a clue.'

He looked at her through the depression lodging over his eyes. 'Great, I think I may have put my foot through it last night. What do I do now, buy some scuba gear?'

'You don't do anything. Just this once, since you're new, I'll do it for you.'

He went with her to her boat, where she gathered tools from the old potting shed lashed crookedly to its bows. He carried back a sheet of marine ply and a mastic gun. Then, feeling redundant but happy to leave it to an apparent expert, he sat down on the cabin roof, which sagged under him, and watched. Without warning, she lifted her shirt over her head and stepped out of it, performed a little mocking pirouette in her bra and pants, and waded into the muddy water. He watched with a mixture of admiration and mild alarm as she came level with where he sat, only her head and shoulders out of the water. 'Not so bad for an old'un, am I?' she said, then ducked under the water, catching him searching between gallantry and caution for a suitable answer. It was certainly true that her body seemed to have covered a lower mileage than her face, but that ranked a long way down the range of emotions he was feeling.

In a few seconds she was up again. 'Found it,' she said. 'Squeeze loads of mastic all round the edge of that plywood, then pass it down to me, would you?'

She took a hammer with her and, lunging down into the thick grey water with every deep breath, fastened the ply over the hole in a few minutes. 'That'll hold it until low tide,' she said, 'then we can do it properly. I'll get my pump over in a while and we can start drying her out.'

She held up a hand to him, and he pulled her up on to the side deck. 'Sorry,' he said, 'I never introduced myself. I'm Steve,' leaving off the surname in the hope it would help retain his anonymity.

She looked at him appraisingly, and he could see the connections being made. 'Rosie, like I said. Webster like I didn't say. Divorcee of this parish and owner of the good ship Venus. Come and dry off, then you can tell me what's brought you to Graveyard Creek.'

Her boat was warm, dry and big, and it had a shower. Twenty minutes later they were both changed and facing each other over mugs of coffee to which Rosie had added liberal amounts of Scotch, strengthening the background smell which permeated the cabin.

'You're a good swap for the gorilla,' she said, eyeing him archly.

'The gorilla?'

'Ted wotsit, the ape who had the boat before. A bigger shit you couldn't hope to meet. Mind you, he only got it as a bad debt in the first place. Nice to have it in steady hands again.'

'Don't make any snap judgements before you meet Nick.'

They talked for another hour. She was just the sort of company Steve needed, though there was a spark in her eye which suggested possible future complications. He was sure she'd worked out who he was by the way she studiously avoided asking him anything at all about his background. In the end she got to her feet. 'You stay here if you want. I'll be back this afternoon, but I've got to fly.'

'Oh, sorry. Have I kept you?'

She laughed. 'No, I mean literally fly. I'm an instructor at the airport. Maybe you'd better ring your friend and warn him we might have to spend a bit of money on the repairs.'

But Steve had been listening to a voice outside which seemed to be shouting his name, and, as it came nearer, he recognized the familiar American accent. 'Warn him yourself,' he said. 'That's him right now.'

They went out on deck and found Nick pacing up and down. The baseball cap was a new clean one, but the T-shirt, jeans and sneakers were the same as ever. 'Thank Christ for that,' he said when he saw Steve. 'That guy must have given me the wrong address.' Then he saw Rosie and his manner changed to old-fashioned gallantry. 'Enchanted,' he said, and gave a little bow. Rosie dimpled at him.

Steve explained about the boat, and Nick was indignant. 'I bet my car against that tub?'

'*Your* car?'

'Well, anyway, it wasn't right.'

They sat on Rosie's deck after she'd gone. 'It's nice to see you,' said Steve, 'but why are you here?'

'I was trying to call you. We've got a job.'

'What kind of job?'

'I called a few people yesterday, and one of them bit on the story.'

'What story?'

'Well, your insider trading story of course.'

'I didn't know I had an insider trading story.'

'Sure you do. All the SEC stuff is heavy-duty dog shit. We can do a lot with that.'

Steve stared at him, horrified. 'Bloody hell, Nick. All it adds up to is a few addresses and a couple of names. What on earth did you tell people?'

Nick looked only slightly embarrassed. 'Well, I may have given it a little bit of Kentucky wind, but it worked.' He leant back in his chair and glanced at Steve. 'I don't think you quite understand the position you're in, old friend. You're dead in the water if you don't do something to prove you haven't gone gaga. The word's out Steve Ross thinks he's a chocolate teapot. I found the one outfit who believe me and don't believe the word. I need to know if you're in because, if you're not, I'll give them their money back.'

'Money?'

'Yeah, money. Development money to chase it up.'

'Who is it, Channel 4?'

Nick laughed. 'Don't show your naïvety,' he said. 'Lovely

people, the Channel, but you don't get cash until you've done the legwork. No, I called up a guy I know in Wessex TV. They'll put up enough to get us going. Not much, but it will stake you for one short trip. If that gets anything, then we can string them along for some more. Are you in?'

'You bet your bloody life I'm in.'

'OK, and I hate to sound like the Beeb, but remember, the *first* target is the insiders. That's what we've got the lead on. If that connects to the Sunny business that's fine, but my ass is on the line with Wessex.'

'OK.'

'Right, where do we start?'

'Either Switzerland or Sark. Sark's nearer and they speak English.'

'OK, let's make it Sark, and remember, we're talking low budget. Buses for transport and McDonald's for lunch.'

Steve looked around him. The sun was out, the river was beautiful and he was back on the road. He grinned at Nick. 'Even a Big Mac tastes good if someone else is paying.'

'Where are you going to start? Do you know anyone there?'

'No,' said Steve, thinking, but then an old memory came back to him. He looked up to the rolling downland beyond the airfield, and there was the familiar outline of Lancing College up on the hill, its giant chapel, the size and style of the average French cathedral, towering over the lower, flint-studded walls of the school itself. The smell of beeswax came back to him, loose wooden blocks from the herring-bone floor of a small classroom in Great School. Sunlight through high, narrow windows, showing motes of dust dancing and inducing warm sleepiness. A black-gowned teacher, sitting at the high desk, intoning with passion. Reading from some-thing ... what? Yes, a book by Mervyn Peake. *Titus Groan* had been a set book, and old Donald Bolton had decided they ought to know something about Peake's other works. He'd read to them from *Mister Pye*, not so much because it was a great book – it was an oddity really – as because it was set on Sark, and Sark, to Donald Bolton, was the promised land. Ever the ham, old Donald, great teacher that he was, used to relish the byplay of the classroom, using little dramas to push the lessons home. This time he'd shut the book with a snap, looked under lowered brows at the class, and growled in his exaggerated Yorkshire accent, 'Saaark. And why do I always go there for me holidays?'

They knew this one. A ragged chorus rose. 'Because it's heaven on earth.'

'Right, right. All right, class. By Wednesday. A short story, nay a VERY short story, in the style of Mervyn Peake, on wherever each of you counts as heaven on earth.'

Ten minutes later Steve was heading up the school drive for the first time in years, slowing the Scimitar just in time to avoid wiping off the leaking exhaust on speed bumps, which looked old but were new since his last visit. He parked on the gravel in front of the dining hall and looked round at a largely unchanged school. He walked up the steps to the cloistered lower quadrangle, looking for someone to ask. On the line of notice-boards along the right-hand cloister he found lists of classes and masters' initials. There was no familiar DB. Lessons were clearly in progress. No one was in sight. He went to the Headmaster's office.

'Mr Bolton?' said the Headmaster's secretary. 'He left before my time, I'm afraid. I'm sure we would have his address somewhere, if, that is ...'

'He's still alive?' finished Steve for her.

'Well, yes, I was only thinking he must be getting on now.'

The door of the office behind her opened. 'Rosemary, can

you get me the Governors' minutes, please?' It was no longer the headmaster of Steve's day, the patrician descendant of great Liberal forebears. This was a more businesslike man, who blinked at the unexpected sight of Steve.

'Headmaster,' said the secretary, 'this is Mr Ross. He's an old boy. He was asking for Mr Bolton's address.'

The man put out his hand. 'Yes, of course,' he said, 'Steve Ross. Let's see now, Sanderson's House wasn't it? I remember looking you up for the new brochure. You know,' he added, seeing Steve's puzzlement, 'achievements of former pupils and all that.'

'Oh dear,' said Steve, 'you'll have to rewrite that one then, won't you,' but the remark was lost on the man's retreating back.

'I had a card from him last month,' he said. 'Yes. Got it. He's living in the Channel Islands now. Balmoral Cottage, Sark. No phone number, I'm afraid.'

When Steve got back to the river, Nick was still where he'd left him. 'We're in business,' he said, 'there's someone I know living on Sark.'

'Will that help?'

'It's a tiny island, Nick. Everyone knows everyone else.'

'OK. I made a couple of calls. There's a boat from Weymouth tomorrow afternoon. Takes you to some place called St Peter Port, then you get another one.'

'Boat? What's the matter with flying?'

'It's five times the price. Go by boat and the money stretches for another day or two when you get there. I told you, we're in the bargain basement now.'

Rosie came back in the afternoon and found them stretched out in the sun on her deck. 'Time to get up, boys. We have a boat to repair, and there's a party tonight. You're both invited.'

'Party, where?' said Nick.

'On one of the boats. There's an amazing old man. We all call him Pugwash. To be strictly honest, he's as mad as a hatter, but it's all right if you're on the same side.'

'What does that involve?'

'Oh, simple really. Not being German, that's the main thing, not being Communist, not being from the local Council, not thinking the European Community is a good idea – that sort of thing. He's still expecting World War Two to start up all over again. He's got a torpedo-boat and it's still got the engines in. Really odd.'

'Why's that odd?'

'They're huge. There's three of them and they fill up most of the hull. Everyone else took them out years ago to make living space. Anyway, old Pugwash spends his whole time oiling them and greasing them, and twice a year he starts them up to make sure they still work. He always has a party to mark the occasion.'

That night, propped in a corner of Pugwash's bridge with a glass of rum, which somehow seemed the right thing to drink, Steve was enjoying himself in the new freedom of not constantly answering questions about his job. The boats had electricity, water and phones, but few of them seemed to bother with television. They weren't that sort of people, so he could just be himself. When pressed, he described himself as a freelance reporter, and found he liked the sound of it.

Pugwash was an eccentric through and through, a retired ship's engineer, who knew all about metal and nothing about wood. 'This is the hydraulic system,' he said to Steve. 'In the war it took half a dozen people to drive this boat. Now I've got everything piped up to the bridge. One day soon, I'll take her out again, all by myself, just to give the girl a sniff of the sea again, maybe down to Brighton and back for a start. If those E-boats ever come back, we'll be ready for them.'

Steve looked at the gleaming pipes and thought of the sad contrast with the patched, lashed-up hull. But the dream was too precious for him to spoil it with practicality.

Pugwash looked at him. 'That Nicholas Ridley had the right idea. They should never have got rid of Winnie. There's more danger from those fellows over there ...' he waved an arm vaguely southward, 'than people remember, you know. There was a time when only these boats and a few planes stood between us and dictatorship.' He stared at Steve. 'You're not one of those Brussels lovers, are you? Because if you are, there's no place for you on my boat.'

'No, no,' said Steve hastily, 'not me.'

'Just as well. I had some little prat up here the other day telling me I had to have my fuel tanks checked or some such damned nonsense, and he started asking me why I didn't fly the European flag as well as the Red Ensign. Bloody fool.'

'What did you say to him?'

'Didn't say anything. Tipped him in the drink. Should have done it as soon as he came on board. Bloody clipboard carrier.'

Steve smiled, sipped his rum and said nothing. Later in the evening, after several more glasses, he looked around for Rosie and Nick, but could find neither of them, so he headed back to the relative comfort of the boat, relieved to find it floating on the high tide, and spread out his sleeping-bag in the dry upper cabin.

Chapter Sixteen

Steve was first off the small ferry when it docked at Creux Harbour, and walked straight past the line of horse-drawn wagons waiting for the tourists. He headed up the steep track to the village on top of the island, giving himself time to take in the atmosphere. There was a deep peace which contrasted with the holiday bustle of St Peter Port in Guernsey, where he'd spent the previous night. He found himself chanting a childhood rhyme: Jersey, Guernsey, Alderney and Sark, Four little islands lost in the dark. No one could say there was anything lost about the first two. They were bustling mixtures of tax haven, rich man's retirement home, yachtsman's cruising ground and, rather despite themselves, holiday destination for the common herd. There was none of that about Sark. The quiet time-lessness of the tiny island wrapped round him immediately. The birdsong seemed more pure, the smell of the flowers in the hedges more powerful.

He stopped at the crossroads in the little village, and hired a bicycle from the shop there. They gave him directions and he bumped off, unsteadily at first, down the green lanes. Everywhere there were grassy banks, small fields and what seemed like all the flowers in the world. The house stood near the road across the island towards the Port de la Joument, set back in a grove of trees. Balmoral Cottage was the exception to the French place-names he had passed, and the house itself was thoroughly English, four-square Georgian with a touch of Yorkshire about it, which told him just why Donald Bolton would have been attracted to it.

Steve cycled down the drive, propped his bicycle against the wall and, seeing the front door wide open, rang the bell.

A well-remembered Yorkshire voice bellowed, 'Come in.' He walked into the dark hallway and the voice, from a room to his left, called out again. 'Is that the water diviner?'

'No,' he said, 'it's Steve Ross, Mr Bolton. One of your old pupils. I don't know if you remember me?'

'Steven! Is that really Steven Ross? Come on in. I'm in here.'

Steve went into a sitting-room or study, it was hard to tell which. There were soft chairs as well as a big desk, and every wall was lined with crammed bookshelves. Donald Bolton sat in an armchair looking towards him. Despite the warmth of the day outside, it was cool in the room and he had a rug over his legs. He was older than Steve remembered him, though he'd always seemed old to Steve. Now the bald head was a little less shiny, the flesh diminishing over the round face with the square jaw, but the expression was that same pugnacious grin which Steve remembered so well.

'Come on in and sit down, my boy. How perfectly splendid. How on earth did you find me?'

'I got your address from the school, and I had to come to Sark on a job, so I thought I'd look you up.'

While he was talking, Steve noticed for the first time that the old man's eyes didn't quite focus on him. Then he saw the low table next to the chair, carrying a tape recorder and a pile of tapes, talking books.

'I wish I could see you, lad,' said Bolton. 'Old Anno Domini has caught up with my eyes and my legs. I used to listen to you on the radio, then you disappeared off that. Someone said you were on the dreadful tellybox, but I haven't got one of those.'

'I seem to be disappearing off that, too, I'm afraid.'

200

'That might not be a bad thing. I never understood why you went on it. All those big heads and their split infinitives.'

'It's not that bad.'

'The trouble with you, young Steven, was that you always hankered after the common touch. What do they call it these days, street cred? You'd rather know how to sell a second-hand car than why John Donne wrote about mandrake roots. You never found it easy to live down being a public-school boy, did you?'

Steve laughed, though he knew the old man was serious, and steered him off into a long reminiscence of old times and of books and of all the things that were valuable to both of them, for an hour or more. Then he felt it was time to broach the object of his trip. 'I'm trying to find out something,' he said. 'It's very sensitive. There's a rather bent company registered here in Sark. It's called Dandycap, and all I know is the address, Les Houblonniers. Would you know it?'

Bolton laughed. 'Les Houblonniers. Yes, of course I know it. I know every house on Sark. It's that old scallywag Joe Thompson. He's no friend of mine.'

'What about Dandycap? It seems a strange place for funny business.'

Then Bolton laughed again, so hard that he started to cough, and reached for a handkerchief. 'Oh dear,' he said finally, 'the things I didn't teach you in school. I never told you about the Sark lark, did I? Mind you, I didn't really know about it myself until I moved here.' He waved his hand across the hallway. 'Go out there and open the first door on the other side. Take a good look.'

Puzzled, Steve did as he was told. The door opened into a small room. On shelves across the end stood a computer with a phone modem, two fax machines and a big old telex. Along the side of the room stood a shredder and a whole rank of filing cabinets. He stared at them for a long while, unable to make sense of it, then went back again. 'I give up,' he said, 'what's it all for?' and he bit back the old urge to put a 'sir' on the end.

Bolton sighed. 'Well, I'm out of it now. Can't see well enough any more.' Then his voice took on that slightly artificial intonation and precise enunciation Steve remembered so well from the classroom. 'One of the many things the average person doesn't know about Sark, Steven, is that it has the highest concentration of fax and telex machines per head of population in the world. You think Jersey and Guernsey are busy financial centres? They've got nothing on Sark.'

Steve looked out of the window at the idyllic rural vision of fields and heathland stretching to the cliffs. 'Why?'

'You're probably aware that the Channel Islands have low taxes, and they're pretty generous with their company law as well. D'you know how much company tax there is in Sark?'

'No.'

'None.' He paused for effect in the old way. 'And do you know how much company law there is in Sark?'

'None?' hazarded Steve.

'Clever boy. So what that means is there's the strangest little racket you can imagine going on behind all these innocent front doors. If you're some filthy foreigner with a problem, all you need do is enlist a couple of Sark locals as directors, register your company here and you've opened up a loophole which you can drive a lorry-load of money right through. No one comes to investigate anything. The folk here make a mint out of directors' fees, and everyone except the rest of the world's tax authorities stays happy.'

'Do lots of people do it?'

'Most of the adult population. There's thousands upon

thousands of companies listed here. It's money for jam.'

'What do you have to do?'

Bolton laughed again. 'Not a lot. Now and then a fax or a telex comes in from the real bosses, saying things like, hold a company meeting and pass the following six resolutions. You read it, walk next door to your fellow director's house, have a glass of wine, solemnly convene a meeting over the kitchen table, and bob's your uncle.'

'As you say, money for jam.'

'Ah, but you mustn't forget the catering. That's the other thing.'

'Catering?'

'The food for the statutory annual general meeting. It's the only time the owners ever come to Sark. They nip over on the ferry, all wearing their business suits, go down on the beach for a quick picnic, declare the meeting open and closed, then head off again as fast as you like.'

'So what chance do I have of getting anywhere with Joe Thompson?'

'Not much of one. He's an old soak and he's not about to start telling tales on the people who pay his booze bill. Sealed lips is the rule of the game. I doubt you'll get past his front door.' He stopped and considered. 'One little tip in case you do. He's always telling war stories about his time in the Desert Rats. Call him Major Thompson and you'll have him eating out of your hand.'

'Do you miss being in it?'

Bolton shook his head. 'Not as much as I miss my beautiful books. You can't get that much on tape, just the obvious things. Nothing like St-Exupéry or Donne or Sterne.'

'Would you like me to read you something before I go?'

Quietly, Bolton said, 'I didn't like to ask. I can tell you're busy.'

'I'd like to.'

'You'll find an old green book on the second shelf there, lying flat. There's a bookmark in it.'

Steve got up to get it, and Bolton chuckled. 'You'll be surprised,' he said, 'but I've wanted to hear it again for such a long time.'

It was a surprise indeed, the passage from *The Wind in the Willows* describing the finding of the otter's child at the feet of the God Pan. In the still room, with the old man sitting there in rapt silence, it was intensely moving.

As Steve said goodbye, a thought struck him. 'Why were you expecting a water diviner?'

'We use him all the time round here. All our water comes from wells. There's a diviner who comes over and drills the wells, and you only pay him if he strikes water at the depth he predicts. He does well. It's a strange and magical place, Sark.'

'Yes, I remember you telling us that in class.'

'You remember that, do you?'

'That and a whole lot more,' and Steve went on his way, leaving behind an intensely pleased old man.

He cycled to Les Houblonniers with a feeling that the phoney war was over. Now it was into the enemy's camp, and, though the camp turned out to be nothing more than a small, grey and unkempt-looking cottage, it was with a heightened sense of tension that he knocked on the door.

The old man who opened it had reddened, protuberant eyes set in mottled pink, yellow and white flesh.

'Yes,' he said aggressively, 'what do you want?'

'Major Thompson?' said Steve. 'I'm sorry to trouble you. My name's Richard Dixon. I'm a researcher for *Down Your Way* on Radio 4. I don't know if you listen to it at all?'

'Used to,' said the man, 'before they changed it all round and ruined it. Didn't know it was still on.'

Neither did Steve. 'Ah well, it's going to be changed back again. I'm working on the next series. I'm told you have some very interesting war reminiscences.'

The door opened. There seemed to be only one main room downstairs and they sat, jammed close together in chairs. At the end of the room Steve could see Thompson's fax machine with a jumble of files and folders all over the table next to it.

'I was in the Eighth Army, you know, the Desert Rats. El Alamein, Tobruk. I could tell you a thing or two.'

Steve listened while the Major launched into a rambling and extremely unlikely story of his exploits, which was recognizably the plot of a war movie starring Telly Savalas recently shown on TV. Whenever he could, Steve glanced round him. He was frustratingly just too far from the table for a good view of the files.

After fifteen minutes of sheer tedium, the Major ground to a halt. 'Would you like a cup of tea?' he asked.

'Oh. Yes, please.'

He went out of the room, and Steve got to his feet, quickly and quietly. He looked at the mess on the desk and lifted a folder which lay on top. Under it was a file marked Telex Log. He started to open it, but the Major's voice came from the kitchen next door, and he quickly put it down. 'Sugar and milk for you?'

'Just milk, thanks.'

He picked it up again and started rifling through the sheets. It took time, far too much time, but down near the bottom of all the boring messages from companies with names he didn't want to know he found a fax headed Dandycap Holdings. Then he heard the noise of cups on a tray held by unsteady hands, and pushed it back under the folder.

He was in his chair before the Major made it into the

room, unable to bear the thought of being so close and yet so far from his objective. In his desperation he thought of simply picking up the file, ignoring the Major's protestations and getting on his bike, but he would have to wait for the ferry, and, although he didn't know how the island worked, he was sure there would be some kind of hue and cry. Then, taking the cup of tea, he thought of the old screen cliché and, with no great attempt at subtlety, tipped it all over the old man's trousers. The results exceeded his expectations. As the hot liquid soaked through the thin polyester, the Major howled his wrath. 'What the hell did you do that for?'

'I'm sorry. I get this spasm. Let me get a towel or something.'

'No, no,' he said crossly, 'don't touch anything. Just stay there,' and he hobbled out of the room, muttering.

Steve was over to the file in a flash. He found the sheet again, took out his pad and began to write furiously. The answer-back address was Dorfstrasse, Waldegg, Zürich. The message told the Major to transfer recent share dealing profits from Mackeson, Shorthouse customer nominee account number 106 to a bank account in Liechtenstein. It referred to 'recent communications from our associate, Herr Morgenstern.' It was signed by someone called Kent Cheeseman.

Steve opened a few other files at random, got nowhere, and was back in his seat well before the Major stumped back in, wearing a different pair of trousers and still looking furious.

The ferry got him back to St Peter Port in plenty of time to catch the Weymouth boat, so he bought a phonecard and found a box. It rang for a long time, and because it was Saturday afternoon he almost gave up. Then he heard a man's voice. 'Pivot Publications. Good afternoon?'

'Hello. Charlie? It's Steve.'

'Steve? There's a surprise. What can I do for you?'

'I'm in Guernsey, Charlie. I'll have to be quick. Can you tell me anything about a nominee account with Mackeson, Shorthouse?'

Charlie was a boyhood friend who had had a parallel career in journalism. Charlie's had taken him into newspapers, then into TV production as an independent, making searing investigative business documentaries. As a sideline he had built up a computer database, the product of endless enquiries using Section 212 of the Companies Act, which revealed many of the real names behind the faceless nominees so often involved in the hotter side of the share business.

'Which account, Steve?'

'Number 106.'

'Aha, I know that number. Hang on a second.'

Steve could hear the computer beeping in the background, and it was less than half a minute before Charlie came back to him. 'You've got a hot potato there. I want to hear about anything you get. It links to Switzerland, and it's come up in at least three really nasty deals we know about. We got one of the companies involved to throw a 212 at them, but it just led to some Anstalt in Liechtenstein, and they couldn't get any more, even when they threatened to disenfranchise the shares.'

Steve could see Charlie in his mind's eye, gazing hungrily at the computer screen, willing it to reveal more. He could hear even down the phone that his blood was up.

'Listen, Steve, if you've got something, you make sure you tell me. To let you in on a secret, I had the Serious Fraud Office on last week, wanting anything we had on that one, and that's something that doesn't often happen to us.'

'As soon as there's anything to tell, I'll let you know.'

'Promise?'

'I promise.'

Chapter Seventeen

Nick was waiting at the boat, in answer to Steve's call, when Steve got there later that night. He was ecstatic with Steve's progress.

'I knew you could do it. That's just what we need.'

'It's still not a lot, and I have a feeling it's going to be much harder to get behind the walls of Zürich.'

'Come on, don't be such a sad sack. You can handle the Swiss. Anyway, it's enough to get some proper money out of Wessex TV, and I've got a friend who can give you a hand in Zürich. He owes me a day's shooting.'

Nick was as good as his word, though it took most of the week. By Wednesday evening Wessex had agreed to put in £5,000 of development money for the next stage, Steve's flight was booked for Friday morning, and Nick's cameraman friend had agreed to help out for a day or two at the other end.

He caught the early morning Swissair to Zürich, suppressed his irritation at a crowd of Swiss standing still right across a moving walkway going at half walking speed, raised his eyebrows at the Schweizerdeutsch *Gruezi* on the welcome sign, and walked out through customs to find a man holding up a large sign simply saying 'Steve'.

Rudi Rohner was a tall, ascetic-looking Swiss of about forty. He had a high, domed forehead with fair, receding hair and a quiet, charming manner. 'So,' he said. 'How is the terrible Nick? Is he still as mad as ever?'

'Yes,' said Steve, 'but I suppose that's the whole point of Nick.'

'I wonder what trouble he will get me into this time,' said Rudi. 'Always trouble with that one. But it keeps you jumping, yes?'

There was a bright spark of humour in his eyes, and Steve liked him immediately. He felt the tension of arriving to do a difficult job in a strange place begin to lift. Rudi took him out to a big black Jeep Cherokee station-wagon parked on a meter in front of the terminal. 'Nick has told me a bit. I suggest I take you first to Waldegg so we can find the house, and then maybe there is someone you can meet who may know something.'

Waldegg was a large, rich village on the western outskirts of Zürich, not far enough out to avoid the infection of the heavy concrete architecture which plagues the city. Kent Cheeseman's house was very big, very ugly and clearly very, very expensive. But all the money in the world doesn't buy much land in urban Switzerland, so it was set back only a short way from the road, protected by high walls and large iron gates. They stopped fifty yards past it and looked back. Steve recognized a small grey shape on a swivel on top of the wall. 'He's got security cameras.'

Rudi looked. 'That's not so strange in Zürich these days.'

'I thought Switzerland didn't have much crime.'

Rudi chuckled sardonically. 'Only if you believe the police,' he said. 'Try to report a crime and they will start by telling you it couldn't have happened. Then they will blame it on the foreign workers. Zürich has almost the worst hard drug problem in Europe, and everything that goes with it.' He nudged Steve. 'It has one of the worst AIDS problems too, so watch your step.'

Just behind where they were parked, a yellow circle was painted on the pavement. There was another one like it a hundred yards further up, with black refuse sacks piled on it.

'What's the circle for?' said Steve.

'Keeping Switzerland beautiful,' said Rudi. 'That is where you must pile your rubbish on the collection days.'

'What would happen if you put it somewhere else?'

Rudi exaggerated a sharp intake of breath. 'Do not ask. Your neighbours would be round to you first thing. It would be nearly as bad as cutting your grass on a Sunday.'

Just then, the gates to the house began to open under some sort of remote control. Steve watched. All that emerged was a small Filipino woman in a grey dress. She was wearing an apron and trailing two black plastic bags behind her. She crossed the road and put the bags neatly into the centre of the circle.

'I want those,' said Steve.

'You want the garbage?' said Rudi incredulously.

'You bet,' said Steve, and began to open the car door.

'Hold on,' said Rudi, 'you cannot do that sort of thing in Switzerland. People will see you and report you. It is theft.'

'Come on, it's only garbage.'

'Where are you going to put it?'

'In the back of the Jeep?'

'But it's clean,' Rudi said.

'So are the sacks. This is Switzerland.'

Further argument was interrupted by the sight of the garbage truck rounding the corner two hundred yards in front of them and coming down the road. Rudi hid his face in his hands while Steve jumped out, opened the tailgate and slung the two bags in the back. After that, Rudi couldn't wait to get away.

'I knew it,' he said, 'you are just like Nick. Always trouble,' but by now he was grinning.

'Where now?' said Steve.

'I have arranged for you to meet a journalist for lunch.

He might be able to help. Then I will drop you at your hotel. This afternoon I have to practise some music.'

'Music?'

'I play in a jazz band.'

The lunch rendezvous was a surprise. They parked in Pelikanstrasse just off Zürich's main shopping street, by an anonymous concrete building, and went through a door into another world. Ireland 1920. It was the James Joyce pub, once the bar of a famous Dublin hotel – transported and rebuilt panel by panel and tile by tile to mark the city's links with the Irish writer. 'We had to do something,' said Rudi. 'How many Swiss writers can you name?'

A hand waved from a dark corner of one of the nests of high-backed wooden benches, and Rudi introduced him to a studious youngster in his early twenties. He wore old-fashioned round glasses and had bad skin. 'This is Hugo,' he said. 'He is not working at present and Nick said we can hire him for a day or two's research. I rang him last night.'

They ordered. Steve thought he'd better go native and asked for Hurlimann lager and a plate of rösti. The others chose Guinness and fish and chips, and when it arrived he wished he'd done the same. Hugo was anxious to impress. 'I have already made some enquiries,' he said. 'You have to ask very quiet questions here, you know. People do not like questions much and journalists do not behave like they do in England or America.'

'I understand. What have you got?'

'Not so much yet. Mr Cheeseman lives a private life. He has a friend who is a Bundesrat, you would say a member of the ruling council of Switzerland, so he has some influence. He came here maybe fifteen or twenty years ago.'

'Where from?'

'I am not so sure. Someone said the country that is now Zimbabwe.'

'Southern Rhodesia?'

'Yes, that is right. He is a big investor, but he is in other businesses as well. He buys and sells art and also expensive cars.'

Steve pricked up his ears. 'Cars?'

Hugo sorted around in his briefcase. 'Yes. I was given this by a friend.' He passed over a magazine filled with car advertisements. A large, boxed-off, two-column advert stood out, ringed in green marker. Steve had to puzzle it out, written in German abbreviations, most of which made no sense to him, but it was clear to see the man was selling a Ferrari F40 and a Porsche 959. That labelled him straight away, a speculator buying very high-priced, limited-edition supercars, who had probably had his fingers badly burnt by the falling market. There was a phone number.

'That is the number of the house in Waldegg,' said Hugo, pointing.

'Useful. Can I keep this?'

'Of course.'

'Anything more?'

Hugo hesitated, then said, 'Excuse me.' Turning to Rudi, he began talking very quietly and urgently in Schweizerdeutsch. Steve couldn't follow any of it. It sounded an almost completely different language to the German he knew. There were lots of interjections and expressions of incredulity from Rudi, and it was Rudi who spoke first when he finished.

'That is very interesting,' he said. 'Hugo has come up with something, but he says it needs some more work.'

'What is it?'

Rudi looked around him. 'It is better that we talk in the car, then we can call Hugo again later.' He turned to Hugo and spoke in English for Steve's benefit. 'I think you should not go further with that one until we talk again.'

When they got back to the Cherokee, Steve stopped Rudi from driving off. 'What was all that about?'

Rudi looked at him with a doubtful expression. 'I am not sure. I think maybe Hugo sees the chance of a few more days' work. He is very young, you know.'

'Tell me anyway.'

Rudi sighed. 'OK,' he said, 'but don't get too excited. There has been a lot of songs and dancing in the media here – even our obedient media – ever since the Kopp affair, about bad smells in high places.' He saw Steve's eyebrows lift. 'You do not know about the Kopp affair? Our Justice Minister, next in line for the Presidency, had to stand down because she was accused of tipping off her husband that his company was implicated in a big drug-money laundering case?'

'Yes, vaguely.'

'Well, of course she got off. The case would not even have come to trial if there hadn't been pressure from the American drug people, but all kinds of things came out of it. First it was revealed that there were security files on a million Swiss citizens who were thought to be subversives, then there was this secret army thing.'

Rudi started the Jeep and pulled out into the traffic as he talked. 'It all came out because of the fuss over the files. They started special commissions investigating everything in sight, and they turned over some stones that they should have left untouched. It is said that they found two secret army units that no one was meant to know about.' He broke off for a moment at a busy road junction. Steve waited patiently until they were through it, swinging right past a big museum, with tram tracks and the railway station to the other side. Rudi waved his hand at scores of shabbily dressed young people standing lining the railings past the museum. 'Needle Park. You see what I told you about drugs. This is where they come to shoot up and buy and sell.'

213

Steve stared at them. 'Don't the police do anything?'

Rudi laughed. 'If they arrested them, then there would be crime statistics. As it is, they just come and bother them now and then, and that keeps the crime sheets clean.'

Steve prompted him. 'The secret armies?'

'Yes, P26 and P27, I think they are called. They did not appear in any files. They were not part of the main military command. They had no official existence or sanction except at the very highest and most secret level. There are supposed to be two thousand people in each unit. They keep their weapons in ordinary houses, rented in the ordinary way for the purpose.'

'But what are they for?'

'They were, or perhaps they still are – who knows? – the final protection for Switzerland if she is invaded. One was for sabotage. The other was to maintain morale during any occupation, whatever that means. That may be true, but many people think the reason was a little different, that they were there to take over if Switzerland looked like falling into the hands of any politicians who might be less keen to keep the invaders out.'

'I don't really follow. What's all this talk of invaders? Who's going to invade?'

Rudi smiled. 'Oh Steve. Be careful. You are trampling on the central myth of Switzerland. The myth which keeps together all these warring cantons who mistrust each other so much. If they didn't think the hordes might sweep in, the social glue would come unstuck and Switzerland would fall into little pieces.'

'But this is a neutral country.'

That was when he really laughed, so much so that the Cherokee swerved towards the next lane and a fat man in a Saab hooted angrily. Rudi waved at him, straightened up and flashed right for a turning signposted Schlieren. 'This is the most militarized neutral country in the world. Tomorrow I will show you. I have a shoot to do for the army. I can take you as, let us say, my apprentice. You might enjoy it.'

'Rudi, how does all this secret army stuff come back to our friend Cheeseman?'

'Aha. Well, it seems Hugo has been talking to some left-wing friend of his in Berne who did research for the commission. He saw some papers suggesting Cheeseman may be tied up in it. Maybe in the financing.' He glanced across at Steve and groaned. 'Oh, no. I can see you're going to get excited. I don't think you should.'

'Why not?'

'Because I think Hugo's imagination is bigger than his knowledge, and his bank balance is a lot smaller than both of them.'

'Why don't you just tell him we will pay for facts but not for guesses?'

Rudi shrugged. 'If you like. But I hope you are good at telling the difference when it comes to handing out money.'

They drew up outside a small and unprepossessing hotel. 'This is where Nick has booked you in, I'm afraid,' said Rudi. 'It is not the best hotel in Zürich, nor even in Schlieren.'

'Schlieren. Is that where we are?'

'Yes. It is what you might call an old industrial suburb of Zürich. We are on the north-west edge of the city. I am sorry I have to abandon you here, but if you want to come I will collect you in the morning at seven-thirty exactly.'

'That's fine. I've got a few things to do.'

Steve took his bag in one hand and the two black plastic sacks in the other. Rudi smiled. 'Only the English,' he said, 'and maybe the Americans . . .'

The hotel didn't run to a porter, which was perhaps just as well, and Steve's room was on the ground floor, only two

215

doors from the reception desk. It seemed higher than it was wide, with a TV set hanging threateningly from a bracket over the bed. There was no phone. Steve sat on the bed, pulled the waste bin over to him and opened one of the sacks. It contained the usual mixture of food packaging, waste paper and kitchen rubbish. Steve checked every piece of paper, scraping coffee grounds off some of them to read them, but there was nothing of interest. It took him half an hour to be sure he had missed nothing, then he turned to the second sack.

This had distinctly different contents. It looked like the product of a workshop clear-out. There was an old car distributor, several empty spray cans and an air filter. Near the bottom Steve found some electronic components, two circuit boards, some solenoids, and a glass and metal tube with terminals on it and a knurled metal ring on the end. He looked at these for a long time but couldn't identify them, and put them carefully in his bag for further examination.

In the end that was all there was of any interest, so he put a knot in the top of each bag. He looked out of the window at the yard behind, and dropped them out straight on to a pile of similar bags waiting to be collected, then he turned back to the magazine Hugo had given him.

He had to go out to the foyer to phone, and a woman's voice answered in German at the first ring. 'Do you speak English?' he said, trying for any small advantage.

'Yes, of course.'

'My name is Williamson. I am in the car business, and I have seen your advertisement for a Porsche 959. I am passing through Zürich and I have little time, so I wonder if I could come to see it today?'

'I am sorry, Herr Williamson. The Porsche has been sold.'

Damn. 'Ah, but I understand you also have a Ferrari F40. I was interested in both cars. Is that still available?'

There was a perceptible and suspicious pause before she answered. 'Yes, it is.'

'Then may I come and see that?'

'If you wish. Where are you now?'

Steve looked out of the window, and thought the truth might constitute an unimpressive answer. 'On the outskirts,' he said. 'I could probably be there in three-quarters of an hour.'

'But how do you know where we are?' she said, and he kicked himself.

'I don't. I was just assuming you were somewhere in central Zürich.'

She gave him the address in a guarded tone of voice and he hung up. The next problem was clothes. He'd come with a limited and casual selection. In the end it came down to a clean T-shirt and jeans under a leather jacket, and, wishing he wore a more impressive watch than the battered Casio on his wrist, he went out to look for a cab.

At the house, the cab fare accounted for a sickeningly large number of Swiss francs, and he looked at the gates with a chill of anticipation. Feeling he was casting a die, he crossed over and pressed the bell-push. The woman's voice, magnified tinnily through a speaker, said 'Mr Williamson?' and he looked up to see the camera on the top of the wall swivelled down at him. 'That's me,' he said.

'I will open the gate. Will you go inside and wait for me please.'

She didn't introduce herself at all when she came out of a side-door, and he disliked her immediately. The pointed nose went with an arrogant manner. She was in early middle age, dressed expensively, and she looked him up and down with something approaching open contempt. 'Come with me,' she said, 'I will show you the car.' Her manner implied she thought it a waste of time. He followed her down a driveway to the back of the house. There was a yard and, on the other side, a startling building, more like a car showroom than an ordinary garage. It had long, plate glass windows all along the front, a rich man's ego-trip to show off his collection to those he was entertaining in the house.

Steve looked all around him, searching for any detail that might help. It was already clear he was only going to see the secretary, not the master. She unlocked a door and he followed her inside. Despite himself, he caught his breath at the sight of the row of cars parked on a spotless tiled floor. It looked like an investor's portfolio, bought regardless of the price. The cars were over-restored, with none of the desirable patina of age. Nearest stood one of the world's most beautiful cars, an Aston-Martin DB4GT Zagato. Next to it was another of Zagato's masterpieces, a rakish body with sweeping wings on a 1930's Alfa-Romeo 1750. Next to that was the brand new Ferrari he had come to see, its squat aerofoiled shape hugging the floor. Beyond that, more cars stretched down the row, a Bugatti, a Maserati 3500 and, at the end, the best of them all, a long-nosed Jaguar D-Type, with the fin on the driver's headrest, in a shiny green, slightly too pale to be proper British racing green. It had a UK registration number still painted on the front beside the oval air intake.

Steve took all this in as the secretary moved over to the wall and pressed a button next to a speaker grille. Steve noted the two surveillance cameras, at either end of the room. She unlocked the car, stood back and said, 'The price in the magazine is not negotiable of course.'

'I would have to have the car checked over.'

'That should not be necessary. It has only done 600 kilometres since delivery and we have the full factory documents.' She had clearly marked him down as a no-hoper and wanted him out. He remembered the button by the speaker grille and calculated that their conversation was being monitored from the house.

'I must talk to my client about the price,' he said. 'By the way, I see a car I know down there. The D-Type Jaguar replica. Has it been here long?'

That got to her. 'It has been here for six months, but why do you call it a replica?'

'Oh dear,' said Steve, 'I hope you didn't think it was genuine.'

'Of course it is genuine. It was bought at auction with full authentication.'

Steve shook his head. 'I know that car well,' he said, pitching everything on one throw of the dice. 'I should do. I was there when they built it, and that wasn't at the Jaguar factory in Coventry in the 1950s either, it was in London in 1988.' A buzzer sounded by the speaker grille, and he thought, 'Bingo'.

'My employer wishes to see you,' said the secretary, when she hung up the phone by the grille. 'Follow me, please.'

He was led across the yard and in through a back door. To one side of the passage was a metal door with an array of high-security locks on it. He could hear a noise from inside that sounded like drilling. He slowed for a second, but the woman waved him on. They came through a door into an ornate hallway with a gigantic naval battle scene in oils on one side and a far more beautiful French Impressionist picture on the other. He had no time to admire them because he was waved into an ante-room of some sort.

There, waiting, stood a thickset man in late middle age. He had a barrel chest and a mottled, red face, radiating aggression. It was the hair that left the strongest impression, sticking up like jagged pig's bristles.

'Michael Williamson,' said Steve, walking forward with his hand outstretched. The man ignored it. 'What's this crap about my Jag?' he said, and his voice had harsh edges as though it had risen from a vast depth past sharp rocks.

'I fear you may have been conned,' said Steve, and the man's eyes widened for a second. 'I saw it being built. It's a replica – a very good one – but a replica nonetheless. Everything's just right, it's even got a genuine D-Type wide-angle engine, but it's as bent as a nine-pound note, I'm afraid.'

'Bullshit. If you really know your D-Types, that car's chassis number XKD405, and I've got all the history. I paid more than two million dollars for it. How in hell do you know you're talking about the same car?'

'I remember the registration and the colour. It's a strange shade.'

The man walked over and stood right in front of him, staring close into his face. Steve could smell acrid sweat. 'You've just been a bit too clever. That car was blue when I bought it. I had it sprayed last week.' He stared into Steve's eyes and Steve tried not to blink. 'So who the hell are you and what do you want?'

Here goes nothing, thought Steve. 'I'm a journalist, Mr Cheeseman. I'm looking into the affairs of Dandycap Holdings, and I thought you might like to answer a few questions about it.'

Cheeseman stepped back and his eyes narrowed, then he turned to one side and pressed a button on the desk. The door opened and two men walked in. One was a burly man in a cotton jacket, the other was older, tanned, in an expensive suit.

'Jacques,' said Cheeseman, 'Mr Williamson was just leaving. Show him out and make sure he doesn't waste a second of his time on the way.' He beckoned the other man into the inner office and they watched on the TV monitor as Steve went out through the front gate, looking behind him. 'Heller,' said Cheeseman, 'pull out all the stops. I want to know who the bugger really is.'

Chapter Eighteen

From the sudden confrontation to his forced ejection on to the pavement took no more than thirty seconds, and Steve knew he had put his foot in a wasps' nest. That wasn't the brightest thing you ever did, he thought as he walked down the pavement, anxious to put some space between himself and the house. At the bottom of the hill was a busstop, and he waited there, thinking a bus to anywhere would be better than staying in Waldegg.

What had he gained? A direct personal impression of Cheeseman, plus confirmation, if that was needed, that Dandycap was a very delicate subject. What had he lost? Anonymity. Now they knew someone was sniffing. At least they didn't know his name. He had an idea they might follow him and he looked at each car that passed, but he'd never seen the man in the passenger seat of the big Mercedes G-Wagen that drove slowly by him, and he couldn't see the thuggish Jacques beyond him in the driver's seat, and anyway they went past just like all the other cars.

He took the bus to the Hauptbahnhof, not realizing he was meant to buy a ticket at the machine by the stop first, and got into an irritating argument with a bus inspector convinced he was only pretending to be an ignorant foreigner. He changed buses and got back to Schlieren, looking around self-consciously, but failing to see any significance in the Mercedes driving past on the main road.

Breakfast the following morning hardly merited the name, the hardest bread roll he had ever failed to eat. It sounded hollow when he tapped it, so he gave up, swallowed the coffee and went back to his room. He came out again a minute or two before 7.30 and, walking into the lobby, stopped in his tracks. A girl was looking through the rack of postcards, the most instantly attractive woman he had seen in months, if not years. Everything about her was golden-brown, a tanned face under a mane of curly red-golden hair. She had a happy, open expression, with a snub nose and a wide mouth. Steve's first impulse was to go over and say something to her, ignoring the daunting difficulty of trying to strike up a relationship in who knows what language at such an unpropitious time of day.

At that same moment he saw Rudi standing by the reception desk and cursed to himself. Rudi was talking to the receptionist, looking a little concerned, but he finished, saw Steve and waved.

'Good morning. How did you sleep?'

'Fine, thanks. Is it time to go?'

'Certainly. We have a long journey.'

Steve glanced at the girl, and to his surprise and delight she turned and gave him a wide smile. Rudi said, 'Oh, Steve. This is Maja – who is the sound recordist,' and the day took on a new aspect. Then he added, smiling, 'She is my new wife,' and Steve's spirits plunged to his boots. She insisted he got in the front of the Cherokee, and he sat sideways for a time just to see her.

Rudi tossed him a map. 'We go to Glarus,' he said, 'then into the mountains beyond the Klausen Pass. You will get a few surprises.' He glanced at Steve. 'I have told Maja about your business here. I hope that is OK with you. If we are shooting for you, it is best she knows what is happening.'

'That's no problem,' said Steve, 'but there's a bit more that neither of you know.' He told them what had happened the previous evening.

Rudi's brow was furrowed when he finished. 'I think you have already stirred things around a bit. When I came to the hotel desk this morning, I heard the man on the telephone. He was being asked questions about how long you were staying and about your passport details. When he finished, I said I was a friend of yours and he told me it was just a routine check by the Fremdenpolizei.'

'They are the special police for the foreigners,' said Maja.

'Do you think it was really them?' said Steve.

'Who knows.'

Steve thought about it in silence for a while. They droned on down the motorway, with the mountains becoming clearer ahead, when Rudi said, 'This is where your lesson begins, Steve.' They were approaching a tunnel, with a big lake beside the road to the left. 'Look at the rocks to the right of the tunnel entrance.'

He looked, but was unsure what he was looking for. 'They're a bit . . . sort of . . . regular.'

'They're not rocks. They're fibreglass. There are cannon behind them, pointed permanently along the road.'

'Good God.'

'That is nothing. On every strategic pass or junction or potential bottleneck, there are these guns and mortars, with their range and aim already set. If you walk in the wrong place in the woods, you will find tree stumps which swing to one side and cover mortar tubes underneath. Switzerland is a porcupine. Further down this autobahn is a straight stretch where the crash barrier in the middle is just wire. There is a special truck which can come along at high speed and sweep the wire and posts out of the way. Then the fighter planes hidden inside the mountains can use it as an emergency landing-strip.'

'Are we going to see any of that today?'

Rudi shook his head. 'If we were, I would not be allowed

to take you. We are going to shoot for a training video on medical evacuation procedures, but you will still see some odd things, I think.'

They drove on, through the old town of Glarus and up a smaller side-road, twisting into the mountains. Steve and Maja talked inconsequentially as Rudi concentrated on the driving, her voice touching some deep part of him. They came to a point where the track was blocked by a barricade and a large notice in several languages, warning that this was an army exercise area and there was a danger of being shot. There was a small, sandbagged command post, and Rudi went to talk to the soldiers manning it.

They were allowed to pass, and went another quarter of a mile before coming out on a small plateau. Five large camouflaged tents had been set up, and a bright-red helicopter sat between them. 'Field hospital,' said Rudi. 'We start filming here. Then, later, you will see a mock battle.'

It was late in the afternoon before they were finished, an afternoon Steve spent divided between wonder at the unfolding military secrets of the mountains and envy at Rudi's good fortune. Rudi had gone to say his farewells to the army doctors in the tents, and Maja was packing the gear into the back of the Cherokee as Steve walked back down the slope towards her, watching her. Despite himself, his eyes had been drawn to her many times during the afternoon. Now she seemed to sense his gaze, turned and smiled. 'Can I give you a hand?' he said.

'Thank you. There is just the tripod to put in.'

'How long have you and Rudi been together?'

'Not very long,' she said, 'only four months, but I have known him for much longer.'

Rudi reappeared then, anxious to leave. Maja drove this time, and Steve climbed in the back, suddenly wanting to be the more distant point of the triangle. It's becoming the story of my life, he thought, Angie in Washington and now this. Some other lucky bastard always gets the pick of them. To break his depressing train of thought he started questioning Rudi again. 'Are all those soldiers volunteers?'

'Certainly. Almost every man is in it. Unless you object and pay a special tax, or unless some friendly doctor says you are mad, you have to serve for a little time each year. That way, all the army is ready for any emergency.'

'But it would take ages to mobilize everyone, surely?'

'Not at all. We all keep our kit at home.'

'Weapons as well?'

'Certainly. Weapons and ammunition and everything we need for each of our specializations.'

'Do you have a specialization, Rudi?'

'But of course.' He turned and grinned over the back of the seat at Steve. 'I blow up bridges.'

'How, or do I mean why?'

'I show you.' He looked ahead for a moment, and talked to Maja in Schweizerdeutsch. She went another half-mile and pulled over beside a small, stone bridge. Rudi got out and Steve followed. He went to the back of the Cherokee and got a little metal tool out of a canvas army bag. Steve followed as he walked across the bridge and used it to unlock and lift a metal manhole cover. Then he swung his legs into the hole and disappeared out of sight. 'Come on,' he said, his voice echoing up from the hole.

Steve climbed down some steel rungs let into the side of the hole and found himself squashed in a tiny, brick-lined chamber next to Rudi. Rudi lifted out a panel set low in the wall and showed him a lattice-work of threaded sockets, set in a rectangle. 'You see,' he said, 'you have to know which one is the right one. Then you screw in a special detonator fuse, set the timer and run for it.'

'What about the explosive?'

Rudi slapped the wall. 'It's already here,' he said, '100 kilos of TNT in this one. Much more in the big bridges. Many of the not-so-important crossings just have empty chambers waiting to be filled, but some in important places – in the passes or over railways – have it there all the year, while the cars and trucks roll over it, never knowing.'

'But couldn't anyone come along and blow it up?'

'You have to have the detonator, and the special code for which socket is the right one in each bridge.'

'How do you get those?'

'They're meant to be handed out in time of crisis, but they once forgot to ask for mine back after an exercise. I keep it in the car.'

They climbed back out and Rudi locked the cover. 'You know the funniest thing?' he said. 'I am one of their special experts in this. I have to be ready to bring the great viaducts crashing down to stop the enemy tanks, but, if it comes to it, I won't be there.'

'Why not?'

'You remember I told you about the secret files on the million subversives? Well, you are now allowed to apply for details of your file. I am listed as one who would be interned if there was a state of emergency. I once played in a jazz band with some activists, and that was all it took.'

They walked back to the Jeep and, just before they got there, Rudi paused. 'By the way, I have the feeling Maja likes you. She likes you very much.'

Steve covered his embarrassment, getting into the back seat again. Rudi got in the front, grinning. Seeking distraction, Steve shuffled through his bag and came upon the bits and pieces he had found in Cheeseman's garbage. 'Rudi,' he said, 'you don't recognize any of these, do you?'

Rudi reached round and took the circuit boards and the

tube, and looked at them closely for a while, turning them to and fro. 'Of course I do,' he said. 'Why?'

'They were in the black bags we took.'

Rudi gave him a surprised look. 'Slide down my back,' he said. 'I mean, what do you say, do not pull my leg.'

'I'm not. They were. Why, what are they?'

'Shame on you. I thought you were an old hand at this business. That's a circuit board out of an old ENG tube camera.' He held up the other part. 'And that's one of the colour tubes itself.'

Steve began to excuse himself. 'I've only ever worked with modern Sony cameras except the once ...' Then his voice trailed off as the obvious but extraordinary thought came careering at him. 'Rudi, can you tell what model it's from?'

Rudi picked up the fresh tone in his voice and looked at him curiously for a moment, then studied the circuit board again. 'Sure. There is the ident printed on the edge here, see. It says IK 79D. That would be an Ikegami 79D.' Steve stared at him. There it was, the final confirmation that both his trails lay in the same direction.

'Why would he have parts from an Ikegami in his rubbish?' asked Maja.

'I don't know, but I do know whose Ikegami they came from,' said Steve. 'I'd better tell you the whole story.'

When he finished, Maja spoke first. 'Nick told Rudi a little bit on the telephone,' she said, 'but we didn't know much of it.' She turned her head and looked behind at him. 'I am very sorry for you,' she said, and Steve felt it had all been almost worth it.

'I've been feeling pretty sorry for myself, too,' he said, 'but now I think it's time to start doing something about it.'

Rudi had been thinking. 'It is too big,' he said, 'this coincidence. You do not know this is the very same camera.'

Maja beat Steve to it. 'Oh, Rudi,' she said, 'of course you

see *so many* Ikegamis in Zürich still, yes? Do you know anybody that still uses one? Are there so many that you find the spare parts in any bin you look in?'

Rudi waved his hands as if to fend her off. 'No, of course, there are not.'

'Tell me the names of cameramen here who still use one.'

'No, I can't, but that does not mean there are not still some lying around.'

'So why would this man Cheeseman have one?' And to that, he had no answer.

As they weaved into the south-western suburbs of Zürich, Steve saw that the yellow circles were in use. There were no bin bags this time, but all kinds of larger objects. He saw a bicycle, a computer and two pairs of skis in one pile. 'Rudi, what's all this stuff they're throwing away now?'

Rudi glanced at it. 'That is the heavy rubbish collection. It happens every two or three months. Then there is the old paper collection, the old clothes collection, the waste metal collection and the garden cuttings collection.'

'It looks like pretty good stuff.'

'You must understand, we Swiss like new things, Steve. There is no point in trying to sell anything second-hand here.'

'Is this happening all over Zürich today?'

'No, just in this direction, I think. Different days in different places.'

'Would it be happening in Waldegg?'

'It could be.' He frowned and put on a joke tone of petulance. 'Oh, no. You're not going to dirty up my nice clean car again, are you?'

A few minutes later they were pulling up a safe distance beyond Cheeseman's house. Steve got out, and suppressed a small thrill as Maja opened the driver's door and followed him. The rubbish pile was overlooked from the house, and

Steve didn't want to linger. There wasn't much there – two garden chairs, an old Hoover and a car seat, piled on top of some large, flattened cardboard boxes. Then he saw the typewriter, almost hidden under the boxes. He bent down and pulled it out for a closer look. It was clean and it wasn't all that old – an expensive electric machine. No one in England would have dreamed of throwing it away.

'What good is that?' said Maja. 'It must be broken.'

'I'll bet it could be fixed,' said Steve. 'I might just take it back with me.'

'Why don't . . .' she began, but then they were interrupted. The camera on the wall had turned to point straight at them, and a distorted, familiar voice issued with surprising volume from the grille by the entry phone. It was Cheeseman.

'Do stop picking through my rubbish, Mr Williamson. Behave with some decorum, or I shall have to send someone to give you a lesson in manners, Mr Williamson . . . or should I not say Mr Ross, Mr Steven Ross.'

It was shock on shock. Steve felt the guilty shock of being caught in the act laid on top of the acute discomfort of hearing Cheeseman using his real name. He straightened up, tucking the typewriter under one arm, gave an ironic bow to the camera, took Maja's arm with the other hand and headed for the Jeep as quickly as he could.

They dropped him at the hotel and made plans to do some discreet shooting at Cheeseman's house the following morning. Rudi offered to take him somewhere nice for dinner, but he felt he had imposed enough, and went back to his room, intending to go into Zürich for some sightseeing later on. But he lay down on the bed, feeling bone weary, and when he opened his eyes again it was 9.30 in the evening. Feeling muzzy-headed, he sat on the bed and found himself staring at the typewriter. He picked it up off the floor and looked it over. There was even a plug on the flex. He pushed it into a socket and switched on. Nothing happened.

He took off the top cover and got nowhere, then he turned it upside down and found a small red button. He pushed it experimentally, and it went in with a satisfying click. Immediately, the machine whirred into life and indicator lights flashed on. Bloody hell, he thought, just a trip-switch. One little push was all it needed, and they threw it away just for that.

Pleased with himself, he opened the drawer in the tiny table and found a few sheets of hotel notepaper. He fed one into the machine and typed 'The quick brown fox jumped over the lazy dog'. It worked perfectly. Cheeseman's type-writer, he thought, or rather, presumably, his secretary's. What secrets you must hold. If only you could talk. He typed out, 'I wish you had a memory becaus ...' but that was as far as he got. The letters stopped appearing.

He felt mild disappointment for a moment, that there obviously was some greater problem with the machine, then he flipped open the top lid and saw that the ribbon cassette inside had simply come to an end. He unclipped it to see if there was some way of reversing it, but it was immediately obvious that it was intended for one-time use. At the front of it he could see the end of the black ribbon connected to the spool by a short length of white plastic tape. He took it out and threw it in the bin.

He thought again about whether to shake off his lethargy and go into town, and decided anything was better than staying in that tiny cheerless room. The bus-stop was only a hundred yards from the hotel and, as he walked towards it, one of the blue trolley buses was just pulling out. He settled down on a bench to kill time, but after a couple of minutes felt restless and started wandering up and down the pavement. There was a furniture shop behind the bus-stop and a pharmacy next to it. Nothing to hold his attention there. Next along was a shop selling cameras, photocopiers and office equipment. He idled away a couple of minutes converting the price of a few Canons and Minoltas into sterling. The answers were depressing. He looked up and there was a bus, three hundred yards up the road, coming his way.

It was only as he turned that he read the huge display placard in the front of the window. 70,000 characters for just 15 francs, it yelled in German. 5 for 60 francs. Summer typists special. He strolled back to the stop and boarded the bus. It had moved off before the meaning of the advert hit him. Seventy thousand characters. Seventy thousand characters all in a row on that one-time ribbon in the cassette. The typewriter didn't have a memory, but its tape did – a perfect memory of seventy thousand characters, and he'd thrown it in the bin.

'Ahhh,' he said, and it sounded like pain. The bus stopped at some lights. Five pairs of curious eyes fixed themselves on this strange young man, who leapt to his feet and began to try to open the automatic door. It wouldn't. The bus carried him slowly on, a hundred yards, two hundred yards, three hundred yards more than seemed reasonable between stops. Then, finally, it came to one, and Steve was running back along the pavement before the doors had finished opening.

Please God, don't let them pick this moment to clean my room, he said to himself as he ran. He developed a stitch halfway back, but kept going, and was panting hard when he got to his room, opened the door and dived for the bin. The small black tape cassette was still there. He pulled some of the thin plastic tape out and held it up to the window. The evening light shone through the clear bits where the typewriter keys had hammered the black film from the tape

on to the paper. He read 'Iwishyouhadamemorybecaus'. He
pulled more out. German words appeared, all joined up. He
went on. The Waldegg address was there at the start of a
short letter which seemed to be about a builder's estimate.
He went on and on, and by the time he had finished there
was the best part of two hundred yards of it, coiling into the
waste bin.

He took out a pen and a notebook and began to read it
from the start.

Chapter Nineteen

By eleven o'clock that evening, Steve had severe writer's cramp and was wishing he had a German dictionary with him. The only way to make sense of the ribbon was to write down the words in longhand, working out where to put the gaps between them. It took him an hour just to write out the first two letters and then to try to work out what they said. One was addressed to a bank in Liechtenstein and was about some kind of special bank account, for which Steve did not understand the German name. It was an instruction to transfer extra funds and it seemed to list conditions under which those funds could be paid to some third party. There were no mistakes in the typing.

The second was shorter and simpler, but its content was unrewarding. It was simply a notification to the Zürich traffic authorities, the Strassenverkehrsamt, of the sale of a Porsche 959 car and the return of its number-plates to them. Steve ploughed on. There were occasional letters in French. Some consisted of orders for goods identified only by catalogue numbers. The amounts of money made Steve whistle, but what one hundred HK33Ks could be in an order worth 185,000 Swiss francs was beyond him to fathom.

One thing almost all the letters had in common was the precision of the typing, which made Steve even more certain that the formidable secretary had been the one doing the work. It was past 1 a.m. when he struck gold. It was the first time he had seen the instantly recognizable pattern of English words come up on the ribbon, and they were familiar words.

FaxtoDandycapHoldings, it began. It was a fax giving instructions to Joe Thompson in Sark to place an immediate buying order through Mackeson, Shorthouse account 106 to buy 50,000 shares in Mellmore Industrial at any price up to £6.50 per share before the close of trading that day. It was dated Thursday July 4th. On Steve's table lay Saturday's Frankfurt edition of the *Financial Times* bought at the Schlieren news-stand, only because it had no other English language papers. He turned to the prices section and found Mellmore's closing price. It was £9.80, up over £3 on the day. He looked through the market report for illumination and read of the hostile takeover bid launched on Friday morning by Bendall Clement, and the surprise it had created in the City.

He felt elation then at this first piece of solid evidence against Dandycap, and decided to share it, so he went out to the foyer to phone Nick. It was only just after midnight in London, and he would surely not be asleep, indeed he might not even be back home. He lifted the pay phone's receiver and got ready with a five-franc piece. There was no dialling tone. He rattled it a few times, but it was clearly switched off. There was no night porter. The foyer was deserted and the front door was locked. He went over to the desk to see if the phone there worked, but couldn't reach it from in front and had to go round behind it.

He picked up the phone, but, though there was a dialling tone, it cut off into a harsh, irritated buzzing whenever he dialled the double zero to start an international call. It was when he put the phone down that he noticed the notepad lying next to it. There were only three short notes written in pencil on it. They were in German. They said '19.45. Dropped at Hotel (Jeep). 21.40. Left hotel on foot. 21.53. Returned to hotel, running.'

He got out from behind the desk as fast as he could and went back to the room to think, locking the door behind him. It seemed unlikely that the Fremdenpolizei would be asking the hotel clerk for details of his movements, unless Cheeseman had somehow initiated it. Or maybe it had been Cheeseman who had called the reception desk that morning? He tried it every way round, and it didn't help, but, when he went back to the rest of the ribbon in the waste bin, he was in a much more troubled frame of mind. He'd been playing the role of hunter, but perhaps he was in fact the quarry.

He began to find other short notes written in English. They were different. There was none of the formality of the letters, and they were badly typed, so much so that it was difficult to make sense of them. It was as if another person would occasionally type out messages to leave for someone else. He could get little out of them that was of any significance until, barely able to keep his eyes open, but unwilling to give up in case some other revelation lay just around the corner, he spotted the word CAMERA buried in a string of block capitals.

Then he forgot to be sleepy for a while, and went backwards and forwards into the German words at either end to be sure he had got the full extent of the English message. It didn't make too much sense. What he had, read KRNTE,GCAKKLLED.THREVISDEOCAMERAISREAD-TYFO GTSDTRESASSUMEYOUWONTTATEBNATTENDBUTIFYO UDO,NEEZMTGLAREWNERLANDNERLANDM-PICKR-BOU NDE7AMTHISMON8.

It was quite clear it had been badly mistyped, then corrected. He tried to work out which letters had been replaced and where the extra letters fitted in. The first seven or eight words could be made out without too much trouble. *KRNTE* had to be Cheeseman's first name, Kent, with the *E* mistyped as an *R* then corrected. It would then seem that someone named as *G* had called, with *K* mistyped twice for *L*, to say that the video camera was ready. After that it degenerated badly until 'assume you won't tatebn attend but if you do', whatever tatebn meant, and from then on it was just pure gibberish. It was quite obvious that many of the other letters were corrections, but, however much he tried, he couldn't sort out which ones they were, or arrange them in any way that made sense.

It was only when he was about to give up that he flipped open the top cover of the typewriter again, more as a distraction than anything else, and saw, tucked almost out of sight below where the ribbon cassette had been, the two little yellow reels of the corrector ribbon. He lifted that out and, looking at it, saw that once again he could easily read off the long line of characters spaced neatly along it where it had lifted the mistyped letters off the page.

It felt like a breakthrough for no more than thirty seconds. That was the time it took him to unroll part of it and realize there were literally thousands of letters on the roll, with no apparent way of matching them up with what he had on the first cassette. He gave up then, and lay back on the bed, intending to rest for a few minutes and try again.

The knocking on the door woke him. It was 7.45 in the morning. He was fully dressed, and his right leg was numb where it lay on top of the hard lump of the typewriter. He stumbled to his feet, brushing his fingers through his hair, and opened the door. The man from the reception desk was waiting there. 'There is a call for you, Herr Ross,' he said.

Steve pulled the door firmly shut behind him, as the man was clearly trying to look inside the room, and walked down the passage. He expected Rudi's voice when he picked up the receiver, but it wasn't Rudi at all. 'Good morning, Mr Ross. This is Kent Cheeseman.'

The tone was level, almost polite. Taken by surprise, Steve decided to say as little as possible.

'Good morning, Mr Cheeseman.'

'I am ringing you to stop you wasting my time and yours, Mr Ross. You asked me about a company. I have nothing to say about that company, but I would suggest you do your homework on the laws of Switzerland. They are very much more free and easy than those of England. I presume you are based in England, Mr Ross?'

Give him nothing, Steve thought. 'I am interested in share deals which fall under the jurisdiction of US and UK securities laws, Mr Cheeseman.'

The thin veneer vanished and the ugly voice grew more guttural. 'I don't give a stuff what you're interested in, Mr Ross. I want you out of my hair. You will get nowhere in this country, and I have many friends here who will not like you asking questions.'

'Why don't you simply answer some of mine then, such as why you are using a Sark company, hidden behind a nominee account in London?'

'Perhaps I'm not making myself plain. There is an old belief that Switzerland is a healthy country, Mr Ross. Your countrymen used to come here to take the air. That is not true any more. Our Alpine valleys are sadly polluted. I would strongly recommend that for your personal state of health, you should go to some other country where the atmosphere is less dangerous to you. That is all. Good-bye.'

Steve looked at the dead phone in his hand, and put it back on the rest. Then, with sudden resolve, he dialled Rudi's number. The man at the desk was watching him, so he turned his back, cupped his hand over the mouthpiece, and spoke softly. 'Rudi? I hope I haven't woken you?'

'You would have to call much earlier to wake a Swiss, Steve. I have already run five kilometres this morning. Are we going to do some shooting?'

'You bet we are, but it's turning even nastier. I think we should be very careful. We'll shoot from inside the car as much as possible.'

'OK. Maybe I borrow a car. The Jeep is not so good for tracking shots. It bounces too much. Shall we pick you up?'

'Thanks. How about nine o'clock? I need some breakfast.'

He went back to the room, looked thoughtfully at the heaped-up ribbon, and put it carefully in his briefcase. He took the case with him into the breakfast room, and was confronted by what looked like the very same bread roll as the day before. This time he carved his initials on it. Drinking the coffee only took five minutes, and, as he walked back to his room, the man from reception came out of it, and stopped in his tracks.

'What are you doing?' said Steve.

'I am sorry, I just had to make sure the television works properly.'

'And does it?' said Steve.

The man smiled, embarrassed. 'Yes, of course.'

'Well, that's strange,' lied Steve, 'it didn't last night,' and noted the alarmed look on the man's face with satisfaction.

The room showed no obvious signs of any interference, but with the all-important ribbons in his case there wasn't anything to find. Remembering where he'd got to, he sat down and studied them again. After a few hours' sleep his brain was working better. The secretary didn't make mistakes. Those were the exclusive province of whoever was typing the English notes, therefore the correction ribbon would last much longer than the main ribbon, and, in that

238

case, the corrections which went with the note should be somewhere near the far end. After that it was easy. Looking through the letters on the correction ribbon, he noticed a string he recognized: *TATEBN*. Working backwards and forwards from that, he came up with RKKRSTGSDT-ATEBNNZEWNERLANDR. Putting the two strings of letters together, it only took him a few minutes to come up with the whole message. It read KENT, G CALLED. THE VIDEO CAMERA IS READY FOR TEST. ASSUME YOU WONT ATTEND BUT IF YOU DO, MEET GLARNERLAND M-PICK R-BOUND E 7 AM THIS MON 8.

Three-quarters of an hour later, he was standing outside on the road, watching the man on the reception desk watching him through the hotel window. He walked up the road to get out of his sight, and didn't for a moment take any notice of the long silver Citroën Safari which pulled up by him. Then Maja smiled at him from the passenger window. 'Good morning, Steve. Here is your limousine.'

He climbed in. 'What a monster. Where did you get it?'

'I often borrow it,' said Rudi. 'I have a friend who likes to drive the Jeep, and this is the perfect car for filming. Very smooth over the bumps and it has big windows.'

'Good. Can you get away from here, then stop somewhere quiet. We have a lot to talk about.'

He told them about the ribbons and about Cheeseman's threat. Rudi was interested, but a little sceptical. Maja was hooked straight away. 'May I see the message?' she said, and studied it for a minute or two. 'No, you are wrong here,' she said. 'It should not read R-BOUND E. I think it is E-BOUND and the R was corrected. That would stand for eastbound, yes?'

'Where is Glarnerland?'

'That is the name of a place – I do not know the right

term – a place with petrol and food by the autobahn.'

'A motorway service area?'

'Yes. I guess so. The one called Glarnerland is on the autobahn between Glarus and Chur. It is run by Mövenpick. That is why it says M-PICK.'

'And MON 8 is tomorrow?'

'Yes, tomorrow is July 8th.'

Steve thought for a moment. 'I can stay an extra day. Are you two free tomorrow?'

Rudi looked at him. 'You want to shoot?'

'I think we should go and see what happens, and be ready in case.'

Rudi looked embarrassed. 'It is just that I told Nick I would do one day for free, for what I owed him, but that is today I think.'

'Don't worry. The risk is down to me. We have enough cash to pay for one extra day. I think it's worth it.'

Rudi was even more embarrassed. 'Nick told me that I must remind you the money is for the share dealing story, not for ... what did he say? Red fish?'

'Red herrings. Rudi, I don't believe this is a red herring. Let's say we'll book you for a half a day, and, if nothing happens by noon, we'll give up.'

Rudi was about to argue again, but a rapid burst of Schweizerdeutsch from Maja silenced him.

Before they reached the house, Steve took over the driving and Rudi and Maja got in the back with the equipment all ready. They stopped down the road and shot every possible combination of wide shot, close-up and zoom of the front and the sides. Then they drove slowly past in both directions, getting a tracking shot of the street and the house. They stopped again, a little nearer, to get a shot with the lens zoomed right in to full telephoto of the surveillance camera

240

on the wall, and, as they did, the camera turned as if on cue and pointed straight at them.

'They have seen us,' said Rudi. 'Do you think it is time to leave?'

'Certainly not,' said Steve. 'Have you got a radio mike?'

They fixed him up with the mike and the little transmitter in his pocket, trailing its short aerial, and he got out of the car. 'You stay inside out of sight,' he said. 'You have to live here. I don't. Just shoot me, keeping in as tight close-up as you can, and I'll cross the road, do a little piece to camera, and ring the bell. We'll see what happens.'

He knew he would only get one go at it, so he worked it all out carefully before moving. Then he crossed to the gate, turned towards the car, and spoke into the microphone. 'This is Kent Cheeseman's house in Waldegg – the address on correspondence giving instructions for Dandycap's illegal share dealings. We are being watched by a surveillance camera from inside. So someone must be at home.' He turned and pressed the bell, hoping for a reply and ideally for more threats. There was silence. 'They're keeping their mouths shut, it would seem. We will have to try again later,' and he walked back across the road to the car.

Cheeseman watched them drive off on the monitor, and turned to Heller. 'He's a persistent little bastard. What the hell does he know?'

'He has heard something about Dandycap. I do not think we should concern ourselves too much. No one here will care about that.'

'He's obviously the man who showed up at Thompson's house. We'll stop using Dandycap. Stick to the Isle of Man companies from now on, at least for a while.'

'Yes, Herr Cheeseman.'

'Tell me everything we know.'

'We have his passport details. We know he is booked back

to London on Swissair tomorrow. We will trace who these friends of his are by the number-plates on the Citroën they are using.'

'Who does he work for?'

'We do not know yet. Enquiries are being made as fast as possible in London.'

'He can't have much. He must be just guessing. Why did he take the typewriter?'

'I think perhaps he just wanted a typewriter, Herr Cheeseman. It can't tell him any stories.'

Cheeseman looked thoughtfully at the monitor, and the empty street outside.

'It cannot be connected with the other thing. His arrival now is only coincidence,' said Heller.

'That had better be right.'

'So we go ahead with the test?'

'Yes.'

It was an early start the following morning. An unhappy Rudi and a smiling Maja met Steve at 6 a.m. The traffic was already building up. In half an hour the Zürich rush hour would be getting into its extremely early stride. One lane of the motorway was closed near Schindellegi for no apparent reason, causing a tailback. 'They are about to wash the road,' said Rudi, and Steve didn't like to ask if he was joking.

It was 6.45 when they got to the car park at the Glarnerland service area, and they parked the Cherokee in a space from where they could see the entry and exit to the motorway. 'I'll have a look round the car park,' said Steve, 'just in case I recognize anyone.'

'That is some chance,' said Rudi. 'The only one you know is Cheeseman and he may not even come.'

'I've seen two of his henchmen, too,' said Steve, but Rudi just sighed.

Maja got out to come with him, and they walked around in silence to start with. Steve felt constrained. He liked Rudi far too much to feel comfortable with the extent of the attraction he felt for his wife, and Maja's warmth towards him only made it more confusing. She touched his arm and he looked at her questioningly. 'You must not mind Rudi,' she said, 'he is very solid, down-to-earth in things like this. He knows you have had troubles and he wants to protect you from any more.'

'Yes, but I'm right about this one.'

'I think you are, too. I will help as much as I can.'

'You know how I left the BBC?'

'Yes.'

They went on looking at the parked cars, but they drew a blank. After that, they sat in the Cherokee, Rudi reading the *Neue Züricher Zeitung* and the other two staring at the slip-road. A few cars came by. Steve recognized no one in them, and none of them looked particularly likely. 7.00 came and went, then 7.15, and Rudi started looking at his watch. 'I think we have to stop soon, Steve. How about we go back to Zürich? Then I will not charge for the time today.'

Steve knew he was on very weak ground. He tried to imagine justifying the cost to Nick. 'I suppose you're right, Rudi,' he began, but Maja stopped him.

'Wait,' she said, 'I would like to see the message once more.'

Steve reached into his briefcase and gave it to her. They watched her as she looked at it again, then smiled. 'I think perhaps there is one more mistake here. This is a very bad typist. You read 7 A.M. THIS MON 8, but I think the 8 is a correction and it should really say 8 A.M. THIS MON perhaps.'

Rudi had had enough. 'Oh no, that is too much. Today is the 8th. Are you saying that is just chance?'

'Perhaps. There is a way we can soon tell. I think Steve did not look far enough on the corrector ribbon. If the next thing on that is the figure 7, then we will know it was corrected.'

They looked. It was. That kept even Rudi's pessimism under control until close to eight o'clock, then he spotted another flaw.

'If the 8 is the time and not the date,' he said, 'then we do not even know that it is meant to be this Monday. It could be any Monday at all. It could have already happened.'

'Oh yes, it's today all right,' said Steve, sitting up straighter and staring at a silver-grey Range Rover pulling in off the motorway. 'It's certainly today. That's the car I chased in Geneva, and the man driving it is the one who was carrying the camera.'

Chapter Twenty

'Don't turn round,' said Steve as the Range Rover drove up the side of the parking area and along the line behind them. He watched it out of the corner of his eye. 'OK, it's past.'

They all looked then, and saw it back into a parking space. No one got out. 'I think there are two people in it,' said Maja.

Steve peered round. They couldn't see from where they were. 'I'll go a bit closer and look,' he said.

'No. Not you,' Maja said flatly. 'Me. Your face has been all over the place lately.'

They watched as she walked past the Range Rover and into the shop by the petrol pumps. She came back, carrying a newspaper and glancing casually round. 'Yes,' she said, 'there are two of them. The other is a woman, very beautiful, dark skinned.' She grinned at Rudi. 'Just the kind Rudi likes, the Black Widow type.'

'You are just saying that to get me interested,' said Rudi, smiling wearily.

'Oh come on, you must believe me now?' said Steve.

Rudi shrugged. 'It's a Range Rover, sure. You think it's the same man. That's fine. If someone comes to meet them, then I get excited.'

No one did. The Range Rover sat there until ten past eight, then it pulled out of the parking space and headed down the slip-road back on to the motorway. Rudi did nothing.

'Hurry up. We'll lose them,' said Steve.

Rudi looked incredulously at him. 'You want me to chase them?'

'Of course I do.'

'This is not a movie, Steve. I am not a stunt driver. And I will have to charge you for the day.'

'Rudi, I'll pay, OK? Now if you don't want to do it, shift over and I'll drive the bloody thing.'

Rudi began to twitter as Steve almost pushed him out of the driver's seat. 'This is not such a good idea. Please be careful. It is nearly new.'

'If I break it, I'll get it fixed, OK?' said Steve, knowing he couldn't.

Rudi looked as if he knew Steve couldn't as well. 'These things do not normally happen in Switzerland,' he said, then seemed to give up, and sat there knotting his fingers together.

Steve turned the key, and the big four-litre engine roared into life. Rudi squeaked almost as loudly as the tyres when he pushed the gear selector into Drive and accelerated hard out of the car park after the departing Range Rover. Steve drove fast until he was two or three hundred yards behind them, then hung back, letting other cars fill the gap between them.

'Can you get the camera out?' he said to Rudi, as much to give him something to think about as anything else. 'I know it won't be a great shot from back here, but it might come in handy.'

Rudi took the camera from Maja and plugged in the umbilical from the recorder. He had to slide down awkwardly in the seat to make space to heft it on to his shoulder, then concentrated on the shooting. 'See if you can come a bit closer,' he said. 'That's good. A bit closer still.'

They followed the Range Rover for about twenty-five

miles, past the junction where the motorway splits off towards Liechtenstein, Germany and Austria. They went on past Bad Ragaz and Maienfeld, with signs off to Heidiland, and then, ahead, Steve saw the Range Rover slowing, and its right flasher going.

'He's turning off. Where are we?'

'This is Landquart,' said Rudi.

'What happens up here?'

'It is a long valley which leads up to the skiing places, Klosters and Davos. If you go on further you come to the valley of the Engadine and then Italy.'

The roads were narrower and twistier, and the driver ahead suddenly seemed in more of a hurry. Rudi had realized by now that Steve was an expert, but was still having trouble keeping his nerves under control. Past Klosters, on the Wolfgang Pass, they ran into low cloud, and Steve nearly missed seeing the Range Rover veer to the right on a hairpin, up a much smaller road.

He braked hard and swung the wheel over. It was a track, and the Jeep lurched and bucketed on the uneven surface. 'Sorry, Rudi,' he said, 'but we don't want to lose touch.'

Now it was doubly difficult. He had to hang right back as the road climbed up through pine woods. On this road any casual backward glance would have alerted the driver in front that he had some unwelcome company. The metalled surface disappeared, and they began to bump over loose stones, in the gloom between the trees.

'Put it in four-wheel drive,' said Rudi, 'the lever nearest you.'

'Do I slow down?'

'No. Just pull all the way to where it says Full-Time 4wd.'

They saw light ahead, and Steve slowed right down as they came to the edge of the tree line. There was a bridge over a small railway line, and Alpine meadows lay beyond.

The Range Rover was half a mile away, still climbing. They waited until it went round a shoulder of rock, then followed. It was hide and seek all the way, short rushes from bend to bend, always making sure the other vehicle was out of sight before going on. They got back into the cloud again, and blessed its concealment, but it was almost their undoing. It blew away for a second, just in time for them to see the Range Rover parked only a few hundred yards ahead, with its two occupants already climbing the steep slope above it.

Steve stopped sharply, and backed up towards the concealment of the last bend. 'Did they see us?' he asked.

Maja said, 'I do not think so. They were not looking round. This cloud helps to cover up the sound.'

Fifty yards back from the bend was a flat section of verge, and Steve parked on it. 'What now?' said Maja.

'We go and see what they're doing,' said Steve.

'You mean, you go and see,' said Rudi. 'Maybe I stay here with the car.'

'You want to shoot, Steve?' asked Maja.

He looked at the steep slopes all round them and the damp cloud blowing past. 'I'd like to, but it's a hell of a tall order to catch them up carrying a camera on this sort of terrain.'

'We have a tiny one also. The Sony Pro Video,' said Maja. 'The pictures are really good. Shall we take that?'

'Will it produce broadcastable pictures?'

'Certainly.' She took it out of its case. It was not much larger than a home movie camcorder. 'Not for regular stuff maybe, but today I think it will be what we need.'

Rudi showed no enthusiasm for moving. Steve looked at Maja. 'Sorry to ask, but do you know how to use it?'

Rudi spoke for her. 'She is as good as I am with a camera.'

Maja pulled a face. 'You only admit that when you don't want to climb a mountain.'

Opening the Jeep's door made an unsettling difference.

248

Inside, the car's cocoon had made it all seem so optional. Filtered through a windscreen, the situation seemed almost fictional, as though they could choose to switch it off or simply drive away from it all. Steve left the soft leather seat for the gravelly grass of the track's verge. The cloud twisted around him, chill and grey, taking the colour from the scene. Just legs, wits and a camera between them and their quarry on a mountainside.

To their left the mountain rose at a steep angle – not quite a walk, nor a climb, but something in between. The bend around which they had reversed to hide them from the Range Rover marked the point where a narrow ridge came down the mountain. The cloud didn't allow much of a view.

Steve turned to Maja. 'If we climb up on this side of the ridge, we should be out of their sight. They seemed to be following the slope straight up on the other side of it. I'll take the camera if you like. Do you mind a scramble?'

She snorted at him and didn't bother to answer, but started up the slope at high speed. Steve chased after her and was out of breath in no time. She waited for him a hundred yards further up, grinning. 'Shall I carry you as well as the camera?'

It took them five minutes to reach the saddle at the top of the slope, where the ridge began to flatten out. The cloud around them was thicker than ever. 'Let's see if we can see them,' said Steve. 'If we crawl up to the edge of the ridge, we may be able to.'

Maja looked around her. 'Over to the left there. You see the rocks with the gap between them? We will be protected from their view.'

They were very cautious, and very wet from crawling on the cloud-damped grass. They reached the little cleft between the rocks, and by squeezing together they could both look through. The ground fell away below them in a grassy bowl, rising again some two hundred yards beyond into another steep, rocky slope, and there were the other two. They were standing perhaps a hundred yards away, down in the bottom of the bowl. The man was carrying the camera, the woman supported the tripod, and they were both watching something on the far slope. Steve could see the camera was an Ikegami.

The cloud blew across again, and they disappeared in the swirling grey. Maja put the little Sony camera to her eye, and played with some of the controls. In the mist they heard a strange, shrill, barking noise. 'What on earth is that?' Steve whispered into Maja's ear, close by him.

'Marmots,' she said.

'What are marmots?'

'You do not know them? They are animals that live in holes in the ground here in the Alps. They look like small beavers. Very nice.'

Another hole in the cloud blew past, and they saw the pair with the camera now on the tripod. Steve saw movement on the far slope and could just make out a brown animal, standing on its back legs to look around, then dropping on all fours to scuttle to another rock.

The cloud came back down, and Maja turned her face to him. The scent and the closeness of her startled him, and he saw her eyes widen for a second before their purpose reasserted itself. 'They are making nature films?' she said. 'Is that what we have come to see?'

He shook his head, suddenly feeling uncertain. 'I don't know. Keep shooting.'

But it wasn't easy. The cloud resolutely blocked their view, lifting just enough from time to time to give them fleeting impressions of what was going on, like a series of still frames clipped at random from a movie. They saw the camera taken off the tripod again, then put back on, then a long period while the woman fiddled with something within the side cover and the man watched. Finally, all seemed ready for the shoot to begin. They saw the man looking through the viewfinder and the woman staring across to the far slope. Then the man stopped, and began to look carefully all around the surrounding mountain. Steve put an arm across Maja's back and flattened her. She had to put the camera down. He whispered in her ear, 'We don't want to be seen. It looks like he's checking.'

He counted to fifteen, then lifted his head carefully, but the cloud was in the way again. There was a sudden series of muted noises, like somebody tapping a rock with a hammer two or three times. It was at least three minutes before the cloud cleared, and it felt like ten. This time the camera stood unattended on the tripod, and both the man and the woman were over by the marmot's rocks, bending down. As they watched, Maja filming all the while, the man knelt, and the woman seemed to pass him something. Then the cloud came back.

'It is just too far away,' whispered Maja. 'Even with the zoom it will not be too clear.'

'Keep going,' Steve whispered back. 'Anything is better than nothing at all.'

They had one more glimpse of them, still in the same place, then a long wait. When they could see again, the scene had changed completely. The camera and tripod had gone, and they could just see the disappearing backs of the other two a long way down the slope towards the track.

'If they drive back the way they came, they'll go straight past Rudi,' said Steve in sudden anxiety.

Maja looked down the slope. 'I think they are too far ahead. Even if we run down they will be there before us. Then they will see us on the slope and know we saw them.'

'But they'll guess that when they see Rudi.'

'If I know Rudi, he will be asleep. That is all they will see.'

Then they heard clearly as the Range Rover's engine started. It moved on up the track, but soon they heard it revving and scrabbling on the loose gravel as it lurched backwards and forwards to turn round. They listened intently as the sound came up to them, distorted by the echo and the cloud. It moved slowly back down the track, seemingly without pausing, until it faded from their hearing.

'They went straight past the Jeep,' said Steve in relief. 'Let's go and look down there.'

They ran down the side of the grassy bowl and scrambled up the far slope to where they had seen the man kneeling. There was nothing in sight, no marmots and no sign of any activity. They searched around, and Maja combed her fingers through the short tufts of grass. She stood up. 'I don't understand,' she said, 'there's nothing here.'

Steve looked at her hand. 'Hey, you've cut yourself on the grass.'

She looked down at it, puzzled. 'No, I don't think so. I didn't feel it.'

They both looked at it. It was indeed covered in smears of bright red blood, but there was no cut. Steve knelt and looked at the grassy tuft through which she had combed her hand. Some broader-leaved Alpine plants grew around it. The top surfaces of their leaves were clean, green, but then he turned one over. The underside was spattered and smeared with blood, and so was the next.

Maja knelt next to him, staring at it. 'Someone's been cleaning up around here,' said Steve, 'but they missed a few bits.'

'I don't understand,' she said. 'They were shooting pictures of the marmots, then there was the noise. Did they kill one?'

'It looks like it.'

'But how? They are nervous creatures. You do not simply walk up to one and hit it on the head.'

Steve gazed in deep thought at the grass. The little scraps of information were starting to click together in his head. 'They were certainly shooting,' he said, 'but maybe not pictures. Don't wipe your hand yet. I want to get some shots.' She explained the simple controls, then held out her hands while he shot close-ups of the blood. She knelt down again, and he filmed her combing the grass. Then they went back down to where the tripod had been standing. The flattened grass showed the spot clearly. He got down on hands and knees again, and made a careful search. Maja joined him. 'What are we looking for?' she asked.

'I don't really know. Anything that shouldn't be here.'

'Like these?' She showed him three curved shards of splintered clear plastic between an inch and two inches long.

'Maybe,' said Steve, taking them. 'I don't know.'

They found four more small pieces, but that was all, and they shot the scene from every angle they could find, though it looked just like any other corner of the mountains. The more Steve's train of thought developed, the less happy he felt about the fact that the others must have seen Rudi and the Jeep at close quarters. He felt nervous on the way back, until he saw the familiar square black shape loom up below them as they climbed down through the cloud, and he was pleased to see Rudi's indulgent smile as he stretched and yawned in the front seat.

'Welcome back,' he said. 'Have you finished playing in the mountains for today?' Then he saw the expression on Steve's face, and frowned. 'Did something happen?'

'Yes it did. Just tell me first, did you see the Range Rover come back past you?'

'Not really. I was dozing a little. The engine woke me as they went by.'

'Did they stop?'

'No.'

'Did they look at you?'

'I don't know, Steve. I thought what would you want me to do, and I kept my eyes closed until they were past.'

'Good.'

'So what is the new mystery?'

Maja gave him a factual account of what they had seen and heard on the mountain. She left nothing out and made no guesses. Rudi looked curiously at the streaks of dried blood still on her hands. The mist swirled around them again, and Steve shivered. 'Let's get back down out of the cloud and find some lunch somewhere.'

They parked in front of the Piz Buin Hotel in Klosters. Rudi brought the camera in with him for safety and put it on the floor next to his chair. They looked through the menu and ordered, then Rudi sat back and gazed across at Steve. 'OK,' he said, 'now I want to hear it. Why do two associates of a respectable businessman from Waldegg go out to film our favourite animals, then start to slaughter them?'

'They never meant to film the marmots,' said Steve slowly. 'I don't think they could have if they wanted to. That camera can't take pictures any more. We found those circuit boards and the tube, didn't we? They've taken out its works and put some sort of gun inside it.'

Rudi laughed a short, derisive laugh and looked sideways at Maja for support, but she was staring at Steve with an expression of fierce concentration. He looked back at Steve. 'You didn't see that.'

'No, but we heard it, with some kind of a silencer, I guess, and we saw the after-effects.'

'All you saw was some blood.'

'We saw them doing something with a bag. I think they

254

took the marmot's body away, either for safety or for proof to Cheeseman that it all works, perhaps.'

'That is still a lot of big guesses, Steve. Why would Cheeseman want to build a gun into a camera?'

Steve shook his head in frustration. 'I don't have any idea at all,' he said, 'at least about specifics. I think I can guess in general.'

'Tell me.'

'Come on, Rudi. I think it should be obvious. You've covered plenty of big news events. You tell me. Take a summit meeting. Security is so tight that your average Red Brigades terrorist with a Kalashnikov can't get within half a mile, right?'

'Yes, so?'

'Well, who gets to stand right in front of any world leader he likes, pointing a bloody great lump of equipment straight at him, looking through an aiming system into the bargain, without anyone taking the slightest notice?'

'A TV cameraman. OK, but you know they have to go through security as well.'

'Oh sure, but have you ever once seen a security guard ask to see the insides of a camera? They wouldn't know where to start.'

'They do sometimes ask you to switch it on for them.'

Maja broke in. 'Yes, but that is only to see the lights come on. They never know what else to look for.'

Rudi was silent now, just shaking his head. Steve went on. 'Look, Rudi, you and I both know that the only real check is the identity of the cameraman. You have to have accreditation organized or you won't pass go. In other words, if you can get the right paperwork from some TV company, no one is going to stop you stuffing the thing straight up the nose of any King, President or Prime Minister you care to name.'

The food arrived, and they broke off. Rudi took a mouthful of rösti, and started wagging his finger in the air to make another point before he had finished chewing. 'Yes, but where does Cheeseman come in? He is not Red Brigades or Baader–Meinhof surely. He is a nice Swiss capitalist, I think.'

Steve took a moment to answer. 'Not nice, and not Swiss, but the rest of it's true. I think, with him, life is all about money – at least, from what I've seen. It must be something about money.'

They ate in silence for a while, each thinking hard, then Rudi spoke again, in a quieter tone. 'Let us say maybe you are right, Steve. Just for the sake of the argument, yes? But it all starts from the killing of your Mr Jordan in the London riot. You would not even be here except for that happening. If this is some secret operation, that was not a very secret way to get a camera. There are lots of cameras in the world. There are even lots in Switzerland. Why kill someone in London just to get an obsolete camera? Surely any camera would do.'

'I haven't a clue,' said Steve.

'Well, I have,' said Maja, and they both looked at her. 'I think it is obvious,' she went on. 'The camera is an Ikegami 79D? Tell me, then, what is special about an Ikegami?'

Steve and Rudi looked at each other. Steve answered uncertainly, 'It's old?'

'Yes, but why is it old? Tell me why isn't it used much any more?'

'Because newer cameras make better pictures, and the U-Matic format has been replaced by a much better system,' said Rudi.

'Go on,' said Maja. 'What else was wrong with U-Matic?'

Rudi shook his head. 'You got a sore shoulder,' he said, and raised his eyebrows when Maja whooped her approval.

'You got it. Why was your shoulder sore?'

256

'Because the thing was so big and heavy.'

'YES. Big. Big enough. Look at this one.'

She bent down and picked Rudi's camera off the floor. 'It is small. Very short compared to the old one. There isn't much space inside it. Certainly not enough space to put in a gun, I guess,' and even Rudi was silent then.

Chapter Twenty-one

For Steve, the rest of that meal passed in a jumble of emotions. The remaining shreds of his recent paranoia fell away. He now knew for certain why Sunny had been killed, and he realized as well that his death had been the result of a casual chance, a simple equipment failure. It was the crew from the training course who would otherwise have been the target of the attack. And what then? he thought. He would still have been working in the BBC, and above all Sunny would still have been alive. He was silent for a while, that fresh and unexpected sorrow turning itself into a new and fierce determination to see it through.

The waitress brought glasses of Pflümli, the fiery Swiss schnapps, and Rudi started picking at the edges of Steve's theory once more. 'There is one problem.' He took up his camera again, and pointed at the lens. 'Multi-element glass. Very thick. Very strong. Extremely obvious if it is not there, and quite possibly enough to push a bullet the wrong way if you have to shoot through it.'

Steve nodded, thinking of the camera lens on display in the Editor's office back in the Spur, mounted on a stand to show the pistol bullet buried in it, a memento of the violent ending of a siege in France which nearly went terminally wrong for the cameraman. He took the handful of convex shards of clear plastic from his pocket and showed them to Rudi. 'They've thought of that. This is the remains of some kind of fake lens which just goes over the end to make it look right. It was scattered across the grass a few feet in front of where the camera had been.'

Rudi nodded, thinking hard, and sighed. 'Well, whatever, it is a very good story. You have covered all the angles. What are you going to do about it?'

'I really don't know.'

'You should go to the police in England maybe.'

'I'm not in very good standing with them at the moment. There is one man I could maybe talk to. What about the police here?'

'Oh, sure. You walk in and say, hello I am an Englishman and I accuse this rich citizen of Waldegg of plotting an assassination. If they laughed you would be lucky.'

'Suppose you went, Rudi?'

'The first thing they would do is look up my file. Subversive, eh? Trying to cause trouble. What proof do you have? And what proof do we have, Steve?'

'Not much, yet. I suppose we'd better get some.'

A thought struck Rudi. 'I hope they didn't see you,' he said.

But of course it wasn't Steve they'd seen, it was Rudi himself. On the motorway, Pfister was coming to the end of a long argument with the woman, Elena.

'He was asleep,' she said for the fifth or sixth time. 'He didn't even look up. He was just some harmless mountain lover, taking a break before he went walking. Maybe he was waiting for the fog to go away.'

Pfister wasn't having it. 'You take any risks you like, sweetheart, but I'm the one on the sharp end, and I believe in safety first.' He picked up the car phone and thumbed the number. 'He's not going to like this at all,' he said, and listened to it ringing.

'Get me Heller,' he said when the secretary answered, then when the man came on, 'Heller. Maybe we have some trouble, maybe we don't. There was a car up the mountain. He wasn't there when we went up, and there was no reason for him to be there when we came back. One man inside. Black Jeep Cherokee, and I don't like the number. It had come from Zürich. ZH 435879. Better find out who it belongs to.' He listened again, then said, 'Understood,' and hung up.

Elena looked sideways at him from the passenger seat. She didn't like him, but he was a lot better than Cheeseman, and he'd kept it strictly professional. He was catching on fast to his new role. 'Well?'

'Seems there's a panic on. We're called to an urgent meeting as soon as we get back. You and me both.'

Cheeseman was beside himself with rage. He seemed concerned less with damage limitation than with damage extension. Someone was going to take the blame for it, that was certain. As soon as they were all gathered, he turned on Heller.

'Your fucking intelligence isn't up to much, is it?'

'It took time. We did not know yesterday. How could we?'

Jacques, the thug, was there too, looking nervous. Cheeseman stood in the middle of the floor, glaring round at them all. 'For those who don't know,' he said, 'we have a small problem. We have had an untoward visit from an English journalist.' He held up a big, grainy blow-up of Steve's face taken from the surveillance cameras. 'This is him. The advice I was given two days ago was that he did not matter. He seemed only concerned in some financial dealings which are not important. Today, however, we hear different.' He turned to Heller and gave a sarcastic bow. 'Perhaps you would like to take the floor?'

Heller looked under strain, but kept emotion out of his voice. 'We now know that Steven Ross, the journalist, lost his job with the BBC a few days ago. That followed an incident of some sort at the OPEC meeting in Geneva. We do not know what the incident was, but the coincidence is remarkable. You were there, were you not?' he asked, looking at Pfister.

'Yes, but we didn't get involved with any of the others.'

'Nevertheless, something happened. The only other significant thing we can discover about Mr Ross is that he was injured during an attack on his cameraman in London, who subsequently died.'

Elena put two and two together and didn't like the sum one little bit. She uncoiled her legs and looked hard at Heller. 'Was the cameraman called Jordan?'

'Yes. How did you know?'

'You should remember. I gave you the book with his name in it which came with the camera equipment by mistake.'

All eyes were on her, and she looked derisively at Cheeseman. 'So we have a dead cameraman, a stolen camera and a reporter sniffing around trying to make it all add up? Brilliant.'

Cheeseman was so angry he could hardly talk. 'How in hell could he know it is the same camera?'

'Herr Heller,' said Elena, 'you said you had an Ikegami brochure. Go and get it please. It is time we took a good, close look at this camera.'

When he came back, they stood the camera on Cheeseman's desk and stared at the pictures in the brochure. It was only then, for the first time, that they realized the little red and gold badge was not part of the maker's logo.

'What the hell do I pay you for?' Cheeseman exploded. 'You bloody loonies fail to spot something as obvious as that. Ross must have seen it in Geneva.'

She wasn't taking that. 'I am not a camera expert. Whose

stupid idea was it to steal the camera in the first place? If you had bought one, we wouldn't be in this mess.'

Cheeseman swung round on Heller. 'Well?'

'That was not my instruction. I thought we had bought it second-hand in the regular way.'

'You'd better make sure the person you bought it from doesn't make that sort of mistake again,' he said with a level voice. 'Now, let's see what other loose ends might need tidying. First we do not know how Ross connected us with the camera. Second we do not know how much Ross has found out. What about the car they were using for filming?'

'Jacques has been checking on that,' said Heller, and they all looked at the leather-jacketed thug as he flipped open a notebook and read from it.

'It is a Citroën Safari registered to Jurg Camenzind. He is nothing to do with TV. He installs swimming-pools, and lives in Hegnau. Yesterday he lent it to a friend, however, who is a freelance TV cameraman. His name is ...' Jacques flipped over the page. '... Rudi Rohner.'

Heller made a curious sound, a half-strangled gasp, and the others all switched their gaze. 'You know the name?' asked Cheeseman sharply. Heller stared at him helplessly and nodded.

'Pfister called me on his way back. Just to check.' He looked at Pfister. 'He saw a Jeep parked down the track on their way back from the test. I checked the number.'

'And?'

'It is registered to Rohner, initial R, with an address in Rumlikon.'

There was a chorus of concern. Cheeseman flushed deep red. 'Incompetence. Complete bloody incompetence. You're all meant to be good and you're being followed around by amateurs.' He swung round to Elena. 'Could Rohner have seen any of the test?'

'The man in the car was asleep, if that was Rohner.' She looked again at the photo. 'Ross wasn't anywhere in sight. We didn't see him up the mountain at all. It was very cloudy and we took away all the remains.'

Cheeseman came to a decision. 'Right. You two go now,' he said to her, waving his hand to encompass Pfister. 'The others stay.'

'What are you going to do?' she said coldly.

'That is our affair.'

'No, it is mine too. If the security of this matter has been breached, I want to know all about it.'

'You can leave that to us. Go.'

He waited until it was just the three of them, then he said, 'We must assume that Ross and Rohner have knowledge that we do not wish them to have. They do not matter, but their knowledge does. It must be deleted.'

'They may have already gone to the authorities.'

'Not here, they haven't. I would know. In any case Ross is a journalist, and I think he will keep it between them until he has more information for his own purposes. Think first, though. It must not be on our doorstep.'

Jacques waved a hand at the door. 'What about her?'

'Our dago lady?'

'Yes. Her heart is not in this.'

'No, but her body is for the time being, and it will be staying in it. I have a very important part for her to play.'

The black Jeep at the centre of the storm was in fact only two miles away from Waldegg, coming off the motorway into Zürich. All the way back the conversation had gone round in circles. Rudi seemed half convinced now, but was still trying hard to search for holes. It came down to two unanswerable questions. Why was Cheeseman doing it, and what could they do about it? It was easier to say what they couldn't do. They all agreed there was no chance of persuading the Swiss to investigate on the scanty circumstantial evidence they had, and the absence of proof of what they'd seen in the mountains.

'There's the video,' said Steve.

'What does it show?' said Maja. 'Just a fuzzy long shot of two people with a camera and some blood on my hands.'

'Who is the woman?' said Rudi. 'There is another thing we do not know.'

'That's right.'

'So, Steve, what will you do?' asked Maja.

'Fly back tomorrow with the tapes and talk to Nick about what we've got, I think.'

'Will you come back?'

He looked at her, and she looked straight back into his eyes, open, friendly and breathtakingly attractive to him. 'Yes, I'm sure. Even if it's just to sit outside Cheeseman's house and see who comes and goes.'

'And be picked up by the police within two minutes for loitering,' said Rudi.

'Well, I'm sure we won't be just leaving it. There's more to come somehow.'

'Make sure it doesn't happen too quickly, then,' said Rudi. 'Tomorrow, for two weeks, the holiday starts and Rohner Video closes up its shop.'

'Oh, I see,' Steve said, with a sudden forlorn feeling. 'Are you going away?'

'Yes, right away. Completely out of touch.'

Zürich without Maja, and of course without Rudi, seemed a less magnetic place to return to. He nodded, taking it in and trying to work out the next step.

At the hotel, he kissed Maja on both cheeks and shook hands formally with Rudi. 'I hope it all works out, and I'll be over again when you get back,' he said.

'Yes. Keep your feet on the ground and your head on your shoulders,' said Rudi.

'Steve, maybe you should go to a different hotel tonight,' said Maja. 'I think it is a risk, because he knows where you are. Shall we take you to another one?'

But back here, in suburban Schlieren, with old hausfraus carrying their shopping past on the pavement and a large advertisement for chocolate on the billboard across the street, that seemed a little too dramatic. 'No, I'm sure it will be OK for one more night.'

'What time are you leaving?' she said, unhappily.

'10.30 flight tomorrow morning. I'll get a cab to the airport at 9.30.'

'No, no,' she said, 'we can fix you some transport. That will be OK.' She spoke rapidly to Rudi, and again Steve couldn't follow the Zürich patois, then she smiled and waved again as they drove off.

Steve went into the hotel, sad at their parting, but still savagely elated by the day's developments. He knew he carried with him enough proof from the typewriter tape to push the film project along. He called Nick to tell him his arrival time, but there was only an answering machine. The hotel clerk was near him, so he didn't go into any detail in his message.

When he finished and turned away, the clerk called to him, 'Herr Ross, you are checking out tomorrow? At what time?'

'After breakfast,' said Steve curtly.

'Do you want I make a plane reservation for you?'

That suddenly seemed suspiciously five-star service from this no-star flea-pit. 'No, thank you,' said Steve, 'I've done it already.'

Back in the room, he thought for a moment about plough-ing on through all the rest of the unread letters and messages on the typewriter ribbon, but decided to leave it until he had a German dictionary available. He took the briefcase with him and went into town to see a movie, delighted to find they were all in English, though the German and French subtitles covered up a large chunk of the lower screen.

It was after 11 p.m. when he came back to the room. The murder mystery he'd been watching and the dark combined to make him wish for a minute that he had moved somewhere else. He found a rubber door-wedge along the corridor and jammed it under the inside of his door, slanting a chairback under the door-handle for good measure. With the window locked shut, he lay in bed for a long time before sleeping, wondering if his precautions were necessary.

They weren't – but only because the two men assigned to watch him had already been through his room while he'd been watching the film. They'd found the notepad with the details of his re-booked flight to London, and they'd found the car park ticket for the Scimitar. Then they'd followed instructions and gone to Rudi's house.

Steve had paid his bill and was sitting in the foyer at half past nine the following morning, wondering if the transport Rudi had promised him would arrive. He had woken with a splitting head after sleeping with the window closed, and was now regretting the previous night's paranoia. He took his bag out on to the pavement, thinking he'd give it five minutes then hail a cab, but then a horn sounded and to his great surprise and delight Rudi's Cherokee pulled up to the kerb with Maja at the wheel.

'Jump in,' she said. 'I am sorry I was not earlier, but someone had broken into Rudi's house last night so we were held up with the police.'

He looked at her in sharp alarm. 'What happened?'

She shrugged. 'They were after money for drugs maybe.

266

They went through Rudi's desk. The police say it was Yugoslavs. That's what they always say.'

He should have asked more, but there was something more pressing on his mind.

'What are you doing here? I thought you had ... I mean, where's Rudi?'

She smiled, baffled at his surprise. 'Well, I dropped him at the airport. He is leaving for Greece this morning. He told you. Why? Is that bad?'

'I thought you were going too?'

She looked even more baffled. 'Me, no. I am staying here.'

'Don't you go on holidays with him?'

'No, of course not. Working with him is quite enough.'

Steve got in the car then, her words clanging in his brain, and stayed so quiet until they were on the Nordring approaching the Kloten turn-off that she kept looking at him worriedly.

She stopped outside the departure building. It was time to go. Steve decided to take the chance of appearing foolish. 'Maja,' he said, 'listen. When Rudi introduced us the very first time at the hotel, he said you were his new wife, so I thought you ...'

Her laughter stopped him. 'That is just an old joke. Rudi always has girls doing sound for him. I am the fourth or fifth. All the other cameramen call them Rudi's wives.' She stopped and looked at him gently. 'Why are you looking at me like that? You look so funny.'

'I don't think there's really time to tell you now. I have a plane to catch.'

'Steve. I thought perhaps you didn't like me. I would be glad if that is wrong.'

'Oh yes. That's wrong. Damn. I've got to go. I wish I didn't.'

She took his hand. 'Rudi has left me his keys. He has

agreed I can use his camera. Here is my number. When you have talked to Nick, call me. I will shoot for you.'

'I'll come back whatever Nick says.'

He left her there and walked through to the departure gate, past the same seated man who had noted the details of Rudi's flight to Greece just half an hour before.

Chapter Twenty-two

This time, Heathrow seemed to hold no horrors for Steve. Completely happy for the first time in weeks, he felt for a moment a slight sense of amused smugness at the brevity of the 'EC passport holders' queue compared to the long, long line suffering at the other desks. He was back in England again, where he knew how things worked. That feeling of belonging for once to the right club disappeared abruptly when the woman behind the desk flicked through his battered passport for much longer than usual, then looked back at him with an unsmiling face.

'Just wait here for a moment, would you Mr Ross?'

'Why?'

'I believe someone wishes to have a word with you.'

Whatever she did next wasn't apparent to Steve, but in answer to the pressing of some invisible button an equally unsmiling man appeared from a side-door. 'Mr Ross? Would you come with me please.'

'What's all this about?'

'I'm afraid I can't tell you.'

They went through swing-doors into a corridor, then into a small, bleak cubicle with a door marked Interview Room. 'Someone will be along to see you in a minute,' said the man, and went out.

Steve sat there drumming his fingers for two or three minutes, trying and rejecting a variety of explanations. The most unnerving possibility was that Cheeseman's ability to cause trouble extended beyond the frontiers of Switzerland.

It was almost a relief when the door opened and Detective Chief Inspector Brian Kitto walked in, though that brief feeling wore off as soon as he opened his mouth.

'Have you been having a good time in Switzerland, Mr Ross?'

'Good enough, thank you.'

Kitto sat down opposite him. 'I was wondering what you might have been doing there?'

'Come to that, Mr Kitto, I'm wondering what you might be doing here?'

'You suddenly disappeared off the face of the earth, Mr Ross. No one seemed to know where you'd gone. Then we had a query about you from the police in Switzerland which landed up on my desk, so it was easy enough to check flight lists after that.'

'What sort of query?'

'Just a query, that's all. They wanted to know what you were doing on their patch.'

Kitto's chosen style was slightly sarcastic politeness. He was watching Steve closely.

'And what did you tell them?'

'Don't worry. I marked their card for them. I told them you had a strong imagination and they shouldn't take too much notice if you started wasting their time.'

'Kind of you.'

'Oh, I promise, Mr Ross, I was very nice about you. I told them you'd had a bang on the head, and it wasn't your fault.'

'Look, Mr Kitto. I'm sure you didn't come all this way just to tell me that.'

'No, I didn't. Like I said before, what were you doing in Switzerland?'

Until that moment Steve had vaguely entertained the idea of trying again with Kitto, of putting to him all that he had seen and discovered. Now he looked across the desk and thought, you could make a crook out of him and not have too much left over. 'I don't think that's got much to do with you, has it?' he said.

Kitto's face darkened. 'Don't get smart with me. Everything you do is my business. Every single thing. Right now you are my biggest problem.' He got up, looming over Steve. 'Next week decides whether Gardiner walks free. You know, Gardiner, the spade that gave your mate the chop? Has that, by any chance, started to bother you yet?'

Steve looked up at him. 'I told you before, I can't help you either way on that.'

'And I told YOU to keep your opinions to yourself.'

'That's my affair, but as it happens I haven't a clue what you're talking about.'

Steve had to twist round in his chair as Kitto walked behind him. 'So you haven't been talking to Gardiner's lawyer?'

'No.'

Kitto nodded to himself. 'Well, when he finds you, do us both a favour and think twice before you start saying too much.'

'I've had quite enough of this, Mr Kitto. I'm starting to think it's about time I went to a lawyer myself, or maybe to your superior. I will tell anyone who asks me, whether it's you, Gardiner's lawyer or the Queen of Sheba, the same thing. I didn't identify Gardiner for the very good reason that I didn't recognize any black person there when it happened. OK?' He was standing too now, and Kitto took a step backwards. 'I would like to go now.'

'I don't think that's a very helpful attitude, Mr Ross. First I need your new address, which you are obliged to give me, being a material witness, then you can certainly go if you wish.' He paused, and the smile of someone about to tell a cruel joke came to his face. 'One thing, though, just a friendly warning. Your car in the car park.'

'What about it?'

'Reliant Scimitar, isn't it? Didn't look too well maintained to me. Front tyres are nearly down to the legal limit. I wouldn't like to see you get into any trouble with the police.'

Steve's bag was the only one left on the carousel by the time he got there, and the zip was half open as if to hammer home the message that it had been searched. He went out through the green channel without any more trouble, and stopped outside to marshal his thoughts. Keith Brice, he thought. I'd better talk to Brice. There's no one else around who's going to be much good.

Brice's number rang four or five times, then a man picked it up. 'Hello?'

'Oh, I was looking for Mr Brice.'

'Well, he's not here any more, I'm afraid. He retired last week. We're still recovering from the party. Can anyone else help?'

'No ... thank you. It was personal. I'll call him on his home number.'

'You'll have to leave it a couple of weeks, then. He's on a cruise. That was his leaving present.'

Steve rang Nick's number. The answering machine came on. 'This is Nick Nielsen. I'm not here at present. Please leave a message after the tone. If it's you, Steve, I'll be down at the boat.'

The courtesy bus took him to the off-airport parking-lot. He paid the bill for the Scimitar, commiserated with the man who brought it round to him about the difficulty he'd had starting it, slung his bag in the back, and settled himself into the sagging leather seat. He drove down the short exit road and stopped at the T-junction with the A4. The road was very busy – fast nose-to-tail traffic thundering along the dual carriageway. He was resigning himself to a long wait when a shadow filled the rear-view mirror. A big brown Transit van was close behind him. Very close. There was a gentle jolt as its bumpers touched his, and he frowned in annoyance. Stupid bugger, what was he playing at? Then the annoyance turned to sudden, penetrating alarm as the Transit revved its engine and started to push him fast into the bacon-slicer stream of traffic across his bows.

He put his foot hard on the brake and managed to stop the Scimitar's forward progress. He craned round over his shoulder to see what was going on, but the van was too high. All he could see was its grille and the bottom few inches of the windscreen. Then it backed off a foot or so, and, in the second before it smashed hard into his rear end again, he saw the round outline of the full-face motor cycle crash-helmet covering the driver's features.

There was a noise of splintering glass fibre as it hit him, and his car was propelled another foot into the traffic before, pushing desperately on the brake until his calf muscles throbbed with the strain, he managed to stop it. Now horns were sounding as the fast-moving traffic in the near lane was being forced to jink round him. The Transit backed up to try again, and he saw the slenderest chance. A lorry went by, horn complaining, barely an inch clear of his front wing. Behind it a black cab had just pulled out into the fast lane and there was the tiniest of gaps before the next car.

He slammed it into gear and dropped the clutch, with the engine revving its heart out. The car slewed sideways on wailing tyres, and fishtailed up the road. The Renault coming up behind locked its wheels to avoid him, and Steve heard the screaming rubber of the chain reaction behind it. The driver of the car beside him was shaking his fist and gibbering at him, but Steve thought, to hell with this, and ignored him.

He turned left, back into the airport, to get down on to the access road to the M4, thinking only of getting clear. As he pulled away from the roundabout, he saw in his rear-view mirror the brown Transit, lurching at high speed on to the straight a hundred yards behind him. Until that moment he had cherished the tiny hope that he'd simply got mixed up in someone else's problem, some villain doing a runner from a raid. That hope disappeared with the certain knowledge that he was the target and, unless Brian Kitto had gone completely off his head, it had to be Cheeseman's doing.

So what do you do when you're going up a motorway followed by a van that's trying to kill you? Go like hell, thought Steve. A Scimitar has to be faster than a Ford Transit. I'll worry about it all later, he thought – but there was a belch from the carburettor as he mashed the throttle open, and a misfire from at least one of the six old spark-plugs. Down the short westbound length of the M4 and left into the stock-car race frenzy of the M25, he was holding his ground with the Transit, ten cars behind him. Then it began to close on him and, with the misfire getting worse, he could do nothing about it. It was coming up on his rear quarter when the Scimitar seemed to pull itself together and leapt forward with all six cylinders chiming in, but it didn't last and soon the big van was looming up behind again.

Steve was doing around eighty-five, trying for every extra mile an hour, when he passed a big artic in the slow lane and saw the police car cruising along in front of it. He felt a tremendous sense of relief and cut in front, slowing down. All I need do is flash left, he thought, and pull on to the hard shoulder. They're bound to stop to see what's wrong. Before he could, two things happened at once. The Transit went past him in the outside lane and the police car's blue lights came on in his mirror.

He was out of the door almost before the Scimitar had stopped, running back to the car behind as the two policemen got out of it.

'Did you see that brown Transit?' he said. 'You've got to stop it. The driver tried to kill me back there.'

'One thing at a time, sir, if you don't mind,' said the nearer policeman, raising his eyebrows at the other one. 'We would just like to take a look at your car. This *is* your car, is it, sir?'

'Look, for Christ's sake. The driver was wearing a crash-helmet and he did his best to shove me in front of a truck.'

'Did you get the number of this van, sir?' The policeman sounded like someone humouring a child.

'No, I didn't. But if you pull your finger out, he's only gone about half a mile down the road.'

'Look, if you don't mind, sir, we were actually stopping you because we wanted to check the condition of your vehicle.'

'*You* were stopping *me*? I was pulling in to get *you* to stop.'

The policeman gave Steve the look of a man whose patience was wearing thin, and walked round to the front of the Scimitar. He bent down to look at the front tyres, and that's when it clicked with Steve that Kitto must have put the word out to give him a hard time.

'Not much tread left on these, I'd say.' The policeman took a little instrument out of his pocket and stuck it into the front tyre. 'Right on the limit.'

'I'll get them changed,' said Steve distantly, realizing there would be no help from their quarter.

They looked all round the rest of the car, Steve sitting on the bonnet, staring at the traffic. Then one of them called him round. 'Would you come and look at this, please, sir?'

The rear-light and indicator cover on the nearside of the car was crushed and splintered. The glass fibre panel around it was split, torn out of shape by the impact of the Transit.

'That's an offence, I'm afraid, sir. Were you aware your rear-lights were defective?'

'That's what I was trying to tell you. That's where this bloody van hit me.'

'Did the driver stop, sir?'

'NO. It wasn't really that sort of an accident.'

'Do you happen to have your documents on you, sir?'

'Why don't you stop calling me sir,' said Steve. 'You think I'm as mad as a hatter and you've been told to hassle me, so why be polite?' So they looked at each other and breathalysed him. Steve found he really didn't mind the pointless delay. At least it was taking the brown Transit further away down the road.

Then there was the paperwork, the careful inspection of his driving-licence, the form requiring him to take the rest of his documents to a police station before the end of the week, and then they'd had enough of him. They sat in their car while he drove off, but he was in no hurry to go anywhere by himself, so he stayed in the slow lane at fifty miles per hour until they passed him, then he tucked in behind them for safety. They pulled off at the Weybridge exit, and he briefly considered following them as far as they were going, for protection. Then he pulled himself together and decided the Transit must be long gone. Five seconds later he was beyond the point of no return, going under the bridge, and five seconds after that he felt the sweat break out all down his spine as the brown van accelerated down the slip-road behind him.

A police Land Rover drove past going the other way, the far side of the crash barriers and as inaccessible as if it had been on the moon. There was dense traffic around him, but it didn't help, and the Scimitar's engine was still fluffing and spluttering. Steve tried to consider his options as calmly as possible and simply couldn't come up with anything useful. He didn't fancy stopping on the hard shoulder with them behind him. He seemed unable to outrun them, and it was four miles to the next exit.

There was a big truck ahead of him in the middle lane. He overtook it and slotted back in front of it, staying as close as possible. There were temporary road signs ahead for a contraflow system. Cones squeezed his three lanes into two, leaving him, still in front of the truck, in the fast lane. It filled his mirrors and he could no longer see the Transit. Then his carriageway ended completely, and the two lanes kinked amid a slalom of cones, through a gap in the barrier on to the other side of the road. The oncoming traffic was using one lane and the hard shoulder. He was separated only by cones from the cars tearing past the other way, two feet to his right, at a closing speed of 120 miles per hour.

He glanced left and was relieved to see an old Ford, full of family, in the other lane. Then it drew slightly ahead, and coming up from behind into its place was the brown Transit. He looked at it transfixed. There was nothing he could do. He had a truck right behind him, another in front. He couldn't go left and he couldn't go right. Then the Transit came at him. He met its impact by swerving left into it and holding his wheel on left lock to combat the pushing. The truck behind started sounding its horn and the Transit bounced off. It came back at him again, and this time he couldn't hold it. Suddenly his windscreen was full of flying cones, tumbling over the front of the car with loud thuds, then he was through into the oncoming fast lane staring at a car coming straight at him. He had time to see the smoke coming off its wheels and the wide-mouthed, horrified stare of the driver as he jinked to the right, missing a coach in the furthest lane by inches in the kind of situation most people only ever experience in video games.

There was no spare room. The hard shoulder was in use as the slow lane. Beyond that was an uneven verge. He hit it, bouncing on the bumpy grass, still doing fifty or more as another truck blared past, a foot away. He hit the brake but the car started to slide. On the grass, at least there was no more oncoming traffic, but there was a steep rise to a concrete bridge support ahead, and there wasn't time to stop. He jabbed the brake pedal in rapid cadence braking, trying to take off as much speed as he could each time before the tyres locked, but he was still doing forty with the bridge only yards away, so he wrenched the wheel over and yanked the handbrake. The Scimitar broadsided, slowing rapidly in a shower of divots of grass. The start of the slope up to the bridge took off the last of its speed, and he stopped, tilted on the slope at forty-five degrees, panting and staring at the traffic tearing past, six feet from the nose of the car.

The traffic going the other way was still moving, carrying the truck and the van away from him, white faces in the first few cars, turned, staring at him. One by one the scattered cones were crushed or sent scudding across the tarmac out of the way, but soon the cars which had seen the incident were past, and the M25 roared on oblivious. He got out and looked at the long gouge in the passenger door of the car, and the smashed front headlamp. Then he got back in, edged down the slope, and waited for a gap in the traffic to go back the other way. He headed for the south coast on the smallest roads he could find.

Chapter Twenty-three

It took Rudi hours to reach his destination, but he was in a holiday mood and not about to make a big issue out of anything. Athens airport was its usual baking, anarchic self. The shuttle down to Préveza left with all the punctuality of a Central American bus service, and there was no sign of the hire-car he'd ordered when he finally got there. Swiss travel agents regarded Greek suppliers like missionaries dealing with cannibals, hope alone sustaining them across a cultural divide they could never bridge.

So Rudi caught the bus from the little airfield, down the coast, past the old Venetian castle, and over the causeway to the island of Levkás. He didn't even bother to try to call Zürich about the car. He knew it wouldn't be worth the time and trouble. He would have been surprised to know how busy those phone lines had already been that morning on the subject of Rudi Rohner, and even more surprised to learn that a car had been specially allocated entirely to his cause, though not his comfort. The battered old Fiat following well back in the bus's dusty wake had nothing else in mind.

He got out of the bus in the square near the small harbour, savouring the random combination of concrete blocks and old stone, Coca-Cola and ouzo, olive trees and motor bikes, which gave it such a permanently temporary quality. The tourist office was easy to find and shady, and the agent was apologetic about the car. He showed him the location of the apartment on the map, a few miles down the coast, then locked the office and ran him down there in his own car, figuring, for a Swiss booking, the extra rent would cover him for any lost business in the process.

It was a two-room apartment with a balcony overlooking the sea. Rudi liked it and began to unpack. The agent left him there and the man in the old Fiat went to look for a phone.

Cheeseman had taken Heller up to his hill. That was the way Heller had come to think of it. There was something about the Uetliberg, with its wooded slopes looking out across the lake of Zürich, which reminded Cheeseman of his far-away childhood, as Heller knew from one uncharacteristically open remark years ago. Normally, neither of them were open people. Heller was a Swiss banker at heart who had adapted perfectly to the role of Cheeseman's major-domo, business fixer and middleman. He provided the layer of insulation between Cheeseman's plans and the sharp end of their implementation.

The summons to the Uetliberg told Heller he was back in favour and Cheeseman was in a mood to play God under the pine trees yet again, getting his pleasure from the planning of far-off havoc as they strolled along the hillside path.

'I hope your man in England does a good job of it.'

'He is very resourceful. He does not give up.'

'What about Rohner?'

'So far so good, Herr Cheeseman. As I told you, we know where he is. There is someone watching his house.'

'I think we must find out what they know and who they have told. It will be easier to do that in Greece with Rohner than in England with Ross.'

'That means moving more men.'

Cheeseman stooped to pick up a pine cone, and stood

staring out through the screen of trees. 'Maybe it means moving a woman first.'

'Herr Cheeseman?'

'Let's put the dago to work. Put her alongside Rohner. Tell her to sweet-talk him. After all, her neck's on the block.'

'She is not easy to persuade.'

Cheeseman pulled one segment off the pine cone with a sharp twist. 'You just have to talk the right language. Tell her she can have the other passport back and all the money when she comes back from Greece. Tell her if she does this, the job is finished. Give her the letter of instruction to the Bank so she knows it's for real.'

'Is it?'

Cheeseman just looked at him and pulled another piece off the pine cone.

'What if it is all too late? What if they have already told people?'

Cheeseman went on tearing pieces off the pine cone. 'I think they are people of little credibility who have stumbled into it flat-footed.' He threw the naked stem of the cone into the forest. 'We can deal with that, but, if not, then my friends had better look for a different route to salvation and you and I had better look for a new source of income.'

It took Steve a long time to reach the boat. First he stopped at a garage and put new plugs in the Scimitar. Even then, with the engine restored to something approaching its former power, he studied each road junction, lay-by and bridge he approached for signs of a brown Transit, or indeed anything else that might pose a threat. He was driving fast, but, every time another car seemed to show any interest, he took random side-turnings until it disappeared. He got lost many times, but found he felt safer when he didn't know where he was.

He went over and over it in his head. Logically, they shouldn't yet know about the boat. Kitto hadn't been able to find him, so how could they? But who were they? How far did their powers stretch? If they could casually arrange for a hooligan to have a go at him on the M25, the answer to that question seemed to be a very long way.

Going straight to the boat seemed unwise, but there was a place to park on the opposite side of the river with a good view across, and Steve took a long, hard look. Nothing was moving. He gave it half an hour to be sure, then drove slowly across the bridge to the main car park. It contained only the usual motley assortment of the boat-dwellers' vehicles, an old coach, a rusty Morris Traveller and a plastic kit car poised somewhere between messy completion and returning to its component parts.

He looked around carefully before going on to the boat. The door was locked – untouched – and opened to a surprising scene. The cabin had been repainted, white, bright and fresh. There was a vase of flowers on the table. Down below too, the dinginess had given way to fresh white paint, and the smell of river mud had vanished. Rosie, he thought to himself, and went to say thank-you.

As he crossed her gangway, loud strains of 'I'm forever blowing bubbles' were coming from her sound system. He walked across the deck to the door, and his footsteps were heard from within, because the sound was turned down and a deep male voice called, 'Is that you, Bubbles?' Nick Nielsen, naked but for the towel round his expansive waist, opened the door. He laughed at Steve's surprised expression.

'Steve. Great. What kept you?'

'Quite a lot. Pour me a drink and I'll tell you.'

It took an hour, and Rosie came back soon after he started, so he had to say some of it twice. The scene on the mountain seemed a million miles away, pushed into the background by the moments of terror on the motorway. He expected to have a hard job persuading them, and was surprised to find them hanging on his every word, but then he couldn't see himself as they saw him. He'd gone away a victim and returned a warrior, a glint of dangerous determination replacing the nervous flicker in his eyes. He took them out to show them the scars on the car, and demonstrated the trick of the typewriter ribbon, and they looked, not for corroboration, but in spellbound interest.

Nick lit a cigarette, and Steve realized he hadn't eaten. Rosie pushed a bowl of fruit across the table to him. 'I'll cook you something,' she said. 'Have one of these to keep you going.' In the middle of the pile of oranges, bananas and pears was a perfect-looking peach. He reached for it, and she burst out laughing. 'I don't recommend that one.'

He picked it up, startled by the cold, hard texture and the massive weight. 'It's alabaster,' said Nick. 'I gave it to Rosie yesterday. Good, don't you think?'

'Not just good. It's incredible. You would never know.' He took a banana instead. 'What do we do now, Nick?' he said while he ate it. 'There's got to be enough for Wessex to go ahead, hasn't there?'

Nick drummed his fingers on the table. 'It isn't that simple, is it? There's a man who seems to want you dead, and that sort of thing tends to get a little bit in the way of making movies, I find. So what do we do about it?'

'I don't know. I'm going round in circles on that. If there was another policeman we already knew, we might stand a chance, but it'll get straight back to Kitto if we go to anyone else, and he'll just rubbish us. What about you and the American Embassy?'

'Same thing. There's just a bunch of ideas. No proof. If they believed it, they'd still contact the police here and in Switzerland straight away.'

'OK, Nick. Maybe it's time to carry the war into the enemy's camp. Let's go back in strength, full film crew, lights, producer, the works. We'll be so bloody obvious about it, he won't be able to do a thing. Put him on tape every step of the way. Don't let him move out of the house without having a camera on him.'

'That means Wessex have to front up with the rest of the money. Do you have enough on that ribbon to persuade them?'

'Yes but that's the next job. I need a German dictionary and a few hours.'

Rosie had been looking increasingly thoughtful. 'It's time to start taking precautions. Why don't you do the work here? It won't do any harm to stay away from the other boat just in case.'

Nick nodded. 'Come on. Let's go buy a dictionary, then we can leave your car somewhere over the other side, in case anyone should be looking for it.'

In the car, Steve paused for a moment before switching on. 'Do we still tell Wessex this is only about insider trading?'

'You bet. You want to scare the shit out of them? Anyway, what else are you going to tell them?'

'Well, this could just turn into a much stronger story.'

'Of course it could, but there's kind of a tradition that detective stories start with a murder and work through the motive and the weapon to get to the suspect, you know? Trouble with this one is you've got it the wrong way round. It might just confuse them a little if we say, hey guys, we've got this great story, the only thing is, all we know at the moment is what they're going to use for a weapon.'

Steve started the car. 'You're right, but if we keep our eyes open maybe something will come up.'

'One thing at a time,' said Nick. 'Anyway, it's good to see

you looking happy again. Switzerland can't have been all bad.'

In the apartment on Sihlstrasse, Heller was cranking up all his persuasive powers. 'You have nothing to lose from this,' he said. 'Your other passport, immediate access to all the money and a further bonus. You will be free to leave here immediately you return from Greece. You may watch as we fax an irrevocable instruction to the bank.'

'I don't know,' she said. 'There's been too much I haven't known about this one all along.'

'There can be no problem. All you have to do is go and talk to him. A few days in the sun at our expense.'

'And if he already knows my face?'

'How can he? He was asleep when you went past his car.'

That made her angry. 'Sure. And he got there by accident? Do you think I am an idiot? Either someone told him where we would be or he followed us there, and in that case he may have seen me.'

He held up his hands to calm her down. 'I know, I know. That is something we do not have the answer to, but Pfister says he is sure the Jeep was not following you.'

He knotted his fingers, thinking for a moment of what Cheeseman had said when he'd raised that problem earlier – one dago bitch looks just like another to any decent white man.

'In any case,' he went on, 'you will know immediately if he is suspicious, and then you will simply leave.'

She still hesitated, and he used the final argument in his locker. 'It is in your interests, too. You must see that we all need to be quite sure that he does not know too much about what you have been doing.'

'And if he does? What will you do then? Will you hurt him?'

285

Extraordinary, he thought, why should that matter to her? 'No,' he said, 'that would only make things worse. We shall simply know we have to abandon our plan.'

She looked at him hard. 'It would make a big difference,' she said, 'if I knew the identity of the target.'

'You know I cannot tell you,' he said, looking at her and recognizing how much it mattered in her decision. 'But I can assure you it is a really bad man.'

She stared out of the window, and he heard a tram rumble past. She shuddered.

'If you go, we will give you your American passport back at the airport,' he said.

'I'll go.'

When she was alone again, she looked at the wall for a long time, rubbing her gloved hand. Her missing fingers were hurting badly.

Back at Waldegg, Heller reported his success to Cheeseman. 'She is very squeamish for someone in her profession.'

Cheeseman smiled. 'Squeamish and just a little stupid for someone so clever. He's coming back in a box, but I still want to know whether he saw anything, and whether he told anyone if he did.'

'She won't be very happy.'

'Her happiness isn't high on my list of priorities, Heller. I don't think she will carry her sorrow into her old age.'

Steve sat in the forepeak of Rosie's boat, staring at the dictionary in mounting excitement. *Genauigkeit* was the word he'd been looking for. Accuracy was the word given, so *auf Genauigkeit prüfen* was to test something for accuracy. Nick sat opposite him, studying the text of the five letters he had already translated. Five letters which, added to the earlier one, gave them enough to crucify Cheeseman and Dandycap, and certainly enough to persuade Wessex TV to commit all the money they could possibly need. Quite apart from blatantly breaking the insider trading laws, Dandycap had clearly been stashing away millions of shares in a recent, highly contested takeover bid, in exchange for a big bribe from a very big name indeed.

What Steve had moved on to was another of those scrappy messages, less badly typed than the last and probably by a different hand because this one was in German, but still needing a certain amount of deciphering. It started off about *ein Termin für Fertigstellung*. Steve didn't need the dictionary for that. A deadline for readiness. Then it went on about the testing for accuracy, then it came back to the question of dates again. July 12th, it said. July 12th was the vital day. Steve double-checked his watch. This was Tuesday July 9th. The 12th was Friday. He looked at Nick. 'We've got a when as well as a what,' he said. 'Now all we need is a who, where and why.'

They had a council of war over spaghetti bolognese and cheap red wine as the twilight chilled the river. Steve peered out at the river bank, and felt exposed inside the brightly lit window. He pulled the curtains. They all looked at the translation of the note. 'The deadline is clearly set,' it said. 'Now that there is a solution to the problem of accuracy, the first deadline date of July 12th at the path is to be definitely adhered to.'

'What's this about the path?' asked Nick.

'I don't know. It doesn't make any sense to me. The original says WEG in capitals. That's as near as I can get. *Weg* translates to path.'

'Who would know what's happening on July 12th?'

'Foreign News would, at the Spur. I can't really call them out of the blue and ask, though.'

'Can you still get into the computer from outside?'

Steve looked at him and smiled slowly. 'That's it. Of course

287

I can. I'll bet they haven't wiped my password yet. Trouble is, we haven't got a computer.'

'Oh yes we have,' said Nick. 'I've got a little Tandy with a modem in the back of the car. If you know the phone number, I can get you in.'

They set up the minicomputer, dialled the external line for access to the BBC's Basys news computer, and pushed the phone handset into the flimsy rubber cups. There were some high-pitched electronic squeals, then a click, and a moment of pure magic as the screen display came up with the BBC's invitation to sign on. Steve tapped in his ident with bated breath. There was a second or two when nothing happened, then the screen filled, and Basys in all its glory was at his service.

He cursored to the right into the home news diary, and scrolled through to the entry for the following Friday. There was a minor royal visit, a test match, a welter of Government statistics and a late-night speech by the Prime Minister.

'Try the foreign diary,' said Nick.

'I'm going to. I thought I'd save the best to last.'

It was more promising. A big Nazi war crimes trial was getting under way in the US. An enquiry was due to report in Italy on the sinking of a passenger ferry. Two Soviet divisions were due to pull out of East Germany. The verdict was expected in the Italian Mafia trial. And then he saw it.

'World Economic Forum. Davos. Switzerland. Start of five days of high-level talks. Many world leaders in attendance. Coverage, Diana Pugh and crew, arriving via Zürich a.m. 11th.' He looked round at Nick and Rosie. 'That's it. That's got to be it. Jesus, they only did the test three or four miles away from there.' He looked at his notes again. 'See? It was another mistake. Forget path. It isn't WEG at all, it's WEF.'

'Fine,' said Nick. 'What the hell's that?'

'Some big talking-shop. To tell you the truth, I've vaguely heard of it, but I'm not quite sure.'

'How do we find out?'

'Now we've got this far, I'll try ringing the desk. It depends who's on.'

He called the direct dial number for the Foreign Duty Editor. It was five minutes after the end of the *Nine O'Clock News*, and he sounded in a hurry.

'Steve? Good Lord, what do you want?'

'Hello, Larry. Look, I wondered if you could just do me a very quick favour and look in the file for the Forum in Davos on Friday. I just need some details.'

'You don't ask much do you? Keeping a man from his drink. You should know better.'

'I'm sorry, mate. I'd buy you a drink if I was still allowed in the building.'

'Well, on the grounds that some of us think it's a crying shame you're not, I'll take two minutes off my drinking time. No more, mind.'

He left the phone for a moment or two, then came back. 'Got it. What do you want to know?'

'Well, what it is, and who's there, really.'

'It's the ultimate talkfest. Run out of Geneva in the interests of world etcetera etcetera. Sort of giant get-together for rubbing your ideas off on each other on top of an alp. Says here there's two thousand political leaders and businessmen. Press coverage is virtually invitation only. Security is as tight as a gnat's arse.'

'Who's on the big name list?'

A trace of impatience crept into Larry's voice. 'Everybody as far as I can see. There's fifteen Prime Ministers for starters. There's even some cock about a set piece debate between Yeltsin and Gorbachev, but that's not official yet. Listen, Steve, if you want to know, why don't you ring Diana? I happen to know she's at home because she's just rung me, and, unlike me, she hasn't got a pint of Guinness waiting for her.'

Steve looked up Diana's home number in his book. She answered on the first ring. 'Diana? Sorry to bother you. It's Steve Ross.'

'Good heavens, the walking dead in person. What on earth can I do for you at this time of night?'

'Can you spare a minute to give me a quick run-down on the World Economic Forum?'

'You're just so romantic, Steve.' She sounded a little drunk, and there was some whispering in the background.

'You're covering it. I just need to know who's going to be there.'

'All right. Wait a mo.' He heard papers rustling, and she came back. 'Prime Ministers of the following, er ... France, Belgium, Spain, Yugoslavia, Poland, Australia, Zimbabwe, South Africa, Colombia, Norway, Nigeria and about six or seven tiddlers. Plus some sort of special Gulf debate with an Iraqi up against a top Kuwaiti, and top ministers from the USA, Britain and so on. Then there's this Gorbachev–Yeltsin thing, but no one knows if that's really happening, plus most of the top brass of the world's top hundred companies. Is that enough for you?'

He thanked her and hung up, then gave the others the low-down. Nick looked at him. 'Great. Now you haven't got a mystery target, you've got two dozen bloody obvious ones. I don't think that makes us much better off.'

Chapter Twenty-four

There was one clip too few, and it was annoying Rudi. He concentrated on not letting it annoy him, with limited success. The throw-away paper tablecloth was held on to the plastic table by small metal clips. It needed four, one for each side, but it only had three. Worse than that, the missing clip was on the upwind side, so the wind kept flicking the cloth up into his yoghurt. In most ways the taverna was almost perfect for breakfast, sitting right by the beach with its patio looking across at the little inlet on the edge of Nydri towards the smaller islands out in the bay.

Rudi had already dealt with the minor irritations, the tepid coffee and the patina on the glass which contained his orange juice. It was just this one big irritation, really, and that produced the first major dilemma of his holiday. He could move round to the other side of the table and put his plate on the flapping triangle. That would stop it flapping, but it would mean he couldn't look out across the sea any more. He could move one of the three other clips, but he was quite sure that would mark him down to the other holiday makers at the tables around him as Swiss, just as surely as if he took out a red and white flag and began to yodel – and Swiss was something that Rudi had come to Greece not to be.

He knew what his problem was. Within Switzerland he was a shade too cynical and a shade too iconoclastic to fit easily into that structured, strictured society. Outside Switzerland he was a shade too clean and a shade too regular to pass as anything else. He should have been born in Germany, or at least in the French-speaking part of Switzerland, he thought – or even in the Tessin, though those Italian speakers were really a bit too sloppy ... He interrupted that train of thought with an angry rebuke to himself and settled for putting the empty yoghurt pot on the loose corner. A gust of warm, thyme-scented wind flipped the cloth, pot and all, up into the air and across the table to land upside down on his trousers.

An hour later, trousers scrubbed and hanging over his balcony to dry, Rudi was lying on the beach below the apartment. Two hours of reading, he thought, with the occasional swim, then maybe some windsurfing later on. He looked down at himself. His lower legs and his forearms were tanned from weekend walking in the alps. The rest needed a bit of sun, then he might go looking for a lady.

Lounging on the sand, propped on one elbow, he found it hard to stop thinking about Steve. It was all very disturbing. He wished he didn't feel involved. It would be nice if he could simply write Steve off as a hysterical Englishman given to fantasy, but it was impossible to think of that quiet, hard man, with the eyes that seemed to look right through you, and not take him seriously. Then he thought of Maja and smiled to himself. She believed Steve for sure, and there was clearly more than just belief involved. I hope he doesn't hurt her, he thought. They have both had bad times and they both deserve some comfort. He looked around the sand thinking, if he'd met Maja here, as a beach girl, not as a professional colleague, he would have wanted a different relationship, but work was work. That was when he noticed the woman lying down twenty yards to his right.

She had spotted him from the pathway through the long grass at the back of the beach, and stood studying him for a while before she took her place, just near enough and just far enough away. She would have remembered his face and that high, intelligent forehead even without the help of the picture, but the sleazy little man called Nicos had insisted she look at it when he met her at the airport. He'd chosen the hotel because it was only two hundred yards from the apartment, he said. She should keep in regular touch with him or his wife by phone. She should get in contact with Rohner as soon as she could in case he moved on.

Now she glanced across at Rudi from where she lay on the sand, and their eyes intersected for a moment before he looked quickly away. She suppressed an urge to giggle. There he was, stretched out on his brand-new straw mat, the towel spread tidily over it, and his blow-up pillow to stop sand getting in his hair. In the plastic box next to him she could see all the necessities of life. Suntan oil, some books, a water bottle and a pair, no, two pairs of dark glasses. Why two? she thought. In case he loses one? Or are they different strengths?

Rudi couldn't believe his first glance. She was the sort of girl you saw on the beach at Rio, not in the Aegean. She had the dark skin of some of the Greek girls, but none of the incipient dumpiness. He took another quick peek. So slim, such incredibly long legs, and the face was something else. Sculptured in complex arching curves, it was not easy to take in all at once. Framed by a cascade of shining dark hair, it was a face you would pause at in a magazine, and be transfixed by in the street. She looked at him then, and he held her gaze for a moment. She looked neither friendly nor unfriendly – more curious, really, and he dropped his eyes first.

He didn't feel relaxed enough yet. French, perhaps he should try feeling French. He put down the book he was reading and sighed. Five minutes went by during which he stared up at the cloudless sky, trying to imagine being a

Parisian, and wound up feeling only slightly depressed. He glanced at her again. She was sitting up, fiddling with something. She had a camera in her hand, with the back open, and was trying to load the film. Rudi watched, glad to have the opportunity of looking at her while she was distracted. She wore both halves of a black bikini, unusually on this mostly topless beach, and it was only then, for the first time, that he noticed the black glove covering her left hand.

He barely had time to notice that before she turned her head and saw him looking. He smiled. She looked bothered. 'Excuse me,' she said, 'do you speak English?'

'Yes, certainly,' said Rudi, 'can I help?'

'Are you any good with cameras?' she said. 'This one is new, and I can't see how to load the film.' She had a pleasing voice, throaty, with a mostly American accent.

He was never more pleased to be asked. He got to his feet, put his box of things on the towel to keep it in place, and went over to her. 'What is the problem?' he said.

'There doesn't seem to be anywhere to push the end of the film into the other spool.'

He took it from her and looked at it. It was a Canon EOS 1000, and he knew the system well. 'It's OK. This is fully automatic. You just pull the film out level with this line and close the back.' There was a whirring as the camera wound all the film out.

'Why is it doing that?' she said.

'Don't worry, it's meant to. It's a good idea. The film rewinds into the cassette with every picture you shoot. That means if something should happen, like the back opening, you don't lose all the pictures you've taken.'

She smiled at him. A bit shy, very charming, he thought. 'That is very kind, how do you know so much about cameras?'

He laughed, 'I am a cameraman, though for TV, not with these, but I also use stills cameras a lot. They're not so different, each one from another.' He stuck out his hand. 'I am Rudi, from Zürich in Switzerland,' he said.

He has a nice voice, she thought, soft and wise. 'I am Elena,' she said, because it seemed suddenly easier to tell the truth, 'and I come from Colombia.'

He squatted on the sand next to her. 'You are a long way from home.'

That's a little obvious, she thought. 'Yes, I know,' she said. Rudi put on a comical face and raised his eyes and the palms of his hands towards the sky. 'Well, I had to say something,' he said. 'Why don't you come to the taverna with me. We will have a cold drink.'

He looked for a table with all four clips in place, and sat opposite her. 'Why are you looking at me like that?' she said.

'I'm sorry. It's just that you are very nice to look at. How do you come to be here in Levkás?' he said, meaning are you by yourself?

'I have been travelling for a time in Europe, and I wanted to see Greece a little,' she said. 'What about you?'

'Oh, no reason. I like the Greek islands, and I had not been to this one before.'

'What sort of camera work do you do?' she said.

'Anything that comes along, but almost always for TV. I am freelance. I work often for foreign TV companies needing to shoot in Switzerland.'

'That sounds fun.'

'Yes, sometimes. It is fun if the client is fun, otherwise it can be terrible. What do you do?'

'I am lucky. Nothing much these days.'

Rudi was a direct person, and he reached across gently and touched her glove. 'What happened to your hand?'

She flinched and pulled it away from him, off the table, then saw the concern in his eyes. 'I'm sorry,' he said, 'I did not mean to offend you, but you were stroking it as if it hurt.'

'It does sometimes,' she admitted, softening. 'It was the result of my work in Colombia.' He waited until she went on. 'I was involved with explosives,' she said, 'for a Government department, and there was an accident.'

'But I too am involved with explosives,' he said. 'What a strange coincidence. I am a demolition specialist in the army as well as a cameraman. Tell me what you did.'

So she did, and the briefest flare of suspicion that had surfaced in him at the mention of explosives was lulled away by the warmth of her voice and the piercing beauty of her face. She told him about her work in DAS and he told her funny stories of the serious make-believe world of the Swiss army, of exercises in blowing up gravel pits because there weren't any spare bridges on which to practise. When they left the taverna to swim together, she was laughing, and Nicos, up the beach, put down his binoculars and decided all was going to plan.

Rudi spent the afternoon thanking his lucky stars he had picked Levkás, and that beach on that day, never suspecting for a moment that this was a lottery he could not have lost. They swam, lunched, and swam some more. By the end of the afternoon she knew enough about bridge demolition to bring the whole of Switzerland to a complete halt, and muscles unused for four years ached from laughter.

In that period between late afternoon and early evening all the prostrate bodies got up one by one, leaving the cooling sand like a rumpled bed. The sun touched the trees on the headland across the bay, and the heat fell out of the colours around them. She suddenly shivered.

'Are you cold?'

'No, but it is getting a little cooler. I must go back to my hotel now. I have some things I must do.'

Rudi looked at her anxiously. 'I have enjoyed our day. I was hoping we might have a meal tonight, unless you have something else planned?'

She hesitated a moment, knowing her mission compelled her to accept, and finding she wanted to as well, but also not wanting to for that same double reason.

'Yes,' she said, 'I would like that. Where shall I meet you?'

Back in her room, she sat for a while musing on the day, then picked up the phone. Nicos's wife answered at the fifth or sixth ring. She could hear tinny bouzouki music in the background. It sounded like a bar or a café.

'Nicos ees no 'ere,' said the woman. 'Soon 'e phone you.'

She waited fifteen minutes for the call. He was abrupt and harsh, no hint about him of the co-conspirator. How does Cheeseman do it? she thought, everywhere he finds men like himself.

'What has he told you?' he said, with a voice corroded by years of chewing tobacco.

'Nothing yet. I must go slowly.'

'Not too slowly. Tomorrow you must push him.'

'Why?'

'That is what they tell me from Zürich to say to you. Tomorrow you must ask questions.'

In the bath, trying to concentrate on a plan of action, one half of her brain ambushed the other by breaking into a little schoolgirl song. She stopped in surprise after three or four bars, recognizing that the brief exposure to the warmth of an ordinary, caring human being had brought a temporary springtime to the long winter of her soul. My name is Judas, she thought. How can I do this? But then she rationalized. Rudi can't know anything, he's too straight-forward to hide it. All I've got to do is to confirm that for

297

Cheeseman, and everyone will be satisfied. She chose some simple clothes with great care and went out to meet him.

Rudi was at the table when she arrived. He saw her as she stepped in from the outer darkness under the string of coloured light-bulbs and thought he had never seen anyone so beautiful or, if he had, he had certainly never been waiting to have dinner with them. He waved, and she threaded her way between the tables to him. He stood. 'Elena,' he said, then just looked at her in frank admiration. She wore the plainest white T-shirt and white cotton jeans, and the effect got them the fastest and most devoted service from the waiter he could ever remember in that unhurried country. He asked for retsina, and she was surprised by the unfamiliar resinous taste of the wine. The meal of kleftiko and salad came, but the food was only an excuse to be there for both of them, and its indifferent quality passed unnoticed.

'Rudi,' she said, 'you told me a lot about the army. What about your real job? Tell me about that.'

'Well, there's not much to it,' he said. 'People pay me to take pictures for them, and I do it.'

'Oh come on,' she said, 'that doesn't tell me much. I know. Tell me about the very last job you did before you came here. Everything about it. I want to hear the smallest detail.'

He laughed. 'Oh no. Not that one. That was not a typical job. If I tell you that one, you will think my life is VERY exciting,' and her heart sank. 'I will tell you about the one before,' he said, and there followed a long and detailed story of a shoot for a documentary producer of the intricate history of the Zürich craft guilds. She let his voice wash over her, relaxing in the knowledge that this was safe ground. She looked at him while he talked. You can see the shape of his skull, she thought, there's so little spare flesh on his face, but he has such kind eyes, and such a funny little smile.

He came to the end of the tale and looked at her quietly,

then he reached out and gently took her gloved hand in both of his. 'Now,' he said, 'fair exchange. You will please tell me the real story of how this happened.'

'No,' she said, a heartbeat too fast.

'Yes,' he said. 'I can guess some of it. It was done cruelly and it hurt you much more deeply than the physical pain.'

She looked up at him then, and he suddenly thought, she's much younger than I realized. This is just a – what? – 25, maybe 26-year-old, hiding inside a hard shell.

'I haven't talked about it for four years,' she said.

'Then all the more reason to tell me now.'

'If I start I might not be able to stop.'

'That does not matter.'

Later they walked back to Rudi's apartment along the beach with their arms tight around each other, in the aftermath of shared sorrow, surrounded by a bubble which cut out everything except the sand under their feet and the trickling sighs of the little evening waves. Standing on the balcony in the moonlight, he kissed her with his hands on her warm back under her T-shirt, then led her across the room to the bed. A motor bike crackled past down the lane outside, but it didn't penetrate to their private, timeless world. She kissed him again, lying over him, her hair tumbling around him to join their faces in a dark, private tunnel. He felt her fingers undoing the buttons of his shirt, but raised a hand and stopped her.

'First this,' he said, and she froze while he gently, slowly, peeled the black leather glove from her maimed hand. She looked in startled wonder while he kissed the remaining fingers and the torn flesh around them with an intimacy she had never imagined sharing.

They made love, in a sensual slippery tangle of damp warmth and suntan oil. The sheet stuck to them and twined around them, so they could not have pulled apart even had they wanted to. Four years of pent-up sexuality exploded in Elena with a fervour that battered and delighted Rudi, and they lay in each other's arms afterwards like survivors of a catastrophe.

At dawn, Rudi awoke from an urgent dream with a memory of a job undone, and sat up in bed sharply. He hadn't given Steve the new message from Hugo. He doubted there was anything in it, but he had meant to pass it on for all that. 'Scheissdreck!' he said, then in the same instant he remembered Elena's presence, missed her next to him, and located her sitting in the chair on the balcony, wearing just her T-shirt.

She got up and came to him. 'What is it?'

'I'm sorry. Good morning. I was dreaming, but it was for real. It reminded me I forgot something very important when I left Zürich.'

She lay on the bed and gazed into his eyes. 'Tell me?'

'Just something I should have told the man I have been working with.'

'Oh, the exciting last job?'

He kissed the end of her nose and smiled. 'Yes, that one.'

'Come on,' she said, 'I woke and I couldn't sleep. Tell me the story. I'd like to hear it.'

So, in this separated, far-away world of their own, he told her, and horror rose in her at how much he knew and what that meant. Before he'd finished talking she already knew she had to create a lie for Cheeseman's ears. At the end he said quietly, 'What do you think? It all sounds a little too unlikely, yes?' but to avoid answering, she covered his mouth with hers. The creaking of the bed, and the rising pitch of her moans, came through loud and clear to the radio receiver on the tape recorder in the motor cycle top-box fifty yards away, and not until sleep quietened the two sated bodies did the voice-actuated microphones hidden round the apartment silently flick back to their stand-by mode.

When they woke again, Rudi watched her. She's sad now, he thought. Perhaps it was all too much too fast, last night. She is blaming herself, withdrawing from me.

'I must go back to my room for some clothes and things,' she said, 'shall we meet later on the beach?' and he gazed after her from the balcony as she walked away.

Nicos was taciturn on the telephone. Elena reported that Rudi knew almost nothing. 'You must phone Switzerland,' he said, 'they want to talk to you.'

'But it is still early there.'

'No matter. They are awake.'

It took four attempts before the Greek phone system could get her that far. Heller came on the phone. 'What have you discovered?'

'Rohner is just a cameraman,' she said. 'He took the shots Ross wanted, but Ross never said why.'

'Why was he in the mountains?'

She had an answer ready for that one. 'He had followed us. We didn't see him. He stayed in the car while Ross went up the mountain, but Ross couldn't find us in the cloud and came down in a very bad temper. He wouldn't tell Rohner what it was all about. Rohner says he does not like to waste his time, and he does not like Ross. He will not work with him again.'

Heller said, 'Wait a minute please,' and the phone went silent, switched off at the other end. It was some time before he came back on. 'You have done well,' he said, 'we are pleased. We will now follow our half of the bargain. Nicos will arrange a flight back and you may collect the rest of your money here.'

An hour later she was sitting on the end of a flimsy wooden jetty, old, faded fishing boats riding the tiny wavelets that rippled beneath her feet, looking out at the wooded island in the bay. Heller was too glib. His reaction was too fast. She did not believe those people would let go so easily and so completely. What to do? Warn Rudi, that was the thing. Take him to some quiet place and just tell him the story, as simply as she could, and then, one way or another, take the consequences.

She rose to her feet, but there was a creak of boards behind her, and a hand came on her shoulder, pushing her down again. She jerked her head round and saw Rudi himself, standing laughing, then dropping to sit next to her, taking her hand in his.

'You were a long time,' he said. 'I came to meet you and I saw you here. What were you thinking about?'

'I was thinking about quiet places,' she said, nodding at the island. 'I would like to go to a quiet place with you today, away from the people.'

'Poet's island,' he said, waving out into the bay. 'Though its real name is Mandouri. Home of the late Aristotle Valaoritis, one of Greece's most famous poets of recent times.'

'How do you know that?'

'I thought everyone knew that. Or if that isn't quiet enough, there is Cape Doukata, where the poetess Sappho leapt to her death after her rejection by Phaon, being dashed to death on a unusual species of freshwater crab.'

She stared at him. 'What are you talking about, what crab?'

'It is true. It is what my book says, look.' He brought from his bag a small guidebook and held it out with the page open. She looked at it. 'Idiot,' she said, 'you turned over two pages. It was the rocks below she was dashed to death on.' But by then she was laughing, and their arms were round each other, and maybe it was all going to be all right.

'Nowhere that's in a guidebook,' she said, 'I don't want to go where all the others go.'

She decided to tell him in the afternoon. At lunchtime they got up off the beach and went to the taverna for fresh fish and salad. An old man with short pepper-and-salt whiskers poking from the creases and folds of a face like a deflating football raised his glass to them from the next table and drank their health. They laughed and drank his in turn. He took his stick from the back of his seat and lumbered over to them, putting his hand on her shoulder as he sat down.

'How do you like my island of Levkás?' he said.

'Very much,' said Rudi.

'You must be sure to see its sights,' said the old man. 'Have you seen the waterfall and the Cape where Sappho leaped?'

'Not yet. We were thinking of going there this afternoon.'

'And Neohori. Have you seen Neohori?'

'That's not in my book.'

'No, Neohori is not in the guidebooks. No one goes there.'

'What is it?'

'It is an old village. On top of this mountain here, behind Nydri. It is deserted since the earthquake and all the houses are falling down but it is very beautiful.'

She smiled at him. 'It sounds lovely. How do we get there?'

'You must have a car or, better, a jeep. It is a steep, bad road.'

Rudi nodded. 'Maybe I hire one later on. We could go.'

The old man looked at Elena, and winked. 'For the pretty lady. I eat my lunch slow these days, then I sit here in the sun until maybe three-thirty. Why don't you take my car? It is outside now, and I am sure it would be honoured to take you up the mountain. Just bring it back in two hours. That will be very fine.'

303

'You are very kind,' she said. 'That would be just perfect.'

He took them to the dusty car park and gave them the keys of a beaten-up Citroën Mehari. The remains of two seats were the only creature comforts in its minimal, open, plastic body, apart from the steering-wheel, but the engine clattered into life when the old man showed Rudi the trick, and, waving their goodbyes, they set off for the track up the mountain, touched by his insistence.

It was more of a goat track, winding up past hairpin after hairpin, affording increasingly spectacular views across the islands, with Skorpios, the Onassis island, in the background. The scream of the tiny engine and the demented rattling and banging from every part of the old machine as they lurched up over the rocks ruled out conversation, so Elena spent the time rehearsing what to say, and what to suggest they should do.

They arrived on a sudden, unexpected plateau and parked under a shady tree by a church which still looked in good condition. The sun was baking down. A lizard perched on the wall watching them, and they looked around at a strange sight. The village street, rock overgrown with wild grasses, meandered away across the plateau. The ground rose slightly to one side, and everywhere there stood the jumbled interlocked remains of the damaged houses, some almost complete still, some showing nothing more than a few stone archways jutting from a mound of loose stone slabs.

She took Rudi's arm and steered him up the street, wandering slowly, thinking, thinking. On a small hill rising above the other houses was a larger building which had stood the earthquake shock better than most. It had open arches through each of its walls into a roofless interior. This is the place, she thought, and led him in. It had a solemn feeling, a tiny Parthenon full of silence. He swung her round to him, to put his arms round her. 'Rudi,' she said, 'I must tell you something.' The noise of an engine sounded for a moment out on the track and she frowned.

'What is it?' he said quietly.

'It's about your friend Steve,' she said, then a rock fell somewhere just outside the walls and she turned her head. Two men stepped in through the archway. Damn it, she thought for a moment, I thought he said tourists didn't come here – but then Rudi was looking over her shoulder with narrowed eyes and the flickering interruptions to the sunlight told of more arrivals. She swung around. The nearest man was heavily built with cropped hair and he was no tourist, and nor were the three others behind him.

There was no weapon to hand but stones, no route of escape but the archways, and each of those was blocked. She knew it was the end of them. In her dangerous life, she had imagined such an ending many times, but always by herself. She would have rushed at one of them, but this time there was someone else to think about, a greater priority. She heard the hiss of Rudi's indrawn breath. 'What is this?'

She gripped his upper arms, forcing him to look away from the men and back at her. 'I brought you here to warn you. I wanted to save you. I did not bring them here.'

But that was all there was time for. Arms grabbed her from behind, pinioning her. She kicked out backwards, but the only response was to find one arm forced agonizingly higher behind her back. She saw Rudi land an ineffectual blow on another man, then two of them had him between them, and he tugged and twisted to no avail, screaming Schweizerdeutsch at them, pulled by panic across a gulf of language from her, separating her even from the contact of his words.

They'll beat him in front of me, she thought. They'll get the information and then what? They'll kill him and I have almost no time to stop them. But she didn't know they already had all they needed. Another man stepped through the arch into the interior and walked up to Rudi. As his head was pulled back sharply by his hair, Rudi shouted one word despairingly, 'Elena!' then there was a flash of steel in the hand of the man in front of him, and a choking, bubbling sound as blood splashed and ran from the great cut from side to side of Rudi's throat. They dropped him then, and she watched as he fell to the ground, one hand moving towards the cut. He died before it could get there.

The man with the knife turned. It was Nicos. He crossed to her and smiled into her face. 'We listened to you both in his room. We knew your treachery. Did you think they believed your stupid tale in Switzerland?' But by then her hands were clenching and unclenching, and a tide of white fury climbed bursting into her brain. The injection they gave her was almost unnecessary. She could have done nothing if she'd wanted to.

They took her to the battered old Nissan Patrol which had been tucked out of sight along the road, and she was unconscious on the back seat when, engine roaring in four-wheel drive, it was backed up against the wall of the building, wheels spinning and pushing until all the old, dry, loose stonework of the wall crashed down over Rudi in a rumbling, dusty heap. One of them took the Mehari down the hill to give the old man his reward, and the rest headed for the airport and the private medical flight booked for the poor, sick lady all the way back to Zürich. She was already in the air by the time the last of the dust settled back to earth, leaving just one more unremarkable ruin among all the remains of Neohori.

Chapter Twenty-five

The sunlight flickered in the doorway and his arms were grabbed from behind. He let out a yell and tried to pull free, then heard Nick's chuckle and relaxed. 'Jesus, Nick, don't do that. I've been jumping every time I hear a seagull land.'

'Sorry, guy, didn't realize it was getting to you so much. You want to hear a progress report?'

Nick sprawled on Rosie's leather sofa and put his feet on her coffee-table. It was half past eleven on Wednesday morning. 'Of course I do, any luck?'

'Maybe. It's nail-biting time. Twenty pounds worth of fax bills so far. These fax bureaux get away with daylight robbery. Anyway, the Director of Programmes likes it. He read it as it came over.'

'And the answer is yes?'

'Not yet. They've got some goddam board meeting most of the day about the franchise. He can't pull the right people together until it's over.'

'He knows the urgency?'

'Damn right. I told him it's a yes today or not at all.'

'They bought the budget too?'

Nick balanced the air with his open palms. 'Pretty much. A few niggles. The usual accountants' crap. Nothing we can't sort out as we go along.'

They'd spent hours burning the midnight oil round Rosie's table, putting together a treatment of the programme to get the final go-ahead from Wessex. As fact went, it was pretty much a work of fiction. What they had in the can didn't add up to much – some fairly indifferent pictures from Switzerland and the transcripts from the typewriter ribbon, but it would have taken an expert in the art of TV flimflam to spot that from the document they had put together.

By the time they added in the other locations – Sark, London and the US – and had pulled out of thin air a notional series of interviews with Stock Exchange officials, it looked like a programme. Adding in the populist angle – the vignettes of the workers in the great industrial company whose livelihood was threatened by the takeover battle won through Dandycap's hidden and illegal help – it looked like a strong programme, and that was without stepping outside the stocks and shares angle at all.

'So if they say yes, it's back to Zürich first?' Steve asked.

'You got it. I told them getting Cheeseman's face on tape was the top of the priority list, so I guess they won't be asking too many questions if we divert through this place Davos along the way.'

'So what do we do while we wait, Nick?'

'Go for broke. Start making the bookings. Call Rudi and have him ready.'

'It's not Rudi. He's away. Maja said she could manage OK, and she'll find someone to do sound.'

He didn't seem able to stop a smile coming over his face as he spoke her name, and Nick looked at him, considering. 'OK, fine by me. She's good news. We travel tomorrow.'

Steve looked out of the cabin window towards the other boat. 'I'm not wild about staying here until then.'

'No one's been yet. I don't think anyone's going to find us. Maybe your man in the truck was just some glue-sniffer with a beef about sports cars.'

'You wouldn't have said that if you'd been there.'

'Well, OK. It won't do any harm to go up to the Smoke.

You can sleep on my floor for the night. As soon as we've got Wessex's answer, we'll go.'

'When will that be?'

'They're sending a fax back around four o'clock.'

From the air, the houseboats looked quite seaworthy. The vertical view hid the worst of the modifications to their upper works. Their hulls looked almost unchanged. Beyond them he could see Shoreham harbour, with its great power station in the process of slow demolition, and, beyond that, the sweep of the sea down east to the white cliffs of the Seven Sisters, and back the other way past Worthing to Goring and Littlehampton beyond.

The Cessna wobbled in an air current, and Nick swore. Steve enjoyed light planes, and the student who'd suddenly cancelled his after-lunch lesson with Rosie had created an opportunity which was too good to miss. Nick wasn't so sure. 'Real airplanes have cabin staff,' he growled, 'cabin staff who give you lots of alcohol so you forget the way the things can fall out of the sky. This is just a buggy with wings on it.'

Steve looked down. There was a haze of blue smoke round the stern of one of the big torpedo-boats. Pugwash must be playing with his engines again. It looked like he'd been working on the hull. He had his little dinghy in the water, bobbing alongside with the outboard on the back. Further up the line there was some serious rebuilding work in progress on one of the Fairmile launches. Its foredeck timber had been lifted, showing a plan view straight down into a bedroom.

Rosie banked the plane round. 'Time to go back,' she said, 'I'll just join the circuit.'

Their approach took them over the edge of Shoreham. Steve looked down on the village, then spotted the car park where he'd left the Scimitar. Someone was bending down, looking in through the window. He stiffened and twisted his head as they passed. It was hard to make him out clearly, squinting down at an extreme angle through the scratched plastic of the Cessna's side-window, but he seemed to be not much more than a kid, a punk haircut and some kind of fluorescent multicoloured jacket.

They bumped down on to the airfield and, while they taxied back to the apron, he brooded briefly on it. Probably just some car-mad youth, and anyway they'd be out of there in a couple of hours. For all that, as they walked back down the river bank, he took a good look around him.

Nick went with Rosie in her car to wait for Wessex's reply at the fax bureau. Steve started packing up the documents in Rosie's boat. He'd stayed away from Nick's own boat completely, but now he realized he would need the clothes in the suitcase in the lower cabin. For a few minutes he found excuses not to go over and get them, waiting for the others to come back, but then he became irritated with himself and his cowardliness and decided to get it over with.

Even then he was extremely careful. He looked all around before crossing the gangplank, and, after he had tested the door to make sure it was still locked, he did a tour of inspection of the upper deck, looking in through the windows of the deck house to make sure nothing had been disturbed. Only then did he unlock the door and go inside. It all felt childish as he folded and packed the clothes in the gloom at the bottom of the ladder. He was glad, when he heard Nick's returning footsteps on the upper deck, that he hadn't been found waiting for them at the other boat. It stopped feeling childish when the legs coming down the ladder turned out not to be Nick's at all, but belonged instead to the punk in the multicoloured jacket who had been looking at his car. Before surprise at the intrusion had

310

even been overtaken by indignation, the bottom of Steve's stomach dropped out as the punk reached unhurriedly inside the jacket and took out a large handgun. Then Steve felt very serious indeed.

There was no sound for a moment or two. Steve stared at the gunman, and the gunman stared back. He was older than Steve had thought when he glimpsed him from the plane. The haircut was more GI tough with some growth in it than deliberate punk. The skin was white and stretched, and he kept blinking, but nothing else about him was unsteady. The gun looked like an American Army Colt. There was a short, bulbous silencer projecting from the barrel, and the hole in the end looked large enough to put your finger down. Under the jacket he wore a green combat-coloured T-shirt. Steve took in all this in the briefest of moments.

'What the hell do you want?' he said, his voice squeaking.

'You. Ross,' said the man in an unexpected Scots accent.

'My name's not Ross. I was just calling in.'

'Fuck that. You're Ross. I saw you, you bastard. I was in the brown truck.' The man grinned. 'Say bye byes Ross.'

In that bizarre second when all that would come into Steve's agnostic mind were the words of the Lord's Prayer, footsteps sounded, running on the deck, and Rosie's excited voice called, 'Steve? Where are you? They've said yes.'

Her foot appeared, groping for the top step of the steep, dark ladder. Steve screamed 'Run!' with lungs paralysed by prickling terror, and the foot withdrew. The gunman swore and raced up the ladder. Steve heard a crash and a yell from Rosie above, and went up it after them. He found Rosie sprawled back against the side of the cabin with the man holding the gun against her stomach. There was a clang and sound of running feet outside, and they all looked at once to see Nick race away across the gangplank and down the path towards Rosie's boat.

'You've blown it,' said Steve. 'He'll phone the police. Why don't you just walk away? We won't stop you.'

The man pulled Rosie in front of him and pressed the gun in her back. 'Come on,' he said, 'we'll go and see what he's doing. All together now, and your friend gets hers first if you start fucking around.'

They went fast down the deserted tow-path, Steve being herded in front. He hoped for a second the man wouldn't know where Nick had gone, but it seemed he had done his homework. He pushed them ahead across the gangplank and into the boat's main cabin, where Nick was just saying 'Police, please' with desperate urgency into the handset. There was a crash of breaking plastic and the phone disintegrated. Steve registered with surprise that the impact of the bullet made much more noise than the discharge of the gun, then decided that was knowledge he would rather not have come by when the gun swung back to him.

'Down the end, all youse,' the man said. 'All in a nice wee line on the couch.'

'These people are nothing to do with this,' said Steve.

'A bit late to say that, wouldn't you think?' said the man. 'They were paying me for one, so I'm sure there'll be a nice bonus for three.'

There was nowhere else to go, so they shuffled to the end of the cabin, forming slowly into a ragged line between the table and the couch, with Rosie between Nick and Steve. She was making a quiet sobbing noise in her throat, and none of them moved to sit down. That seemed too final.

'So who's going first?' said the man, but he didn't seem to expect an answer. His eyes were unnaturally wide and he was breathing fast.

If this were a film, we'd jump him, thought Steve. If this

were a film, I would have some mysterious way of leaping through twelve feet of intervening space in far less than the time it takes him to move his finger an eighth of an inch. What a load of shit, he thought. This man is going to shoot us and there is nothing we can do. His mind raced fruitlessly, and as he started to accept that there really wasn't any way out, the cold fuzz of panic began to take over. He glanced sideways and saw Rosie blinking uncontrollably, her lips moving. Then he looked at Nick and saw in his face only calm determination.

Nick moved an arm and the gun barrel swung sharply towards him. 'Keep still,' the man barked, 'and I told you to sit down.'

'Whoa,' said Nick, 'I just want an apple, that's all.'

The gunman stared hard at the fruit bowl, then looked at Nick. 'OK, take one. Move slowly.' Then he laughed. 'But that makes you the first. Two bites and it's bye-bye time.'

Nick took a pace forward to the table, and reached deliberately for an apple. He picked one up, then put it down and reached back to the bowl. His hand fastened on a peach.

'You said an apple.'

'So? Does it matter?' Suddenly Nick was raising his voice. 'What goddam difference does it make to you whether I eat an apple or a peach? Jesus, as if it wasn't bad enough already being shot by a goddamned amateur.'

The man raised an eyebrow, still smiling. 'I'm no amateur, my friend. Cut the bullshit and eat the peach. One bite now, that's all you get for the cheek, then bang.'

He was well out of their reach. Steve tensed, ready to move if Nick moved, and rating their chances at zero. But Nick was furious. 'One bite? That's not what you said, you fucking limey scumbag. What's it to you if I have two goddam bites.' His face was turning purple, contorted in anger, and the man was starting to giggle. 'If it's one bite,

313

you eat the goddam thing,' and, fuming, he drew back his hand and threw the peach straight at the gunman.

The man was laughing aloud, and raised his gun, not even bothering to avoid the hurtling fruit, so that, when it hit the side of his forehead with all its alabaster mass behind it, the gun went flying from his hand and he sprawled back over a chair and down on to the floor with a surprised screech. Nick and Steve dived after him, colliding with each other. Steve got his fingertips to the trigger guard of the gun and flicked it back along the floor behind him, away from the man's reach.

The man got to his feet and ran through the door and across the gangplank. Steve dithered for a moment, but Nick roared 'Come on' and they all went after him. The gunman took a few paces along the path, stopped, and turned back towards them. There was a click, and a long steel blade sprang out of the black object in his hand. He took another step towards them, one eye glaring and the other already closing under a massive swelling.

Nick and Steve both took a pace backwards, but then there was a popping noise from just behind them and the concrete in front of the man's feet exploded in a fan of dust and splinters. A second pop produced a sound of breaking glass from the houses beyond him, and he took to his heels. They turned and Rosie stood there, holding the silenced Colt out in front of her with both hands. She fired again. The bullet ricocheted, whining off the concrete, and the man swerved wildly and plunged down the bank between two boats.

'Attagirl,' yelled Nick. 'After him.'

They heard the sound of an outboard starting and, as they came level with the place, saw him making off across the river in Pugwash's little dinghy, its blunt bow rising steeply out of the water under full throttle. Alerted by the sound, Pugwash came out on to the bridge of his boat and bellowed in rage when he saw his property disappearing across the Adur. The old man bent down, fiddled around, and then the river bank erupted into noise and smoke as the three great Packard engines came to life. Pugwash was shouting to them, but they couldn't hear. He ran forward and cast off his bowlines, waving furiously at them as he raced back to the bridge.

'Oh shit,' Rosie screamed above the noise, 'he's going after him. He wants us to let go the stern lines.'

She started to run forward, but Pugwash had given up waiting. The rumble of a dozen lorries turned to the lumpy roar of a Lancaster bomber taking off as he opened the throttles. There was a moment when they couldn't see through the smoke cloud and could scarcely breathe, then a loud crash as the gangplank came to pieces and a pile of old bicycles cascaded into the river. Two twangs marked the parting of the ancient stern lines, but Pugwash had forgotten the chain secured to the Samson-post halfway along his stern. The boat was moving forward fast now, and there was a tremendous lurch as the chain came up tight, followed by a splintering crash as the transom and half the stern was ripped out of the patched-up old hull.

They stood aghast on the shore, watching as, despite it all, the old MTB, trailing furniture and carpets out of the gaping wound in its backside, bellowed out in furious pursuit of the tiny dinghy, Pugwash waving his arms from the bridge. The spitting, coughing Packards forced the old hulk through the water at enough speed to send the bow rearing out of the water. It was a dying leopard racing a healthy Pekingese. By the time the boats were halfway across the river, Pugwash was abreast of the dinghy, towering over it a few feet away.

What he intended to do about it never became clear,

because there was an audible scream as one of the MTB's ancient propeller shafts seized in its old bushes, then snapped, and the great boat, heeling ponderously under the sudden asymmetric thrust, turned sharply to starboard, straight over and through the dinghy and its occupant. Pugwash cut the engines and the boat slowed, settling drunkenly by the stern into the water. The smoke cloud it had trailed behind it dispersed in the fresh sea breeze. The rumbling echoes of the exhaust bounced under the road bridge and fled away into silence. In the last of the wake, a few bits of glass fibre bobbed slowly along the surface of the Adur towards the sea, and that was all.

Nick took the gun from Rosie, rubbed it hard all over with his handkerchief, and tossed it down the bank to land near where the dinghy had been. The MTB was slowly turning, listing heavily, struggling back against the tide with its engines ticking over. Pugwash was peering over the side at the water with a worried expression. Somewhere on the far side of the river, a police car's two-tone horn started wailing.

'Anyway,' said Nick, 'I wish people wouldn't keep interrupting. We were coming to tell you Wessex have bought the whole story. The money's there. It's time to go to war, boyo.'

Chapter Twenty-six

The high drone of the little jet's engine still filled her ears long after the plane had come in over the low hills north of Zürich and landed at Kloten. The drugs made her dip in and out of consciousness, incapable of speech, floppy as a rag doll. She was faintly aware of the conversations that got her through some minimal officialdom and into a private ambulance waiting on the tarmac at the bottom of the plane's steps. The world reeled and whirled around her when she opened her eyes, and it was easier to stop trying, to wait for the next wave of nothingness to take away the memory of red frothing blood.

There was a second injection from a woman in nurse's uniform in the ambulance, and, when she next had any awareness, the motion and the noise had stopped. She opened her eyes, and the light just brought pain. It took minutes of blinking to get the tears away from her eyes and then, through a headache of almost unbearable intensity, she could make out her immediate surroundings. She lay, spread like a starfish, on a large wooden bed in a wood-panelled room. Her wrists and her ankles were bound tightly to the four corners of the bed. She had no sensation in her legs except for a painful prickling, and could not move at all. The room was fairly bare, just a few shelves and a picture of a lake, but through a small window on the right-hand side she could see a steep spur of mountain with blue sky beyond, and heavy cables on pylons up the profile of the slope.

Her tongue was like a piece of old cardboard, and she had no moisture in her parched throat, so, when the door opened and Cheeseman walked in, she could say nothing. He sat on the end of the bed and stared at her with a look of private amusement. 'So,' he said, 'in spite of all I paid you, you changed sides. Not very clever. Did you think I would just let you walk away?'

She made a thick noise, and he shook his head, then got to his feet. There was a basin in the corner, and he filled a glass, then poured it, at arm's length, all over her face. Thirst forced her to open her mouth, despite her pride, and she took as much water as she could, trying to hold it for long enough to soak through the crust on her tongue and the clogging in her throat. She swallowed with sharp pain, and lifted her chin to look at him as he sat down again on the side of the bed.

'You're just a silly girl playing men's games,' he said. 'We had your room wired as well in case you went there. We had someone watching you wherever you went.'

'You said you wouldn't hurt him.' She could still only mumble, and couldn't put the venom she wanted into her voice. It came out like a child's complaint.

He looked at her with brutal amusement on his face. 'I said he wouldn't be hurt, not that he wouldn't be killed. Knife cuts don't hurt for the first few seconds, you know. Anyway, don't you tell me I didn't keep a bargain. You fucked him, and you told us lies.'

She looked away and closed her eyes, but she couldn't keep his voice out of her ears. 'Now you're going to make up for it,' he said. 'You're going to carry the can for our little escapade here. There's a car down the road, rented in your name, and there's enough paperwork in the back to hang it all on you to the full satisfaction of any policeman who goes looking. I can just sit tight and no one will come near me.'

There was a slight sensation of pressure around her numb legs, and she opened her eyes to see his hand moving up the inside of her thigh, under the thin cotton dress she had put over her bikini to go up the mountain in Levkás. He stared down at her with contemptuous lust, and his hand came up hard into her crotch. She flinched, but kept her eyes on him, filled with cold, cold hate as he squeezed and fingered her. 'I know what you did with him, you stupid slut. I listened to it all, every little whimper. I reckon what's good enough for him is good enough for me.'

She felt the sharp tug as he put his hand in her bikini bottom and ripped it away, then he fumbled with his own clothes for a while before he lowered his body on top of her. She tried to bring her legs together against the bindings, but he reached down, hooked a hand under one of her knees, forcing it out and sideways, then pinioned her with his weight, and forced his way, dry and brutal, into her. She smelt his sweat and she concentrated on hating him, not even closing her eyes, but staring into his with a message of death which only seemed to fuel his frenzy. But as the pain mounted, the sickness, which had served her so ill so many times, finally came to her rescue, and the whiteness rose into her head, blotting him out in a thick fog.

When she came back to her senses, it was with the muddled sleepiness which always followed her fits. The bonds which still held her spreadeagled and the growth of burning pain between her legs soon brought her out of that. She opened her eyes, and they wouldn't focus properly. The room was empty. The window was less bright. On the wall facing her was something which hadn't been there before, something large, square and grey.

She tried to make it out, but it swam in and out of her

blurred vision. She could see it was a face, and that something was written above it. She blinked her eyes, and it came suddenly into brief, sharp focus. The words above it in thick, felt-penned letters said THE TARGET. She stared at the face. She knew it at once. It was a face of peace and wisdom, familiar from a thousand newspapers. She used her voice then, screaming and yelling as loudly as she could, but no one came.

Steve and Nick had passed the first hurdle of the check-in desk and were standing in different lines for passport control. This was the moment it might all come unravelled, and Steve was wondering whether Rosie had been able to give them the time they needed. It was almost a disappointment when the man simply looked at the cover of his passport and waved him through.

He waited the far side and watched Nick's successful passage with relief. 'So far, so good,' he said. 'Good old Rosie.'

'Time for a drink before they call the flight,' said Nick. 'Maybe even time for two.'

'Then we can drink her health. She deserves it.'

In the shocked aftermath of the hold-up and the sinking, they'd had to make their plans at great speed. 'You two mustn't stay here,' said Rosie. 'If you start trying to explain you'll still be here this time next week. Get going now. Phone me later.'

'We can't,' said Nick. 'Your phone was the first casualty, remember?'

'OK,' she said. 'Phone me at the Flying Club at exactly 9 p.m.'

'Right, but what are you going to tell them?'

'I'll think of something. It'll be a while before they sort themselves out enough to get round to me. Just go.'

'Hold it a minute,' said Nick. 'This is the final proof that Steve is right. Maybe we should stay and explain.'

Steve made up his mind. 'Rosie's got a point. Once my name comes into it, we'll have Kitto down here in a flash, then no one will believe a damned thing we say. Whatever happens, if we have to start explaining, there's no way they'll let us disappear off to Davos in time.'

Rosie started pushing them physically back along the bank. 'Stop talking. Just get going, will you?'

So they'd grabbed their bags and gone, walking down the river bank while the police car tore into the car park, then across the bridge to where they'd left the Scimitar, and away. They hadn't even gone to London. They'd driven to a country pub in the quietest part of Surrey, checking in under assumed names and making sure the Scimitar could be tucked out of sight in a barn, on the pretext it wouldn't start any other way. Steve spent some time on the phone, changing flight bookings, and Nick persuaded Wessex TV to fix travellers' cheques for collection at Heathrow.

At 9 p.m. they had rung the Flying Club number. Steve had the phone and was holding the receiver sideways so Nick could hear too. 'No problem so far,' she had said. 'Pugwash beached the boat before it sank, and the police have been looking at it. They can see one of the shafts broke, so they know he didn't try to kill the guy on purpose.'

'He's definitely dead then?'

'Oh yes. The body was pulled out down at Portslade. One of the Sergeants told me they're quite excited about it, because he's got a record as long as your arm.'

'Have they questioned you?'

'Yes. I thought I'd better go straight to them before they came knocking. There was a real crowd there after you went. One of the bullets went through the kitchen window of a house in the estate. When they found the gun they got really enthusiastic.'

'What did you tell them?'

'Oh, I came over all helpless and wobbly. Said the man appeared in my boat, shot the telephone to bits when I tried to call the police, and ran away when I threw the peach at him.'

'Do they believe you?'

'So far. They want to see me again tomorrow.'

'Rosie, listen. We'll be gone by 10 a.m. If you have to mention us, don't say anything about Switzerland. We've got to get to Davos without anyone stopping us.'

'I'll do my best. By the way, there are reporters all over the place.'

Nick took the phone from him. 'You take care, lover. When I get back, I'll teach you to shoot.'

There was a rude noise from the other end, and Nick hung up. 'Lover?' said Steve.

Nick looked shifty. 'Great girl,' he said, 'lots of guts. Anyway, down to business. What next?'

'Precautions first of all. We have to start stepping more carefully. First, we're not going straight to Zürich. I've booked us into France, near the Swiss border. We'll pick up a hire-car and drive into Switzerland on one of the small roads, where there won't be any computer and where there won't be any nosey people waiting to tip off Cheeseman.'

'Good. What's second?'

'I think we need to write out an account of everything we've got so far. We send one copy to Rosie and tell her to hold on to it in case anything goes wrong on Friday. We send the other to Keith Brice, so it's sitting on his mat when he gets back from his cruise, just for safety in case it all gets really nasty. I'm sure he's still got enough friends to count.'

'Last will and testament? Or just insurance in case we're banged up in some Swiss dungeon?'

'Let's hope it's neither.'

They'd had to change at Paris's Charles de Gaulle airport to an Air Inter internal flight, so there were no more customs formalities when they walked into the foyer of the provincial airport in the old French textile town of Mulhouse and went in search of a hire-car. They chose a big Renault 25 in case they needed the speed, and took a roundabout route across the Rhine to Müllheim and then east through the peaceful fields and woodlands of southern Germany until they crossed into Switzerland over a picturesque stone bridge at Kaiserstuhl, only fifteen miles north of Zürich. There was just one bored Swiss official, who didn't even look inside their passports before waving them through.

'Where are we meeting Maja?' asked Nick as they followed the signs to Zürich.

'She gave me instructions. It's on the edge of an airbase called Dübendorf somewhere just east of the city.'

'Anything I need to know which might account for the silly grin on your face whenever her name comes up?'

'Well, not really. Just that I think she's very beautiful and very sweet and I sort of like her.'

Though they were late, she was waiting where she had said she'd be, in the car park by the airbase. She jumped out of the Cherokee when she saw them pull in, yelled 'Hi, Nick,' and threw herself into Steve's arms. After a while in which Nick stood by politely whistling and looking at the planes taking off, Steve let go and saw her smile fade at his expression.

'We shouldn't hang about here in plain view,' he said. 'There's been a bit of trouble.'

They got into the Renault and the two men brought her

up to date. 'We have to assume they saw the Cherokee up on the mountain,' said Steve. 'Rudi's out of harm's way, and they probably have no idea we're back in Switzerland, but they might know about you.'

She was calm about it. 'That is fine,' she said, 'I have my things here. We do not need to go home. We just have to go to Rudi's house to collect the camera equipment.'

Steve was about to suggest that they park the Jeep in case it was spotted and all go in the hire-car, but then he thought how much he needed to be alone with Maja, and persuaded himself it wouldn't matter.

'Why don't you go on ahead, Nick, and fix us up with rooms, and we'll meet you in Davos later on.'

'Sure,' said Nick, 'if that's what you want,' and grinned. 'Where shall I meet you?'

'There is a café on the other side of the road to the main cable-car station, just where the one-way system starts, the Konditorei Weber. We should be there by eight o'clock,' said Maja.

They waved goodbye to Nick, and Maja drove the Jeep on small country roads to the southeast. The warm air was whistling through the open windows, and Steve had his arm along the back of the seat, resting gently on her shoulder. As long as that lasted, all felt right with the world.

Rudi's house was a surprise after all the concrete monstrosities Steve had seen before. It was a chocolate-box farm, all wooden with intricate carvings and painted shutters, beyond a peaceful little lake called the Greifensee. A rutted driveway led down to it, through small, well-tended fields, opening into a courtyard of timber barns flanking the house.

'Rudi inherited it,' said Maja, smiling at the expression on Steve's face. 'I think it suits him.'

From the gravel yard outside, the old, carved front door opened into a cool interior of sun-dappled wood panels.

Outside, the world had been full of movement, doubts and pressures, but the door, closing behind them, blocked all that off, leaving them alone together in sudden silence. In the shadows of the hall Steve was suddenly acutely aware of Maja's physical presence.

She was standing in front of him, looking through a bunch of keys, and he touched her gently on the shoulder. He felt a tingle like static electricity and she jumped, looking round at him. Her lips parted in a surprised half-smile, then she took his hand and gazed at him for a long time. He stepped towards her, but she turned and led him up the stairs. At the top a large landing, with a battered wardrobe, richly decorated with intricate painted patterns, against one wall, had four doors opening off it. She opened the door directly opposite the head of the stairs and he followed her into a large bedroom. The bed and most of the furniture was ancient – robust peasant-carving the colour of honey. But against one wall was a massive steel cabinet, painted in military olive drab, with a big padlock securing its double doors. Maja tried the key and it opened. On the shelves inside, Rudi's equipment was neatly stacked – camera, recorder, mikes, leads, lights and boxes of tapes. Maja stood looking at it and, over her shoulder, Steve saw that the right-hand side of the cupboard was filled with equipment of a different sort. An assault rifle was clipped to the back of the door, while a stuffed backpack, boots and a helmet occupied the shelves. Steve heard Rudi's voice again – 'We keep everything at home. That way, the army is always ready. Then, no one will dare attack brave little Switzerland' – with that self-mocking half-smile on his face.

Maja picked up the camera, standing hunched over it with her back to Steve, then put it down and turned to him. She looked directly into his eyes. 'Steve, I do not know what's going to happen in Davos, and I know we have to go there because no one will listen to us, but I feel this may be the only peace we have together. We should make the most of it while we can.'

She was gazing at him in the soft, dusty sunlight, golden and open, and Steve thought she was more beautiful than he had ever seen her before. The world inside slowed to a halt. He stepped towards her and put his arms round her, feeling the skin of her back warm through the silky, sliding material of her shirt.

'Nick will just have to wait,' he said.

She laughed, 'No, he won't. That's why I said eight o'clock.'

There was no time-limit on their kiss, except the growing urgency it generated in both of them. They were lying on the bed without really knowing how they'd got there, rushing to get rid of the clothing that was keeping them apart. Then they met again, skin to skin with a blast of overpowering sensuality from their nerve endings which suspended all the rules of foreplay. They moulded to each other, moving together, straining to be closer and deeper than their bodies would allow, rushing to a bursting climax which left them stunned by its power. They lay, still locked together in wonder, content just to hold each other, then drifted into sleep.

Steve woke, gazing up at the ceiling to find the late-afternoon shadows lengthening in the room. Maja was lying half across his chest, her hair cascading down across it, gazing at him. 'Hello,' she said.

He looked at her and smiled. 'Lovers in the act dispense with such meum-tum sense,' he said.

'What is that?'

'It's an English poem I read a long time ago. I didn't know what it meant until now,' he said.

326

'Teach it to me,' she said, and her voice turned husky as her lips approached his.

Then, into their secure island of peace, there came a crunching of boots on gravel from the courtyard. They froze, and Steve slipped quickly out of bed and moved cautiously to the edge of the window. A man walked past the end wall of the barn, coming into the yard from the track. He was burly and dark-chinned and Steve had seen him before. It was the man called Jacques who had bounced him from Cheeseman's house.

The man glanced briefly at the Cherokee, unsurprised to see it there, and then rapped on the door. Steve held his breath, but only a few seconds passed when, with a heart-wrenching shock, they heard the breaking glass of a forced entry, made with all the noisy confidence of one who knows there is nobody at home.

Chapter Twenty-seven

He didn't even get as far as the door before the man with the gun had him. He had been hoping that with the right air of breezy confidence he might just sail right past the security check into the conference centre, but Nick's clothing was against him. The baseball cap wasn't the best of camouflage in the circumstances. Men in very expensive suits or even more expensive casual clothes were being checked through one by one, the photos on their passes being studied carefully before they were allowed to slide their pigskin attaché cases through the electronic scanner. Nick's attempt to walk briskly, smiling and waving in all directions, right through the middle, didn't look like working for a minute, and the policeman who grabbed his arm, machine-gun halfway raised with the other hand, didn't have any discernible sense of humour.

'*Wohin gehen sie?*'

'I'm sorry?'

'I said, where are you going?'

'To the Press Office. I need to get some accreditation. Where is it?'

'Inside.'

'Then can I go there?'

'Not without a pass.'

'That's why I need to go there, to get a pass.'

Two more policemen came over. Nick frowned. 'Look, I need a pass to get in, right? But the only way I can get a pass is to go in and see the Press Office. Right again?'

The policemen shook their collective heads. One reached for a clipboard with a long list on it. 'Are you from a newspaper?'

'No. TV.'

'What name?'

'Nielsen. Wessex TV.'

The policeman didn't even check the clipboard. 'There is nothing arranged for you. You are not here on the list.'

Nick took a deep breath. 'I know. That's why I have to go and see them to arrange it. That's the point.'

The policeman laughed and put the list away. 'No, sir. This had to be done before. Since two weeks you should have arranged this, then you would have the special temporary pass to get you to the Press Office where they would give you your badge.'

Nick gave up and went in search of a way. There was a public route down the side of the conference centre, an elevated concrete walkway screened off by plywood shuttering. He peered through a gap. Below was a yard with a back entrance. Two catering trucks were being unloaded. The men carrying in the equipment wore blue trousers and red shirts. Nick went looking for a clothes shop.

After that it was a doddle. The shirt was a shade too dark and quite a bit too tight, but it worked. He chose his moment, when the guard on the back driveway was busy, to wave and slip through the barrier, then picked up a crate of beer bottles from the back of the truck and wandered in through the door, held open for him by an obliging policeman.

In a subterranean corner of the basement, through a network of tiny passages, he found the press area. A room full of telephones with temporary soundproof bubbles around them. Fax machines, telexes and a table of bored operators waiting for business. Then came a small room with notices of coming events and pigeon-holes stuffed with multilingual press releases, advance copies of speeches no one would read, and finally the press office itself. He stood at the door and weighed up the possibilities. There were three or four young girls, too junior to be of any use to him. A middle-aged woman in glasses was rushing about. Too senior, too busy and too Swiss. She was in the middle of what looked like a furious exchange with another woman, in her late thirties, clearly a subordinate and clearly hating that fact. Nick's interest quickened. The woman was tall, with long, glossy dark hair and strong, handsome features set in the profile of a Cherokee Indian. They were talking English.

'Why don't you just listen to me?' she was saying. 'The way you want it won't work. Believe me.' Her accent was German, but there were overtones of east coast American.

'Marlene, just do it. That's all. Just do it,' said the other woman in a low, intense voice.

'I go for coffee. Then I decide if I do it,' said the woman called Marlene, and swept out past Nick. He followed.

In the coffee-shop upstairs, he bought a cup for what seemed a phenomenal number of Swiss francs, and sat down beside her. She was staring fiercely at the wall.

'Mind if I join you?' he said.

She looked at him with sudden interest. 'American?' she asked.

'On the button. Nick Nielsen,' he said and held out a hand.

'Marlene Heydrich,' she said. 'I worked in America a long time for German TV.'

Bingo, thought Nick. 'Heard you in the Press Office. I wondered why you were speaking English.'

Her lip curled. 'I don't understand that woman. These Swiss speak such dreadful German. She makes no sense. Anyway she is stupid.' She looked at Nick, and her expression softened. 'So what are you doing here?'

'Ah,' said Nick, 'that's something you might just be able to help me with.'

Maja gave a little suppressed gasp as the last piece of broken, cascading glass reached the floor and silence resumed. Then the door below creaked open, and footsteps sounded in the hall. He didn't need to do that, thought Steve. We came in that way. It was open. So he knows Rudi's not here, and he doesn't know we're here. The comfort that gave him wasn't great. He felt extremely vulnerable, standing naked by the window. Maja was sitting up in the bed, staring down as though she could see through the floorboards to the man searching below.

Steve took a cautious step towards her, and the floor creaked slightly. He bent his mouth slowly down to her ear and whispered. 'Is there any way to get out from up here? Anything like a balcony?'

She thought, and shook her head. 'Only the stairs,' she whispered back.

They listened. He was moving around below, opening cupboards, pulling out drawers. 'He's searching everywhere,' Steve whispered. 'He's bound to try this room, but he doesn't know we're here.' He clenched his fists, trying to keep down the panic, knowing it was just a matter of time before they would hear those feet climbing the stairs – to what? To discover witnesses to his casual housebreaking. How would he react? Violently, certainly, but to what degree? A deep conviction came uncomfortably over Steve that the degree would be total. Maja was off the bed and beside him, warm against his skin, but the only feeling that aroused in him now was anger at the interruption to their time together.

Maja listened intently. 'He is in the kitchen now, I think. At the other end.'

They moved slowly across the floor, one step at a time, trying not to put too much weight on the aged, noisy boards. The door was open a crack and they could see a corner of the hall below. The man came out of the kitchen, stood irresolute for a second, moved towards the stairs, then turned to a small cupboard and began to look inside it. I could stand behind the door, thought Steve, and hit him with something when he comes in. I wonder if it really works? He looked desperately around for something solid enough, and his eyes fell on the open metal locker with Rudi's assault rifle clipped to the door. For a moment he rejected the idea. Too much escalation. He wasn't sure he could carry it through. Then he thought, to hell with that. Let's fight fire with fire. At least it should frighten the bastard. He moved carefully towards it and pulled it free of the clips, opening them with his fingers so they would make no noise. It was lighter than he imagined, a square metal butt, a curving magazine in front of the pistol-grip and a folding stand at the barrel end. He eased out the magazine and looked at it. It was empty.

But Maja was ahead of him. She moved past him like a ghost, lifted the rucksack carefully out of the locker and on to the bed, and started opening the side pouches. She brought out a bayonet and then a white tin, which she passed to Steve. He looked at it without understanding. It looked like an old-fashioned tin of cigarettes. On it was a legend in French, *Cette munition de poche est destinée exclusivement à la protection individuelle.* On the other side it said '24 7.5mm 591–1100.' It was sealed by a soft metal band, and underneath, stuck on the bottom, was a little key of the sort you used to find on sardine tins.

Footsteps approached the bottom of the stairs. Steve

opened the tin. Packed inside were two dozen gleaming, cupro-nickel bullets. Time seemed to stretch in two different directions. His mind was racing but his shaking fingers were moving at leaden speed. One by one he eased the bullets against the spring and into the magazine. Nine went in, and then time was nearly up. There were footsteps on the stairs. Maja jammed Rudi's steel helmet on his head – the only protection she could give him – but it made him feel all the more vulnerable having nothing else on, and he quickly and silently pulled on his underpants. Then, keeping his eyes fixed on the door, he reached round behind him for his trousers. The footsteps were on the landing now and all he could hear was his own breathing.

His groping fingers brushed the heavy rucksack. It swayed and toppled off the bed with a crash. There was a loud exclamation from outside and a surge of adrenalin took over Steve's brain. Fuelled by pure terror, he held the assault rifle in front of him and burst out through the bedroom door, screaming at the top of his lungs. The man, standing rooted to the spot only feet away, took one horrified look, turned and tripped headlong down the stairs, sliding painfully down on his shoulders, feet rattling on the banisters before over-taking his head in a backward roll at the bottom. He lay still for a moment, then picked himself up and ran hobbling outside. Steve stood watching his disappearing back, rifle extended, relief flooding through him. He turned and went back into the bedroom, suddenly aware of his nakedness. He threw the helmet on to the bed and moved quickly to where Maja was crouching by the open window. She pointed.

They saw the man limp as far as the end of the barns. Then he seemed to collect himself. He stopped, reached inside his jacket and, bringing out a small automatic, turned back towards them. Oh shit. I'd better frighten him again, thought Steve. We've got to keep the upper hand or we're dead. He raised the gun and, aiming to the left of the man, pulled the trigger. Nothing happened. He tried again with no more success. Then he saw the cocking lever sticking out of the side and, remembering a hundred war films, pulled it back. Still nothing.

The man outside was growing bolder and beginning to come back towards the house. Steve studied the gun. He'd never seen one like it. The maker's name, SIG, was stamped on the side. Near it was a little lever with three positions marked M, E and S. It was on S. Figuring it had to be a safety-catch, Steve flicked it forward and down to M. He stuck it out of the window and, aiming near the man's approaching feet, squeezed the trigger again.

Violence erupted all around. The gun, set to full automatic fire, sprayed its nine bullets out in less than a second. It had very little kick, but the hammering noise and the destruction it wrought on the yard outside took Steve completely by surprise. He'd been expecting just one warning shot and wasn't prepared for the deafening roar as the gun took control. Bullets hurled gravel in all directions and whined off the cobbles. The man took to his heels and ran down the track as fast as his limp would allow. In the sudden silence, appalled at crossing a threshold which left them no friends on either side of the law, Steve heard a car engine start out on the road and accelerate away.

It was only then that he became aware of the faint whirring noise to his left. Maja had Rudi's camera on her shoulder. She switched off and put it carefully down on the ground.

'You got it? The whole thing?' he asked in amazement.

She nodded, and her voice had just a small tremor in it. 'You chose your weapon, I chose mine,' she said. 'Anyway, it was much easier when it was all black and white in the viewfinder. Then it wasn't so scary. It was like make-believe. I jumped a bit when your gun went off. I hope that didn't spoil the picture.'

He held her for a moment, but they both knew they had to get away. 'We must warn Rudi,' she said. 'He must not walk back into this without knowing.'

'You're right. Do you have a number?'

'No. He didn't know where he was staying, but he calls in here every two or three days. We must leave a message on the answering machine.'

They dressed and, before they went downstairs, Steve loaded the remaining fifteen rounds into the assault rifle's magazine. He put the safety-catch back on and took the rifle with him. He watched the yard from the door while Maja fiddled with the answering machine.

'There's no instructions,' she said, and tried another button. There was a click and a hiss from the speaker, and then the machine began to play out the messages recorded on it by callers. There was only one, but that was enough.

'*Rudi,*' said a distorted voice, '*hier ist Hugo. Ich habe etwas sehr wichtig zu sagen.*' Steve tensed and raised a questioning eyebrow at Maja, who bent to listen intently. Hugo spoke rapidly in Schweizerdeutsch for a minute or two. At the end she stared at the machine until Steve broke the silence.

'What did he say?'

'I'm sorry. I forgot you don't understand.' She looked drawn. 'He says he has found out some more about Cheeseman, but Cheeseman's men have been asking many questions about you and about Rudi. He says do not underestimate Cheeseman. If he doesn't like you looking into his affairs, he will find a way to stop you. He says Rudi should have believed him when you met at the James Joyce. It is the secret armies that lie behind this. He has sent Rudi a

335

letter with more details.' She looked at him. 'Does this mean much to you? I don't understand it.'

'Where would Rudi's post be?'

'In the box outside the door.'

The letter-box was a flap in a metal case, which pivoted out of a recess in the wall. In the back was a locked door to allow the householder to get the mail out. Maja looked through the bunch of keys.

'I can't find it here. Maybe it is in the house somewhere.'

'We can't hang around here. I'll break it open.'

She watched unhappily while he levered the door apart with a big screwdriver from the hallway. 'Don't worry,' he said, 'I'll fix it for him when this is over.'

In the box was a load of junk mail, film processing envelopes and books of special offer supermarket vouchers. There wasn't much personal stuff, just a couple of postcards, a phone bill and a large brown envelope with a hastily scrawled address on it. Steve opened it and found several stapled sheets of typewritten German. The name Cheeseman leapt out at him. 'This is it,' he said, 'let's go. We can call in from Davos and leave a message on the machine, then he'll pick it up when he calls next.'

Keeping a careful watch, they loaded the camera gear into the back of the Jeep. Steve looked at the gun. 'I think we should take this just in case,' he said. 'I'll put it on the back seat with something over it.'

Maja made a face. 'Rudi will get in trouble,' she said. 'It should stay locked away.'

'Don't worry, I'll give it back to him.'

'No. He is in trouble anyway because we opened the bullets. The tin is inspected once a year when he goes for annual service to make sure it is intact.'

Steve heard genuine anxiety in her voice. 'Hey, those bullets saved us,' he said. '*La protection individuelle*. That's what it said on the tin. We've just got to make sure we've got something to justify it at the end of all this.'

She nodded. 'I drive, you watch,' she said.

'Maybe we shouldn't go the obvious way. He could be out on the road.'

She looked around without speaking, tugged the lever into low-ratio four-wheel drive, and steered the Jeep, lurching and bouncing, into a field.

Chapter Twenty-eight

The Konditorei Weber was almost empty, lying fallow for the winter skiing crowds who would pour out of the claustrophobia of the Parsennbahn mountain railway across the road when the season began in four or five months. It lay at the start of the Promenade, the interminable one-way street through Davos's concrete ugliness which allows occasional glimpses of the soaring beauty of the Jakobshorn, Schatzalp and the great Parsenn itself, looming above.

Time was Steve would have walked in with a smile on his face, slapped Nick on the back and simply sat down. Now, though, they first checked out the café by driving past, then moved warily through the shop which served as its ante-room, past the trays of chocolate truffles and meringues, until they could see diagonally into the room, to where Nick sat alone. He had chosen a table in the far corner, where he could see passers-by much more easily than they could see him. He waved.

'Saw you driving by,' he said, then his eyes narrowed as he looked at them both. 'I was going to say you'd taken your time, but it looks like you've been to war again, right?'

'Right,' said Steve, 'and we won.'

Maja pulled a face. 'This time, maybe.'

'OK,' said Nick, 'drinks first, then tell. You'll be pleased to hear I've been putting in some research for you. The Skiwasser isn't as good as the Jagertee. The Lumumba is short on rum and long on chocolate, and the Pflümli is the best of the schnapps.'

Steve sat back, drinking something hot, sweet and alcoholic, and let Maja tell the story in a low voice, pitched to fall short of the elderly couple in walking clothes at the only other occupied table. 'Steve was so brave,' she said, 'chasing him out of the house, then aiming bullets all round his feet to make him run away.'

He let that version of events ride. 'You should have seen this one,' he said, putting his arm round Maja's shoulders, 'filming away in the middle of it all, like it was all in a day's work.' But there was an undercurrent to their voices. Not far below the levity and the relief of being able to tell the tale, all three knew there was a deep hollow, filled with black doubt and impotence in the face of an adversary who seemed to hold all the cards.

'I hate to say this,' said Nick, 'but maybe it's time we tried the Swiss police.'

Steve and Maja looked at each other. 'You haven't heard the rest of it,' Steve said.

He told Nick of the documents in the envelope from Hugo, documents from a left-wing sympathizer in the fringes of the Berne government. Photocopies of photocopies with codes, dates and far too many names whited-out along the way. 'The main one is a report of some sort. I read it out to Maja. She filled in the bits I couldn't understand.'

She broke in. 'It sounds the real thing to me, Nick. It claims to be an internal report prepared for a member of the Federal Council. It is very bureaucratic.'

'What does it say?'

Steve and Maja looked at each other. Maja inclined her head and Steve went on. 'Well, first I'd better give you the quick history lesson on P26 and P27.' He told Nick about the way the veil had been lifted on the secret armies by the fallout from the Kopp affair, and how Rudi had poured cold

339

water on Hugo's belief that Cheeseman might be involved.

'Whatever these bits of paper are, if they're real then maybe Rudi was a bit quick with his judgement. The main one says Cheeseman has been of great service to the Swiss Federation in providing certain items of equipment for the use of the secret forces. There's a note from Hugo saying, according to his source, they'd run into a problem trying to divert enough weapons from the regular forces without it becoming conspicuous, and one or two people in the trade had stepped in with alternative supplies.'

'So our friend is an arms dealer?'

'Looks like it. There's apparently no shortage of them in this country.'

Nick shrugged. 'So what's the problem? All the more reason to think he's a bad boy.'

Maja shook her head. 'Maybe in America, but this is Switzerland. You have to understand it is not so open here.'

Steve nodded. 'Hugo's papers say it is believed Cheeseman can now count on a very high level of tolerance and personal latitude for his business affairs because of what he's done.'

'You mean he's bought off the politicos?'

'I don't suppose that's the way they would see it, but it means they would have to be very, very convinced before they would listen to us.'

'And by that time someone may be dead.'

'Yes,' said Steve, 'and we don't have a clue who that someone is going to be, so what do we do next?'

'First, I'll show you our room.'

Steve raised an eyebrow. 'Room? As in singular not plural?'

'You spotted it. Only one in the whole place that's not booked solid for the meeting. Four bunk-beds in an attic. That's one each and one for the camera gear. They're meant for children, but if you lie sideways and sort of hunch up you can just about fit. After that there's the wee problem that we don't have any accreditation to get us inside, but I've got a secret weapon to help us through that one.'

'What sort of secret weapon?'

'The sort we're meeting for dinner in half an hour's time.'

The Konditorei Weber gave way to the bar at their hotel and then to the Restaurant Gentiana in the seamless way that the presence of Nick Nielsen always seemed to ensure, but being surrounded by harmless people indulging in harmless eating and drinking was what they all needed. Out on the street, their eyes and neck muscles were on overtime, trying to spot members of an opposition they weren't even sure they'd recognize before they themselves were spotted.

Marlene came into the restaurant like a storm cloud looking for a receptive drought to fall on. In the little upstairs room, decorated with discoloured Victorian adverts for English steel corsets, she barely waited to be introduced before she launched into a full-scale denunciation of the idiocy of those for whom she worked.

'She is a cow, that woman. She tells me what to do all the time and she has no idea, no idea at all.'

Steve raised an eyebrow at Nick. 'Who are we talking about?'

'Freya Stäheli, the media coordinator. I come and work for the Forum twice every year, just for the big events, and each time she is worse. She should leave the television crews to me. That is my responsibility, but she interferes all the time. It is impossible. I shall walk away and then they will see.'

A large vodka and tonic arrived and she downed it almost in one gulp. 'Now she demands separate photo-calls tomorrow for the TV and for the stills photographers. Two minutes

341

each. Can you imagine? Two minutes for the crews? They will hardly have got switched on and white-balanced. It is nonsense.'

'Crazy,' said Nick. 'Really dumb,' said Steve. Maja nodded. Marlene ground to a halt and looked at them. 'So why are you guys here?' she said.

'We're putting together a documentary for Wessex TV in the UK,' said Nick, 'and we'd like to do some shooting here. Only thing is, the company seems to have screwed up our accreditation.'

Marlene looked at them, surprised. 'I see all the TV applications, and there wasn't one for you. The lists closed a whole month ago.'

'I guess they sent it to the wrong address or something. The problem is we're going to be in real trouble if we can't get in.'

She shook her head. 'Big trouble. I don't know. It is all so tight here because of the people who are coming and the theme of the conference. The whole point of Davos is that all these rich businessmen can rub their shoulders with any world leader they want. So that means lots of security outside so they can all move freely inside. Procedures are very strict. There has to be an application already in. There are only five crews at the moment allowed inside.'

'Who are they?'

She ticked them off on her fingers. 'SRG, that's to say Swiss TV, BBC, two from the Forum itself to do all the shots for the big screen behind the speaker, and then the EBN crew.'

Nick looked at her enquiringly. 'EBN?'

'Oh, it's just some satellite TV outfit from Zürich. It does business shows.' She drained another glass. 'Anyway, what is it about, your documentary?'

Nick looked at Steve, who thought, thanks a bunch.

'Well,' he said, 'I suppose it crosses over with your theme. Remind me, how have you phrased it?' Please, he thought, not a one-word answer. This is a talking-shop after all, they always have wordy themes.

She laughed. 'It was going to be Cashing in the Peace Dividend, but now they've made it After the Gulf, Is There Still a Peace Dividend?'.

'Exactly,' he said in relief. 'That's almost exactly our working title.'

Wine arrived and they ordered fondue chinoise. Nick and Marlene chatted their way through the staff lists of the US TV networks, never quite knowing the same people. Steve, sitting opposite Maja, moved in and out of warm awareness of her presence, as obsessive worry about their situation kept reasserting itself, half listening to the other two. Then he heard Marlene say, 'Did you know the BBC guys in Washington at all?'

Nick waved at him. 'Ask Steve about that. He worked for them.'

Marlene looked at him with renewed interest. 'You were with the BBC?'

'Certainly. Right up to last month. I was in TV News.'

'Why didn't you say so? Maybe that is the answer. There is a woman here from the BBC. Miss Pugh. Do you know her?'

'Diana? Oh yes.'

Marlene carried on with artless candour. 'Well, excuse me if she is a friend of yours, but I don't like her. She is very bossy. Anyway, the BBC had booked for two crews and they have only brought one. She has given me a letter to cancel the other accreditation, because there is an administration fee for each one, you know. But she was a bit rude so I have not yet processed the letter.'

'So you mean we could come in as the other crew?'

'If she agrees.'

'But the names wouldn't be right.'

Marlene sighed. 'Well, that is maybe the loophole in our watertight security. You know how it is with crews. They get stuck somewhere. They get sick. They take time off. If we know the company they are working for, we let them change the names. What matters is that the request has been in since before the deadline. That means I can change the names without trouble.'

'I'll go and find Diana in the morning.'

'You could go and find her after this,' said Marlene. 'I remember from her form, she is staying in the Sport Hotel just along the road.'

An hour later, leaving the others lingering over their coffee, he was knocking on the door of room 213 of the Sport Hotel. He could hear Diana's voice raised on the phone inside. 'A minute,' she called out. The conversation lasted more like five minutes, while Steve paced up and down outside, rehearsing possible openings. Then the door opened and the pale, unmade-up chrysalis from which the Diana Pugh butterfly emerged every morning stood in the doorway, wrapped wet-haired in a dressing-gown, blinking at him in surprise.

'Good God, Steve Ross,' she finally said. 'Well there's a thing. Come in. Sorry, I had *Breakfast News* on the phone.'

'Bad luck,' he said. 'I just need a quick word.'

'What are you doing here?'

'A doco. I need access. You're the only person who can fix it.'

He explained the accreditation problem. She just looked doubtful. He begged. Then she started to get a bit tetchy. 'You're not the flavour of the month in the Spur, Steve. The word on you is that you fell off your trolley and started seeing things that weren't there. Mike Page reckons you set his promotion prospects back by five years. I don't intend to let you do the same for me.'

'There's no risk to you.'

'Oh isn't there? You've been a bit disaster-prone lately, haven't you? If you go berserk in the middle of Davos and start biting people, I don't want it coming back to me.'

She fiddled with her hands, then looked up at him. 'Sorry, Steve, the answer's no.'

'Listen, Diana. This is no fantasy. I think we are on the edge of a very big story. Nick Nielsen's in this, too, and he'll tell you the same. We've got proof of it, and it was good enough to get a lot of money out of Wessex TV.'

She looked at him in disbelief. 'Tell me about it.'

'No, I can't, but I'll give you a break on it when it happens if you help.' He was getting nowhere.

There was steel in her face and self-preservation uppermost in her mind. She shook her head and got to her feet. 'It's time for bed, Steve, and that doesn't include you.'

He went to the door, feeling it all slipping away, and then the gut fear of the off-base reporter came to him and gave him the key. He turned back to her. 'All right,' he said, and his voice had an edge to it that made her stop in her tracks. 'I'll tell you something you had better listen to, Diana, because it's an experience I know all about. Some time in the next two days, just as you're getting ready to call room service, or getting in the shower, or maybe just nodding off to sleep, that phone is going to ring and the desk is going to tell you that you have just missed the biggest story of your life. You'll be running your ass off, shit scared, trying to cover yourself, but it will be far too late. I'll be the only one with the pictures, and I'll be selling them to ITN. Is that what you want, or maybe would you like to talk?'

He saw a momentary shadow of fear in her eyes as she looked at him, and he waited. She sighed. 'Come back and sit down,' she said.

The Gentiana was used to staying open late, and there were still one or two other diners there when he rejoined them at the table. Marlene was smiling with slightly drunken indulgence at Nick, who was in the middle of some unlikely anecdote, while Maja sat back, keeping her thoughts to herself. She saw Steve approaching first and her face lit up. Nick stopped in mid-flow and looked enquiringly at him.

'It's fixed,' he said. 'She's agreed.'

'That is good,' said Marlene. 'Give me the names now, then I will have passes waiting for you at the door to get you in tomorrow.'

'Well, Maja's doing camera,' said Nick.

'Maja what?' asked Marlene, looking at her, and Steve realized with a start that he didn't know her surname.

'Frey,' said Maja, and Marlene wrote it down.

'And who is doing sound?'

'I am,' said Steve and Nick simultaneously.

'Can we get three in?' asked Nick.

'No. Two only,' said Marlene.

'You'd better do it then, Steve,' said Nick. 'I'll have to hang around outside.'

'Aren't you the reporter?' Marlene asked Steve curiously.

'Yes, but we're short of a person, so I can do sound.'

'Steve what?' she said.

'Ross,' he said, and her face changed. For a moment he thought the story of his downfall must have penetrated even this far into mainland Europe. She looked at him in wonder, then she said, 'You can answer a mystery for me then.'

'I'll have a go. What is it?'

'A man has been asking about you. I couldn't think why.'

346

'Who was it?' demanded Steve, leaning towards her.

'A man named Heller. From Zürich. Do you know him?'

'I know the name. What did he want?'

'Just to know if you were accredited to the conference. I said no.'

'Fine.' But it wasn't fine at all. She looked distant and unhappy. He went on, 'You don't like him?'

'It is not him. It is a man he works for. I know it is the same man because last year he was making such a fuss about hotel bookings for his boss. A man called Cheeseman. I am very worried by him.'

There was a sudden silence, then Nick said casually, 'So what's with this Cheeseman that bothers you?'

'He caused so much trouble last year. We had a big session on Eastern Europe. Lots of ministers from the old Warsaw Pact countries talking about the changes. Klaus was there.' She looked around at their blank faces. 'You know, Klaus, the Czech finance minister? He is such a nice man. He just wished he had time to go skiing but he couldn't. Anyway, Cheeseman stood up in one of the public sessions and started shouting at him, abusing him. It was really very embarrassing.'

'Why did he do it?'

'We had to find out in case something happened again.' She stopped suddenly. 'I shouldn't be telling you this.'

Nick laid his hand across his heart. 'Off the record, I promise.'

'Well, OK,' she said, and smiled at him. 'As long as you promise. It seems he had some very big contract with a Czech engineering company to buy goods over a long period, and when the new regime took over they cancelled it. It has put him in big troubles financially.'

'Why did they cancel it? Surely hard currency is just what they need.'

She shook her head. 'You should know that Václav Havel changed a lot of things when he came to power. He is still a gentle playwright at heart. There are some trades which were traditional in Czechoslovakia that he does not like.'

'Like what?' said Nick into the silence.

'Oh, come on,' she said, looking around at them, enjoying their ignorance. 'You don't know about the Czech export trade for all these years, suppliers of goods to keep the wheels of terror turning, goods like machine-guns and Semtex?'

This time the silence extended until she broke it herself. 'So this year, we have to be very careful. We will not let Mr Cheeseman have a ticket for the session.'

'What session?'

'The discussion with Václav Havel, of course.'

Chapter Twenty-nine

The moon was bright on the shoulder of the mountain, showing the cable-car pylons standing out, black, down its profile. Steve looked at his watch. 3.30 a.m. near enough. Two hours' sleep at best and then his over-active brain had nudged him out of bed. He stared out of the little window, wondering what the morning would bring. Wood creaked behind him and an arm circled his waist. Maja, in an oversized black T-shirt, nestled against him.

'You can't sleep either?' he said, and she shook her head.

'I keep thinking,' she whispered. 'If they are going to use the camera to do something inside the meeting, they must have accreditation, too, so which one are they?'

'Mind if I join the party?' said Nick from the top bunk. 'I've been thinking the same thing.'

'Well, they're not the BBC crew, for sure. They've come out from London with Diana, so it must be one of the other four.'

'I think it is time to decide what to do,' said Maja. 'Marlene said most of the VIPs have already arrived. We don't have much time.'

'OK,' said Nick, 'accreditation first. Then you two prowl round inside looking for familiar faces. If you see the crew, stick to them like glue. I'll do the outside.'

'You don't know what they look like.'

'No, but I know an Ikegami when I see one.'

Maja sat down on the edge of her bunk. 'Do you think it is definitely Havel?'

Steve shook his head. 'Nothing's definite. There's still the Gorbachev–Yeltsin debate, and God knows what else. Marlene said she'd give us the full schedule.'

She nodded. 'I think we must have a cut-off. If we haven't got any further by lunchtime, we must tell the police.'

'What do we tell them?'

She thought for a moment. 'Well, at least we can tell them to look inside the camera. They might listen.'

There was a silence. Nick broke it. 'End of the doco if we do.'

'Not necessarily,' said Steve. 'Not if we make sure we're there to shoot it when they grab the guy.'

'We won't have much.'

'Nick, what is the alternative?' said Maja firmly. 'Are you saying we stand by and do nothing so we get good pictures of a killing? Suppose we can't stop it? Suppose it is Gorbachev or Havel?'

'OK,' he said, 'you're right. Lunchtime it is. But that's assuming we find the guys. They may not even be here.'

Marlene was as good as her word, waiting with passes at the security barrier at 8.30. 'You all look terrible,' she said, 'did you drink too much?'

Steve shook his head, the weight of the recorder unfamiliar on his shoulder. 'We didn't sleep much. No matter. Are these the passes?'

'These get you in as far as the registration area. You must go there now, and they will take your photo and give you the proper laminated badges.'

'I'll sit outside here and wait,' said Nick. 'See you later.'

Steve and Maja followed Marlene downstairs through a large foyer to a room where a security guard waited with a chair, a Polaroid camera and the badge-making machinery. 'Come to the press office at 9.30,' she said. 'We will have the list of today's events for you,' and she left them to it.

'Sit in the chair, please,' said the man, and they took turns to sit and stare ahead while he lined up a spot of light on their foreheads and took their pictures. Then they had to wait while the photos dried. He cut them out, typed their details on the badge blanks, then, one by one, he put them through the machine which heat-sealed them into a plastic sleeve, to a faint smell of scorched hydrocarbons. Steve's came out first and the guard handed it to him, unsmiling, and slipped a second copy into a box file marked Press.

'May I take a quick look in the box, please?' he asked.

The man stared at him. 'Why?' he said.

'I saw someone I know from a long time back. I can't remember his name,' said Steve, and the man pushed the box towards him. There were maybe a hundred and fifty cards – stills photographers, journalists and TV. It was almost at the end. The mug shot wasn't immediately obvious as the man on the mountain, and Steve looked on through the rest before coming back to it, but then he read the details printed on the card and he knew with complete certainty that this was indeed the man they were looking for. PFISTER, DIETER was what it said, then, underneath, TV: EUROPEAN BUSINESS NETWORK. He showed Maja, thanked the man, and, badges clipped on, they walked out into the foyer.

The crowd was building up. All along one wall, sets of double doors led into the auditorium, but the first session wasn't due to start for half an hour and the early arrivals were milling round the tables in the foyer where coffee was laid out. The bar was opening for business at one end. Within seconds Steve spotted the elderly figure of a former French Prime Minister standing chatting to the British Trade Secretary. Behind them, a tall man with receding hair was looking around with a worried expression.

'That's it,' said Steve, 'I know that guy. He used to work at Lime Grove on some BBC2 programme. Of course. European Business Network. He was head-hunted a year or two back to start something up in Switzerland. That's what it was.'

'You had better talk with him. You go, I'll come behind,' said Maja.

Steve followed the other man out of the hall, trying hard to remember his name. Then he got it. 'Hunter,' he called out, 'Hunter Williams.'

Williams turned, smiling uncertainly, looking fairly blank. 'Hello,' he said with enormous *bonhomie*. 'Oh, it's er ... John, isn't it?'

'Steve, Steve Ross, remember me from the Spur?'

The truthful answer was clearly 'No'. 'Yes, of course,' said Williams with gusto, 'how are you?'

'Fine, fine,' said Steve. 'I suppose this is right up your street. Are you shooting much here?'

'Oodles and oodles. It's jolly good. Nice to, er ...' and his voice trailed off as he looked vaguely around the crowd.

Steve remembered his reputation for rarely finishing a sentence, and persisted. 'Who are you using as a crew?'

'Oh, that's a bloody disaster,' said Williams, suddenly switching his full attention back on with considerable vehemence. 'Tragedy really. Our man went and crashed his car yesterday on the way up. Did himself no end of damage. Pushed off the road by someone who didn't even stop. We got baled out by some local who just happened to be here on spec. Trouble is, he's a bloody awful cameraman. We've had to have a strict word or two about the quality. Only about a quarter of what he's shot so far is any good at all. He doesn't seem to have a clue and he keeps pissing off when we need him. Still, I suppose we have to be grateful for ...' His voice died away again as he clearly saw someone much more interesting elsewhere in the crowd.

'What's his gear like?'

Williams looked surprised at the question. 'What on earth do you mean?'

'Well, has he got up-to-date equipment?'

'Wouldn't have a clue. You'll have to ask one of my technical types if you really want to know. We're cutting in a sort of mobile home thing out back. Is it important?'

'Just a thought.'

'Anyway, if you happen to see him, thickset, stubbly sort of chap, tell him I want him, will you? He's left a message saying he's going up the mountain for some bloody photo-call, and I need him for an interview downstairs.'

'I'll tell him. What's the photo-call?'

'Oh, it's the Václav Havel shoot. We don't even need it.'

The man in the maroon waistcoat looked indignant as he was sent staggering back into a pillar, spilling his coffee, reaching for the place where the swinging recorder had hammered into his side. 'I'm sorry,' said Steve. But he didn't stop to help. He was moving as fast as he could through the knots of people, Maja coming after him, her questions for the moment ignored, threading his way towards the staircase down to the press office.

There was no one else on the stairs, and she tried again. 'What's happened, Steve?'

He was panting, racing downwards. 'Havel, photo-call up the bloody mountain. Pfister's already on his way.'

Marlene was gathering up papers from a desk. He slowed to a less question-provoking speed as he came round the corner. 'Marlene, we just heard about the Havel shoot. Can we go?'

She looked at her watch. 'Sure. There's time. The special train is in ten minutes from the Parsennbahn station. I am going now myself. Just come with me.'

Nick was sitting on a wall when they got back into

353

the fresh air. He jumped to his feet. 'We're going up the mountain, Nick,' Steve said loudly, 'Havel is appearing up there for some pictures. The other crews are going up as well.'

Nick got the message. 'Don't suppose I could come too?' he said to Marlene.

She looked a little doubtful. 'You're meant to have a badge to get on the train,' she said, 'but, if you stay with me, I'll get you through.'

The Parsennbahn station was closed for normal business for the morning. A few disgruntled Alpine walkers were being redirected along the far end of the Promenade to the Schatzalpbahn. Two security guards checked their passes, listened to Marlene's explanation of Nick's presence, and let them through into the gloomy interior of the station, where the zigzag barriers for the winter crowds stood superfluously. Electric doors opened to let them on to the platform, and Steve, feeling a touch on his shoulder, looked round to see Nick proffering a pair of mirror-lensed sun-glasses and his baseball cap.

'In case your face gets spotted,' he whispered. Steve nodded and put them on, glad he did so when he saw the twenty or thirty people already waiting on the platform, heads turning to inspect the newcomers.

Most carried the paraphernalia of the professional photographer – Nikons strung round their necks, equipment bags over their shoulders. The little red train was waiting, but its doors were still closed. The entire train was tilted up at a steep angle, with its carriages subdivided into compartments going up like a staircase. The platform rose in steps to match it, each bay opposite a matching door of the train, railed off.

At the far end, up the slope of the platform, Steve could see Diana Pugh with Neville and Ted, her crew. Then a cold shock of recognition hit him, and it all began to turn from theory into practice. Just beyond the BBC crew, through a gap between them, he saw Pfister's profile. The man was talking to someone else, his soundman, a young fair-haired guy he had never seen before. Then the doors opened and they got in.

The train was capable of carrying twenty times the number of passengers, so they had a compartment completely to themselves. It was designed mostly for people standing, but across each end was a fold-down wooden bench seat, and there was enough space for the four of them on one of those.

'What happens when we get there, Marlene?'

'There is a sun terrace at the main restaurant and lift-station, the Weissfluhjoch. Havel is already there, having a private meeting. He will come out for just a few minutes for pictures. It is very beautiful there, just a sea of mountain tops all around.'

'How close do we get?'

'Right up as close as you like.' She opened her briefcase. 'By the way, while we are waiting, here is the rest of today's programme.'

Steve took it and looked through it, with Nick and Maja craning over his shoulder.

09.30	Opening session. Welcoming remarks from Chairman and Mayor of Davos.
10.00–12.00	First Plenary. 'After the supply-side: Economics for the end of the century.'
12.00–13.45	Lunchtime discussion groups. See other list.
14.00–16.00	Second Plenary. Gorbachev–Yeltsin debate and questions.
17.00–18.30	Third Plenary. 'South Africa after

19.45   Cocktails. Main Hall. Provided by the
         Municipality of Davos.

It was the second plenary which grabbed him, and with it returned all the uncertainty of not, after all, knowing if this slow train ride was taking them up to the conclusion they feared.

Nick was ahead of him. 'Marlene, what's the access like for Gorbachev and Yeltsin? Can we shoot arrivals, or is there something special laid on?'

She laughed with the doubting tone of someone who doesn't know if their leg is being pulled. 'Arrivals? That would be difficult. You have time to go to Moscow?'

Nick's incomprehension showed clearly in his face. 'What do you mean?'

She laughed again, this time more derisively. 'You didn't think they were coming here, did you? It's just a stunt. They're on a satellite teleconference link from a studio in Moscow. They're only doing half an hour, then they're taking five questions each from the floor here.' She leaned forward conspiratorially. 'To be honest, I am not even certain Gorbachev will turn up. There are stand-ins from the Soviet press ready to take their places just in case. Are you disappointed?'

'No,' said Steve, 'no, not at all,' and, turning to look out of the window, he began to flex his hands and arms as if limbering up.

They had to change trains halfway up at the Höhenweg station, walking across the angled platform to another identical train for the last leg. Steve avoided looking up in Pfister's direction. Then it was a shorter ride up past an increasingly lunar landscape of scree slopes, hidden from time to time by

356

avalanche shelters, to the bulky blockhouse of the Weissfluhjoch, where the cable pulling the little train slowed to a halt and they got out into a network of echoing concrete tunnels. Policemen were everywhere.

'The sun terrace is just up that way,' said Marlene, pointing. 'I must hurry. Shall I see you up there?'

'Yes,' said Steve, glad of the excuse to hang back out of the way while the other crews went ahead. They were left alone for a moment in a large hallway. Overhead signs with symbols showing cable-cars pointed to the Schiferbahn, the Gipfelbahn and the Parsennhüttebahn.

'This is it, guys,' said Nick. 'Any ideas?'

Steve felt slightly dizzy and short of breath, and realized it must be the altitude, but his brain seemed to be working with great clarity. 'Yes,' he said. 'No more risks. We'll find a place which overlooks the photo-call. When you can see we're up there, ready to roll, you tell Marlene there's a problem. Tell her to get the police to grab Pfister and take the side plate off the camera. We'll shoot it.'

'Do I wait for Havel to come out?'

Maja answered, 'For God's sake, no. That could easily be too late.'

Nick went to the terrace. Maja and Steve found some steps leading to a sun-deck up above it. A policeman barred the way, then checked their tags and, to their relief, let them through. They came out on a concrete balcony and looked around. The view was as spectacular as Marlene had promised. In the clear air, mountain peak after mountain peak serrated the sky, mostly on the same level or slightly below them. Then, as Maja prepared the camera, Steve looked down and caught his breath. They were immediately above the terrace, which was crowded with photographers and policemen. Nick was looking up desperately for them because, at the end of the terrace, leaning back at ease against the railings, the familiar figure of Václav Havel was already standing.

'Are you ready?' he asked Maja. She nodded. He put up a thumb to Nick. Nick pushed through the crowd to Marlene, Maja filming every move, and began talking urgently to her. She swung round to him, displaying the body language of utter astonishment, then disbelief. He began to wave his arms around emphatically. Marlene looked pale and put one hand up to the side of her face. She stood, showing indecision, while Pfister lifted his camera to his shoulder, and then she crossed to a policeman, showed her pass and started talking rapidly, pointing at Pfister. The policeman talked into a radio and, with bewildering speed, everything happened at once. Two men in plain clothes and two other policemen closed in on Pfister and his soundman.

Then, when it was too late for second thoughts, the first doubts struck Steve. This was all wrong. Pfister looked like a mercenary, not a fanatic. There was no way out from up here. He wouldn't have stood a prayer of getting away. He watched in an agony of doubt as the men were frogmarched to the back of the terrace, arguing loudly. Maja, out of their line of vision, panned with them, zooming in. The rest of the crowd, intent on Havel, stirred momentarily, then got on with the job in hand, filling the gap where Pfister had been. The policeman laid the camera on the table, Nick and Marlene coming back to see. Maja zoomed in to tight close-up and suddenly Steve heard her mutter a swear word. Then he saw what she had just seen. The side plate had come off to reveal nothing inside except the normal circuitry, which was not surprising because the camera was a shiny new Sony.

Chapter Thirty

Steve slipped again on the loose shale and swore. The weight of the recorder kept swinging him off-balance on the steep, rocky pathway. Maja, bounding down in front, seemed to be having no such problems and turned to smile encouragement at him. It was her idea, and he had to admit she was right.

As the angry security men led Nick and Marlene away from the terrace, leaving a thoughtful-looking Pfister to get back to his filming, Maja had ducked down behind the parapet of the sun balcony, pulling Steve down next to her, out of sight. 'Better we get clear now,' she said. 'Marlene might tell them we are here.'

'How?' he said. 'There's only the one train down.'

She shook her head and pointed to the steps down from the side of the balcony. 'We have our feet,' she said. 'We go down the path to the halfway station at Höhenweg and get on the lower train there. It gives us a better chance.'

'Unless they put the word out on the radio.'

'Sure, they might. Stay here, and they're certain to find us. Then you lose your badge straight away. Come on.'

There were marmots running across the further slope of the rugged valley down beside the railway track. Steve remembered their blood on the grass, what seemed like months before, and his resolve hardened again. Two policemen stood on guard at the entrance to the middle station, ready to turn away ramblers, wearing the air of men unsure why their morning was being wasted in this way. They looked surprised to see them, but Maja told some story about getting general shots of Davos from above and, after having their badges inspected, they were allowed on to the waiting train. They went right to the lower end and huddled in silent tension for ten minutes, and, when the top train finally came down with all the photographers and cameramen on board, no one else bothered to come down the platform as far as their compartment. Craning to look through the side-windows up the slope of the platform, they saw Pfister and his soundman for a moment, but there was no sign of Marlene or Nick.

At the bottom station they got out first and ran down the steps to the street, rushing to get clear before Pfister or anyone else came in sight. From a vantage point behind a coach they watched Pfister come out of the station and stand for a minute talking to the younger man, looking at his watch. The other man nodded and walked off along the Promenade towards the conference centre, while Pfister crossed the road towards them and disappeared into the side-street that led downhill to the car parks. They went after him.

When they got to the entrance to the side-street, they could see him a hundred yards further down, carrying the camera by its top handle. Whatever he had made of the incident on the mountain, he didn't seem too bothered now, just sauntering along, looking straight ahead. He was in an open area, the main wintertime parking lot for the mountain railway and the buses to the other ski lifts. It was fuller than was usual in summer because of the conference. One end was fenced off and contained a fleet of fifty or more shiny black Audi V8s, brought in from Germany and being marshalled there for their job of transporting the VIPs to and from the conference.

Steve and Maja had a clear view from above, and didn't need to get any closer.

'Kneel down,' said Maja, 'I will use you for a tripod.'

She steadied the camera against the side of Steve's head, switching in the doubler and zooming to the full extent to reduce the distance. Pfister strolled over to the Audis, looked through the windscreen of one of them for a minute in casual interest, then turned and crossed the parking lot. He threaded his way between the lines of cars, and they could see his objective long before he got to it – the familiar Range Rover which had cost Steve his job in Geneva, and which they'd last seen on the slopes of the mountain.

Pfister unlocked the rear hatch, reached inside and took out something grey. Steve thought for a moment it might be the Ikegami, but, from the way Pfister was holding it, it was too light. Then he got a clear view as the camera went on whirring next to his ear, and realized it was only a big directional microphone, bulky inside its long, cylindrical wind cover. Pfister took it and, still holding the camera in his other hand, moved off through the car park, heading back along the lower road, which paralleled the Promenade, towards the back entrance to the conference centre.

'Let's go and look in the Range Rover,' said Steve. They waited until Pfister was out of sight, then circled around from the other side of the car park, keeping as many cars as possible between themselves and the direction in which he'd disappeared. They peered in through the back window. The load space behind the rear seats was full of boxes and equipment. A rug was spread over it, but, protruding from under it, right at the back, was an inch or two of familiar grey and black metal casing. It was the Ikegami.

'For God's sake. It's here. It's just sitting here,' he said in disbelief. 'Let's just grab it. They'll have to believe us then, and they'll have to pick up Pfister.'

'And no one gets killed,' said Maja.

He looked around, weighing the odds of discovery. 'OK, first things first. Can you get a shot through the window which shows the Icky in the back of the car?'

'Sure.' She plugged in the camera and white-balanced it, zooming in on the white cloth patch on the recorder bag. Then she leant against the side of the Range Rover, hefting the camera up awkwardly so that she could shoot through the glass and twisting the viewfinder down on its pivot so she could see properly. She wasn't satisfied with the reflection to start with, and did it again through a different window while Steve sweated out the seconds, staring round to watch for a returning Pfister.

'OK,' she said, 'I have it. What do you want to do now?'

'Could you go and get the Jeep and bring it here. We're going to need it. I'll wait. You can leave the camera here.'

She reached up a hand to his cheek. 'No, it's OK, I'll take the camera. If he comes back, I would prefer it if you were able to move fast.'

When she'd gone, Steve went in search of some wire. He knew exactly what he needed from years of driving ancient cars with unreliable door-locks: a strong length of straight wire, like a section from an ordinary wire coat-hanger. He couldn't find anything like it. He searched in rubbish bins, on the building site next to the car park, and on the ground under the cars. Swiss cleanliness was working against him. The black Cherokee was nosing into the car park before his eyes lit on the solution. A large wooden sign advertising a nearby pizzeria was wired to a bracket on the back wall of the car park. He went over and inspected it. There was enough thick, soft wire bent round the bracket, through each of the two holes, for his needs.

He went to the Jeep. 'Maja, does Rudi keep any tools in the car?'

'Yes, I think so. There is his special army gear in a brown bag in the back there.'

He put the recorder on the back seat and opened the tailgate. The bag was lashed carefully to the side of the rear luggage space, to a set of metal rings which Rudi had clearly installed for the purpose. When Steve untied it, he realized why. The bag was filled with the special tools of Rudi's army trade, strange-shaped wrenches, some coiled fuse cord in a plastic bag marked with warning skull and crossbones, and a large, yellow, metal cylinder with a screw thread on one end in a separate, carefully padded container. He found a pair of pliers in the bottom of the bag, replaced everything else with great care, and went to work. It took no time to undo one piece of the wire, but the sign looked conspicuous, hanging drunkenly off the wall, so Steve started on the other one. He was halfway through when a voice challenged him, and he looked round to see an angry-looking Swiss policeman striding towards them.

Maja intercepted him before Steve had a chance to say a word. She spoke fast and reassuringly in Schweizerdeutsch, with a note of distinct authority. The policeman broke in a couple of times, but she didn't give him a chance to interrupt the flow. Inside a couple of minutes, he was nodding, waving and going on his way.

Steve let out his breath in a long sigh. 'What did you say to him?'

She shrugged her shoulders. 'I just told him we were from the Cantonal inspection department, doing a survey to see whether the acid rainfall has had any weakening effect on metalwork in the area, and we needed to test this wire to see if the sign had become a safety hazard to passers-by.'

'Wow.'

'You better hurry. He might come back for another look. Anyway, what do you need the wire for?'

'To get into the Range Rover.'

Maja moved the Jeep so it screened the driver's door of the Range Rover from view. Steve used the pliers to straighten the wire, then turned the end a quarter-inch at right angles to make a short hook. While Maja kept watch, he pushed it carefully down between the glass and the sealing rubber of the window, and rotated it, feeling for the short metal bar inside the door casing which operated the lock. He touched it, and pulled back on the wire to hook it under and lift. The wire bent and the hook slipped out. He cursed and tried again, but the same thing happened.

'What is wrong?' asked Maja, frowning, but continuing to stare round the car park.

'The wire's too soft. It's bending.'

She looked. 'Can you make it work?'

'I don't think so. I'll have to search around for some more.'

She shook her head. 'I have a way,' she said, 'shall I try it?'

'Does it work?' he said, surprised.

'It always works.'

'OK then, go ahead.'

She went to the back of the Jeep, chose a heavy Stilson wrench from Rudi's bag, looked all around her, then swung it once, hard against the Range Rover's window. The noise of shattering glass seemed to fill the car park, and Steve jumped out of his skin.

'Jesus, I didn't know that was what you meant. I'm not sure ...'

'Just get the Ikegami and let's go,' she said.

He reached through the remains of the window and opened the door. The central locking clicked, and he lifted the tailgate. Then the Ikegami was in his hands, lighter than he expected, and he was putting it in the back of the Jeep.

Maja started up. 'Stay in the back there,' she said. 'Pack Rudi's stuff away carefully while I drive. Be very careful with that yellow thing.'

Steve looked at the metal cylinder in its packing. 'Why?'

'Because it is a detonator.'

In the little bedroom, Elena woke again, but the drugs had been weaker this time and it was a more controlled wakening. She kept her eyes closed and her breathing regular, because the noises in the apartment told her there were others there beside her. She listened and heard Cheeseman in the next room.

'Good,' he said, 'that's the last of that. All clean in here. If there's anything left worth checking, they won't find a thing.'

'What about the second device?'

That was Heller. Then it was Cheeseman again. 'Put it in the car, with the papers.' He laughed. 'Just in case they're a bit slow at putting two and two together. That should give them a pretty big clue as to what happened to this place. I've jinxed the timer on that one. When they take it to bits in Bern, they'll find it would have gone off as soon as she began to set it, so they'll guess the same thing happened here.'

'We had better get her prints on it, before it goes in the car.'

'Good thinking, man. Go and do it, will you? Oh, and put the passport in her bag. We'll leave that with her.'

She let all her muscles relax as footsteps came into the room, and a rather fastidious hand took hers, pressing three of her fingers against a cold, smooth surface. Glass, she thought, or very highly polished metal.

The footsteps left and she heard Heller go out of an outside door. A minute later he was back. 'I have done it. It is in the boot.'

This will never be believed, she thought. With a target like that, what could the motive be? But immediately, she knew that was naïve. Money would be enough motive. A paper trail of money, artfully constructed, leading back across two continents, its deep black footprints filling up with the blood that would result, the sudden reversal of the rapid progress towards peace and reconciliation.

'That's it, then. You go to the meeting point to make sure Pfister gets clear. I will come back later to do what needs to be done here. I'll put the clothes on her then.'

Footsteps approached the door. Heller's voice came from the doorway. 'Shall I give her another shot?'

Cheeseman's voice was scornful. 'NO, for crying out loud. Didn't you get the point? If there's anything left to check, they must not discover she was drugged. She should be waking up soon. It has to look like an accident.'

When the door slammed, she waited another minute before she opened her eyes. The room was empty. She lifted her head as far as she could and looked around. Everything was as it was before. The target's picture was still on the wall. What was new was the large glass container on top of the chest of drawers – a container full of maybe four litres of an amber-coloured liquid. The square box on top had a switch and a digital electric timer built into it. The switch was set at OFF.

Maja turned right off the road, bumping over a railway crossing, which had Steve grabbing to steady the brown bag, then climbing the road towards the Fluelapass. A mile further up, she pulled into the deserted car park of the Pischa ski-lift.

'I will set the camera up, then I film you opening the side cover.'

'Right,' he said. 'Once we hand it over to the police, I don't suppose they'll let us see it again.'

The four fasteners had wide slots in their screw heads, and, when Maja had the camera set up on the tripod and ready to roll, he used a coin to undo them. Moving slowly to give the best shot, he took the cover off and lifted it out of the way. Maja pressed the rocker switch to zoom in, and he looked into the side of the camera. There should have been a neat rank of printed circuit boards, but there wasn't. Beyond them, towards the front of the camera, there should have been the ends of its colour tubes, but those weren't there either. That much was confirmation of all they had suspected, but there also should have been something else, the barrel, magazine and breech mechanism of some kind of gun. The trouble was, that wasn't there either.

Maja switched off her camera and took the Ikegami from him, turning it in her hands and staring at it. It was little more than an empty casing, gutted of almost everything. She pointed inside it. 'Look, here and again here. There are new brackets inside. You can see where something was attached to this one. They have taken it out.'

The lens casing was empty as well, not even the fake plastic lens itself had been left in place. Maja put the camera back in the Jeep. 'Should we take this to the police?'

He shook his head slowly. 'What would you say, if you were a Swiss policeman?'

'I would say, you are making a joke with me, yes? I would say, you say this is a camera made to have a gun inside, but there is nothing inside. I would say you and your friend Mr Nielsen are wasting a lot of our police time.'

'Yes,' said Steve, 'that's what I would say, too.' He put both hands to his face and rubbed his eyes hard.

Maja stood there watching him, a troubled expression on her face. He stretched out his hands to her, and twined her fingers into his. 'Well then,' he said, 'it's just you and me against the bad guys.' She smiled sadly and nodded. 'Not fair, I would say,' he added, as they climbed back into the Jeep. 'On the bad guys, I mean.'

Chapter Thirty-one

The first obstacle was the security barrier on the way into the conference centre. They stood, deliberately apart, in the line of delegates and tried to look bored as they came up to the man who lifted every badge, read every name and compared every face to its photo.

Maja went first and got through. Steve followed, expecting a challenge, but it was all plain sailing, just a quick impersonal look and then a nod. Whatever was happening up the mountain, word about them hadn't yet reached its foot. Inside, they checked the main rooms, but there was no sign of Pfister or anyone else they recognized. Back in the foyer, they stopped and looked around. 'All we can do is keep our eyes open. Time to take a breather and think hard,' said Steve. 'We need a place where we're out of sight, but where we have a good view.'

Maja pointed upwards. 'By the coffee lounge,' she said. 'See the balcony?'

It stuck out above the foyer, a quiet corner for businessmen to do deals and swap cards. For what they wanted now it was perfect, shielded by a screen of decorative trees in tubs, but allowing them a panoramic view across the whole of the entrance and registration area, and the main foyer below.

It was an out of the way corner, but revenge is a powerful driving force and Marlene found them inside half an hour. Steve turned round when he heard her cry of recognition, and just had time to think, oh shit, we've run out of time, before she was upon them. She pitched her voice low, but its tone was venomous.

'You have maybe cost me my job,' she said. 'You and your stupid friend. I wish I had never helped you.'

'Nick was just trying to . . .'

'He is telling such stupid tales to the police you would not believe,' she said. 'Full of nonsense about plots. They want to know why I took him up the mountain. I have to write a report this afternoon.' She sat down and glared at them. 'And after I did so much for you.'

'Where is he now?'

'Where do you think? They are holding on to him at the police station. You do not just say stupid things like he said in the middle of an event like this and walk away.'

'Marlene, maybe what he said isn't so stupid . . .'

But she was off again in full flood before he could continue. 'No, no, no. I do not want to hear.' She was scratching the back of one hand with the fingernails of the other.

'Havel may still be in great danger.'

She rounded on him. 'Bullshit. Havel is in no danger. Havel is in a helicopter. He has gone, just like they always planned. No one shot at him, no one attacked him, no one even shouted at him.' Then she seemed to run out of steam and her voice trailed into little more than a whisper. 'I don't know what to do about you two.'

A little feeling of hope crept back into him. 'Didn't you tell them about us?'

She looked uncomfortable. 'It is very hard for me. Nick is bad enough. With you two it is worse. I really broke all the rules. I have let you inside. That is why I was looking for you. I want to know what you will do. Are you going to make any more trouble for me? Because if you are I must tell someone right now.'

Steve shook his head. 'No trouble. We'll just shoot pictures and keep our noses clean.'

'I don't know,' she said, 'maybe I should go now and think. I don't even want to be seen with you.' To Steve's alarm she was crying as she spoke, and, before they could say anything further, she got up and walked rapidly away.

As she disappeared down the spiral stairs, a man in a white linen suit got up from a nearby table and Steve heard a voice he knew well say, 'Annoying the ladies, Mr Ross? Dear, oh dear, we shall have to do something about your manners.'

'Anthony?' he said, and so far away was he from the familiar feelings of journalist's camaraderie that the not-at-all-surprising presence of an old colleague at this news-worthy event seemed the strangest thing in the world. For a moment the pressures of their dangerous situation seemed to weigh less heavily on him, and he waved the man eagerly to Marlene's recently vacated chair.

'Maja, this is Anthony Conrad. An old friend of mine. He's with BBC World Service. One of the intellectuals.'

Conrad kissed her hand with exaggerated courtesy. 'Delighted, which is more than I can say at seeing this walking scarecrow here. I wouldn't have recognized him but for his voice.'

Steve remembered the baseball hat and the mirror glasses and, looking round cautiously, took them off. 'Sorry, I forgot.'

Conrad brought a pipe out of his pocket and began to stuff it with aromatic Dutch tobacco. 'Things must be bad if you have to take on a job as soundman, then dress up to hide from your friends.'

Steve shot a glance around the foyer, remembering what they were there for, then looked back at Conrad. He'd spent a while working for the World Service at Bush House in the

Strand, and enjoyed every moment of it. It was an ivory tower compared to the glossier world of the BBC's domestic services, and, perhaps because of that, the people had a special quality. Old-fashioned objectivity came first in a way the other services might regard as pedantic sometimes, but which had kept the special World Service reputation intact around the globe.

Anthony Conrad was an old Africa hand, but he'd been everywhere else as well – a man who knew almost everything but would never make that obvious unless you asked. He was thin to the point of gauntness, with a high forehead and a cleft chin. Long-fingered hands with surprisingly hairy backs stuck out from the frayed linen suit which he seemed to have been wearing ever since Steve had first met him. The only concession to the passing of time was the small Sony Pro-Walkman tape recorder he had put on the table in front of him in place of the giant Uher reel-to-reel machine which had always been the standard equipment in the past.

'What are you here for, Anthony? The Gorbachev debate?'

The older man made a rude noise. 'Come on. You can get better than that on Soviet TV any day of the week. No, it's the South Africa stuff I'm after. That's getting on for real news.'

Steve was distracted by a movement down in the foyer, and glanced rapidly round to check faces. Conrad took his blank look at face value. 'Haven't you been keeping up with the news?'

'Which particular news?'

'Well, you know the USA has dropped trade sanctions.'

'No, really? When?'

'This week. God, Steve, where have you been?' He looked at him more closely. 'I thought you were joking, but you really didn't know, did you?'

Steve shook his head. 'No, I've been a bit out of it for a

few days,' thinking to himself, I haven't heard a news bulletin since before we left Shoreham.

'It's all come tumbling down. They're back in the Olympics too.'

'What brought all this on?'

This time Conrad really stared at him. 'You do know de Klerk's abolished apartheid, don't you?'

Steve glanced around the floor again to cover his confusion, realizing just how much life had changed since the days – when ? – only two or three weeks before, when he would have been suffering severe withdrawal symptoms after only a couple of hours without a news bulletin of some sort. He looked back at Conrad. 'Anthony, one day I'll tell you the story, but things have been a little odd just lately.'

Conrad raised his eyebrows, taking in the distracted glances both Steve and Maja were constantly casting over the balcony. 'So it would seem. Am I getting in the way of your work?'

'No, not at all. We're just watching out for someone. Are you doing stuff for Bush newsroom?'

'I'll do a piece for Radio Newsreel if it's strong enough. No, in fact I'm doing a special on the end of the pipeline. Half an hour, for next week.'

Steve had had enough of looking blank. 'What pipeline?' he said.

Conrad looked at Maja and winked. 'Your soundman used to be a bright boy once, before he went to pieces. Don't worry, Uncle Anthony will now explain.' He looked at Steve. 'You do remember what sanctions were, don't you?'

'Get on with it.'

He pretended to look hurt. 'Well I'm sure you know that one of the major effects of sanctions was to make huge amounts of money for the people who knew how to break them, and this charming country we're in has maybe the biggest concentration of specialists and front companies helping all those goods on their way, with no questions asked. Hence the pipeline, and hence a great big hole in a lot of big bank balances now sanctions are disappearing, right?'

'Yes, of course,' said Steve, looking across the foyer again.

'It's not quite that simple of course, because the UN arms embargo is still there, but even that probably has its days numbered now.' He looked around and chuckled. 'Funny, really, isn't it? Here's Switzerland playing host to the UN in Geneva and, at the same time, it allows all these people to live here who are doing their best to drive a coach and horses through some of the things the UN is trying to achieve. Lots of little neo-Nazi middlemen, living in the sunshine, creaming off their forty per cent.' He looked thoughtfully at Steve. 'Your turn. That's what I'm doing. How about you?'

There's no point in holding back, thought Steve. Any extra pair of eyes right now would help, and the clock's running. 'Strictly between ourselves until I say so?' he said.

'Of course.'

'We're shooting a doco. It started off being about insider trading. Now it looks like being about murder. We think something nasty is going to happen here.'

Conrad took the pipe out of his mouth and rocked forward in his chair. He looked at them silently for a minute and saw something in their faces which removed the bantering cynicism from his voice as if it had never been there. 'How can I help?' he said.

'Well,' said Steve, 'there's a man called Kent Cheeseman.' He looked around again as he spoke, and experienced that disorientation you get surfacing from a novel set in an airliner, and only then remembering you're in one yourself –

Cheeseman was walking across the floor below, heading for the registration desk.

'Maja,' he said urgently, 'crank it up. There he is.'

She had the camera on her shoulder, and he bent to check the recorder, while Conrad tried to crane past him through the narrow gap. By the time they were all in a position to see, Cheeseman had his back to them, bending over the desk talking to the girl down below. He talked for a long time.

'Turn round, you bastard,' muttered Steve. Then he had an idea. 'Anthony, go and see if you can get him to turn round, will you? Just ask him something, anything you like.'

'I'm on my way,' said Conrad.

'One other thing. It looks like he's registering for one of the sessions. See if you can read the list and find out which one.'

Conrad waved a hand and headed for the stairs. There was a groan from Maja. 'Battery. Oh no. Quick, pass me one.'

Steve's fingers fumbled with the straps of the equipment bag. He was holding his breath, feeling the sharp pain of knowing just how many perfect shots had been ruined by the sudden death of a battery. His fingers found the edge of one of the heavy black rechargeables, and Maja's hand was waiting for it. She slotted it into the holder on the back of the camera, which hummed reassuringly, and panned as Conrad appeared below them and walked across the foyer.

To start with, Conrad played his part perfectly. He stood next to Cheeseman, keeping out of the way of the shot, while he looked down at the transaction going on at the desk. The girl behind the desk was writing something down on a piece of paper. They saw Conrad saying something, and to Steve's delight Cheeseman lifted his head and turned to show his profile to the camera.

Just keep him talking, he willed, just thirty seconds or so, but it was not to be. As Cheeseman and Conrad looked at each other, they both reacted with stunned surprise. Conrad's jaw dropped and Cheeseman recoiled as if he'd been slapped. They stared at each other in silence for a count of three, then Cheeseman turned back to the desk, ripped the piece of paper from the girl's hand, ignoring her startled protest, and strode away across the floor. Conrad stood staring after him.

'Come on,' said Steve, picking up the recorder. He took the cable from Maja as she undid it from the camera, then went down the stairs two at a time. They met Conrad at the foot.

'You knew him. We could tell. What happened?' demanded Steve.

Conrad blinked at him. He looked shocked. 'Jesus Christ,' he said, 'I never expected to see *him* again. Kent Cheeseman.' He nodded to himself. 'He's Anglicized it. That's not Kent Cheeseman, that's Coen Van Kaasman, Connie to his friends. Not that he has many because he's about the most evil bastard you could ever hope to meet.'

'Van Kaasman? He's Dutch?'

'God no. Well, only if you go back a few hundred years. He's South African. He's Boer through and through.'

'Quickly as you can, Anthony. Tell me what you know about him. We've got very little time.'

'It was a long time ago. I was covering the Biafran war. He was mixed up in some weird business when the Nigerians changed the currency almost overnight. There was a heap of potentially worthless money sitting in Biafran bank vaults the wrong side of the lines. He was trying to get in with the bunch of guys who were planning to smuggle it through before the deadline for changing it. Needless to say, it all fouled up.'

'You mean he was on Ojukwu's side in Biafra? I thought they were all idealists.'

Conrad managed a half-grin. 'Idealists and mercenaries. Some of them were bloody nasty, but Connie took the biscuit. After the currency scam went wrong, they blamed him. Word went round he was working for the other side. People even started saying he was a BOSS agent working for the South Africans for some devious reason of their own. They locked him up. That's why I remember him so well. I spent two hours in his cell trying to interview him. They were planning to shoot him the next day, but he didn't hang around to give them the pleasure. He strangled the guard that night and legged it. I haven't seen him since. I wonder how the hell the Swiss let him in?'

But Steve knew all too well. It was suddenly, belatedly, crystal clear. 'The pipeline, Anthony. Your own words. He's been living here for years. He's in the arms business.' He stopped. 'De Klerk. Oh God, it's got to be de Klerk. If he gets de Klerk, he could screw it all up. When's de Klerk coming?'

'Soon. The debate's this afternoon. That's what he was putting his name down for.' Conrad's face was pale. 'Why just de Klerk, Steve? Why not both of them at one go?'

'What do you mean, both of them?'

And then Conrad's frightened voice was almost a scream in Steve's ears. 'Jesus. Don't you know anything? Mandela's coming. That's what the debate is all about, de Klerk and Mandela.'

Chapter Thirty-two

'Come on, Steve. It's been on the cards for six whole bloody months. You must have known.'

'Well, I didn't. Mandela wasn't on the list I saw.'

'That was just WEF theatrics. They love last-minute surprises, but everyone knew, really.' Conrad stopped talking and shook his head. 'Anyway, that's not the point. Just tell me. No bullshit. Do you really think your man is going to try to kill them?'

Steve looked at him hard. 'No bullshit – yes, and I'm running out of ideas. The police won't believe a word I say. We've already blown our hand. Where did Cheeseman go?'

'Out that way,' said Maja. 'To the entrance, I think.'

'Look, Anthony. You might just bring this off. The police are holding Nick Nielsen. He's an American. He's working with us.'

'I've heard of him.'

'He tried to tip them off. It went wrong. We had the wrong target. If you went to them and you told them who Cheeseman really is, and who he must be aiming for, they might just believe you.'

Conrad looked doubtful. 'They might not.'

'No, they might not. I can't force you and I haven't time. It's up to you. If you do it, tell them, and Nick too if you can, that the gun's been taken out of the Ikegami. It's somewhere else. We don't know where.'

'What gun? What Ikegami?'

'There really isn't time to explain. Nick will understand.

Tell him we've got the Ikegami, OK?'

Conrad's face was a picture of indecision as he grappled with that one. Steve gave it one last shot. 'We're going to try something else to see if we can stop him. You're the only other chance. I'm going now. You make up your own mind.' He turned on his heels and took Maja by the arm, and they left Conrad standing there.

'Where are we going?' she said.

'Outside, to see if we can find Cheeseman.'

'No,' she said, 'inside first. What about asking your friend at EBN?'

'Asking him what?'

'Asking him where his cameraman is. Cheeseman is not the kind to get his own hands dirty.'

Out through the back door and into the long concrete yard, they saw the TV vehicles lined up against the wall fifty yards further down. Three big SRG outside broadcast trucks were first in line, festooned with cables looping up to windows above. Beyond them were four Portakabins. The third in line had a sticker on the door, a waving flag showing a stylized map of Europe and the initials EBN below it.

They heard a man's voice raised in anger inside before they even got to the door. Steve knocked, opened it and looked in. The windows were screened off. In the half-light, Hunter Williams's face was lit by the flickering image on the two monitors in front of him. He was holding his large head with his hands, in a pose of theatrical disgust. A nervous-looking girl with glasses was half-turned towards him, frozen with her hand on the control knob of the tape player.

'Go on,' he said, 'spin through it. There must be a shot in it somewhere that's actually in focus if only by the law of averages.'

He turned to them. 'Oh hello,' he said. 'Er ... John. Sorry, not a very good moment. We're having a lot of camera problems today. Can you come back?'

'No, not really,' said Steve, improvising fast. 'Actually, after what you said before, we thought you might have a problem, so we decided to offer you a hand. We're shooting the Mandela–de Klerk debate this afternoon. If you want to give your bloke a rest, we'll let you have a copy.'

Williams swung right round in his chair, radiating puppyish enthusiasm. 'Well, I must say, that's jolly decent of you. What a helpful thought. Normally I'd jump at it, but we're not really terribly interested in, er . . .'

He looked back at the monitor. Steve counted to five. 'In what?'

Williams turned back to him in surprise. 'Oh, in Mandela. In fact we're using Pfister to interview some bankers this afternoon. You might be interested. It's a jolly good story. Even some of the Brits are starting to realize that a strong, independent Central Bank is . . .'

'Hold on a sec,' said Steve. 'We're short of time. Your man isn't going anywhere near the Mandela debate?'

'No. Kind of you to ask though.'

'Not at all. Bye.'

Confused and in some despair, they'd gone twenty yards when his voice came from the door of the Portakabin, provoked by some slight pang of conscience at not reciprocating the offer.

'I say. Hold on a minute.'

They turned to look at him, and he ambled towards them across the yard. 'If you want Mandela pictures, our man's shooting the arrival. He says he knows just the spot.'

Time stopped. A shiver ran through Steve. He could only see Williams's huge face at the centre of a blurred world. 'Where?' he managed to ask, and it came out sounding strangled.

'Don't know exactly. Somewhere down the valley. Good idea of his, really. He said a motorcade coming up the pass with the mountains behind it would make a jolly good opening shot. He thought there'd be so many police around for Mandela and de Klerk, their car would be the ideal one to do.'

'Their car?'

'Yes, apparently de Klerk went down to fetch Mandela from the special train at the bottom. Gives them a chance to talk again before the debate.'

'Do you know when?'

'About an hour's time, I think. The thing is, though, from what I've seen so far, there's only a one-in-ten chance the pictures will be worth using.'

'Thanks,' shouted Steve over his shoulder as they ran.

'Funny people,' mused Williams as he went back to his edit.

They were both out of breath when they reached the Jeep.

'Over the pass?' panted Maja.

'Yes. We'll just have to go like hell and look for Pfister. If we don't find him, we'll try to stop the motorcade.'

Steve leapt into the car, grabbing for a steering-wheel that wasn't there. In the heat of the moment he simply forgot it didn't have right-hand drive. A deeply hidden layer of male chauvinism exposed by the stress of the moment made him curse, but Maja's storming start out of the car park showed it wouldn't have made any difference.

She hit the Promenade with tyres squealing. 'But what do we look for? We know it is not in the Icky.'

'Pfister. We'll just have to look for Pfister. Why are we going this way?'

She was heading along the Promenade, weaving in and out of slower cars. 'Because it is one way,' she said calmly.

381

'We have to cut down left as soon as we can and come back on Talstrasse.'

They were almost level with the conference centre when the traffic all stopped. Ahead, steam was rising from the bent bonnet of a tourist's Volvo which had found out the hard way that, despite the one-way system, buses are allowed to go both ways. The cars ahead waited patiently while the bus driver climbed out and bent down to look at the damage. Maja's hands were clenched on the wheel and Steve, desperate to get moving, leant out of the window to see if there was space to squeeze by on the pavement. There was a lamppost in the way, and a man walking rapidly past it, away from them. The man was Cheeseman. He turned right off the Promenade into a climbing side-street.

'Maja, look,' said Steve. 'I'm going after him. The traffic's about to move. Come up slowly behind me when you can.'

He was out of the door before she had a chance to answer. A sign said the side-street was Richstattweg. He stood at the corner until Cheeseman was a good way up it, then followed, keeping in as much cover as the projecting walls allowed. They crossed Symondstrasse and Scalettastrasse, and Cheeseman kept right on going. Steve was acutely aware of the ticking seconds passing, but here was something solid, and the instincts he had followed all his professional life were busy telling him it was worth sticking with it. Rossweidstrasse stretched across them, and the terrain began to open out with just a few concrete blocks of skiing apartments and a hotel spaced out along it. Trees were visible above.

Steve paused to let Cheeseman cross the open space, and heard the Jeep growling up behind him. He turned and waved Maja to the side of the road, and she stopped and turned off the engine. Then he started off again.

Above Rossweidstrasse, Richstattweg continued for a little

way, curving into a small group of more traditional small chalets, with the first alpine meadows starting above them. From a copse of trees on the left of the road, Steve was able to watch as Cheeseman climbed some outside steps to the door of one of the chalets and let himself in with a key. Steve stood there for two minutes, wondering whether to risk going closer. I'll give it one more minute, he thought, but, before half of that had elapsed, the door opened and Cheeseman came out, locked it, and ran down the steps. He looked flushed. He went quickly back down the road past Steve to the cross-street below, where a green Mercedes G-Wagen was parked. Steve shrank back into the trees. Cheeseman jumped in and gunned the big, square machine down the road, gravel spraying from all four of its chunky tyres. Then he was gone.

Steve ran down to the corner waving his arms to Maja, and in a few seconds the Jeep was stopping next to him. He jumped in. 'Up the hill,' he said. 'Cheeseman came out of a house in a big rush. I want to see what's in there.'

The steps up to the door were concrete. Steve took them cautiously, Maja right behind him. The front door had a glass panel and he could see a dim hallway beyond. There was no sound. Shading the glass with both hands, his face pressed against it, Steve could just see into a more brightly lit room beyond, its door half open. He tried the handle gently, but he'd seen Cheeseman lock it and wasn't surprised when it wouldn't open. Then a tiny movement caught his eye. It was at floor level, almost hidden in the shadow below the brightness. He stared, but it didn't move again. Then, as he strained his eyes to see, a cloud passed over the sun. The contrast between the sunlit part of the room and the floor diminished, and he could see the shape of a foot, sticking out from behind the door.

'There's a body lying on the floor,' he said. 'We've got to get in.'

He rammed the door with his shoulder, but the frame was solid. 'Time for your special method again,' he said, and ran down the steps. Next door stood a concrete mixer beside a heap of sand and a pile of concrete blocks. He picked up a block, ran back up the stairs and rammed it through the glass. He put his hand through and opened the door, then stopped and listened. There was no sound from inside.

He waved Maja back, but she took no notice and followed him into the hall, step by cautious step. 'Shall I get the camera?' she said.

'No, this feels a bit too much like real life.'

The room at the far end of the hall was a small bedroom, with a single window high up in the wall. A dark-skinned woman lay on the floor. She wore jeans and a cotton shirt in some disarray, as though they had been pulled on her as she lay there. The strap of a leather shoulder-bag was round her neck. Steve knew instantly it was the woman they had seen on the mountain, and he knelt down to her. She was breathing, and a large bruise on the side of her forehead, its centre split and oozing blood, showed where Cheeseman must have hit her.

He glanced round the room and saw the picture fastened to the wall – Mandela. At that moment Maja exclaimed from the other side of the room, 'Steve, quick. I think it is time to go.'

He looked across to where she stood in front of a chest of drawers. She was staring at a large glass vessel standing on top of it, a vessel full of liquid and surmounted by a square metal box. The switch on the box stood at ON, and the green figures of a digital timer were counting down as he watched, flickering from 1.02 to 1.01 then 1.00 then .59.

'Shall I turn it off?' said Maja.

'No,' he said, 'don't touch it. Let's get out.'

'And her?'

'Grab her feet. Let's go.'

They were out of the front door inside fifteen seconds and inside the Jeep in another fifteen. Maja got in the driving seat, Steve in the back supporting the limp, light body of the woman. 'Back down the hill. Fast as you can,' said Steve, but the instruction was superfluous.

They were just joining the main road when a dull, thudding wave of pressure swept through their open windows, and looking back they saw a fireball rising above the roofs. Steve padded the unconscious woman's head with a jacket, studying her. Even in these circumstances she was striking, and he wondered what to do. My enemy's enemy, or just another baddy they decided was disposable? Either way there seemed nothing to do but keep her in the Jeep.

They were on Talstrasse, heading back to the road east out of Davos. There was traffic, and Maja was weaving through it with skill. As they passed the lake, and the concrete buildings thinned out, the woman groaned and stirred. Steve looked at her. Her eyes flickered open, blank and unfocused, then closed and opened again with clarity back in them. She moved her head and gasped with pain.

'Do you speak English?' said Steve, and she swivelled her head to look at him.

'Yes of course,' she said. Her voice was thick and slurred, but the accent sounded American.

'Keep still. You were hit on the head. We need to talk to you.'

'You are Ross,' she said. 'How did you get me here?'

'We pulled you out of a building just before Cheeseman blew it up.'

She looked at him in silence, then at Maja in front. Blood was trickling down the side of her face. She did not sound or look dangerous. Steve folded a handkerchief into a pad and handed it to her, and she held it to her head. She nodded towards the front. 'Is this Maja Frey?'

'Yes,' said Steve, surprised.

'Rudi told me a lot about you both,' she said in a voice that sounded suddenly empty.

'Rudi?' said Maja from the front seat, in amazement. 'How could you know Rudi?'

'I was sent to Greece to talk to him. I liked him very much. We had a little time together,' she said simply. Then her tone changed, hardened. 'Now I will kill Cheeseman for what he did.'

'What did he do?' said Maja, while Steve began to feel an awful hollowness in the pit of his stomach.

The woman looked at them for a moment. 'You didn't hear yet that Rudi is dead?'

Maja swerved on to the side of the road, slewing to a halt, and turned her face back to them, pale and staring. Steve answered for her. 'No,' he said, 'we didn't know that.'

Then the woman, recovering fast, seemed to click into gear. 'Cheeseman had him killed,' she said. 'I was ... close to him. I tried to stop them, then Cheeseman decided to kill me too. We must find him.'

Steve tried to push down the rising grief and anger which was getting in the way of his ability to rationalize. 'Your friend Pfister is somewhere down this road, waiting to kill de Klerk and Mandela, right?'

'Yes,' she said, 'on the far side of the Wolfgang Pass, from a lay-by where the road takes a sharp bend.' She looked out of the window. 'Maybe three miles from here.'

'You want to stop them?'

'You bet, and then go after Cheeseman if I can. He's set me up.'

Steve looked at Maja. 'First things first, then. Are you OK to drive or do you want me to?'

She inhaled deeply, wiped a hand across her eyes, and let the breath slowly out. 'I do it. I'm OK.'

They howled over the Wolfgang like a low-flying plane, braking hard whenever they came to one of the knots of traffic police standing waiting beside the road. Steve fired questions at the woman. 'We got the Ikegami. It's in the back. Where's the gun gone?'

'The brackets inside kept breaking. He couldn't aim it too well. We needed more time, so we put it inside a microphone instead. It was simpler.'

Steve remembered the long grey mike he had seen Pfister take from the Range Rover, easily long enough for a barrel of eighteen inches or more hidden inside the cigar-shaped wind cover, and with a perfect wooden pistol-grip underneath it.

'How was Cheeseman going to blame it on you?'

'Papers, in a car, showing payments from Chief Buthelezi's Zulus. He told me. He said the blacks would finish each other off and the whites would help them.'

The woman had turned and reached over the back seat, pulling the rug away which was covering the Ikegami.

'What is this?' she said suddenly, as she uncovered the end of a barrel, and Steve remembered what else was hidden there.

'Rudi's army rifle,' he said.

'Is it loaded?'

'Yes.'

'Well, I guess that is very fitting,' she said.

'How will Pfister get away?' said Steve, grabbing at the seat back to steady himself as Maja opposite-locked the Jeep, swaying through the first bend on the downhill side of the Wolfgang.

'There's a route worked out. You will see. We will soon be there.'

'Is the soundman in it, too?'

'No, not this one. He's just a stooge. Cheeseman wanted a fall guy to distract the cops afterwards.'

'But he'll be pulling the trigger on the mike.'

'No, he won't. Pfister will let him take the pictures just this once as a special treat. Every soundman's dream, right?'

'What are we going to do about it?'

'Stop them.'

Maja slowed as they passed another group of policemen, waiting beside the road with a van and three motor bikes. 'We shouldn't take risks. Let's tell them.'

'No,' hissed the woman. 'There is no time, and I do not want to go to jail. You do it my way or you find Pfister yourselves.'

Before Steve could stop her, she reached into the back and pulled out the gun, holding it awkwardly in the confined space, pointing vaguely between Steve and Maja. 'If it helps your consciences, you can say you had no choice,' she said.

Maja kept quiet and kept going. The woman peered ahead. 'Round the right-hand bend, then slow right down,' she said. 'There is a tiny track going up to the left. Take it very slowly and very quietly, and stop when I say.'

Steve recognized the spot. It was just before the other track which they had taken the day they saw the marmot killed. Maja eased the Jeep up, branches scraping its sides.

'Stop here. Now we must be silent. Follow me.'

Playing an unfamiliar game by rules he didn't know, Steve fell back on a well-tried set of values. 'Camera,' he said to Maja.

'No pictures of me,' said the woman. 'Try it and I'll shoot your camera to pieces.'

She took the rifle and they followed, pushing carefully

through trees and bushes until they could see through a final screen down on to the bend in the road, now well below them. They looked down on to an ambush waiting for its target. The other track branched off where the road turned right in a sharp, descending hairpin about fifty feet below them. On the outside of the bend was a gravelled area, between the verge and the rock-face. The familiar Range Rover was parked there. Next to it were two motor cycle policemen resting astride their BMWs, paying no attention to the camera crew set up next to them.

The young man was squinting through the camera on the tripod, nervously practising the pan and focus adjustment he would need to get his one chance of a good shot as the cars came by not more than ten feet away. Pfister sat on a rock next to him, with the big microphone across his knees. Then he was getting to his feet as a message crackled over the police radio sets and the policemen thumbed their bikes into life.

Chapter Thirty-three

They were lying flat on their stomachs, peering through the foliage, and Steve knew he had a choice. To his right the woman lay, wriggling into a comfortable firing position with Rudi's rifle at her shoulder. To his left was Maja, doing the same with Rudi's camera. He could get up and go down there, couldn't he? He could maybe tear the mike from Pfister's grip, show it to the policemen? Maybe he could and maybe he couldn't. The alternative was to stay up here and let events take their course.

The woman nudged him and pointed left. Just above the lay-by, up a steep path which joined the track, he could see the back of a motor cycle hidden in the bushes. 'Kawasaki trail bike,' she whispered. 'Pfister's route out of here, up and over the mountains. Helmet, suit, money – everything he needs waiting in the panniers.'

She concentrated on Pfister again, and Steve went back to balancing action against inaction. She seemed to know what she was doing, but just lying here must make him an accessory to something or other. It went round and round in his head. Should he launch himself into some sort of physical action which he didn't know if he could bring off? He needed time to think it through. But then, suddenly, he didn't have time any more.

Down to the right, from round the next bend, came flashing blue lights. Four motor cycles were coming up the pass at speed, with a black Audi saloon, headlights burning, behind them, and a police car bringing up the rear. The two policemen in the lay-by eased their bikes off the stands and sat more upright in the saddles, looking round in every direction except the right one for possible threats. The camera came to life next to Steve's ear, red light flashing on the recorder to show it was working.

Pfister was holding the mike out with a straight arm, headphones on, peering along it at the approaching cars, when the police radio squawked again. The message had an electrifying effect on the two motor cyclists. They both looked round at Pfister and his helper. While one started to put his bike back up on its stand again, the other revved his engine, let in his clutch, and slid the back wheel round in a shower of dirt to close the narrow gap to the camera crew. Anthony, thought Steve in a sudden burst of exultation, you did it.

Then Pfister turned and pointed the microphone at the approaching rider. There was a flash and a sharp noise as the end cap of the mike disintegrated and the policeman folded in the saddle, the bike swerving crazily to fall sideways in the road, back wheel still spinning. The other policeman reached for his gun, but Pfister fired again long before he could get to it, hitting him in the shoulder and throwing him back over his bike.

Then Pfister was out in the road, raising the mike with one hand towards the oncoming motorcade, which was slowing sharply, and pulling a grenade from his pocket with the other. He got no further. The SIG rifle next to Steve's ear went off, deafeningly, twice. The microphone spun out of Pfister's hands, through the air, and he fell to the ground clutching his thigh, while the youth with the camera finally stopped looking through his viewfinder and realized there was something wrong. There was bedlam on the road below, but they didn't stay to watch. Wriggling backwards through the tree screen, they were almost at the Jeep when they heard an engine burst into life higher up the track, and saw the green snout of Cheeseman's Mercedes edge into view.

'He was watching it all,' said the woman. 'I knew he couldn't resist it.' She raised the rifle, but he saw her and the Jeep blocking his escape route at the same moment. The Mercedes slammed to a halt, then shot off backwards up the track, transmission whining.

'I don't think he can get through that way,' said the woman, 'I checked it all. On the bike, yes, but not in that.'

'We'll go after him. The Jeep can go anywhere that thing can.'

'You go. I'll stay,' the woman said.

'The police will be all over this place when they pick themselves up down there,' said Maja.

'Don't worry about me. You go,' said the woman. 'Don't let him get away.'

Steve beat Maja to the driving seat. 'You keep the camera ready,' he said.

The woman pulled the driver's door open again. 'Quickly,' she said, 'just one thing. Rudi told me he kept a bag in the car with his army equipment in. Where is it?'

'In the back, tied up to the side,' said Steve in surprise, and she had the tailgate open almost before he'd finished. It slammed shut.

She shouted, 'Go.'

He had his foot flat, and all they could see to the edge of the tree line was the dust from Cheeseman's car. Then they were clear of the woodland, and the green Mercedes was bobbing up the track three hundred yards ahead of them, slewing from side to side on the loose surface, and leaving daylight beneath its wheels as it leapt the small stone bridge over the little railway line that runs from Landquart up the valley. Maja was trying to shoot through the windscreen, but the jolting, crashing ride had the camera all over the place, and she put it down.

'What will you do?' she asked.

'Don't know,' he grunted, whirling the wheel as the front tyres found a deep rut and skittered towards the side of the track. 'Keep him in sight. That's the first thing.'

Beyond the point where they had parked in the mist that first day, the track swung round the shoulder of the mountain then disappeared down a large dip and climbed steeply up the far side. As they reached the cleft in the top of the shoulder, overlooking the dip, Steve braked sharply to a halt.

'Got him,' he said.

They could see the rubble piled across the track at the top of the further slope. Ten cubic yards of rock had lost its fissured grip on the side of the mountain and no one had yet seen any reason to clear it all away on a track that would be no use to anyone until time came to prepare for the skiing season. Cheeseman must have seen it too, but decided to hope for the best from his Mercedes' all-wheel drive. They watched from their vantage point as he tried to force the G-Wagen, swaying and lurching, over the first obstacle, but the rocks were too big and the angle was too steep.

There was a moment when the machine just sat there as if exhausted by the effort, then they saw it move backwards down the slope and, finding a small, flat verge beside the track, start a laborious multi-point turn.

'He is coming back,' said Maja. 'What will you do now?'

But Steve hardly heard her. He was thinking about all the indignity and suffering he had been through because of this man. He was thinking about his job and about Tom, but most of all he was thinking about Sunny's body flattened on the dirt of a London street, and Rudi – gentle, kind Rudi – done to death and they hadn't even known.

The Mercedes hit the bottom of the dip at enormous speed and began to weave up the slope towards the point where the black Jeep sat squarely, blocking its path, engine idling.

'Move out of the way, Steve. He cannot get away.'

He sat there, just staring fixedly down the hill ahead.

'Steve. If you make him stop, he will certainly have a gun. You will be dead.'

But hatred had taken him over. He wanted to see the fright in Cheeseman's eyes as he found his path still blocked. He wanted to see the man get out so he could use Rudi's Jeep as a battering ram to even the score.

'I've lost too much to stop now,' he said in a stranger's voice.

The Mercedes was still travelling fast. Fifty yards, forty yards, then Maja's voice found its way to his ears. 'You haven't lost me,' she said. 'You have gained me, but not if we are both dead.' He looked at her, and saw love in her eyes through the fear. Then the camera was once again on her shoulder, pointing at the oncoming Mercedes. 'Come on,' she said, 'we have a film to make.'

Cheeseman was almost on top of them, clearly prepared in his desperation to try to smash them out of his way. Steve rammed the selector into gear and mashed the throttle open, wheels scrabbling on hard-right lock as the Jeep tilted, protesting, up the steep bank. Then a scream of tearing metal filled the air as Cheeseman reached them, side-swiping them hard as he scraped past to slide down the other side of the shoulder. Maja jumped out of the Jeep with the camera, and Steve tried to turn the vehicle, but thick metal had been pushed and folded by the impact down on to one front wheel and it was stuck fast.

He switched off and got out. Maja stood, panning with

Cheeseman's Mercedes as it slithered back down the track, the way they had come. The crest on which they stood gave them a grandstand view. Ahead of the Mercedes was the little stone bridge over the railway and, parked near it, hidden mostly from view by a rock outcrop, was the Kawasaki trail bike. But even at that distance Steve could tell it was the dark-skinned figure of the woman who knelt by it, now dressed in motor cycle gear.

In the same instant he realized what Cheeseman was attempting to do. Another small track branched off into the trees, heading back towards a lower section of the Wolfgang Pass. There were still no policemen visible this side of the tree line. They clearly had not yet realized where the rest of the shots had come from. If he reached the track, Cheeseman stood a chance, and there was nothing they could do.

He wondered if the woman still had the rifle, but he couldn't see it and, from where she knelt, she would have no clear shot at the track.

But just as the Mercedes reached the bridge there was a flash and a big puff of smoke. It seemed to come to pieces, merging with a rising spray of stone fragments with flames at its centre. The bang reached them as the remains of the car and the centre of the bridge fell in bits on to the railway line below.

The woman got to her feet, pulled a black crash-helmet on to her head, and straddled the bike. She looked in their direction, gave a quick wave with one black-gloved hand, and rode off down the railway track.

Maja lowered the camera and slumped to the ground. Steve sat beside her and put an arm round her shoulders. Out of the tree line, far below, came a police van. It went cautiously along the track to the remains of the bridge. Several policemen got out, and two men in ordinary clothes.

Maja lifted the camera to her eye and zoomed in. 'It's Nick

and your friend Anthony,' she said. 'I suppose it's over.'
Then she looked at him. 'What changed your mind? Was it
what I said about the film, or what I said about us?'

He tried to kiss her, but she pushed him away. 'I am
serious.'

'So am I. That should answer your question. As for the
rest of it? You know, it's only television. Mind you, Nick will
be very pleased with the pictures.'

She looked worried. 'Not very, I think.'

'Why not?'

'At the end there, I didn't zoom in. I stayed very wide. It
will all look tiny, just a little toy car then a puff of smoke. I
was sure the police would insist on seeing it.'

He looked at the railway track, where the motorcycle had
disappeared well before the police had reached it.

'We'll let her have a head start,' he said. 'Anyway, I've
got a terrible memory for faces.'

They looked down in exhausted silence for a long time,
close to each other but not touching. Then Nick spotted
them and began to shout, his voice tiny in the distance. One
of the policemen followed his gaze and started to wave his
arms, beckoning. Maja tried to climb to her feet, but Steve
stopped her. 'Why don't we let them do some of the work
for a change?' he said.